# HEART OF THE RAVEN PRINCE

TESSONJA ODETTE

TESSONJA ODETTE

# HEART
## OF THE
# RAVEN
# PRINCE

A CINDERELLA RETELLING
ENTANGLED WITH FAE

Copyright © 2021 by Tessonja Odette

All rights reserved.

No part of this book may be reproduced in any form or by any electronic or mechanical means, including information storage and retrieval systems, without written permission from the author, except for the use of brief quotations in a book review.

Cover illustration and design by Tessonja Odette

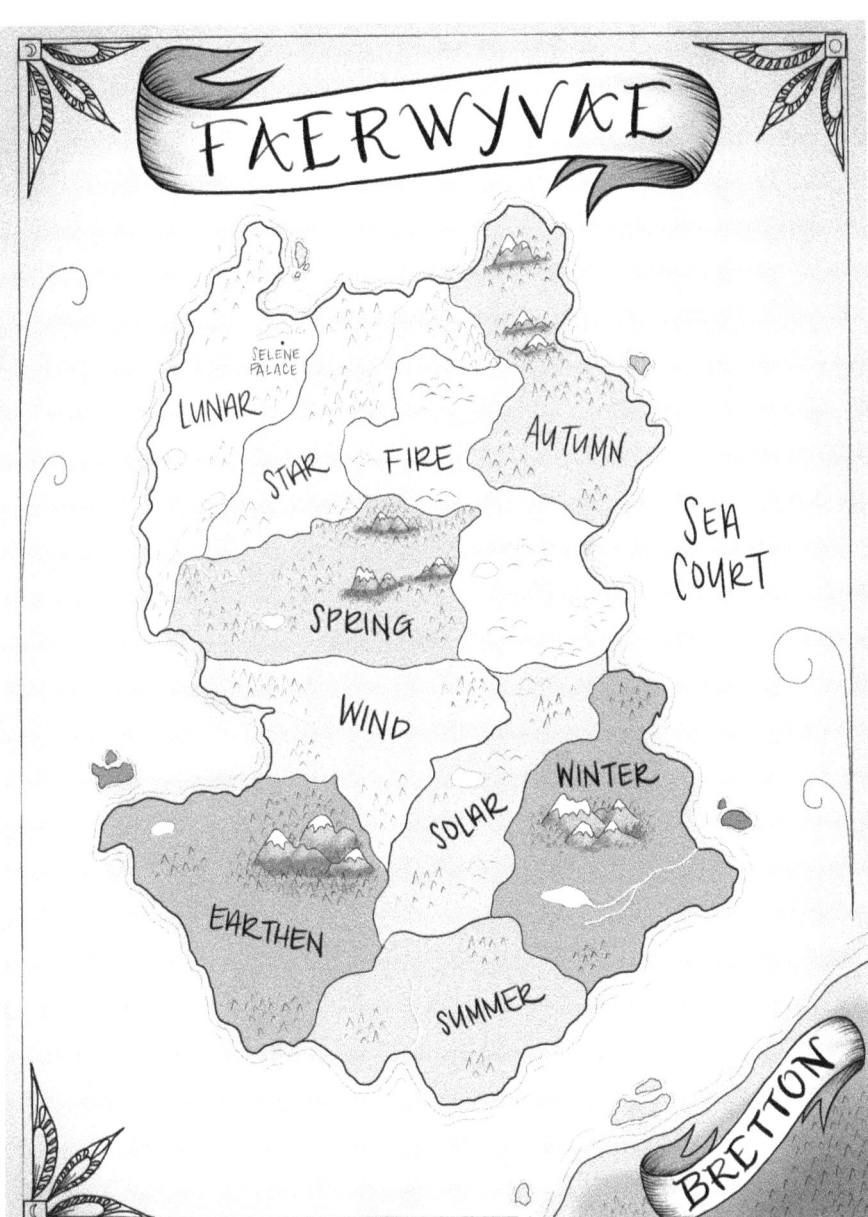

# 1

**EMBER**

There's a certain music about being alone. One I rarely get to hear outside of a single hour each morning. It's my peaceful respite before the sun rises, before anyone seeks to fill my day with a cacophony of demands. After dawn, I'll have to climb down from my rooftop hiding place and return to my chores and obligations. But for now, at least, I hear it. The subtle song of a sleeping city.

The hoot of an owl brings my attention to the adjacent rooftop where a pair of bright yellow eyes in a dark silhouette watch me. The owl hoots again, as if eager for me to acknowledge his contribution to the predawn song. "I hear you," I whisper, then lean my head against the brick chimney behind me. My legs, shielded from the chill air by thick wool hose, extend along the flat narrow ledge that rests between the two sloping sides of the roof. This, in all its unkempt, soot-dusted glory, is my sanctuary. My seat at the unseen orchestra.

Closing my eyes, I let the music wrap around me—the owl,

the soft wind whispering in the black sky, the echo of crickets chirping from the countryside surrounding the city. Then I hear a familiar beat, the pitter-patter of a raccoon approaching the many waste bins that clutter the narrow alley between my apartment building and the next one over. "I hear you too," I tell the raccoon and wrap my wool coat tighter around my nightdress.

I let the lullaby continue to play around me while I bask beneath the fading moonlight that kisses my closed eyelids. It's only a matter of time before the sun's light will conquer the moon's territory. Not even here in the Lunar Court are we free from daylight's domain and the bustle of activity it brings. Of the eleven courts on the isle of Faerwyvae, Lunar is the only one that hosts a perpetual twilight quality during daylight hours, diffusing the sun through an eerie haze. Still, the morning hour will bring the chiming of bells, just like any other court. The city of Evanston will wake from slumber.

And I will face another day paying off the stupidest bargain I ever could have made.

At least I have this moment.

Soon, I'll have more moments like this. Soon, music will fill my days and illuminate my nights. Soon, I'll be free from my stepfamily, free from my past and everything I've had to endure. I'll be able to become someone new.

Only then will I find a place I belong.

The thought brings a smile to my lips. I open my eyes and reach into the pocket of my coat, retrieving a treasure I always keep at my side—a train fare voucher—my literal ticket to freedom. In two weeks, I'll be leaving everything I know behind and boarding a train from Evanston Station to the city of Lumenas in the Star Court. As the music capital of Faerwyvae, Lumenas is famous for offering boundless opportunities to aspiring musicians. I have every intention of joining a musical troupe once I'm there. After that, it's the open road. No attachments. No stifling bonds. Music at my fingertips.

I caress the smooth paper, careful not to smudge the date or proof of fare. After saving for nearly a year, I was finally able to purchase the ticket in secret last week. Now I can hardly believe it's real. That freedom is truly so close.

So close.

Two more weeks.

The ticket suddenly flickers a shade of blue. With a startle, I look up to find three bright blue wisps bobbing above my head. I'm surprised to see them. While Faerwyvae is both ruled and inhabited by the fae, Evanston is a primarily human city that is seldom frequented by wild fae creatures like the wisps. This close, I can see their tiny faces amidst their bright, round, flame-like bodies, and their stubby arms and legs. They stare down at my ticket with curious expressions.

"Traveling, yes?" one says with an ethereal, feminine voice.

I gently fold the ticket and place it back in my pocket, saying nothing in response.

"Why take a train," says another, her voice slightly higher than the first, "when we could guide you where you want to go?"

I snort a laugh. Everyone knows wisps are not to be trusted, especially when it comes to journeys or directions.

"Come with us," says the third. This one has a more masculine tone. "We will take you there now."

"I'm not ready to go right now," I say, which is only half true. If it were up to me, I would have left my stepfamily long ago. But the bargain I made deems it impossible until the day I turn nineteen.

"Then perhaps you should play with us instead," says the first. She floats in a spiral higher overhead. "Come fly."

I level a stare at her. "I can't fly."

"You're of the wind," the second one says.

A hollow ache throbs in my chest. How can she tell? "I am. My mother was a sylph."

"Was," she echoes.

"She died eleven years ago."

"Then fly with us," the male wisp says. "Honor her."

"I already told you I can't. Just because I'm half fae doesn't mean I can fly like my mother could. I'll not let you use my grief against me."

The first wisp clasps her hands in an innocent gesture. "But you'll miss the sunrise. It's nearly at the horizon. Don't you want to see it?"

Sunrise. That means my peace is almost at an end. My heart plummets at the thought of all the chores, mending, and verbal insults that await once I return to the apartment. I glance toward the horizon but can see no evidence of the sun, not with the towering smokestacks that invade the view. Yearning tugs at my unruly fae side, urging me to give in. With it comes an echo of a promise made long ago.

*Always be wild. Promise me.*

Setting my jaw, I rise to my feet, keeping my balance steady on the rooftop ledge. I pivot to face the chimney. Extending my arms, I rise to my toes and grasp the chimney's crown, ignoring how the soot darkens my hands. The wisps swirl around me, giggling as I pull myself up. Climbing has always come easy to me because of my mother. She taught me to climb my first tree, helped me scale the roof of our manor so we could watch the sunrise together. The memory threatens to pull me down, but I use it as fuel instead. Once I've heaved myself onto the crown, I rise to stand, bracing my feet on opposite sides of the gaping flue, and face the horizon again.

"Jump. Fly," the male wisp begs, but I ignore him.

"Sing," says the first wisp, a hint of taunting in her eyes. "I know you want to."

My shoulders tense at the dare while a sudden tightness in my throat begs to be freed. Climbing this high up, giving in to even a portion of my fae nature, always tempts me to sing. Just considering the action of setting my voice to a tune, letting it mingle with the quiet music of the morning, sends a painful longing through me. My throat bobs, pleading for a hum, but I swallow it down.

I shake my head. "I don't sing."

*Not anymore.*

The wisps continue to taunt and tease, but I tune them out. Instead, I focus on the view, gazing above the smokestacks and factories that make up the Gray Quarter, a neighborhood as bleak as its name. I look out at the rest of the sprawling city beyond my neighborhood, then at the mountains and countryside in the distance.

I don't notice when the wisps get bored and float away, but soon I'm alone again, frozen in place, letting the breeze rustle my coat and dance through my hair while I listen to the shift in music.

First comes the beat of opening and closing doors, then the quiet pound of footsteps on cobblestones as the factory workers leave nearby apartments and workhouses for another grueling day of labor. Next comes the rhythm of horse hooves and carriage wheels, then of gears turning, of machinery roaring to life. My fingers flinch at my sides, eager to tap along to the tune, each digit haunted by the ghost of piano keys. It's been months since I last played. Months since I felt that comforting, familiar weight of ivory against my fingertips, of sound reverberating through my bones. Even though I refuse to sing, I still find comfort in playing the piano. Still find a connection to my mother through it.

Or at least I did. Before my stepmother sold my pianoforte.

Sinking into the song, I allow my fingers to tap against my thighs. A crying babe screeches out, disrupting the melody like a missed note. As if on cue, the first blush of sun peeks over the mountains beyond the city, painting the sky in muted shades of blue and gold. I watch as it bathes the countryside at the base of the mountains. My breath hitches. Somewhere amongst that gold-flecked green lies my childhood home. The modest country estate where I spent the happiest years of my childhood.

Until it all changed.

Until the last time I sang.

And killed the only living person who loved me.

I swallow the searing lump in my throat and return my attention to the rising music, listening to it grow louder and louder, letting it drown out my hidden sorrow until it's nothing more than a whisper in the audience. The tempo both quickens and slows as multiple musicians battle in disharmonious tandem. My fingers resume their tapping, chasing one beat, then the next.

Then I hear it. The chime of morning bells.

Good sense tells me I should get down and cleaned up before my stepmother seeks me out, but as the sun continues to rise, I find myself unable to look away. I remain in place, watching the golds grow brighter. The sun kisses more and more of Evanston. Any moment, it will illuminate even the Gray Quarter.

A flash of panic rushes through me, but a rebellious fire has my feet rooted to the chimney's ledge. I will remain. Just a second longer...

"Ember!"

The grating voice has my back stiffening as it reverberates through the apartment below, sending all prior sense of rebellion leaking from my bones.

"Ember Montgomery!" my stepmother calls again.

Closing my eyes, I clench my jaw and reach for the locket at the base of my throat. Squeezing it tight to steady my nerves, I take a deep inhale and a slow exhale. Then, releasing the locket, I climb down from the chimney. From peace. From music.

All to fulfill a bargain I never should have made.

# 2

## EMBER

Every human on the isle of Faerwyvae is taught never to bargain with the fae. It's a tenet learned long before the human lands merged with the fae lands twenty-one years ago and unified under fae rule.

And yet, no one ever tells a fae—or a half fae like me—never to bargain with a human. I often wonder…if I'd grown up with a warning like those the humans are given, would I have gone through with the bargain three years ago? Would my grief and guilt still have been so overwhelming that I would have neglected to pause long enough to see the truth? The lie? The deception?

Not that the question does me any good. It won't change that I'm bound to the bargain I made. Bound to my stepmother.

For two more weeks, that is.

I hear my name called again, closer now. Driven by urgency, I drop from the rooftop ledge to the awning over my bedroom window. Luckily, the apartments in the Gray Quarter are rather narrow, leaving me very little space to traverse. Still, I always get a rush of panic in the split second between letting go of the ledge and feeling my slippered feet touch the awning. Like always though, my feet meet their mark. Then it's a matter of careful balance as I drop from the awning to the windowsill, through my window, and onto my bed. On swift feet, I hurry behind my faded dressing screen. A second later, my door swings open.

"Ember!" my stepmother barks. "Why aren't you downstairs?"

"So sorry, Mrs. Coleman," I say with as much regret as I can fake.

Her footsteps approach the dressing screen but—thankfully—stop on the other side. If she sees the state I'm in, she'll know I've been outdoors. "What excuse do you have today?"

I clench my jaw as I pour water into my washbasin and begin to rinse the soot from my arms. "It's barely sunrise, Stepmother."

She releases an irritated huff. "We have errands to run first thing this morning. If we don't get to Sonsbury Square before..." She trails off as if realizing I'm not worth explaining to. Instead, she uses the same weapon she battles me with time and time again. Her words come out slow, her tone laced with a sinister chill. "Do not argue with me. Just *obey*."

The fear hits me first, then the pain. It's sharp, like an iron blade twisting in my gut. I bite back a cry as sweat beads on my brow. My fingers grip the edges of the washbasin so hard I fear the porcelain might shatter beneath my hands. *I'm obeying, I'm obeying,* I repeat to myself until the pain starts to lessen.

That's my least favorite part about bargains. They hurt when broken. If I were full fae, my disobedience could kill me. Since I'm only half fae, the mysterious magic that rules fae bargains isn't as detrimental.

"I'm obeying." This time I say it out loud, my voice barely above a whisper.

The magic seems satisfied by my assertion, for the pain quickly retreats. It's still enough to leave me quaking with the reminder of what happens when I truly refuse my stepmother's direct orders.

Mrs. Coleman takes another step closer to the screen. "Did you hear me?"

I clench my jaw, my body still trembling in the wake of my momentary agony. It's a struggle to keep my voice even as I say, "I'll be down as soon as I'm cleaned up and dressed."

A long pause. Then, "Very well. Be quick about it. And close that damn window! You'll send a draft through the entire apartment." With that, her steps retreat.

My fear shifts to rage, my unspoken retort swirling through my mind like a storm. *My bedroom is always drafty, regardless of the window being open or closed. That's what happens when a bedroom is an attic, you breezing daft cow!*

I bite the inside of my cheek, glaring down at the dirty wash water. "Two more weeks," I whisper. That's all I have to tolerate. After that, I'll be nineteen and free from this stupid bargain. Free from *her*.

With a slow exhale, I release the washbasin and finish scrubbing my arms. Then I strip off my nightgown and hose, replacing them with my regular daily wear—stockings, shift, corset, chemise, blue wool skirt, and a cream cotton blouse. All articles are faded hand-me-downs from my stepsister Clara, and the corset is so tattered I'm surprised I haven't been impaled by my own stays yet.

Honestly, that sounds like a picnic compared to how I spend most of my days.

I pat my locket and arrange the gold chain around the high collar of my blouse. Then I don my manacles. Actually, it's a bonnet, but it might as well be a ball and chain. The bonnet suppresses the part of me my stepmother hates. The part she wants no one outside our household to see.

My hair.

Unlike my mother's pale blue, mine is turquoise, the same color as my eyes. A shocking thing to see amongst the stuffiest circles of human high society, setting me apart, providing proof of my fae heritage and evidence that my sylph mother lives on in me.

*Always be wild. Promise me.*

Gritting my teeth, I pin every teal strand beneath the bonnet. Not only is the hat hideous—a monstrosity of floral-patterned linen and nothing like the pretty bonnets that were fashionable twenty years ago—but it is also enormous. Perfect for keeping my face in shadow while making me look utterly ridiculous.

With a deep breath, I enjoy one last beat of being gloriously and peacefully alone, then join my already-bickering stepfamily downstairs.

A HALF-HOUR LATER, I TRAIL BEHIND MRS. COLEMAN AND MY two stepsisters as we make our way through the Gray Quarter toward the heart of the city. The three figures walk clustered together, nearly identical in looks and height, all with blonde curls and pale, snooty faces. Clara, the shortest of the three by an inch or two, is seventeen—a year younger than me—while Imogen, a near-spitting image of Mrs. Coleman, is nearly twenty. They wear their best dresses, hats, and coats reserved only for public outings, a façade to hide the truth of our poverty.

Following the rule that I must act as a maid in public and remain separate from the family unit, I maintain several steps behind as we continue our walk, weaving through the outskirts of the Gray Quarter to avoid the foot traffic of factory workers. Soon smokestacks and industrial buildings are replaced by rows and rows of tightly knit apartment buildings, just a slight increase in luxury from ours. My stepfamily keeps a hurried pace, as if that will help them flee their association with the Gray Quarter. Finally, we cross Chairman's Street where the housing grows sparser, larger, giving way to townhouses. The colors are brighter here, the streets cleaner. Mrs. Coleman releases a heavy sigh and slows to a more casual stride.

"Remind me why we came back here," Clara whines. "Why couldn't we have stayed in the Earthen Court? Things were fine there."

"Fine, but going nowhere," Mrs. Coleman snaps. "Neither you nor Imogen managed to secure a husband *yet again*. We've attended every court's social season, one after the other, for three years in a row, and still, my daughters fail me."

Imogen scoffs. "We haven't been to *every* court's social season. Why won't you take us to Autumn or Fire? Doesn't Aunt Marie have a cottage near Maplehearth Palace?"

"Marie leads an impure and unchaste life," Mrs. Coleman says, her tone sharp. "I won't have you associating with her ilk."

"But why did we have to come *here*?" Clara asks. "Couldn't we have entered the Lunar social season in a different city? One where we could live somewhere nicer than the Gray Quarter? Or couldn't we have asked to stay at the manor?"

At first, I'm confused by what she means. Then I realize she's talking about my father's house, where we all lived together before he died. After his death, Mrs. Coleman didn't hesitate to sell it in exchange for funding a lavish lifestyle chasing social seasons. Since each court hosts their month-long social season during a different month, there was always somewhere new to go all year long. A new house to rent. New dresses to buy. New schemes to get closer to the aristocracy.

Look where that's gotten her. Where's it's gotten all of us.

"The manor doesn't belong to us anymore, Clara dear," Mrs.

Coleman says. "We can't simply ask to stay somewhere uninvited."

"We could if we knew anyone important here. At least we had friends in the Earthen Court—"

"You know why we're here, Clara," Imogen says, silencing her sister. She then casts a withering glance over her shoulder at me. "It's almost time for Ember to claim her dead father's fortune."

I keep my gaze fixed straight ahead, refusing to acknowledge her mention of my dead father and my inheritance. I harbor no doubts about whether they'll try to steal it from me, for they most certainly will. Even though it's only a modest fortune, my stepfamily's financial situation has fallen greatly the past couple of years, and I know they're growing more desperate by the day. Regardless, they'll never see a single moonstone chip—the currency of the Lunar Court—after the money is legally mine. Neither will I, in fact. I'll be giving it to charity as soon as I claim it. That way Mrs. Coleman has no one to steal it from. No one to hound and harass.

Besides, while Mrs. Coleman is undeserving of my father's fortune, so am I.

I'm the one who killed him, after all.

"Your sister's right," Mrs. Coleman says. "When it's time for Ember to claim her father's wealth, we'll need to go to Selene Palace. This is as close as we can get while still maintaining somewhat respectable company."

There is some truth to that, considering the city of Evanston is the only human city within a twenty-mile radius of the unseelie palace, where my inheritance is being held until the day I turn nineteen. It's not normally the duty of the unseelie ruler to deal in human matters of life and finance, but after the death of Father's executor earlier this year, his estate was turned over to the crown. His will and finances were moved to the nearest royal vault, which is, of course, at Selene Palace.

My stepmother lowers her voice. "Just think. If the late Terrence Montgomery's executor hadn't joined him in the grave, we wouldn't have this chance to visit Selene Palace at all."

Imogen eyes her mother with a smirk, expression calculating. "Did your decision to bring us here have anything to do with the fact that Prince Franco is still unwed?"

I suppress a groan at the suggestion of yet *another* scheme to marry Imogen to fae royalty. Prince Franco is the brother and heir of Queen Nyxia, the Unseelie Queen of Lunar, and he is just as unlikely to fall for Imogen's nonexistent charms as every other royal she's tried to woo.

Mrs. Coleman lifts her chin and returns her daughter's sly look. Her voice takes on a sing-song quality. "Perhaps. Can I count on you to snag his attention?"

Imogen purses her lips, all amusement leaving her face. "Of course, Mother. That is, if we ever manage to steal a moment in his presence."

"We will, my dear. I promise."

"Before Ember claims her inheritance? I won't be wooing the Raven Prince over the fulfillment of contracts. Not when Ember could very well ruin everything." Imogen says this last part under her breath, but her words reach me just the same. As does the scowl she burns me with.

"I have my ways," Mrs. Coleman says, a swagger in her step.

Clara gasps, eyes going wide. "That's why we're going to Madame Flora's shop, isn't it?"

I furrow my brow in surprise; I hadn't known of our destination until now. Madame Flora is a fae glamourist who specializes in weaving glamours for human entertainment and cosmetic purposes. While I've never been to her shop, I know her wares don't come cheap. Why would Mrs. Coleman spend her dwindling finances on a visit to Madame Flora?

Imogen must have the same question as me. "What is your latest scheme about, Mother?"

She gives a haughty shrug. "One must be prepared should an invitation to a certain glamoured ball—one hosted by the Raven Prince himself—come their way."

My stepsisters exchange a delighted glance, but Imogen's excitement quickly sobers. "Mother, the New Moon Masquerade is tomorrow night," she says. "How do you expect us to procure an invitation if we haven't already received one?"

"I told you, my dear. I have my ways."

I shake my head at my stepmother's back. Of course she has no reservations about wasting money on a ball she has no invitation to. Of course she scrimps on food and coal for the furnace in favor of the latest fashions. Of course she sells my pianoforte—

As if she can sense my burning resentment, Mrs. Coleman whirls around in time to catch my frown before I steel it behind a neutral mask.

Imogen catches it too. "What was that look for, Ember? Jealous you won't be going to the ball?"

I don't bother answering her. The truth is I've given up on being envious of my stepsisters. It used to hurt more, being treated as a maid, forbidden from attending balls or coming out to society. But after three years of helping my sisters prepare for one grand event after another, I've learned society dances are less about the parts I like—the music and dancing—and more about marital schemes and following a careful set of rules labeled as frivolity. I've come to believe the best place to be during a dance is in the orchestra, not on a man's arm.

"Wipe that sour sneer off your face," Mrs. Coleman says before facing forward, even though I know I wear no such expression.

Imogen, however, continues to eye me with disdain. She snorts a laugh. "Is that soot on your cheek?"

I try to hide my alarm, but a flush of panic rushes through me. Did I forget to wash my face this morning? With the sleeve of my coat, I wipe my cheeks.

This seems to amuse Imogen even more. "Just because your namesake places you amongst ash and cinders, doesn't mean you should seek cosmetics from a chimney."

"At least an ember still burns," I say under my breath.

Clara joins Imogen to smirk at me. "You think you're a poet now? Little orphan Ember with her clever words and nothing to show for it."

"Ignore her," Mrs. Coleman tells her daughters, as if I was responsible for the teasing. "It doesn't matter how brightly one burns if no one cares to look."

∾

We arrive at Madame Flora's shop with fifteen minutes to spare before it opens.

"We're too early," Clara says, shoulders slumping.

Mrs. Coleman's lips curl into a satisfied smile. "We're right on time."

Imogen studies her mother's expression. "What do you mean by that?"

"You'll see. Now we wait."

"Can't you just tell us?" Clara peeks through one of the windows, but it's obvious the lights are off inside the shop.

Mrs. Coleman tugs her daughter away from the window, then ushers her and Imogen close. "I have it on good authority…" Her back stiffens, and she whirls around to face me. "Why are you here?"

I clench my jaw. "You gave me no indication I shouldn't be here, Stepmother. You brought me along."

"Don't talk back to me, girl," she says through her teeth. "You know what I'm asking. Why haven't you made yourself scarce? Did you honestly think we'd bring you into Madame Flora's with us?"

"You've yet to send me on any other errand. Oddly enough, I can't read your mind." I know I shouldn't have said the last part, so I plaster on a pleasant smile.

Mrs. Coleman's nostrils flare, her eyes shooting daggers. After a tense pause, she reluctantly reaches into her purse and retrieves a piece of paper. I take it from her, finding a short list of food items. Nothing but the essentials, of course. Especially since every other moonstone chip will be spent on my stepmother's frivolous fancies.

She shoos me with a wave of her hand. "Go, and don't you dare come back until we're done. If you finish early just...wait in the alley."

The alley. Of course.

*Two more weeks. Then it will all be over. Just go through the motions and obey.*

"Very well," I say, voice flat. I leave my stepfamily behind, but not before I catch a few words of Mrs. Coleman's whisper.

"...the Lunar Prince!"

Imogen and Clara's excited squeals are the last thing I hear before I round the corner toward the market.

# 3

## FRANCO

"You've truly outdone yourself," I say to the fae standing next to the mirror.

Madame Flora claps her dark, slender hands. "I thought you would like this one," says the floating porcelain mask that is her face, her voice deep yet feminine. She has no neck to connect the mask to the rest of her short, stout body, which is covered in an elegant black robe. The robe's many folds writhe around her like shadows pulled by a nonexistent wind.

I turn in a slow circle, assessing my reflection, and try my hardest not to laugh. Not that Madame Flora would be offended if I did. It's more that I must learn to keep a straight face while wearing this ridiculous—no, *marvelous*—glamour. Satisfied with my product, I remove the black silk cravat from around my neck. As soon as it leaves my flesh, the glamour disappears.

Flora takes the cravat from me and reverently folds it within sheets of tissue, then packs it into a gilded black box. No matter how many times I've told her not to waste such pretty packaging on the likes of me, she ignores me. Hisses, actually. That one request is the surest way to offend her. "Would you like to try the other?" she asks, the painted red mouth on the porcelain mask never moving.

"Absolutely." I take the strand of black tourmaline beads she offers and face the mirror, then drape the necklace around my neck and settle the length of it over my chest. My reflection shifts in a flash, leaving...me. Same silver hair, haphazardly parted, drifting just past my jaw in places. Same pointed ears. Same eyes. I crack a smile and find she's even managed to weave in the elongated tips of my canines.

Flora floats over, assessing me with her painted, unblinking eyes. "A near-perfect imitation, is it not?"

"Better, I'd say. How did you come up with this outfit?" I turn from side to side, admiring the cape of black feathers that trails almost to the ground, the heeled boots, the tight pants that hang low on my hips. I brush the cape to the side, and—as if it were a real cape—the glamour obeys, revealing the back of my pants. "My ass looks amazing. Did you make it bigger?"

"I had to cater to your vanity, didn't I?"

With a grin, I release the cape and face forward to study the front of my shirt, a flowing confection of pink ruffled lace. Free of waistcoat and cravat, the neck is left unbuttoned. I pull the collar aside and find a hint of black ink. "You even got my tattoos right."

She shrugs. "It wasn't hard to do."

I face her with a smirk. "Is that because I rarely care to don a proper shirt?"

"That's part of it." Even though her face reveals no expression, I hear the amusement in her tone.

"Well, I learned from the best. Have you seen what Nyxia

wears?" I keep my eyes on my reflection as I remove the necklace. In an instant, the real me returns. I look mostly the same but without the flamboyant costume. In its place are black trousers and an indigo linen shirt. As tempted as I am to replace the glamour and wear it for the rest of the day, it's far too early for pink lace. Or is it too late? The best parties that involve ruffles and lace last at least until sunrise...

Flora takes the necklace from me and wraps it just as carefully as she did the cravat. "Speaking of your sister, how is she?"

The question sends an iron weight to my stomach. "She's... doing well. Aside from the fact that she's abandoning me and all." I try to say the last part in jest, but wince when I hear the bitter note that mingles with my words.

The fae pauses and gives me the expressionless equivalent of a pointed look with her mask. "I take it you aren't pleased about hosting the human social season."

"It's my duty," I say, not bothering to hide my dark tone this time. I turn away from her, hands in my pockets, and walk slowly along the row of floor-to-ceiling shelves that line the walls. On each ledge rests a seemingly innocuous item—a pair of gloves, a hat, a necklace—but I know each holds a different glamour. Some are customized according to the buyer's tastes, like the ones she made for me, but others are entirely random concoctions from Madame Flora's brilliant mind. I pick up a pair of cufflinks, wondering what glamour they hold. "Nyxia has been hell-bent on improving my reputation so that I can earn the respect of the human population. To do so, she insists I must host this year's social season alone. All in the name of training me to be a proper heir."

*Not that it matters*, I think to myself. Unless my sister dies, there's no reason for me to take her place as king. Like all fae, Nyxia is immortal. So, aside from the unlikely chance she's mortally wounded by ash or iron—two materials that are illegal in Faerwyvae—the odds that I'll outlive her are slim.

"Isn't it the seelie ruler's responsibility to gain the approval of the humans?" Flora asks.

"Yes, that's how it *should* be." Again, my bitterness is clear. And she's right. Each court in Faerwyvae has both a seelie and unseelie ruler who rule from two separate palaces and serve on the Alpha Council. The seelie ruler oversees the more civilized aspects of the court, such as maintaining peace and integration with the humans, day-to-day petitions, matters of economy and finance. The unseelie ruler, on the other hand, keeps the traditions of the Old Ways and oversees matters of nature and advocates for the wild fae creatures. The unseelie rulers, like my sister, aren't expected to open their palaces to humans or hear their petitions. At least, that's how it was before the rebellions. Ever since a few short-lived skirmishes broke out in Lunar, Wind, and Spring eleven years ago, our three courts have taken measures to ensure more cooperation with the human population. Since I butchered our first attempt at demonstrating our goodwill, we've now resorted to opening Selene Palace one month a year to host the social season.

This will be my first year acting as host. A fate most cruel indeed.

"Surely, you can handle one month of fine dinners and balls." Her tone tells me she finds my plight rather shallow. Maybe she's right, but still...

I huff a laugh. "The last time I took part in such activities, I came out the other side a vile rogue." I set down the cufflinks to face Flora. "Besides, it isn't just that. Nyxia wants me to interact with the humans on a deeper level than even she dares to. I am to attend garden parties, visit the theater, kiss the hands of aristocrats' daughters—"

"How dreadful," she says, tone mocking. "You'll have to leave your palace once or twice to visit your subjects."

"Technically, the humans aren't *my* subjects. They *should* belong to the seelie king."

"What are you afraid of, Your Highness?"

I put a hand on my hip. "Afraid? Me? What would *I* have to fear?"

"Only you know that answer."

My first instinct is to brush her off, but the gravity in her tone has my normally thick defenses growing thin. There isn't much I can hide from Flora, nor do I find it pertinent to do so. She may be an artisan now, but she once worked in politics. Many years ago, she served on my mother's advisory council and has been like a grandmother to me ever since. In fact, she's been in my life far longer than my mother cared to be. Not once in hundreds of years has she shied away from giving me brutal honesty. It's what I like about her because seldom do I receive that level of candor. Everyone else is more concerned with kissing my ass.

"You know what happened last time I interacted with the humans," I say, my tone wary. "And now...well, you know how I feel about these ridiculous human practices. I detest their restrictive codes of conduct. Even worse than that are the mothers and fathers who throw unmarried daughters at me, eager for one to snatch me up like I'm some war prize."

"I've worked in this city for a decade now," she says with a light laugh. "In that time, I've learned much about humans and their strange ways. A husband *is* a war prize, and it's far from silly. For some women, it's the difference between comfort and poverty."

"That's only because of their own outdated traditions. They choose to follow these strictures of chastity, etiquette, and social hierarchy, values leftover from when the humans on the isle bowed to a human king. When the fae won the war, we liberated them from King Grigory. Now it's almost as if they expect their fae rulers to take his place."

Flora steps closer, her tone soft. "It's what they know, my

prince. The isle has only been unified for twenty-one years. You can't expect them to change so soon."

"That's just it. The humans aren't the ones changing. The fae are. As every year goes by, I can't help but think we're becoming more and more like them."

"Is that a bad thing?"

"It is for the unseelie," I say. "If Faerwyvae becomes too civilized, the unseelie will cease to be. You know it's true." A shudder runs through me at the thought. Long ago, before humans came to the isle, all fae were unseelie. I wasn't alive back then, but I've heard the tales. Fae were wild creatures, ethereal spirits, forces of nature. Then the humans discovered the isle and made first contact with the fae. They taught us language, shared food, offered clothing. Those who accepted these things began to transform on a physical level, adopting human bodies, opening themselves to human emotions. The result is what we now call *seelie*. There once was much debate over the *right* way to be fae. Was it keeping to ancient tradition or embracing evolution? Blood was shed over that very question, battles were fought, won, and lost. At the end of the last war, our isle united under the principle that each side should be allowed to be who and what they want to be.

I suppose that right belongs to the humans as well, for better or worse.

My shoulders slump, an unsettling feeling stirring in my gut. This conversation has put me highly on edge, drowning out all the pleasant mirth I felt mere moments ago. So, I do what I always do when I'm uncomfortable. I make light of it.

"Honestly, Flora. You wouldn't be arguing if you attended last year's season. It's almost as bad as watching harpies breed, minus the only fun part—the sex. No, instead it will be polite conversation, stiff dances, and *so* many rules."

She chuckles. "Then maybe I'll come this year, if only to watch you suffer."

I brighten at that. "Please do, Flora. In fact, you should take a room at the palace all month. You can even set up shop. You'll get loads of business, as I plan on making all the dances glamoured occasions. You know everyone wants their next glamour to be even more dazzling than the last."

"Do I sense desperation?"

"Absolutely. Please save me from boredom. Nyxia will be gone on her lovers' holiday with her mate all month. The rule of Lunar will rest solely on my shoulders."

"How can you expect to be bored if you're running a kingdom?"

"I'd hate to find out. Come on. Your glamours make life so much more interesting." My words are more than just flattery. While most fae are capable of conjuring glamours, myself included, we are limited by our own particular strengths and imaginations. Flora's creations are artistic marvels unparalleled by the capabilities of the average fae. She has the distinct talent of connecting a glamour to an object. I don't know any other glamourist who can do that. And where most fae glamours are nothing more than illusions, hers take physical form, forging with its wearer.

"I'll consider it," she says unconvincingly and hands me my two boxes. "Which glamour will you wear first?"

I waggle my brows. "Wouldn't you like to know? Besides, what if I'm planning to use both at the first ball?"

She says nothing, but I sense an invisible eye roll. Her mask bobs toward the door that leads to the main portion of the shop. "I suppose this might be a good time to warn you that an audience awaits. A horde of women, to be exact."

I glance back at the door, my eyes widening with horror. "What? They're waiting in the shop?"

"They aren't inside yet," she says. "They're waiting outside. Regardless, it seems you've been found out. Why else do you think I kept you in the backroom this whole time?"

"I thought this was where you serve your most important shop patrons." My tone is teasing, but the thought of exiting the shop to a cluster of husband-hungry socialites has the blood leaving my face. I wonder who at the palace I have to thank for flapping their loose lips regarding my whereabouts. I'll have to interrogate later. First, I need a way out. Perhaps if I shift into my raven form...

Flora snorts a laugh, clearly amused by my distress. "Go out the back door. I'll distract your many admirers."

"Thank you," I say, closing my eyes with relief. Flora leads me to the door at the opposite end of the room. I pause and face her, startled when I find her suddenly standing a head taller than me. Gone is the stout body and flowing robes, replaced with a tall, slender figure in a black silk evening gown, her arms covered in long white gloves. Her mask remains, but it now rests over a humanlike head with strands of long, black hair falling around it.

"Is this the form you wear for your human patrons?" I ask. Like all fae, Flora can shift between two physical manifestations—her unseelie and seelie form. A fae's unseelie form is their natural shape, while one's seelie form is modeled after human likeness. It's what some humans refer to as *lesser fae* and *high fae*. Which is quite rude, honestly.

"I find it's more comforting for them," she says. "There's nothing like comfort mixed with a dash of mystery to loosen one's purse strings."

"The same can be said about bodices." She swats my arm with her gloved hand but lets out a low chuckle. I shift my tone to a more serious one. "Will you at least come to tomorrow's ball? Please say yes."

"I'll think about it," she says, tone flat.

Holding both of my boxes under one arm, I push open the door, waving as I back out of it. "Thanks for everything, Flora."

She waves back and closes the door between us.

I turn around with a sigh, relieved to find the alley gloriously empty.

Or...not empty.

Damn.

# 4

## EMBER

The nine o'clock bells have come and gone and still, the shop hasn't opened. I know this because my stepfamily remains outside the door when I return from my errand. Not daring to pause at the end of the street for fear of my stepmother's wrath, I head straight for the alley to wait. Then I return to check. Then again. And again. Each time, they are still by the door. Not only that, but a line of people—particularly young women around my age—has grown behind them. Can they truly all be here to buy a glamour for the ball? Surely half the ladies of Evanston can't have been invited. Royal events are far too exclusive.

I return to the alley after what is probably my sixth time checking the front of the shop. It incenses me that I have to wait in an alley at all. What's the harm of bringing me inside so long as I act as a maid?

I lean against the back wall of the building and release a groan of frustration.

*Two more weeks, two more weeks,* I repeat to myself, thinking of my train ticket tucked safely inside my coat pocket. That's all I have to tolerate. Then I'll be free.

My fingers flinch at my sides, begging for piano keys. It's been too long since I've played. Too long since I've been able to release my bottled angst through song. Closing my eyes, I lower my head, resisting the temptation to tear off my bonnet. Then I let my fingers tap against the sides of my thighs, following sheet music in my mind—

A sound to my right startles me from my imaginary song. I whirl to the side as a door swings outward, and two voices come from behind it. I bring a hand reflexively to my locket as I take a step back, then another. Finally, the door closes, revealing a tall, slim figure dressed in fine, dark clothing, and carrying a pair of small boxes. He's fae, as evidenced by the pointed tips of his ears. Face averted, he looks down the opposite end of the alley and releases a sigh, then turns on his heel toward me.

For a split second, a dazzling, contented smile warms his face, his lips parted to reveal the delicate tips of two pointed canines. I'm unable to move, stunned by his striking beauty. Most fae males are gorgeous in their seelie forms, but this one, with that breathtaking smile...

His silvery blue eyes meet mine and the expression dissolves in an instant, leaving a scowl in its place. I feel cold at the sudden shift, as if a cloud has covered the sun. That's when an even more chilling realization dawns on me.

Silver hair.

Pointed teeth.

Showing way too much skin above his carelessly unbuttoned shirt collar.

I know who this is. It's Prince Franco. While I may not have seen him in person before, I've heard both him and his sister described. And not just in physical appearance.

Fearsome.

Powerful.

Vampire.

It doesn't even matter that he *supposedly* doesn't drink blood. It doesn't matter that he's spoken of as a highly sought-after bachelor. The disdain in his glowering, silver stare is enough to make my knees quake.

"This is a bit much, don't you think?" he says, his voice a lazy, disinterested drawl.

I blink a few times. When I find my words, they come out with a tremor. "Pardon me?"

With a roll of his eyes, he looks away from me and shakes his head. His gaze remains averted as if I'm no longer worth looking at. "Clever, I must admit. What's your next move? Pretend to have a fit of the vapors in hopes that I'll lift you into my arms and fall desperately in love? Or are you the kind to simply throw yourself on me without pretense? Let me guess. You aren't wearing undergarments."

His condescending tone has me bristling, my fear blown away like a leaf in a storm and taking my idiotic short-lived attraction with it. On second glance, I see not his lean frame and sensuous lips but his arrogant posture, his domineering sneer. He's just like every other stuck-up aristocrat I've met through my stepfamily. In fact, he's like *them*. Like Imogen, Clara, and Mrs. Coleman. My knees cease their trembling, and my fingers curl into fists. I know I should keep my mouth shut. I'm practiced at it. It's what I do every single day at home. This man being the prince makes it even more imperative that I play the meek and humble servant. I should bow low, move to the side, and pretend I never saw him at all.

I *should*.

But there's something about him that sparks a tempest inside me, one that explodes from my lips before I can stop it. "What are you talking about?"

He scoffs. "Playing coy, I see. That tactic is familiar to me as well. Congratulations, you aren't special."

My mouth falls open and heat rises to my cheeks.

Before I can form a retort, he speaks again. "No, that was rude. Forgive me." There's no apology in his tone, but he returns his gaze to me, assessing me from head to toe with a quirked brow that says he isn't impressed. He puts his free hand on his hip and stands with a casual slouch. "You were clever enough to corner me back here without alerting anyone else of your scheme. So, go ahead. You deserve it."

I narrow my eyes. "Deserve what?"

"Tell me what you came here to say. What is your proposal? Shall we run off together and get married at once? Have a tryst against the alley wall? I assure you my answer is no, but you've earned my ear for..." he glances at his palm, miming that he holds an invisible timepiece, "thirty seconds."

My shoulders heave with rage. The sensible part of me screams to swallow my pride and simply walk away. But another part—and I have no doubt it's my fae side—refuses to be silenced.

I take a step toward the arrogant male. "You assume too much, Your Highness—"

"Ah, so you do know me. I suppose that means we aren't doing the old *I didn't recognize you* bit."

"—I did not come here to corner you, throw myself upon you, or offer you a *tryst against the alley wall*." I say this last part through my teeth. "As hard as it might be for you to believe, not every young woman in Faerwyvae goes weak and mewling in your presence, begging to bed and marry you. In fact, anyone with half a brain would know to avoid you entirely."

He barks a laugh. "Is that so? Because of my impressive reputation?"

He means his rakish reputation. Everyone knows the prince

is nothing but a rogue. I've heard the rumors about his many lovers, how he breaks hearts with hardly a care. I never gave these sensational tales much weight before, but now...

"Well, this is cute," he says flatly, "and yet I've heard it all before. You hate me, you find me despicable, you're not like other girls...and yet it always ends with someone trying to kiss me." A corner of his mouth lifts in a suggestive smirk that has my cheeks heating further.

"You couldn't pay me to kiss you!" I say. "I would rather kiss a troll's—"

"Your thirty seconds are up," he says, and I startle as an enormous pair of black feathered wings sprouts from his back as if from nowhere. They expand nearly from one side of the alley to the other. I leap back as they lift and beat the air around us, nearly sending my bonnet flying off my head. Then, pushing off from the ground, the prince darts into the sky.

"It was a valiant effort," I hear him call overhead before he soars over the buildings and out of sight.

"I would rather kiss a troll's *ass*! That's what I was going to say!" I shout at the empty sky but get no response. For several minutes, I remain in place, scowling at the clouds. No matter how much time ticks by, my anger refuses to dissipate and instead roars through my veins. My curled fingers dig so hard into my palms, I'm sure they've left crescent moons. I release my clenched fists, shaking out my hands. If I had a piano right now, I'd probably smash the keys to pieces while expressing my rage. With no musical outlet at my disposal, I'm left to growl under my breath. And when that doesn't work, I point a rude gesture at the innocent sky.

"Ember, what is taking you so long?" I lower my hand and whirl to find Clara standing at the mouth of the alley. She crosses her arms and pins me with a glare. "We've been finished for an entire minute at least."

With a few steadying breaths, I gather my composure, smoothing my skirts with trembling hands. "Sorry," I say as I hurry toward her. She walks away before I reach her, which allows me a few more moments to try and forget my irritating exchange with the prince.

∼

"The prince," Clara says with a wistful sigh as she turns in a circle. The skirts of her glamoured dress swirl around her ankles and brush up against the cramped furniture in our apartment's front room. "Do you think he'll like my glamour?"

The honest answer is no. After my meeting with that crude son-of-a-harpy, I'm convinced the prince only likes himself. But since the question isn't directed at me, I swallow my remark and continue to scrub the floor around the stove. Harder. Like it's the prince's face.

"It won't matter if he'll like it or not if we can't secure an invitation to the ball," Imogen says, turning the page of a book I doubt she's even reading. She reclines on the couch, no longer in the fine outfit she wore to town. Instead, she wears a threadbare morning dress, something she never would have dared to wear a year ago. After Mrs. Coleman sold all but a few articles of the family's finest clothing, what remains must be worn sparingly to avoid stains and tears. "I wish Mother would tell us her plan."

Clara ceases her twirling and peels off a pair of silk gloves. As soon as the first glove is removed, the glamour disappears, leaving Clara in a drab gray skirt and blouse. "Mother's original plan already failed," she whispers, casting a quick glance toward Mrs. Coleman's bedroom. "Why didn't we see the prince? He was supposed to be there."

Imogen shrugs. "Maybe Madame Flora wove him an invisibility glamour."

I smirk at the ground as I continue to scrub the filthy floor. Shortly after rejoining my stepfamily to make our way back home, it became clear something had gone amiss. Even though their shopping appeared successful, the proof being the three boxes they had me carry home for them, my stepmother was in an even pricklier mood than she normally is. If only they knew how little they missed in not having seen the prince. Then again, I would have paid dearly to see one of my stepsisters ridiculed in my place. Would he have treated them the way he treated me? Or would the playboy prince have been flattered by the attentions of someone not dressed like a maid?

Clara takes a seat next to her sister on the couch. "Maybe he went out another entrance."

Imogen freezes, slams her book shut, and whirls toward me. "Ember, did you see him? Did he exit through the alley?"

For not the first time, I'm grateful I can lie. Only the pure-blood fae are plagued by the inability to tell direct untruths. "I did not."

"Can you imagine Ember meeting the prince?" Imogen says to Clara. "What would she even say to him?"

I'd tell him I hope the All of All smites him in his sleep and drags him to hell in a burning iron chariot. The thought makes me smile as I scrub the stones even harder.

Clara faces me with cruel mischief in her eyes. "Ember doesn't care about meeting the prince, I'm sure. She's of no mind to marry."

I say nothing to argue her statement because it's true. Even if Mrs. Coleman hadn't forbidden me from marrying until both her daughters are wed, I still wouldn't harbor any hopes for matrimony. No one wants to marry someone like me, a girl too wild to be human, and too tame to be fae. A girl who fits nowhere with no one. A girl guilty of killing the person she loved most...

A knock sounds on the apartment door, making me pause

my scrubbing, brow furrowed. We rarely receive visitors, since Mrs. Coleman likes to pretend we don't live here at all. Not even the post comes to our door, for my stepmother insists on picking it up in town. We already stopped there on our way home today, and after Mrs. Coleman flipped through the sparse letters without opening a single one, she shoved them into her purse with far more contempt than necessary. It was clear she'd been expecting something important.

"What are you doing down there?" Imogen eyes me with a sneer. "Go answer the door."

With a sigh, I drop my scrub brush into the wash bucket and dry my hands on my apron. By the time I reach the door and open it, there's no one there...

I glance down, finding an enormous white owl perched upon a slender box. In one taloned foot, it holds an envelope. "Are you Ember Montgomery?" the owl asks, the deep female voice coming not from her beak but somewhere within the creature.

"I am," I say with no small amount of hesitation.

"Parcel and letter for you."

I'm frozen in place as I stare down at the owl. It isn't that a talking owl surprises me. Not in the least. All fae—both seelie and unseelie alike—can talk if they choose to, and owls are no strangers to the Lunar Court. However, owls aren't used for delivering the post in Evanston. It's a human city with human postal carriers. What's more surprising than all of this is that I have mail. *Me.* I don't think I've ever received a letter in three years, much less a parcel.

The owl tilts her head. "Are you going to take it? I'm an ambassador, not a carrier pigeon. I have other places to be, you know. I'd rather not linger on your doorstep on one leg if I can help it."

"Forgive me," I say and crouch down to take the envelope from her foot. I'm too puzzled to ask what an ambassador is doing delivering parcels, if that's really what she is. Ambassadors work for royals, for the kings and queens of Faerwyvae. What reason could a royal ambassador have with someone like me? I'm about to ask if she's mistaken me for someone else, but as soon as I grasp the envelope, the owl flies off, leaving me with my mysterious gift.

# 5

**EMBER**

Balancing the parcel under one arm, I close the door behind me and lean against it. I turn over the envelope to study the elegant script. Sure enough, the letter is addressed to me. As for the sender...

My eyes go wide as I read the name on the return address. It's from Gemma Bellefleur, mate to the Unseelie King of Winter. It's been over a year since we've spoken. We became warm acquaintances when my stepfamily lived in the Winter Court last year, but things never felt the same after Imogen made such a scene over the king choosing Gemma over her. And even though Gemma asked me to write to her when we moved, I never did. Partially because I was embarrassed about my family's behavior, but mostly because it's hard to believe someone as important as she truly cares to hear from me. She was kind to me, but we weren't *actually* friends. Were we?

"What is that?" Mrs. Coleman stands before me, eyes wide as she stares down at the parcel. I'd been so wrapped up in my thoughts, I hadn't noticed her approach.

"It's for me—"

"Of course it isn't," she says as she snatches the letter from my fingers and wrenches the package from under my arm. Brushing past me, she storms into the front room.

Heat burns my cheeks as I follow hard on her heels. "It's addressed to my name," I say, voice quavering with suppressed rage. "It's from Gemma Bellefleur."

"Gemma Bellefleur!" Imogen rises to her feet from the couch, an appalled expression contorting her face. "What could that filthy harlot possibly want with *you*?"

"It's of no one's concern," Mrs. Coleman says, whisking my package past the couch and toward her bedroom.

Imogen's mouth hangs on its hinge. "Mother! What is this about?"

I'd like to know the same and am about to say as much when my stepmother halts outside her room with a cry of alarm. Dropping the letter and parcel, she leaps back as if she's been burned.

I lunge forward at the same time as my stepsisters do, but I reach the fallen objects first and gather them in my arms. The box is cold to the touch, with tiny ice crystals receding from where Mrs. Coleman's hands had been. Beneath my palms, the ice quickly disappears.

Mrs. Coleman's lips peel back in a sneer. "What is the meaning of this? I said it wasn't for you." She tries to take it from me but snatches her hand away as soon as she touches the box, revealing a fresh patch of ice crystals.

"It seems the parcel claims otherwise," I say. My stepfamily stands around me in a tight half circle, expressions mutinous.

"Why does *she* get a gift?" Clara mutters.

Imogen's face burns crimson. "How does Miss Bellefleur know where we live?"

"Quiet," Mrs. Coleman hisses. Then to me, she says, "Open it. You will open it in front of me or not at all."

Part of me wants to rebel, to say it can go in the fire for all I care. Clearly, she's hiding something about this, and refusing to allow her to witness the contents of the package would enrage her greatly. But as much as I'd love to thwart whatever scheme my stepmother's concocted, I'm too curious to leave the gift unopened. Not to mention, my wretched bargain with Mrs. Coleman enforces my obedience.

"Fine." Tucking the package under my arm, I start with the letter. Sweat prickles behind my neck as I slide my thumb beneath the seal. Inside the envelope, I find four rectangular cards with gilded edges. Before I can read what they say, Mrs. Coleman tears them from my fingers.

I expect her to be burned by ice again, but it seems I have no such luck this time. Clara and Imogen huddle close together as they read, erupting with squeals a second later.

"We're going to the ball!" Imogen shouts, taking Clara by the shoulders. "Mother, how did you do it?"

It makes little sense why Imogen would credit her mother when the invitations came in a letter from Gemma Bellefleur to me. However...a creeping dread tells me there might be more truth to that sentiment after all.

The girls continue to squeal, bouncing on the balls of their feet, while I slide what remains from the envelope. My first glance reveals a brief letter, addressed to me and signed by Gemma. As I start read silently to myself, the girls go rigid, and I feel Mrs. Coleman's eyes burning into me.

*Dearest Ember,*

*I admit, I was thrilled to hear from you after so long. I've missed your presence dearly since your family moved away, although the same can't be said for those you reside with. I was equally pleased to hear of your interest in attending the dance at the Lunar palace. I hear it will be a glamoured ball, and quite a lavish night. Although, it surprises me that you'd be so taken with* the prospect of attending a ball that you'd write to me asking for invitations. Not only for you but your three undeserving family members as well. How unusual! It's almost as if...as if you hadn't been the one to pen the last letter to me at all, but...but perhaps Mrs. Coleman? No, that's just silly, for only the most desperate and repulsive creature would stoop so low as to impersonate one's stepdaughter for personal gain. Anyhow, my answer is yes. I am happy to procure you invitations to the ball. I'm so happy, in fact, that I've had my dearest Mr. Rochester—the King of Winter, if Mrs. Coleman needs a stern reminder—enchant the invitations. They will remain valid so long as you, Ember Montgomery, attend the ball. In addition, you must wear the dress I've provided in the accompanying parcel. If you are left behind or without the gown I've gifted you, the tickets will turn to ice and shatter, rendering them useless. So don't even think about trying anything clever, Mrs. Coleman. Not that you could ever be clever, but I understand one must always try one's best. Have a wonderful time at the ball, Ember.

*Kindest regards,*
*Gemma Bellefleur*

I have to bite my lip to keep from grinning. It's no surprise Gemma wasn't fooled by Mrs. Coleman's scheme, for I can't imagine even the smartest person outwitting the bold Miss Bellefleur.

My stepmother stomps her foot. "What does it say?"

With as much neutral calm as I can manage, I hand her the letter. "You can read it for yourself if you wish."

She takes it from me, and again her daughters huddle close. I can't bring myself to watch their horrified expressions as they read, for it will only set me off laughing. Instead, I stand still, my unopened parcel clutched to my chest.

"The nerve," Mrs. Coleman says, balling the letter in her fist.

"She was quite rude," Clara says. "And why should Ember go to the ball, anyway?"

My stepmother ignores the question. "Show me the dress."

As much as I'd prefer to open the parcel in private, it's folly to think I'd be allowed the luxury. So I do as I'm told, placing the box on the floor and lifting off the cover. An unexpected lump rises in my throat as I peel back the layers of tissue. It's been so long since I've received a gift; it reminds me of cheerful birthdays, solstice, and Yule celebrations I had as a child.

With the tissue out of the way, I get my first glimpse of the box's contents—folded pale blue taffeta with a silver domino mask resting upon it. The mask is lightly decorated with floral filigree but is otherwise unadorned. Setting the mask aside, I lift the dress and rise to my feet. I suppress a gasp as I examine the pleats and layers of the flowing blue skirt, the elegant yet modest neckline. It's the most beautiful thing I've ever—

"It's so boring!" Clara says with a snicker. She stoops down to pick up the mask. "And is this supposed to take the place of a glamour?"

Mrs. Coleman joins her daughter's teasing laughter. "You're quite right, dear. Is that not the most insignificant dress you've ever seen? Miss Bellefleur may fancy herself a clever girl, but she clearly has questionable taste in fashion. Your friend made a poor choice, Ember."

At first, I'm stunned. How can anyone look at this dress and not see its understated elegance? I open my mouth to argue the dress' finer points and defend Gemma's taste but stop myself. It occurs to me that Gemma's choice in dress was far more calculated than my stepfamily will ever know. While the gown is finely made, it is neither as daring as current fae fashions nor as impressive as the most coveted human ballgowns. It's modest enough not to spark envy but lovely enough to allow me to fit in at a ball without drawing much undue attention.

A lump rises in my throat again, and with it comes a hefty

dose of shame and regret. This gift shows just how well Gemma knows me, even after all these months apart. Why did I insist on not keeping in touch with her? Why did I ever think we hadn't truly been friends?

"I wouldn't be caught dead in that," Clara says. "What about you, Imogen?"

My elder stepsister is strangely quiet, but a glance at her face tells me she's fuming. Finally, she rounds on her mother. "You wrote to Gemma? You asked a favor of the one person I despise more than any other?"

Mrs. Coleman meets her daughter's glare with a flippant shrug. "Of course I didn't. Did you not read the letter? Ember wrote to her."

"Mother—"

"Do you want to go to the ball or not?"

Imogen snaps her mouth shut, then slowly turns her gaze to me. "Not if we have to depend on *her*."

"Honestly, Imogen." Mrs. Coleman releases a heavy sigh and rubs her brow. "Do you think I like this any more than you do? I will do whatever it takes to get you and Clara introduced to Lunar high society, and this is our best chance."

Imogen continues to hold my gaze. "She's only going to show off and you know it."

"In that plain dress? Please. She doesn't even have a glamour to wear. She might as well be invisible."

The way they speak about me as if I'm not standing a mere two feet away sets my teeth on edge. I fold the dress over my arm and lift my chin in defiance. "Fret not. I don't want to go."

Silence settles over the room as the three women stare at me as if I have two heads. My stepmother takes a step closer. "Excuse me?"

"I don't want to go," I repeat, slowly this time. As grateful as I am for Gemma's heartfelt gift, and as exciting as it would be to attend my very first ball as a guest, I can't allow my stepfamily to use Miss Bellefleur's generosity for their schemes."

Clara gasps, cheeks flushed. "But if she doesn't go, none of us can!"

Mrs. Coleman scoffs. "You'll go, Ember. I demand it. You *will* obey me."

A sharp pain clenches my stomach, and I nearly double over. Squeezing my fingers into fists, I force myself to remain upright, to keep the pain from reflecting on my face.

She shakes her head with a bitter laugh. "You will obey me, Ember. You can't fight it. The longer you hold out, the more additional punishments I'll find for you."

I've heard that before, which is why I now find myself the sole servant of the household. It's why Mrs. Coleman sold my pianoforte. She's made several demands in the past that I tried to ignore, tried to take the pain and bear it. Maybe this time I'll succeed. Maybe this time I'll outlast her...

"Ember, please!" Clara shouts. "After everything we've done for you, it's the least you can do for us."

Her words drench my rebellious fire, leaving me chilled to the bone. They reverberate through my mind, echoing memories I'd rather leave forgotten.

*It's your fault he died, Ember. After everything you've done, after everything you've taken from us, it's the least you can do.*

Father's eyes flash before me, so bright and alive as he grins at me over his teacup. In the next moment, they turn empty, hard. His hand clenches over his heart. My voice, rich with song, shifts into a scream—

"Obey!" Mrs. Coleman shouts, and I jump at the sharpness in her tone. I shudder at how it mingles with the wail still haunting my mind. My head begins to spin as the memories refuse to abate.

The clatter of tableware.

Father's lifeless eyes.

*It's your fault he died...*
His hand clenched over his heart.
*After everything you've taken from us...*
"Obey!"

"All right," I say, the words coming out with a gasp and leaving me trembling, breathless. "I'll go to the ball." The pain releases me, but the memories linger at the edges of my mind. My knees buckle, sending me sprawling to the ground. I heave a sob as tears stream down my cheeks. When did I start crying?

"That's more like it," Mrs. Coleman says. "Now, get this dress out of my sight and finish cleaning the floors." She stalks away, as does Imogen, but Clara remains before me. I only know by her shoes, for I can't bring myself to lift my head.

"You're so selfish," she mutters coldly. A second later, my silver mask lands on the floor in front of me, thankfully unbroken. Then Clara follows the other two.

Unable to stand, I remain with my sobs and a tear-stained ballgown.

# 6

## FRANCO

Standing on Selene Palace's rooftop balcony, I rest my forearms on the railing and stare down at the sprawling lawn. Beyond it, the forests and mountains gather shadows as the setting sun leaves inky blue twilight to descend upon my kingdom. Soon night will fall, which is when most of the Lunar Court population comes alive. I can already see tiny blue wisps bobbing over Lake Artemisa as well as the flaming tails of a few kitsune who dart between the trees.

It's peaceful up here, alone, with everyone else inside preparing for tomorrow's ball. I dread how busy the palace will be in the coming month. Several elite families will be taking rooms at the palace, and overall, we'll be hosting far more guests than usual. Many have already arrived in anticipation of tomorrow, filling the palace with dense, unfamiliar energy. Energy I can taste and feel with every inch of my being.

As a rare type of fae that feeds on emotion—a psy vampire—I sense energy as easily as I breathe. When I'm used to a person's energy, or their energetic signature, as I call it, it's easier for me to tune them out at will. But when I'm near too many new people at once...it's a lot to get used to. It's one reason I've never been great at making new acquaintances. I much prefer a quiet palace, solitude, and spending my time at home with the very few people I know and trust.

Sudden movement catches my eye, and I straighten. From the line of trees emerges a carriage coming down the road from the north. It's too dark to see much detail from where I stand on the rooftop balcony, but as it approaches, I note the pearlescent sheen of the coach and a pair of puca that draw it. I furrow my brow. The vehicle can belong to none other than the Sea Court. However, as far as I know, we aren't entertaining any fae dignitaries during the social season, since it's a human centric event. Could Nyxia have invited sea fae to attend the ball?

I ponder the question until the answer becomes painfully clear.

Damn it, I know exactly what this is. I'm willing to bet my wings Nyxia has invited a princess to parade before me. It's been years since she's meddled in my love life, although she has dropped several hints as of late.

*Are you still courting so-and-so?*

*Any prospects for a future mate?*

*Have you called on such-and-such? They have a daughter you'd find pretty...*

Is this the real reason Nyxia appointed me to host the social season? So she can display me front and center in hopes that I'll finally snag a mate? Why does she care so much? I grit my teeth, fingers clenching tight around the balcony rail.

Footsteps sound behind me, shaking me from my aggravation. The balcony was empty when I arrived, so curiosity has me turning toward the newcomer. An enormous glass dome rests at the center of the circular rooftop, obscuring my vision of the staircase on the other side. I extend my powers and quickly recognize the energetic signature of my unseen guest. It's my sister's mate. "Greetings, Lorelei," I call out.

A second later, a petite figure with rich brown skin and dark curly hair appears on the walkway, rounding the bend toward me. "It's creepy when you do that, you know," she says with a smirk. The wood nymph wears loose pants and a sleeveless tunic, both in bronze silk—an outfit that tells me she must have just arrived from the Fire Court where she is ambassador to Queen Evelyn.

I meet her halfway down the walkway with an embrace. "I thought you'd be used to it by now, considering you're in love with my sister."

"She, at least, knows better than to use her powers on me anymore." Her tone is indignant, but I've known her long enough to tell she's amused. She pulls back and grins up at me. "How are you, little brother?"

I snort a laugh. "Little brother? There were times you called me much worse."

She scoffs. "There were times you deserved it. Besides, according to human tradition, aren't you what they call my brother-in-law?"

"I suppose you're right." While Lorelei and Nyxia haven't participated in a human wedding, they've held a mate ceremony, which is the fae equivalent according to our traditions. "Are you and my sister ready to leave for your romantic getaway? Is it the Summer Court you're headed to? Perhaps a warm beach?"

"No, it's the Winter Court, actually. I've had enough hot sand beneath my toes after serving the Fire Court for so long. It's plush snow I now crave. Although, I'd still take a beach if it meant time off. I've needed a vacation for...twenty years, at least."

I chuckle and extend my hand toward a pair of chairs nestled against the balcony railing. "Politics, eh?"

She lets out a dark laugh and slumps into one of the seats. "Politics." Her eyes unfocus as if she's lost deep in thought. I resist breathing in her energy, not wishing to invade her privacy, and claim the empty chair. A glance at the lawn shows no sign of the carriage that had been approaching. It must have pulled up to the palace by now. Lorelei shakes her head as if to clear it and returns her attention to me. "What about you? Are you ready to take on the great and terrible burden of running a kingdom while we're gone?"

I swallow hard, feigning as much confidence as I can. "What's the worst that can happen?"

She taps a finger against her lips and pretends to ponder. "Having to host a human social season would be pretty dire—oh, wait. That's already happening."

"If that's the worst, then I'll just have to bear it. Although, I'm almost positive Nyxia has a new marital scheme underway. Did you happen to see the regal-looking coach coming this way? I have a sneaking suspicion it contains a princess."

"I wouldn't be surprised," she says. "But I thought my mate was done with all that."

"Our dear Nyxia will never cease trying to auction off my virtue."

She snorts a laugh. "If only you had an ounce of virtue left to offer."

I put my hand to my chest. "You wound me, Lorelei. I promise, my colorful reputation isn't nearly as bad as it sounds."

A ripple of trepidation clouds her energy, and she nibbles her lip before saying, "I know it isn't." I'm taken aback by her serious tone, the way her eyes bore into me. She leans forward. "Why do you do it, Franco? Why do you let others think you're some roguish playboy? Why didn't you just...explain yourself when everything happened?"

I shrug, trying to appear nonchalant despite how her words pierce my hidden truth. "My reputation may be exaggerated, but it isn't entirely false. I've courted many women without ever taking a mate."

"But...it's not like you set out to break hearts."

"How do you know?"

"Because I know you. I know you deserve love. I also know you haven't seriously courted anyone in years. You've given up."

A cocktail of emotions floods my senses, and I suppress the urge to wrinkle my nose at them—pity mixed with sympathy and encouragement. I hate the way it tastes. Rising to my feet, I face the balustrade and brace both arms against it. "What's your point?"

She stands and settles in next to me. Her eyes burn into my profile, but I refuse to meet them. "My point is I want to see you happy. You should be allowed to find love in your own time—"

"It isn't that easy."

"Why?"

I purse my lips. There's no answer I can give. Not one she would understand, at least. We've been acquainted long enough that she's learned I'm not the confident male most people think I am, but it's not like she can relate. Lorelei is brave and wears her heart on her sleeve. Meanwhile, I...Well, meeting new people and wooing strangers doesn't come easily. When I try to be myself, I'm as awkward as a newborn kelpie on land. To make up for what I lack, I try to play it cool. I make jokes. I laugh easily. I flirt and tease and taunt. That, in turn, either pushes others away or makes them think I'm someone I'm not.

When I finally *do* manage to get to know someone while revealing my true self, it's my powers that get in the way. I can't count the occasions where I've drummed up hopes for a relationship to succeed only to sense the other's ulterior motive. Very rarely have I had a lover who likes me for *me* and not my title.

Then there's good old-fashioned rejection, my least favorite conundrum. Not because I'm being rejected; that I can understand. It's because I have to experience my own emotional response to being broken up with as well as the emotions of the one doing the breaking-up. Double the discomfort for a fraction of the fun.

In the end, I'd rather flirt my way to someone's bedroom for the occasional roll in the sheets without having to take things further. But even that has grown old. Even that can lead to heartache on both sides.

Lorelei's right. I have given up on love, but I'll be damned if I admit it out loud. Lorelei is the absolute worst when she knows she's right about something. Instead of giving her the truth she wants, I do what I do best. Pretend I don't care.

Forcing my shoulders to relax, I lean against the balustrade with a slouch and a smile. "Since when do you give a banshee's tit about my love life?"

She barks a laugh, then stares out at the lawn. "I don't know. I suppose ever since I saw how you courted Evelyn. Before that, I thought you were nothing but a playboy too. But then...with her, I got to see the real you."

My cheeks grow hot, but I divert her attention with a roll of my eyes. "Oh, for the love of the night, don't bring up Evelyn. That was decades ago. I'd like to forget I ever courted the famous Unseelie Queen of Fire, thank you very much."

I expect to taste more pity coming from her. Instead, she seems to buy my lighthearted response and turns to teasing. "I'm willing to bet she'd like to burn the memory from her mind as well. Don't worry, I won't tell her you still pine for her."

"I don't *pine*. There was never any pining."

She winks. "If you say so."

"Oh, come on. She and I are friends. That's all we've ever been."

"Is that why you still ask her to go to bed with you whenever you get the chance?"

"For one, I only do that because it annoys her, and I enjoy the flavor of her aggravation. For another, I ask her *and* King Aspen to go to bed with me, but the answer is always a mind-boggling no. Followed by so much delicious rage."

She shakes her head, and for one shining moment I think that might be the last I'll have to hear of this *love* conversation. But her expression quickly turns pensive, brows furrowed. "I've learned a lot about love these last few years."

"Is that so?" I say, my tone high and mocking. "Lorelei has fallen in love and now she's an expert."

"I'm not an expert," she says, leveling a stare at me, "but I'll confess I once thought I'd never give love a second chance. You know...after Malan died." Her emotions dip into sorrow, and I breathe it in. It feels heavy on my tongue, surprising me that after two decades, she still feels such poignant grief over her former lover.

I know I should say something consoling, but I can't find the words. It's nothing I've ever experienced myself.

Lorelei continues. "I'd hate to see you give up on love and miss out on something amazing. Like what me and Nyxia have."

I lean in close, my expression soft and sincere. "Lorelei, has anyone told you lately...just how completely and utterly annoying you are?"

She punches me in the arm. "I'm trying to have a serious conversation with you."

"That's your first mistake. Honestly, I think love has addled your brain."

"I'll addle your brain," she says, reaching up to slap the side of my head.

A light laugh reaches my ears, and we both pause to face the approaching figure. My sister, Queen Nyxia, strolls casually along the pathway, although her outfit says anything but casual. Dressing to impress is probably her favorite hobby, although

I'm not sure if her target was her mate or whomever just arrived in the coach. Whatever the case, regality drips from every stitch of her slim black pants, her low-cut silver blouse, and her indigo jacket decorated in silver stars. A pair of glittering earrings dangle from beneath the cut of her short silver hair.

We look quite similar in our seelie forms. We have the same towering height, slim stature, and pointed ears. Even our eyes and hair are the same color. But never—*never*—could I evoke the same confidence she does. Never could I wear the mantle of king the way she wears hers as queen.

Lorelei goes to embrace her mate, and I can't help smiling at their height difference. It's cute. In an annoying sort of way, as romance always is. "Can we get out of here already?" Lorelei asks Nyxia with a pleading expression.

The look my sister shines down on the wood nymph is so heartwarming it's almost embarrassing. For whom, I'm not sure, but it's just...painful to look at. "Yes, darling. We leave in an hour. I need to speak with my brother first."

Lorelei nods and pulls away from my sister. Then, with a parting wave for me, she leaves us alone.

Nyxia gestures me over to join her, and I do. We walk along the circular path with leisurely steps. "We have a guest who has come to stay during the social season," she says, her tone hesitant.

I quirk a brow. "You mean, a princess?"

She lifts her chin, revealing not a hint of shame. "Princess Maisie is the youngest daughter of King Ronan. She's a selkie, and this is her first extended visit on land. You will host her stay and make her feel welcome."

"You mean I am to court her. Just say it plainly if that's what you intend."

She stops and faces me. "Yes, Franco, you are to court her."

"What happened to you no longer interfering with my love life? Do you recall what happened last time?"

"Yes, I recall. We both made mistakes then. Afterward, I said I wouldn't meddle unless I had to."

"Oh, and now you suddenly have to?" My shoulders tense and my fingers clench into fists. "Is this about my *training* again?"

Her tone turns sharp. "Perhaps you should speak plainly too, brother. I can tell you're holding back."

A flash of guilt sinks my stomach. Of course she can tell. She's an even more powerful psy vampire than I am. I run a hand through my hair, forcing my anger to calm. "It's just...I know I'm your heir, Nyxia, and I'm happy to do my duty. I always have and always will support you in any way you need. But you and I both know I'm never going to be king. So why do you continue to train me like I am? Why have you been pushing me harder and harder into a position you know I'll likely never have to take?"

Her lips pull into a frown, her energy plummeting. I breathe it in. It's sharp and cloying and full of unspoken secrets.

A shudder runs down my spine. "What aren't you telling me?"

She sighs. "There was a time I thought I'd rule forever. For a very long while, I wanted to."

Her tone has my stomach turning. "Does that mean you no longer want to?"

She glances over at me. "You know I love Lorelei, right?"

I nod. How could I not know the enormity of my sister's affection for her mate? It's so strong I can feel it across the room when they so much as look at one another. It's powerful enough that it terrifies me. How could I ever find what she has?

Nyxia continues. "I ruined my chances with her once before

and thought I'd never win her back. Now that we're together... you know I can't lose her."

Although I've sensed my sister's love for Lorelei, I've never heard her express her feelings out loud. She and I are the same in that way. We are masters of disguise when it comes to our own internal workings, always keeping a strong outer persona to hide what lurks within. Hearing her words paired with the energy radiating off her is almost enough to overwhelm my senses. My head spins for a moment and I'm forced to widen my stance for stability. "What does your love have to do with me being your heir?"

Her energy contracts with a hint of trepidation. "Lorelei is ready to retire from politics. After two decades working through some of Faerwyvae's most tumultuous times, she's eager to live a simple life. And I want to give that to her. Share that with her."

"What exactly does that mean?"

She folds her hands at her waist, a demure posture for someone who's normally so fierce. "The reason I've been pushing you to find a mate the last few years is because I want you to challenge me to the throne. As soon as your standing is strong in the eyes of Lunar Court's people—the humans included—I'm ready for you to succeed me."

My mouth goes dry. No, this can't be. I was always meant to rule by her side, to be her heir, a safeguard against her unlikely death. I was never meant to rule.

Alone.

Without her.

"I'm sorry I didn't tell you sooner," she says. "I didn't want you to feel pressured."

"Well, thanks for that." I don't bother masking the iron in my tone. "Instead of warming me up to the idea, you're now hitting me with it all at once."

"I thought I had more time to give you, but I can't make

Lorelei wait any longer. I've felt how exhausted she is. She won't say so, but she doesn't need to. Even when I shield myself from tasting her energy, I can read it as clear as day."

My heart clenches as I recall how tired Lorelei looked when she first sat down with me tonight. Now it all makes sense. The realization clears my head, dampening some of my bitterness and fear. Being king might not be what I desire, but I do want to make Nyxia and Lorelei happy. I release a heavy sigh, which only unwinds the merest fraction of my tension. "What do you need me to do?"

Her face brightens, a spark of hope pulsing around her. "I need you to be king, Franco. To do that, you must gain the respect of the people. That way, when you challenge me to the throne, no other contender will dare line up behind you."

I shift from foot to foot. While the rule of each court is often passed through bloodline, anyone is eligible to make a bid for the throne at any time. The magic that infuses the isle—a force we call the *All of All*—makes the final choice, and it isn't always the heir who is selected. In the end, the best safeguard against losing the right to rule is to prevent anyone from thinking they stand a chance. That's what has protected my sister's reign. Being the most powerful lunar alpha in generations has kept anyone from daring to bid for Lunar's unseelie throne.

But me...I'm not as powerful as she is. I'm not as feared by other fae. When it comes to the humans, I'm certainly not as respected. Not after what happened last time I was in their midst. At least now it makes sense. "That's why you've been pushing me to take a mate."

"Not just a mate, Franco. You must marry."

I bristle. "Marry? I thought you'd given up on trying to force me to marry. You and Lorelei only held a mate ceremony, and that's been deemed good enough."

"Only because I am feared and my rule has a history of being uncontested. You will face different obstacles that I haven't had to endure. You'll have other strengths to prove. The Lunar Court needs us, it needs our unseelie values. We can't afford to have your reign challenged. The best thing we can do to prevent that is to prove you're an unshakable king. To the humans, that means royal marriage and the ability to produce heirs. To the fae, it means a respectable political alliance."

"Hence Princess Maisie of the Sea Court. My potential future wife." I rub my brow. I've never once considered a lover to be my mate, much less thought of making one my wife. In the fae tradition, selecting a mate means deeming someone your committed partner. While mate relationships aren't always eternal, it's a significant label, even for the fae who prefer to have multiple mates simultaneously. But marriage... that's even more significant. With marriage comes vows. And vows are impossible for a fae to break since they are a form of bargain.

"I want you to court her," Nyxia says, a note of desperation in her voice. "I want you to at least *try*. Show me you're trying. Show the people you're trying. Court Princess Maisie publicly during the course of the social season. Be seen with her on your arm. If you find her abhorrent at the end of the month, I'll find someone else. But damn it, Franco. *Try*. Promise me."

"I'll try, Nyxia," I finally say.

Her shoulders relax and gratitude spills from her, wrapping around me like a suffocating blanket. She steps forward, a dazzling grin replacing her serious expression. "Thank you, Franco. I do hope you'll like Maisie, but I trust you to make the right decision."

Guilt burrows inside me, but I try to force it away before Nyxia can sense it...and the reason behind it. While I'm determined to keep my word and court the princess, it's not with the hope that things will work out between us. My romantic history has told me those chances are slim. But I will do what it takes to make Nyxia *think* my efforts are real.

Sooner or later, I know I'll have to let go and settle on a wife. I love my sister and Lorelei. I want them to be happy. But for now, I just want more time before everything changes. Before the one person I've always been able to depend on leaves. Before I'm forced to be king and stand beneath the scrutiny and pressures of a crown I never thought I'd wear.

I tuck those thoughts away and hide them behind an arrogant façade. Standing tall, I say, "You know, I always thought I'd look better on that throne than you anyway."

Her sentimental mood shifts in an instant, matching mine, her grin widening with a mixture of pride and mischief. "That's the spirit, little brother." Her eyes flick over my clothing, a mock sneer on her lips. "But if you want to fill my shoes, you'll have to learn to dress better."

I chuckle as she walks away, but as soon as she's gone, my smile slips. My shoulders sink. All I feel is empty in her wake.

# 7

## EMBER

In the hours leading up to the ball the next day, I lose myself in my chores, trying to become as small and inconspicuous as I can to avoid further altercations with my stepfamily. I make it my particular mission to speak as little as possible, argue none, and do as I'm told. Keeping focused on my tasks, I dare not listen in on my stepsisters' conversations as they gossip throughout the day, speculating on what tonight's festivities will bring. I dare not even look their way.

Instead, I scrub. Mend. Polish. Cook. Scrub. Mend. Cook.

I can get through this. It's a single ball. A single night where my stepfamily will use me and my friend's generosity for their own gain. As much as I despise giving in, I can't bring myself to reignite yesterday's fight, the memories Clara's words stirred, or the pain Mrs. Coleman's demand created.

Two more weeks.

Then I'll be free.

Scrub. Mend. Cook. Scrub.

My hands are raw and red by the time the afternoon draws

near to dusk and Mrs. Coleman announces it's time to get ready for the ball. My stepsisters erupt with cheers and race off to their shared bedroom. Once the door closes behind them, my stepmother turns her gaze to me. It's the first time she's so much as looked my way since yesterday's argument.

I don't wait to be told what to do before I rush for the attic stairs and head to my room to get ready. There's no electricity in my attic bedroom, so I light a lamp on my bedside table. Then I throw open the shutters of the single window over my bed to reveal the hazy illumination of the setting sun. Everything in me itches to get outside, to climb up to my rooftop perch and watch the sun's descent. But no. The New Moon Masquerade awaits.

I wish I could be as excited as my stepfamily is. This is my first ball, after all. I *should* be thrilled. Under any other circumstance, one where I hadn't been granted an invitation under deception and coercion, I think I would be. Not that I care for the restrained human dances I've never been allowed to learn or the tense social formalities that are expected at such formal occasions; it's the music I've always yearned for. The music I always wished my stepsisters could bring home with them. There was a time, years ago, when I'd sneak out of bed after my stepfamily came home from dancing. I'd seek out their dancing slippers and hold them up to my ears, hoping I could tease out strains of music written in the wear of their soles.

Then I got caught by Imogen.

*Stupid Ember, listening to a shoe! Such a wild fae creature. Are you fifteen or a child? You're lucky we don't bring you out with us. You'd be ridiculed to death!*

I turn away from my window and face my cramped room. Piles of chests and boxes line the walls and clutter the floors, leaving me just enough space for my tiny bed and dressing area at the far end of the room. I skirt toward my wash table and set about cleaning the day's filth from my hands, arms, and face.

Our apartment has no proper tub or washroom, unlike the finer townhomes we've lived at in the past. Which means by the time I'm done cleaning up and dressing in the nicest undergarments and petticoats I have, it still feels like a crime to don a beautiful gown.

The gift from Gemma hangs on the back of my dressing screen, as out of place as a poorly tuned piano key. In this case, however, the dress is the only fine-tuned object in the room and everything else stands in stark disharmony.

Including myself.

Handling the dress as if it were glass, I slip it over my head, cringing when any part of it brushes the dusty walls and furniture. Once I have it on, I find more to appreciate about it as well as Gemma's foresight. Unlike most ballgowns, this one requires no help to close myself into it. The back is low enough for me to reach, with hooks for closures instead of pretty laces. And the puffed sleeves that cover my shoulders and upper arms make up for the modesty that the low back lacks.

I step out from behind my dressing screen to the cracked mirror propped amongst a pile of boxes, surprised at what I find.

Elegance.

My hand moves to my locket as I assess my reflection. I'm delighted at how much I look like my mother in this moment. I may not have her pointed ears—only full fae have that feature—but I have her hair, her eyes, and her smile, things this gown seems to bring out more than anything has before. I flip open my locket to reveal the portraits of my parents. A lump rises in my throat as I study them. My heart clenches as my eyes rest on my father, and I can't bear to look at him for long. It hurts too much. Fills my stomach with the iron weight of guilt. When I look at Mother, I can almost recall the sound of her voice, the graceful way she walked, her smooth motions when she danced...

I shake the ruminations from my mind and snap my locket closed. Training my focus on my appearance, I note my hairstyle leaves much to be desired. Free from the bonnet, my turquoise strands hang in tangled waves around my shoulders. I take a brush to it, only to realize I have no skill with pinning my hair up for formal occasions. Then again...will Mrs. Coleman even allow me to forgo the bonnet for one night? Surely, wearing a tattered bonnet with a ballgown will draw far more undue attention than teal hair will. The ball is being thrown by a fae prince, after all—

The blood leaves my face at the thought.

Damn it, why haven't I confronted this until now? I'm about to attend a ball hosted by the very royal fae I not only insulted but was also ridiculed by. My face grows hot at the memory of his lewd suggestions about my mistaken motive. I'm not sure whether I should be more fearful of being recognized by him or irritated that I'll have to see him at all. In addition, I'll be expected to pay him respect like I'm the simpering maiden he thinks all females are.

I grit my teeth and brush my hair harder, attacking my tangles as if they were his arrogant face.

At least I have one comfort.

He *won't* recognize me.

I wore my bonnet yesterday. I was dressed in rags. Furthermore, I doubt he has any room in his tiny, self-obsessed brain to remember the likes of me, someone he assumes is yet another girl in love with him.

Footsteps sound on the stairs leading to my bedroom, startling me. I lower the brush and whirl to find my stepmother clearing the threshold. She pauses just inside my room and studies me through slitted lids. "The dress will do." Her words come out clipped.

She moves closer, and I brace myself, muscles tensing with

every step she draws near. Her eyes flash to the brush. She extends her hand, palm up.

I hand her the brush and she motions for me to turn around. With bated breath, I do as she wants, turning my back to her. The brush comes to my head. I flinch, expecting the bristles to dig into my scalp, but she simply drags it down the length of my hair. My heart leaps into my throat at the closeness, the uncharacteristically gentle gesture. She's never brushed my hair before, never done anything a mother would do for a daughter.

The last person to brush my hair besides me was my true mother.

I breathe away the tears that prick my eyes and refocus on the feel of the bristles running through my hair, waiting for the moment the motions turn rough, punishing.

"We must speak of your expected behavior tonight," she says, and I shudder at the proximity of her voice. "You will say and do nothing to sully my name. You will not show off or draw attention to yourself."

I bristle at that. Even after all these years, she still expects me to do what she considers *showing off*. Not once have I sought attention for myself, and never have I desired to outshine her daughters. It isn't my fault I used to get more attention for my accomplishments back when Father was still alive. I didn't ask for it. All I wanted was to play the piano.

And sing.

It was the singing Mrs. Coleman hated.

It was the singing that killed my father.

Mrs. Coleman lowers the brush and hands it back to me, but when I try to turn around to face her, she squeezes my shoulder to make me stay in place. I wince as one of her fingernails digs into the bare flesh above my puffed sleeve. Then, without a word, she hands me several hair pins. The plain kind, not ones with jewels and baubles like she and my stepsisters are keen on wearing. I take them from her.

"Keep them where I can reach them," she says.

I hold the pins near my shoulder and feel her gather my hair off my neck. Again, I brace myself for pain, but it doesn't come. I squeeze my free hand tight to steady my nerves.

Mrs. Coleman takes a pin from my fingers and slides it against my scalp. She takes another and speaks again, maintaining a quiet, chilling tone. "Do you know why I took back my maiden name for myself and my girls after your father died?"

I don't dare shake my head, don't dare disrupt her ministrations. My answer comes out barely above a whisper. "No."

"Because I didn't want my daughters associated with the likes of you."

I already figured this was the answer, but I've never understood the reason behind it. My stepmother acts like she's better than the fae when we're amongst human society, speaks as if the fae are no better than animals. Then when we're around faekind, she boasts about how well she understands them, brags on and on about the fae figures of great importance she knows, naming all her supposed fae acquaintances and connections. She constantly seeks their favor, hunts for husbands amongst the royals like there's nothing greater to aspire to. Then with me...with me, she acts like I'm no better than dirt. A tear breaks free from the gathering pool and trickles down my cheek. Thankfully, I have no cosmetics to ruin.

A word unbidden comes from my lips. "Why?"

She slides another pin into my hair, and this one grates against my scalp, making me cry out. "You know what you did. You're the reason your father is dead."

My lungs contract at her words, my throat dry. Another tear streams down my cheek. She's right. It was my fault. It was all my fault.

She pushes me roughly away from her, and I stumble before righting myself. "You were a thorn in our marriage and now you're a thorn in my side every day."

I turn to face her, trembling, a cold sweat beading behind my neck.

"I should have dropped you in an orphanage when I had the chance. It would have saved me three years of grief."

I go still. Not because her words sting but because they're full of lies. I focus on them, inviting a whirlwind of rage to overpower my shame, my sorrow. "You made me stay with you," I say through my teeth. "Begged me."

Her eyes go wide. "I did not beg."

"Is manipulated a better word?"

"You ungrateful, wretched girl. Where would you be if you hadn't stayed with me these last three years?"

I shake my head, biting back my answer. If she hadn't manipulated me into staying with her, if she hadn't dragged me to a bargain broker and convinced me to enter a legally binding agreement, I would be exactly where I want to be. Away from my stepfamily. Free. I'd already be touring with a troupe of musicians, the way I plan to do once this is all over.

If only I hadn't been so blind. So vulnerable. Her words seemed genuine, and I was stupid enough to believe them.

*I promised your father I'd take care of you. The only way I can keep that promise is if you make a bargain to stay with me. Give me this peace of mind so I can fulfill my promise. It's your fault he died, Ember. After everything you've done, after everything you've taken from us, it's the least you can do. You are a bad girl. Dangerous. You know this. You need someone to guide you. Someone to obey.*

While half of what she said was true—that I am guilty of my father's death, bad, and dangerous—her motive had been a lie. But she won. I hardly gave it a second thought before our bargain was set in stone.

*Until you turn nineteen, you will remain in my care and live under my roof. And you will obey me. Do you agree to this bargain?*

*Yes.*

My stepmother takes a step closer, lips peeled into a snarl. "For three years, I've provided for you, cared for you. Gave you a roof over your head, let you play your infernal music. And how do you repay—"

A dark laugh escapes my lips. "Do you think I don't know?"

Her chest heaves. "Know what?"

"You didn't trick me into a bargain so you can *care* for me. You did it for the money. You did it because of my father's will. Did you think I'd never find out?" My body quakes as anger storms through my veins. I pin my arms close to my sides to still them.

Mrs. Coleman folds her hands at her waist, a smug smile tugging her lips. "I don't know what you're talking about."

"Your stipend. The two thousand moonstone chips you get every month because of *me*," I say. According to my father's will, she receives a generous allowance for my upkeep until the day I turn nineteen—so long as I remain under her care until then. After that, I claim my inheritance whether I live with her or not, and the choice to continue paying her falls to me. She's yet to discover my plan, however. After I donate my inheritance to charity, neither she nor I will see that money ever again.

She doesn't bother looking ashamed. In fact, she seems more amused than anything. "How did you find out?"

"Being easily forgotten has its uses," I say. "I overheard you lamenting over your woes to Imogen."

Her cheeks redden at my answer. Averting her gaze, she wanders over to my bedside table where my silver mask rests. Taking the mask in her hands, she says, "I had to do what was necessary to care for my girls."

"You could have just asked me." My voice quivers with restraint. All I want to do is yell. "You could have *asked* me to stay and ensure you'd be provided for. You could have treated me like family—"

She whips her gaze back to me and takes a forbidding step closer. "You are not family. And don't you dare say I haven't asked."

"Manipulating me into making a bargain isn't asking."

"Manipulating, pah!" She takes a few slow steps to close the distance between us and stares down her nose at me. "You may think you have it rough, but you know nothing of pain. You know nothing of hardship."

My current circumstances beg to differ, but I purse my lips to keep from arguing. She isn't worth my breath. She'll never see her own vileness. I'll always deserve her hatred, always be the villain in her story. And not for killing her husband. After he died, she made it quite clear it was his fortune she mourned, not his life.

She burns me with a scowl for a few tense seconds, then hands me my mask. I clasp the other end, but she doesn't release it. I tug harder, but it makes her step uncomfortably close. "When you claim your father's inheritance, you don't plan on giving us a single moonstone chip, do you?"

I could lie. I could tell her I'll consider it, perhaps manipulate her the same way she's manipulated me. And yet, I don't have it in me. Not now. Not when I'm so tired and *so* close to freedom.

Holding her gaze steady, I speak the truth. "No. You'll never see another chip of my father's fortune for as long as you live."

"I could force you. I could order you right now to hand it over to me."

I shrug. "It would be an order made in vain. I could neither obey nor disobey, for I have no right to those funds yet. And when I do, our bargain will be fulfilled, and you will have no control over me."

Her expression darkens, her tone barbed with iron. "Your father should have taught you to be kind."

"He did," I whisper. He's the only reason I bother being even remotely civil to my stepfamily at all. Father saw good in Mrs. Coleman, saw a broken family in need of his love and support. Even when I told him they treated me badly, he assured me if I responded with kindness, they'd never truly hurt me.

However, perpetual goodness in the face of cruelty is not in my nature. Not with my mother's blood flowing through my veins. Not with her final request echoing through my heart.

*Always be wild. Promise me.*

My stepmother snorts a cruel laugh, then finally releases the mask and brushes past me. When she reaches my door, she pauses.

"When we get to the ball, you will behave. You will obey and you will not overshadow my daughters in any way."

I lift my chin, standing tall despite having only the back of her head to witness it. "It's like you said yesterday. In a dress like this, I might as well be invisible."

# 8

## FRANCO

The New Moon Masquerade has yet to begin, but already the throne room reeks of human desperation. I stand in the doorway with a glass of wine in hand, nose wrinkled at the neatly made tables and chairs that line the perimeter of the room. One hosts a display of refreshments that bears only a single variety of fae wine, and it certainly isn't the fun kind. I take in the rest of the room, then narrow my gaze at the dais. Upon it sits my sister's obsidian throne, where I am to be put on display tonight to greet aristocrats and smile at the eligible daughters they thrust before me.

Why anyone seeks to pawn a daughter off on a prince with such a despicable reputation is beyond me. For a couple of years, it was enough to save me from the attention of hopeful lovers. As time passed, my reputation somehow shifted into an open invitation, emboldening men and women alike to try their luck at wooing me. It was amusing at first. Pleasurable, even. Until it wasn't anymore. Now it's just insulting.

Thank the All of All I won't be forced to dance tonight. I swore off ballroom dancing years ago, for reasons I'd rather forget. Of course, if this were a traditional new moon revel and not a human ball, I'd be more than happy to dance. If that were the case, I'd be standing under the open sky, preparing for a night of unrestrained debauchery. We'd have *good* wine like Midnight Blush, the kind that makes you far happier than one should ever feel. We'd have drums and wild, unpredictable music. The dances would be chaotic and sensual and...and nothing like the trite ass-clenching etiquette I'm about to witness tonight.

Lifting my wineglass to my lips, I take a heavy swallow of the bittersweet liquid. It isn't Midnight Blush, but hopefully it will lower me to at least a semi-conscious state before the night is through.

"Drinking already, Your Highness?" asks a grating voice.

I turn toward the man that approaches and give him a contrived smile. "Brother Marus, I didn't realize you were fond of dancing."

"I'm not," he says, eying the room with almost as much disdain as I feel. "And yet, there are certain necessities required to secure one's desires. I just so happen to be in want of a wife."

"And where better to procure one than at the county fair—oh, forgive me. That's livestock. Although, I'm not sure your kind treat bride selection any differently." I say this last part under my breath and take another gulp of wine. Brother Marus, however, doesn't seem amused as he watches me with a blank look. The man would be handsome, still in the prime of his youth with his dark hair and eyes, were it not for his lack of humor. Then again, I haven't come to expect much else from the brothers of Saint Lazaro's Church.

He takes a step closer to me, his hands behind his back. "There have been speculations, my prince."

"I'm sure there have been many, although I've never found their existence to be an interesting topic of conversation. Surely, they've been around since the dawn of the thinking mind. For, if one can think, then surely one can speculate." Brother Marus doesn't even quirk a brow, the stone-faced bastard. "You know what *is* interesting? The word *bastard* and humankind's assertion that it's an insult. Your people have some truly fantastic swears."

This, at least, I get an eye-twitch over. Marus clears his throat. "It is said there's a reason behind Queen Nyxia's absence from this year's season. It is also said you may be taking the throne before long."

"Who is *it* and why is he talking about me? The nerve, really." I attempt to take another swallow of wine only to find my glass empty. With a sigh, I head for the refreshments table to refill it.

Unfortunately, Marus follows hard on my heels. "Your Highness, I simply wanted to say how much the Church of Saint Lazaro appreciates your sister's support of us—"

"Not killing you isn't the same as support, but go on."

"—by giving us representation at court. All we want is to be recognized as a primary human religion and given the freedom to follow our faith." He pauses, and for one glorious moment, I think that might be the last I hear of him. However, I sense him inching closer as I pour my wine, his energy swarming around me like murky streams of sewage. "Prince Franco, I do hope that when you succeed your sister to the throne, we can continue to maintain the same peace we have now. It would be in both our best interests."

The hair on the back of my neck stands on end. His energy is calm, but I can't help wondering if his words hold a veiled threat. Saint Lazaro's Church is responsible for sparking the rebellions eleven years ago, after all. While the skirmishes were supposedly instigated by radicals in their number and not the church as a whole, I don't fully trust anyone from their brotherhood, regardless of the peace treaties they signed after the rebellions were quelled and their radicals were exterminated. It never ceases to infuriate me that my sister allows a man from the brotherhood to take up residence at the palace at all. Nyxia has assured me time and time again that giving proper recognition to their religion will keep history from repeating, and I have to trust she's right. But why in the name of the night did the brotherhood have to select Marus? Couldn't they have selected someone less...intolerable to represent them?

"Should that day come, I am sure we will talk," I say with a forced grin. He opens his mouth to speak, but a four-legged fae near the door offers me salvation. "It's been great, but I must speak with my ambassador. Enjoy the ball."

I down my drink in a single gulp and slam the empty glass on the table. The smile slips from my lips as soon as I brush past Marus and join Augie, the Lunar Court ambassador, at the door. The bushy-tailed black and gray raccoon utters an unsettling hiss, yellow eyes fixed on the man behind me. "I don't like him," he says. "He smells like something..."

"Like corruption, unbridled ambition, and the particular stench of a man who hasn't passed wind in public for over a decade? I know. Butt clenchers, the lot of these humans."

"Can I eat him when he dies?" Augie asks as we turn away from the throne room to walk down the hall.

"Well," I say, drawing out the word, "that's probably not for the best. For one, the humans will want his body for their burying and chanting and crying bit that they do. For another, you're an ambassador. Even the unseelie ambassador is supposed to have seelie sensibilities, not a taste for human flesh."

"I can be seelie," he says. Then, with a shudder, he rises on two legs, his fluffy raccoon body replaced with his humanoid seelie form. He waggles his brows, a dark charcoal color to match his short-cropped hair. His eyes are no longer yellow but more of a dark amber. The thing that stands out most about his seelie form are his ears. Instead of the lightly pointed tips most seelie fae have, his ears are furry and triangular, set on the top of his head, much like they are in his unseelie form. "Is this better?"

I chuckle and elbow the younger fae in the ribs. While we look about the same age in our seelie forms, he's a good two hundred years younger than me. Which is probably why we get along so well. The older generations of fae can be almost as stuffy as the humans. "What news do you have for me, Augie? Has anyone interesting arrived, or are we in for the most boring night of our lives?"

"Madame Flora is here. She's taking a room for the night."

I brighten at that. "She decided to come after all. Splendid. Speaking of Madame Flora...did you happen to mention plans of my trip to the glamourist's shop to anyone earlier this week?"

He grimaces. "Not on purpose."

"Augie." I drag out the name with a growl.

"Well, there's this female I'm seeing. A servant. And she...well, we were talking about the ball, and I had to tell her why I won't be able to dance with her—"

"Damn it, Augie, you know better than to blab about my private matters. Have you any idea what you did? I had a horde of women waiting to jump me outside."

"To...hurt you?"

"No, not to hurt me. They wanted to waltz, I'm sure. Horizontally. Followed by a marriage proposal."

Augie grins as if I'm bragging and not relaying horrors of the utmost severity. I point a finger at him. "I'm serious. You can't tell anyone about my private travels. Especially when I'm going to a human city."

He gives a resigned nod. "I'm sorry. It won't happen again."

"Very well. You're lucky I don't tell my sister. Half the time I think she regrets taking my word of recommendation and hiring you. Anyhow, where is Madame Flora staying? I'd love to pay my respects."

"She's been settled in the Dawnstar wing, down the hall from your selkie princess. Speaking of, shouldn't you be paying your respects to her instead? Have you yet to meet her?"

"I've tried, I swear, but the few times I've called on her, a male voice at the door says she isn't feeling well. Should I be worried there's a man in the bedroom of the female I'm supposed to be courting?"

"That could be her voice, you know. Besides, shouldn't you be more worried she isn't feeling well?"

I shrug. "I think I'm more worried that I'm not more worried."

Augie rolls his eyes. "Well, I take it she's feeling much better now, for I heard she's paying calls to her neighbors. In fact, I spotted her coming out of Madame Flora's room not long ago."

"Wait, you've seen her even before I have? That's hardly fair." A pinch of indignation moves through me before I remind myself I don't care. Still...could she have been faking ill to avoid meeting me? It hadn't occurred to me that she could dread our courtship as much as I do. "I suppose I should at least confirm whether she's coming to the ball, although if she's gone to see Madame Flora, I assume it was to procure a glamour for tonight. But if I don't have to parade her around on my arm all evening, our night proceeds as planned. Agreed?"

His lips quirk with a sly grin. "Agreed."

∽

WITH A DEEP BREATH, I KNOCK ON THE DOOR TO PRINCESS Maisie's bedroom.

"Who is it?" asks the same male voice I heard before.

"Prince Franco," I say. "Again."

A shuffling sound comes from inside the room, followed by a rhythmic clacking. Unlike the last few times, no one tells me to go away and come back later. Finally, the door creaks open. I step inside the room, but there's no one there.

"She's outside," says the male voice. I turn toward it, just in time to glimpse a dark shape falling from the door handle. When it lands, I see it's a crustacean covered in a cluster of mushrooms. I furrow my brow. He isn't an unusual type of fae. Being lovers of any dark, wet, or warm climates, his kind are found in many of Faerwyvae's courts. However, he's personally unfamiliar to me. He certainly isn't a servant at the palace. "And you are?"

"Podaxis," he says in a bored tone, then snaps his pincers toward the other end of the room. Shuffling sideways, claws tapping against the marble floor—the source of the clacking sound I heard—he leads me to a pair of closed balcony doors.

"Are you the princess' servant?"

Podaxis stops and fixes two beady eyes on me. "Servant? Please. Have you never heard of friends, Your Highness?" He taps his pincers against the door.

"Come in," says a feminine voice from the other side.

I'm about to tell her *come in* is incorrect, considering I'm exiting the room onto a balcony, but stop myself. My first words to her should probably be something other than an annoying remark. I swing open the balcony doors to greet the darkening sky. A female fae in humanoid form sits on a chair at the far end of the balcony, staring at the horizon where the sinking sun paints its final streaks of color. Her skin is tan, cheeks flushed with a rosy hue. Her hair is pale pink, styled in a flawless updo, leaving curling tendrils to frame her face. I can't make out the color of her irises, but I think they might be blue or gray.

"Greetings, Princess Maisie," I say with my most winning smile. "I'm Prince Franco."

She glances at me briefly but doesn't meet my eyes. "A pleasure," she says, voice devoid of all feeling. Podaxis scuttles across the balcony floor and climbs up the blanket draped over her legs. After turning in a circle, he settles on her lap. Maisie gives him a pat, then adjusts the blanket more securely around her hips. I sense a spike of panic and wonder what could have her so alarmed. The way she fiddles with the blanket, ensuring it fully covers her bottom half, makes me think she might be self-conscious about the way she's dressed. I can see nothing below her waist aside from the elegant pair of shoes that peek beneath the bottom of her blanket. They're made of a pale blue silk dotted with tiny pearls.

I take a step closer only to realize there isn't anywhere for me to go. There's no other chair out here, and she doesn't seem keen on standing to converse with me. It seems odd to hover and talk down to her, so I lean against the balcony railing.

And. Say. Nothing.

Neither does she. I can't tell if she's simply nervous or doing her best to make me feel unwelcome. Normally, I'm the one to put off unwanted advances in such a way. It feels odd to have the tables turned on me. At least she isn't batting her lashes and calculating my net worth.

I clear my throat. "How do you find the Lunar Court so far? Is it to your liking?"

"It's rather dry."

"Yes, I suppose any court on land would feel that way to a sea fae." I watch her face, wondering if she'll crack a smile, but...nothing. I breathe in, sensing her emotions, and find a blend of annoyance and frenetic energy. It seems like she's itching to be anywhere but with me. "So...what brings you here?"

Finally, she meets my eyes with a pointed look. "I'm sure you know, Your Highness. We are to court. Father expects us to marry by the month's end." There's no bitterness in her tone, but there's no warmth either. It feels more like...anxiety. But why?

"Princess Maisie, if you came here against your will, I won't force you to stay." I'm torn between relief and disappointment as the words leave my mouth. If she leaves, I'll be free from the chore of courting her. But that also means I'll have failed my sister's expectations before I've even begun. I sigh. "If you want to leave, I'll—"

"No, please," she says, sitting straighter. Her energy darkens with a hint of desperation. "I am willing to be here. I...need to be here. Please forgive me for my rudeness. I've never lived outside the Sea Court. You...you can't imagine what it's like being thrust into this body, going from warmth and blubber, only to come up on land with two legs that don't behave and air that sucks all the life from your skin."

I get the sense she's hiding something, but at least I've gotten her to talk. It seems she responds not to charm but sincerity, much to my supreme discomfort. I'm not used to being so serious with strangers. It's an effort not to fidget as I deliver the words she needs to hear. "I understand far more than you realize. I too shift between forms. As a raven, I'm agile, but this body is far different. When I first learned how to shift, I had to get used to alternating between my two forms."

She nods and gives me the first semblance of a smile. "Thank you for saying you understand."

Although her words sound more like what she *thinks* she should say rather than what she *wants* to, it's something. And now that I've gotten her to talk, I feel like I should keep it going. "So...did you not take seelie form often before you came here?"

She shakes her head. "I rarely removed my selkie skin. I wasn't much for dancing after sundown like my cousins, nor did I have a taste for visiting the coastal pubs at night with my brothers."

I ponder that for a moment. Selkies are one of the few types of fae who don't shift between their seelie and unseelie forms at will. Rather, they remove their sealskins to reveal a human form underneath. It's fascinating, bordering on delightfully morbid. I'm almost of a mind to ask her more about it when I sense her energy shifting again, contracting this time. I've already lost her interest.

"Why did you agree to our courtship?" I ask, my curiosity genuine.

"Father wants a marriage with a royal on land," she says, though I still taste a deeper truth lingering beneath her words.

I wink. "And he didn't find me attractive enough to woo for himself?"

She stares at me blankly, unamused.

I clear my throat, regaining my serious composure. "Regardless, I am pleased you are here. Will I see you at the ball tonight?"

"I don't know. Like I said, I was never one for dancing."

I furrow my brow. If she hadn't planned on attending the ball, then why did she visit Madame Flora? Based on our conversation so far, it's hard to believe she's the friendly type to call on strangers for courtesy's sake alone. Or is her cold composure meant just for me? Whatever the case, I'm not upset that she doesn't want to come, for I already have alternative plans that will be far more enjoyable...

I push off from the balustrade and offer her a bow. "If you end up coming to the ball, I'll be honored to see you. Otherwise, I'll call on you in the morning."

She nods, and I return to her room. Once back within the halls of the palace, I suppress the urge to erupt with agitated laughter. Maisie isn't anything close to the worst female I've courted, but we are far from compatible. A pit of dread forms in my stomach as I consider what it will be like to spend time with her for an entire month. She hated my charm and barely tolerated my sincerity. I'm starting to think she'd like me best if I were to have a lobotomy.

Then again, isn't our situation ideal? With someone so clearly wrong for me, one who makes her disinterest plain, there's no one to disappoint when it's over.

Not me. Not her.

At least this way, no one gets hurt.

# 9

## EMBER

The carriage ride to Selene Palace is a tense affair, with my stepfamily acting far more bristly than usual. Their mood was all bubbly excitement until they discovered the state of our hired cab. Without many options available in the Gray Quarter for a four-seater on such short notice, we were forced into a rusty old thing with squeaking wheels and cramped, musty seats.

"I feel like we're riding in a rotting pumpkin," Clara whines from her place next to me, scowling at the patches of rust that have even marred the interior.

"Blame Ember," Mrs. Coleman says. "If her friend had gotten us our invitations sooner, we would have had more time to prepare."

I bite back my response, keeping my eyes fixed on the scenery out the window. It's hard to begrudge the sorry condition of our cab when it offers such a lovely view of the countryside. It reminds me of the lands outside my childhood home. Despite my visual distraction, I can feel my stepmother's glare burning into me. My scalp still hurts from where she scraped it with the hairpin. She never did finish helping me with my hair either, so I was left to complete the haphazard job myself. Which, of course, has given my stepsisters plenty of fuel for their insults. As if they needed more. I tap my fingers against my thighs, wishing I had piano keys.

"Your gloves are stained," Clara says. When I don't respond, she says it again, bumping her shoulder into mine.

I pull my gaze from the window and turn my palms over, finding the white silk has turned to gray. It doesn't surprise me, considering these are the only formal gloves I own. The last time I wore them was when I played piano for the Winter King's ball last year. The only other ball I've attended. Even then I served as a musician, not a guest.

"Unlike mine," she says, holding out her hands to examine the pristine silk gloves she got from Madame Flora's shop. The glamour attached to them has her dressed in a lavish emerald gown covered in peacock feathers, her face shimmering with gold dust, lashes composed of curling green feathers. It looks so real. And whenever her skirts brush mine or her feathers tickle my arm, I'm surprised to find the glamour feels real too.

"Don't tease," Imogen says. Her glamour is woven to a black feathered hair clip, her hair turned a similar shade and piled high upon her head. Her glamoured gown is midnight blue with raven feathers adorning the bodice. Her kohl-lined eyes lock on mine, and her voice turns cruel. "I'm sure she already feels ugly enough as it is, dressed in that plain gown when we have such stunning glamours. Besides, we have our dear stepsister to thank for tonight's invitations."

"Ember knows it's *she* who should be grateful," Mrs. Coleman says. Her glamour, bound to a ruby necklace, covers the top half of her face in a black mask swirling with moving galaxies. The conjured gown is black and silver with a high neck and long, flowing sleeves.

And then there's me. Simple, beautiful gown. Plain unglamoured mask. "I am grateful," I say, although what I really am is anxious. Ever since my argument with my stepmother, I've felt more and more unsettled, a feeling that weighs heavy in my gut. Contrasting that, my heart races faster the closer we draw to the palace. Perhaps I'm finally feeling some of that excitement I earlier yearned for. Or is it dread?

"You *should* be grateful," Clara snaps. "Have you any idea what an honor it is to go to a royal ball?"

"I do hope the ball is civilized," Imogen says. "Wearing a glamour is already quite vulgar as it is."

I bite the inside of my cheek to keep from laughing. If Imogen thinks a glamour is vulgar, just wait until she meets our host.

"The prince is hosting the ball for human society," Mrs. Coleman says. "I trust a prince must know the difference between a ball and a revel. Even though he is of the unseelie reign."

Clara shifts uncomfortably in her seat. "The prince isn't *really* a vampire, right?"

Imogen shrugs. "I've heard he's an emotional vampire, whatever that means. I'm certain he doesn't drink blood. Prince Franco is said to be one of the handsomest royals. No one sane would say that about a bloodsucker."

I doubt anyone sane would call the prince handsome when there are several equally true adjectives to use about him. Of course, I don't say so out loud.

"I heard he has tattoos, though," Clara says. "Is that not vulgar as well?"

My stepmother waves a dismissive hand. "Never mind any of that. Prince Franco is an eligible royal, and that's all we need to concern ourselves with. I'm sure the ball will be quite a proper event."

Our cab approaches the palace, pulling up behind a long line of far more elegant coach-and-fours. I catch my first sight of the palace, an extravagant structure of moonstone columns and walls of opal and obsidian.

"Get out, quickly," Mrs. Coleman orders.

Clara's mouth falls open. "But we aren't even there yet."

"I don't care. We'll walk the rest of the way. Get out before anyone notices where we came from."

The three of us obey, pouring out of the cab with haste. My stepmother drops the fare into the coachman's open palm, then leaps away as if he could burn her. Then we walk the rest of the way up the sprawling drive. The fuller the palace comes into view, the more awed I become. I've never been to a palace, much less a glamoured ball. As we approach the front steps, we join the swarms of guests filing out of their coaches. Each person's glamour is more fantastic than the next. I try not to gape as we begin our ascent up the stairs alongside them. I do, however, trail behind my stepfamily like I always do. It allows me to take care with each step and resist lifting my skirts too high. Owning no pair of dancing slippers like my stepsisters wear, I'm determined not to reveal my plain, worn shoes hidden beneath my hem.

Halfway up the stairs, I hear the first strain of music coming from inside the palace. As it hits me, it nearly steals the breath from my lungs. The tune is lively and upbeat, the musicians expertly weaving a song that already makes me want to dance. My fingers flinch, eager to play along. A steadying calm mingles with the buzz of excitement, like a playful wind that makes my feet feel lighter, my heart less heavy.

Perhaps this won't be a miserable occasion. I may have no interest in dancing with strangers or casting nets to lure in marital success, but that doesn't mean I must dread what awaits. I might even be able to accept that tonight could potentially be...dare I say, fun?

We reach the top landing and approach the door to the main hall. My stepmother hands over our invitations to an impeccably dressed fae footman. His ears are pointed, his hair a shade of crimson rarely seen on a human. Beneath his nose extends a ridiculously long, curling mustache of the same vibrant red. Mrs. Coleman's shoulders go rigid as the fae studies the four cards. His eyes widen, and I glance at his hands to see a sheet of ice crystallizing over the invitation bearing my stepmother's name.

"Ember!" she hisses, snapping her fingers at me.

For a split second, I consider remaining in place out of spite. If I hold still, will the ice continue to grow? Will it shatter the cards? The thought of destroying my stepmother's schemes is almost tempting enough to root my feet in place.

But now that I've heard the music...

I dart past my stepsisters and stand before the footman. Mrs. Coleman takes a step back, and from the set of her jaw, I can tell she's furious at having to do so. The footman glances from the invitations—three of which have now been coated in ice—to me. I offer him a smile, and when our eyes fall back to the four cards, all are in perfect, iceless condition.

The footman chuckles, making his mustache twitch. "Powerful magic." Then, with a nod, he ushers us through.

No sooner than we clear the entry does my stepfamily brush past me, forcing me back to my proper place behind them. One warning glare from over my stepmother's shoulder tells me not to associate with them for the rest of the night. It doesn't bother me in the least. Not when it means freedom from their cruelty and control. Not when the music grows louder with every step.

I slow my pace to gain further distance from them, letting the crowd of strangers swallow me, rendering me invisible amongst their stunning glamours. I hardly know where to look as I follow the current of guests through the hall toward what must be the ballroom. Everything is breathtaking, from the moonstone walls to the obsidian rafters high overhead.

Finally, we reach an open doorway and funnel inside. The music wraps around me, sings through my veins, dances in my blood. It's everywhere, filling the ballroom and my heart with its song. I head toward the center of the room, where a large group of dancers perform the quadrille. I watch for a few moments but dare not linger in case I'm asked to join. While I may recognize the dance, I've never learned the steps or attempted to perform it. Of course, with so many gorgeous glamours, who would ask the masked girl to dance?

I study said glamours as I skirt around the dance floor, swept away by how creative some of them are. While there are an abundance of glamours featuring dainty beaks and raven feathers—in a rather obvious attempt at paying homage to the prince—I also see a pair of elephant tusks, a lion's mane, two more peacocks even more extravagant than Clara's costume, and an array of glamours that are eccentric concoctions of shape and color. A few guests have chosen simple formal wear paired with a mask, much like myself, but they seem to be mostly men.

I reach the far end of the dance floor and turn my eyes to the ceiling where an enormous glass dome rises overhead. Thousands of stars speckle the black sky, brighter and clearer than I've ever seen before. There's no sight of the moon, which makes sense, considering this is the New Moon Masquerade. My eyes leave the dome to rove the perimeter of the room. That's when I realize the starlight is the main source of illumination, shining off walls of moonstone and opal, giving the dancers a dazzling, dim glow. Adding to this are several orbs of blue light—wisps—fluttering about the ceiling and bobbing to the music.

*The music!*

I turn toward the sound of the orchestra, only to nearly trip on a stair. Righting myself, I gather my bearings and find a dais before me, which hosts the musicians at the far end. The ensemble is larger than anything I've had the honor of playing in, comprising of piano, harp, flute, violin, and horn. My fingers tingle with their desire to claim the keys of the pianoforte, and I can feel my hips starting to sway. The musicians' faces are bright, their playing so lively and exuberant it almost brings tears to my eyes.

My gaze rests on the violinist, and I'm surprised to find he has pointed ears. He looks otherwise human. His youthful face and the way he grins while he plays reminds me so much of another violinist I once had the pleasure to meet. He was half fae, and the first person to teach me the true meaning of freedom and how it can be found on the road. It was last year, before Stepmother had expressly forbidden me from going out after dark. We were staying in a townhouse at the Spring Court, and nearly every night I'd climb from my window to visit the music hall downtown. Unlike the formal ballrooms and opera houses my stepfamily frequents, the music hall was a place for traveling musicians, where unfamiliar tunes blared from the stage and songs were often accompanied by dazzling vocalists.

That's when I met the violinist from a visiting band. A half-fae boy whose name I never knew, not even after we spent the night together in a loft backstage. Eager to get home before Mrs. Coleman found me missing, I left before the sun rose, not even offering a goodbye. The next night, a new band had already taken the previous one's place, and I thought I'd never see him again. To my surprise, it wasn't disappointment I felt but...comfort.

When I did see him next, we had moved on to the Summer Court's social season. Again, I sought out the local music hall, and there he was. I expected him to act cross with me if he remembered me at all. But not only did he recognize me at once, he greeted me like an old friend. A lover. Both cherished and stranger at the same time. I still didn't learn his name that night, but he told me where to go if I sought a life like his—the city of Lumenas, where all music lovers belong, and where almost any musician can get their start.

That's when I decided, as soon as I turn nineteen and escape my bargain with Mrs. Coleman, I'm going to the Star Court to join any troupe that will have me and make my home on the road—the one place I might finally fit in, despite being different. Too human. Too fae. With a life on the road, I can become anyone. Take a new name. Let my music speak for me. Form no attachments. No bonds.

Freedom. Only freedom.

The violinist catches my stare and winks. I'm frozen for a moment, surprised by his attention. I toss a look over my shoulder to see if it was someone else he'd noticed, but everyone behind me seems to either be dancing or engaged in conversation with someone else. Emboldened by the memory of my former lover, I fix a smile on my lips and return my gaze to the violinist...only to find my previous view blocked by a new figure, one that saunters across the dais toward the obsidian throne.

I clench my jaw, all previous joy flooding out of me at once.

It's the prince.

# 10

*EMBER*

Prince Franco wears a crooked silver crown, a lacy pink shirt unbuttoned to reveal half his chest—which is decorated in black geometric tattoos—and a pair of heeled boots. Strands of black and white beads hang around his neck, and on his shoulders rests a feathered cape. Gone are the wings I saw sprout from his back yesterday, which means he must be able to summon and dismiss them at will. Based on his uneven gait and the enormous golden goblet in his hand, he's already thoroughly drunk.

Every arrogant word he said to me yesterday echoes through my head and dampens all the peace I felt just moments ago. Part of me wants to step back from the bottom of the dais and disappear into the crowd, but rebellion roots me in place. My chin lifts in defiance, daring him to recognize me.

The music stops as Prince Franco pauses before the throne. The dancers halt as well, and all eyes turn toward him. His guests dip into bows and curtsies, some genuflecting all the way to the ground. I, on the other hand, keep my curtsy shallow.

When we rise, applause ripples quietly over the crowd, a reminder that—despite the fae luxury and wild glamours that surround me—this is a human ball, not a revel.

He extends his arms and raises his hands slightly, as if he's a conductor lifting the tempo. "You see your prince, and all you have is applause?" His words are slightly slurred, his tone higher than it was yesterday. Further proof of his inebriation.

The crowd claps again, a little louder, but this time, wisps whistle overhead, unseen owls hoot, and the musicians strike a note. Franco lifts his hands again, bringing another wave of hoots and whistles, another note from the band, and even a few exuberant whoops and shouts from the crowd.

With a smirk, his eyes sweep the room from one side to the other. I hold my breath when his gaze briefly lands on me, but it leaves faster than it was ever there. A giddy smile tugs at my lips. He doesn't recognize me. Not even a little.

Unimpressed with his assessment, the prince scoffs and gives a half-hearted shrug. "Enjoy the New Moon Masquerade." With a dismissive wave at the orchestra, the musicians commence playing, and after a few beats of chaos, the dancers fall back into the quadrille. Franco slouches onto the throne and swings a leg over one arm while leaning his back against the other. Then, as if we lowly humans are worth no more of his time, he turns all his attention to his goblet, which he drains in a gulp. With a snap of his fingers, a female fae with moth-like wings and a petite stature even smaller than mine flutters over to refill his cup. I don't miss the heated gaze that passes between them, the finger she brushes along his arm, the way he bites his lip in response, or how his eyes linger on her backside as she flutters away.

Shaking my head with disgust, I turn away from the dais and, to my regret, the musicians upon it. If I have to look at that vile prince a second longer, I just might vomit.

∼

I SPEND THE NEXT SEVERAL SONGS WANDERING THE BALLROOM, watching the dancers, and even indulging in a glass of wine. No one seeks an introduction to me nor does anyone ask me to dance—which is exactly how I want it. My beautiful ballgown seems to be serving its purpose perfectly, helping me blend in with the crowd while rendering me delightfully invisible. The only creatures who pay me any heed at all are the fae servants and the wisps. The servants, which includes the moth pixie the prince had ogled, only notice me when I approach the refreshments table. The wisps, however, are far more eager to interact with me. They hover over my head from time to time, tempting and teasing with their tiny mischievous voices.

"Sway to the music."

"Fly with us."

"Dance on the dais!"

Not wanting their attention to linger, I do my best to ignore them and mix back into the crowd whenever they gather too long. When I notice very few others being harassed by wisps, it makes me wonder, why me? Is it only because I'm not dancing? Because they can sense my unmet desire to sway, move, and play? Or is it because my heritage is of the wind? Since wisps are creatures of both air and fire, we share an element in our blood.

I'm in the middle of evading a rather persistent cluster of said stalkers when my stepmother's voice reaches my ears. "Ember, dear. Oh, there she is."

My heart leaps into my throat at her tone. Never has Mrs. Coleman called me *dear*, and I certainly wasn't expecting her to sound happy to see me should we accidentally cross paths tonight. Until now, my attempts to keep my distance from her, Clara, and Imogen have been successful.

I pause and turn toward the voice, glimpsing her glamour

behind a chatting couple. My wisp pursuers catch up to me, but after looping once above my head, they retreat with a squeal. Smart on them. I too dread whatever reason Mrs. Coleman has sought me out for.

"Ember," she says, skirting around the guests to reach me. When she does, she lays a hand on my shoulder as if to claim me. As if—for once in our relationship—she's eager to demonstrate our connection. Her smile is wide, and my first thought is that she's been tricked by some fae creature, put under an enchantment or compulsion. Or perhaps she drank the bad kind of fae wine. Then I see the smile doesn't quite reach her eyes. And she's not alone.

A man stands at her side. His hair is dark, reaching just past his shoulders, and his clothing is modest, especially for someone at a masquerade. Dressed in all black, his trousers are well tailored, his jacket buttoned to the top of his neck, leaving no sign of shirt or cravat. The style of jacket tells me he must be a man of the clergy. The top half of his face is obscured in a simple black domino mask, making it hard to tell quite how old he is. The stubble-free jaw and lack of creases around his lips tell me he's likely no older than four-and-twenty.

Of course, age can be a tricky thing in Faerwyvae. When the wall that once divided the humans from the fae came down twenty-one years ago, fae magic was freed over the entire isle. While magic can only be wielded by the fae, it still affects human day-to-day life in visible ways—infusing the land and giving each court distinct climates and terrains, powering our electricity through webs of ley lines. Additionally, there are many hidden ways magic can impact human life, the most recent discovery being a decrease in aging. Not all humans seem affected, but evidence has shown that those closest to the fae, especially those in loving, intimate relationships with them, begin to age slower. Only time will tell if that means immortality for such humans or just a lengthy lifespan.

As half fae, I expect I've already begun to stop aging. But for the stranger before me, he could be four-and-twenty or four-and-forty, for all I know.

Hand still on my shoulder, my stepmother faces the man. "Brother Marus, this is Ember Montgomery, my stepdaughter. She's half fae."

"A pleasure," he says with a nod.

I belatedly return it. My mind feels slow, still reeling from not only being acknowledged by Mrs. Coleman, but openly referred to as half fae. She's never once wanted me to show my teal hair or speak of my heritage. Why would she be so open with this Brother Marus? What church is he from that has her so eager to make him my acquaintance?

Then I see it. The tiny emblem at his lapel—a pair of crossed swords over a black flame.

Brother Marus is from Saint Lazaro.

The church that sparked the rebellion.

The rebellion that killed my mother.

I try to take a step back, but Mrs. Coleman squeezes my shoulder, holding me in place. Brother Marus' forehead wrinkles above his mask, a concerned expression not lost on my stepmother.

"Forgive her," Mrs. Coleman says, pinning me with a glare. "She does not mean to be rude."

He offers me a tight-lipped smile. "I take no offense, and I understand her trepidation, but Saint Lazaro is not what we once were. We no longer have radicals hiding in our midst who wish to rebel against our fae monarchs, and our gracious kings and queens have publicly acknowledged that. As my church's representative at court, I have the queen's ear, rooms at the palace, and vast influence over the court. You'll find me quite civilized."

"Oh, how nice," Mrs. Coleman says with wistful warmth, but his words do nothing to placate me. Eleven years of obedience and a few royal privileges won't change what Saint Lazaro did. Furthermore, I find it hard to believe it was only their radicals who promoted violence with their claims that fae aren't people but the progeny of demons. Many died for those beliefs. Both humans and fae alike.

My mother was one of those fae.

I still remember her final days. The way the life was leached from her as black veins of iron poisoning crisscrossed her body until it covered every blue inch. The way I couldn't even hug her or feel her touch because the pain of the iron bullet embedded in her stomach made it impossible for her to return to her seelie form. Instead, she was trapped in her unseelie body—her sylph form—blue and incorporeal with an iron bullet fused within her. Impossible for the surgeons to operate on.

Forced to suffer.

Forced to die.

*Always be wild. Promise me.*

I try to wrench free of my stepmother's grip, but her nails dig into my skin. "Hold still," she hisses under her breath, and I dare not fight her further for fear that she'll use our bargain to enforce the order.

Brother Marus steps closer, and his eyes slowly sweep over me, his gaze like knives sliding over my flesh. "Is this her true form, or does she wear a glamour?"

"She wears no glamour," Mrs. Coleman says.

He reaches a hand toward my face, and I flinch back. His grin widens. Keeping his eyes on mine, he grasps an errant strand of my hair between his fingers. My fear tells me he'll pull it, but instead, he twirls it around his fingertip. "Blue," he whispers, "the same shade as your eyes."

Panic, anger, and disgust storm through me. Despite his gentle tone, his smile, and the pleasure in his gaze, I can't look at him without seeing my mother. Without seeing everything

Saint Lazaro's zealots did eleven years ago. I burn him with a glare, my chest heaving with suppressed rage.

He releases my strand of hair and turns to my stepmother with a light chuckle. "She's exactly as you described."

"Yes," she says with a forced smile, although her tone is unamused, "she's a rather untamed creature."

My insides revolt at her words. *Untamed creature.* Just like how Saint Lazaro sees all faekind. It's no coincidence she had me meet Brother Marus. She knows how my mother died. She knows how I feel about Marus' brotherhood. This is just another cruel punishment, another reminder of how she feels about me.

I bite the inside of my cheek to keep from saying something I'll regret.

*Two more weeks. That's all. Just go through the motions and obey.*

Finally, she removes her hand, and I feel like I can breathe again.

Brother Marus faces me. "Miss Montgomery, may I—"

I take a step back, far enough from my stepmother's reach, and nearly collide with a servant carrying a bottle of wine. "I am unwell," I say to Marus. Mrs. Coleman hisses my name, but I dart between a cluster of guests conversing nearby and flee to the other side of the ballroom before I can hear whatever she'll say next.

I keep moving, stopping only when I cross the threshold and reach the hall. That's when I realize I have nowhere to go, nowhere to be alone. The hall is far from empty, teeming with people coming to and from the ballroom, dining room, or drawing room. If I leave the palace, what then? Do I expect to walk all the way back to Evanston? It would take at least an hour. As much as my skin crawls with the thought of sitting in a cab with my stepmother after what she just pulled, I've dealt with worse from her before.

Perhaps if I act as shaken as I feel, she won't seek to punish me further.

For now, I just need a moment of peace, a moment to collect myself, to breathe, to dab away the tears that have begun streaming down my cheeks before anyone notices the distraught girl in the unglamoured ballgown.

Blue lights flutter overhead, and I turn my glazed eyes to another cluster of wisps that swirl above me.

"She wants to fly."

"She wants to sing."

"Come dance with us."

Their voices, though much like the rest of their kind, sound suspiciously similar to the three who tried to get me to fly off my chimney yesterday morning. I clench my jaw, my trembling hands curling into fists. "If ever you wanted to be helpful, now is your chance."

"Helpful. We always are," says one of the females.

"Climb upon the rafters," says the male, pointing to the obsidian beams overhead, "then jump. We will join you. Then we'll fly."

"I need a place to hide," I say through my teeth, glad no one seems interested in watching me converse with the creatures. "Somewhere I can be alone. Do you know these halls well enough to find a place like that for me?"

"Oh, we know how to navigate all the places," says the other female.

That's the opposite of what wisps are known for, but I don't say so out loud. Desperate times call for desperate alliances. "Please, just take me somewhere like I've asked. Promise you won't lead me astray."

The male crosses his tiny arms over his orb-like body. "What will you promise in return?"

"Will you fly?"

"Will you sing?"

I squeeze my eyes shut, about to refuse, but an aching fills my bones, begging to be freed. At this point, it doesn't matter what I do, so long as I can release the rage and fear that continues to blow through me. "Fine, I'll sing," I say in a rush. "I promise to sing for you if you promise to take me somewhere according to my exact specifications. Somewhere in the palace that's private, safe, and where I won't get in trouble for being."

The wisps exchange excited glances, then swirl in a circle. "Agreed," they chorus, then take off down the hall. I follow them past the dining room and drawing room, then down a short corridor that ends in an open doorway. They fly inside, but I pause outside the threshold, examining what awaits. It seems to be a large parlor with tall windows that glow with starlight. The wisps squeal as they spin about the room. Thankfully, it appears vacant. With hesitant steps, I enter, assessing the sitting area, finely furnished with a set of chairs, a couch, and a tea table. My eyes rove over the rest of the room, and I see a desk, exquisite paintings cluttering the walls, another sitting area, a card table, and—

*For the love of the breeze.*

My heart hammers against my ribs, but not with fear. With longing. For there in the far corner of the room is that which I've craved more than anything else.

A piano.

# 11

### EMBER

My feet move before my mind catches up, drawn to those black and white keys. The grand pianoforte shines white beneath the starlight with an iridescent sheen. The piano bench is covered in a plush black cushion, one that begs to be rested upon.

Sanctuary. Safety. Home.

I barely realize what I'm doing as I sweep across the room and settle onto the bench. The three wisps circle over my head, then hover above my hands as I lift the fallboard to reveal the keys. My fingers tingle in anticipation, but I know better than to start playing at once. A musical instrument is more than a tool. It's a partner. A friend. Something that deserves as much courtship as a lover.

Lighting my gloved fingertips over the surface of the keys, I press nothing, and instead familiarize myself with the tactile experience. I do this from one side to the other, then settle my fingers over a chord.

Then I press. Lightly.

The sound reverberates through my bones, loosening the tension trapped within me. Brother Marus' face flashes through my mind, and I close my eyes. Then I see his lapel pin, the insignia of Saint Lazaro.

I press again, slightly harder, the chord rumbling to my very core.

Next, I recall my stepmother's smug grin, my stepsisters' teasing, the prince's lewd suggestions in the alley. It all comes tumbling forth, spilling from memory and shifting into a rage that radiates down my arms, my fingers, and flows over the piano keys.

I play. With my eyes closed, I let my fingers fly. I need no sheet music, for I play no existing song, following only what my rage wants to say and how my fingertips want to say it. The resulting song fills the air around me, replacing my anger with relief I haven't felt since Mrs. Coleman sold my pianoforte. The music continues to bleed out of me, and after a while, I open my eyes.

The three wisps rest upon the shelf where the sheet music should be, expressions tranquil.

"You promised you'd sing," whispers one of the females. For once, there's no taunting or teasing.

A spark of anxiety surges through me, one reflected in the chord I play. She's right. In my urgency to get away, I promised to do something I haven't done in over three years. Ever since...

Ever since...

My song takes a chaotic turn, my throat burning as a lump rises within it. I try to swallow it down, but I can't. Fae promises are nearly as binding as bargains. I must keep my promise.

I have to sing.

My bass notes grow louder, deeper, the treble cascading down to meet it.

A rumbling builds in my throat, eliciting a desperate

craving with it. For three years, this is as much as I've ever given in to. A hum. And it's never been enough. Never.

The hum shifts from a rumble to a tone—one still trapped beneath my closed lips. A tear slips from the corner of my eye, and a burning fills my lungs. Then finally, I part my lips.

My fingers go still, ringing out a bass chord. My voice meets it two octaves higher, a simple and quiet *ah*.

The relief I felt just moments ago is insignificant compared to what I feel now, the tension melting out of me, every remnant of rage whisked away as if snatched by a gust of wind. My fingers dance lightly over the keys, a slow progression to meet the octave of my *ah*. There the notes join, the piano and my voice, and a much gentler song emerges. I weave a wordless vocal tune to harmonize with the music of the keys, and the combination feels so much like happiness I could weep.

I glance at the wisps again, finding all three frozen in place, leaning forward from their perch to gaze at me with wide unblinking eyes. I pause my singing and offer them a smile. They return it, and I'm about to ask what their names are when, all at once, they glance up. With a squeal, they dart from the piano and out of sight.

Startled by their sudden exit, my fingers halt on the keys.

That's when I feel it. The sensation I'm not alone.

I whirl around on the piano bench to find a raven hovering behind me.

Biting back a shout of alarm, I rise and stumble back, a dissonant chord ringing out as I catch myself on the keys. As much as I regret such indelicate treatment of the poor pianoforte, I can't bring myself to move off it. The raven simply stares at me, equally as frozen as I am. And it isn't *just* a raven. That is, I'm not sure it's a raven at all but a person—one of towering height with humanlike arms clad entirely in tight black gloves and draped in dark feathers, legs adorned in orange hose and ending in rather convincing claw-like feet. At its neck is a black cravat, and above it rests its raven face, over-large and expressionless, looking more like something you'd find stuffed and mounted than existing on a living body. My gaze falls to the raven's middle, which is of wide girth.

The creature moves, first taking a step back, then glancing down at its stomach. When it looks back to me, it says, "I'm a fat raven." The voice is male, youthful, and heavy with amusement.

"I see." Steadying my breathing, I slowly push off from the piano and right myself.

"I didn't mean to startle you. It's a glamour."

I shutter my eyes a few times but say nothing.

The raven cocks his head, then nods. "Ah. This is more about me sneaking up on you unannounced. For that, I apologize."

"I should go," I say, sidestepping the raven.

He steps before me, blocking my progress. "Wait, please don't go. I'm deeply sorry for interrupting your song. I was just...drawn to it. Announcing myself would have been the gentlemanly thing to do, I'm sure. Even more gentlemanly would have been to leave you in peace, but I couldn't resist a closer listen."

I pause at how flustered he sounds. There's something about his voice that has my brow furrowed as I stare at that ridiculous glamoured raven head. Is it familiarity? Kindness? Eccentricity? Whatever it is, my fear begins to settle.

He extends his arms. "So...do you like my glamour?"

I glance over him once again, taking in the plain feathers, the clawed feet, the comically large belly. Without my permission, the corners of my lips begin to lift.

"You *do* like it. I think you're the first who does."

"Well, Mr. Raven," I say quietly, "everyone else seems to honor the prince in subtler ways. You know, dainty beaks and feathered headdresses."

"Meanwhile, here I am in all my spectacular glory and nobody cares. I'm one of the very few people dressed in a full-body glamour. I was certain there would be more. What's the point of a glamoured ball if one is only partially glamoured? Isn't the goal to be unrecognizable?"

"You should ask the prince." As soon as the words leave my mouth, I wish I could stuff them back in. Surely, he heard the scorn laced within them.

He snorts a laugh. "You aren't fond of Prince Franco?"

"I said no such thing." I try to sidestep him again, my eyes fixed on the door, but again the raven intercepts me.

"Do tell. I love a juicy piece of disdain about the prince. Have you met him?"

I'm about to cross my arms but think better of it. I may be in hiding, but I'm still at a formal ball. Instead, I fold my hands neatly at my waist. "I've met the prince but once and have nothing to say on the matter."

"Oh, come on. You must share something."

I lift my chin. "You are reading too far into this. I simply brought up the prince in response to your statement that glamoured balls are events in which one should be unrecognized."

He flourishes his hand in an encouraging gesture. "Because..."

"Because he's the only person at the ball *not* in a glamour."

The raven snaps his fingers and points at me. "Exactly! You're literally the only person who's noticed. I'm astonished by the density of these ballgoers."

"Are you not a ballgoer yourself?"

He shrugs. "I prefer to lurk in corners and make fun of people while getting thoroughly drunk on wine. When I'm not hiding from them, that is."

"Is that what you're doing in here then?"

He taps the underside of his overlarge beak as if it were his chin. "I could ask you the same."

I give him a small smile. "If you care to recall, I was just leaving." I skirt around him, and this time he doesn't try to stop me. Not until I reach the door, that is.

"Wait." I pause and turn back to face him, suppressing a chuckle as I take in his wonderfully hideous costume yet again. He closes the distance between us, his tone suddenly tenuous. "What about you? Do you wear a glamour? Or is this your real face behind that mask?"

I say nothing, suddenly aware of my proximity to a stranger, a man I'm unfamiliar with, whose name and appearance I don't know. It should unsettle me. I should find it vulgar to be alone in a room with an unknown male, I should fear for my honor. But I don't. The impropriety paired with mystery reminds me so much of my violinist lover, of our temporary, meaningless tryst, that it brings a rush of exhilaration instead.

The raven studies me with his glassy, sightless eyes, but I can sense his true gaze burning behind the glamour. It's a rare thing that I'm seen, noticed, and studied. Even rarer when the sight of me is enjoyed. It happens so seldom that it's easy to recognize how it feels when it occurs. Like now.

He lifts a hand toward my face, gloved fingers lighting on a strand of loose hair, just like Brother Marus had done. But where I felt disgusted with Marus, I feel bold with the raven. I stand tall, feet rooted in place as he runs a finger along the strand without grasping it, and then slowly lowers his hand.

"Is this its true color?" he asks, voice far quieter than before.

"Wouldn't you like to know?"

"I would," he says, and I can still feel his stare drinking me in. "I want to know who you are. Your true face. Your name."

I take a step back. "That would defeat the purpose, Mr.

Raven. For isn't the point of a glamoured ball to go unrecognized?"

"Does that mean I would know who you are if I saw you? Are you someone of renown?"

With a shrug, I turn away from him. Then, tossing a grin over my shoulder, I say, "I suppose you'll never know."

With that, I enter the hall, a giddy smile spreading over my face.

## 12

FRANCO

I stare after the girl in the blue ballgown as she strides down the hall, leaving me stunned after our delightful interaction. It was the most authentic exchange I've had with a stranger in a long time, if not ever. I suppose that's one benefit of being so thoroughly disguised. There was no pretense, no need for her to put on airs, act nervous, or try to impress me. While she started off so timid, she turned a delicious shade of taunting by the time I said I wanted to know her name. She flirted with me—*me*, not as the prince but a fat raven. It couldn't be attributed to her guessing my true identity, because the momentary disdain she revealed for *the prince* was genuine. Regardless of how she tried to deny it, I could taste her abhorrence on my tongue like bitter lemons.

But that's not how she treated *me*.

And yet none of that is as surprising as the reason I snuck up on her to begin with—her song. That haunting, passionate tune. I could feel it long before I heard it. I'd been perfectly content stalking the dining room and delighting in the disgusted sneers at my costume before I felt that melody tugging at my bones, an odd mixture of peace and grief. The way it pulled me to her reminded me of a siren's song. Is that what she is? Is my mystery guest a siren? Tonight's ball hosts very few fae guests, considering it's a human event, and her ears were most certainly rounded. Could she have been half fae? Or a siren glamoured as human? No sea fae were invited to the ball, aside from...

My eyes widen.

Could she somehow be...Princess Maisie? Selkies don't have the power of a siren's song, but based on what I've heard of her father's—*ahem*—virility, her mother could be anyone. And after our less-than-stellar first meeting, it would make sense why she isn't fond of my true identity. Then again, when we met earlier, she didn't seem keen on coming to the ball. Or standing, for that matter. Could she have changed her mind? Augie did say he saw her visit Madame Flora...

And if she isn't Maisie, then who is she?

My feet fly beneath me, propelling me into the hall after her, a buzzing excitement humming through my veins. Glamoured ball or no, I must know who she is. I'm too fascinated not to.

She slips into the throne room seconds before I get there. As I enter, the music, dancers, and chatting guests invade my senses. Streams of energy writhe about the room, overwhelming me. I try to reach out toward one specific signature, but I'd been so entranced by the mystery girl, I hadn't been conscious enough of her energy to try and establish a baseline. I'd been more aware of...my own emotional response.

Stalking the perimeter, I look this way and that, but it seems the ball has already swallowed her whole. A challenge, then. With a grin, I move toward the dance floor.

"Very clever, Your Highness."

I halt as Madame Flora approaches me. She's in her

towering seelie form with her black evening gown and porcelain mask. Her long hair has been pinned up in a formal style, but she appears to be without any noticeable glamour. I would have thought the fae glamourist would have the most spectacular glamour of anyone.

Not wanting to be rude, I shake my previous train of thought from my mind. "Madame Flora, my ambassador told me you'd come. I'm pleased you're here."

"I had to see what you'd chosen to do with my work, didn't I? However, when I sold you two glamours, I didn't expect I'd be an accomplice in helping you hide from your own party."

"I'm not hiding," I say. "I'm...spectating from the shadows."

She chuckles. "Is that so? And what have you spectated thus far?"

I sigh, remembering the girl and her song. "A rather delightful mystery."

"Does it have anything to do with your missing other half?"

I furrow my brow, wondering what she's referring to. If she's somehow gleaned my distraction over an unknown female, it's strange she'd refer to her as my *other half*.

Noticing my confusion, she waves a gloved hand toward the dais. "He who wears the second glamour."

I cast a glance at the throne and find it...empty. Only now do I realize the collective energy in the room has shifted since earlier in the night. Their *prince* is nowhere to be seen. "Damn it, Augie!" I mutter.

"Hmm," she says, and her energy morphs into teasing. "So that isn't what had you on the hunt after all."

"It does now," I say, looking about the room for any sign of the ambassador. "I must find him before he ruins everything."

She nods but doesn't curtsy, which I'm grateful for. My glamour is only effective so long as no one suspects who I really am. "Do what you must, my prince, but do try to have fun."

I smirk. "That's the point of this glamour. Well, I suppose I shall hunt down my unruly *other half*. Thank you for coming tonight."

"Of course," she says, then weaves back into the crowd.

I dart back the way I came mere minutes ago, out into the hall, and down an empty corridor, reaching out for the ambassador's energy. Unlike my mystery pianist, Augie's signature I know well enough to track. It's close and flavored with something else—*Oh, I see.*

Feathered hands on my hips, I take in the sight. Despite the enormous glamoured raven head that rests on my shoulders, I can see through it as clearly as if it wasn't there at all. And what I find is...*me*—or at least the glamoured version of me—lips locked with a moth pixie. She has shoulder-length black hair and enormous black eyes. I recognize her as a palace servant, although I don't know her name. Considering where her hands are on the front of my pants, she thinks we're well acquainted.

"Augie! What the hell is this?"

The two pull away with a startle. Augie has the decency to look surprised, but the pixie doesn't seem at all alarmed to be caught kissing the prince by an oversized raven. Augie faces me but keeps an arm around the pixie's waist. She, in turn, slides her hands up his glamoured chest, beneath the pink lacy shirt, and over his tattoos—no, *my* tattoos.

"Sorry, Franco," Augie says with a crooked grin. "This is Seri. Seri, you know the prince."

She offers me a smile and somehow manages to curtsy without taking her hands off my ambassador. "Your Highness."

My eyes shutter. "Wait, so you know he's not actually the prince? And that I *am*?"

She nods and plants a seductive kiss on Augie's jaw. "Augie-boy tells me everything," she says in a juvenile voice.

I quirk a brow. "Augie-boy?"

"We're into this sort of thing," Augie says with a blush.

"You're *into* this sort of thing? Does that mean the two of you have been an item? For how long?"

Augie shrugs. "I told you I've started seeing someone. We've been together...maybe a month now?"

Seri swats his chest with a mock gasp. "Two months, you dirty rake."

"Two months," he says, a sheepish smile curling his lips.

I wave a dismissive hand. "Well, you should have told me sooner. I'd have offered you my congratulations."

"Thank you, Your Highness. Say, do you mind if I keep the glamour overnight?"

I narrow my eyes. "The night is far from over, Augie. Why aren't you at the ball on my throne like we agreed?"

He gives me a pleading look. "I'm so sorry, but it's ridiculously boring in there. Stuffy men started bringing their daughters and nieces for introductions. All the while I kept looking over at Seri." He turns toward her, a sappy look on his face, one I doubt my visage has ever been graced with before, glamour or no. "She looked so cute serving wine. I couldn't resist her for long."

I roll my eyes. "You can't go around kissing people in public while you're wearing my body, and you need to get back to the ball. You're *supposed* to be tolerating those introductions for me. It's what we agreed. The humans want their prince and I'm having too much fun not being me tonight. Besides, you said you *wanted* to be a prince for a day."

"You're right. I'm sorry." Augie takes Seri's hand and tugs her forward. They pause before me, and Augie lowers his voice. "So, what do you say? Can Seri and I borrow the glamour tonight?"

Seri makes a purring sound and runs her hands over Augie's chest again, her moth wings buzzing with excitement. Then her eyes flick to me. "You could join, if that's what's holding you back."

My eyes widen as they fall on Augie—on *me*—and I watch myself wink with a seductive grin. I cock my head to the side. "Is it weird I'm turned on by this?"

"It's only weird if you make it weird," Augie says, biting his lower lip. Something I'm sure I never do.

"It's definitely weird," I say with a chuckle and take a step back. "Go finish your job, Augie. If you two can manage to keep your hands off each other for the rest of the ball, then I'll let you...have your way with my glamour."

Seri lets out a delighted squeal that Augie swallows with a kiss.

"Stop, you two, it's gross. Now, get back to the ball." They giggle and dart down the corridor. "Separately, please."

Seri tosses a pout over her shoulder but releases Augie's hand and falls back behind him. I follow at a slower pace, ensuring the two return to their proper places when we reach the throne room. As soon as Augie settles back onto the throne, the room's energy returns to what it had been before—excitement mingled with desperation and a hearty dose of desire.

Meanwhile, I return to the shadows and my search for the mystery girl.

# 13

**EMBER**

Playing the piano set me so much at ease that I return to the ball without fear. I could credit my conversation with the raven for my change in mood, but I doubt I would have had the gall to flirt with a stranger if I hadn't released all my trapped fury beforehand. Now all I have to do is evade him, hide from my stepfamily, and try not to hate the rest of the evening.

I catch a glimpse of the raven now and then, and I wonder if he's looking for me. A small part of me wants to let him find me and spark our conversation back up again, perhaps see who resides beneath that eccentric glamour. But the majority of me is satisfied with what transpired. It's better not to know. It's better to disappear before anything like hope or attraction can stir on either end.

Several songs go by, and I get lost in the music once again. Each time I see any hint of either of my stepsisters, I subtly turn course before they notice me. Same goes for Mr. Raven. My stepmother, oddly enough, is nowhere to be seen, and neither is Brother Marus. I can only guess they've gone to dine, and good riddance to them both. Of course, my reprieve from Mrs. Coleman is only temporary, for as soon as the ball comes to an end, I'll be trapped in our cramped cab with her, then back to the Gray Quarter.

After that, this ball will become nothing but a dream. A memory.

I wander toward the dais to get another look at the orchestra, keeping my gaze fixed firmly away from Prince Franco, who had the decency to return to his ball not long ago and now sits slumped on his throne again. I rather enjoyed myself quite well during his brief sojourn, but I'm used to not getting my way.

As I watch the musicians, yearning rises within me again. Despite my time at the piano, it seems I'll never be sated. Even now, with the feel of piano keys still so fresh on my gloved fingertips, all I want to do is climb up on the dais and claim a seat next to the pianist. I'm so entranced, I nearly miss the familiar head of blonde hair as it enters my periphery. A second too late, I glance to the side and see Clara making a beeline for me. I quickly turn away from the dais but get no more than five steps before her gloved hand grasps my upper arm.

"Don't pretend you didn't see me, Ember," she says as I turn to face her. "Do you think I want to follow you through the entire ballroom?"

I lift my chin, emboldened by the music. "I was only trying to avoid getting in your way. Is that not how you prefer it?"

Clara sneers, an expression so at odds with her elegant glamour. "You are so irritating. I wouldn't be talking to you at all if Mother hadn't sent me to find you."

My stomach drops. "Why does she want to see me?"

"I don't know," Clara says with a scoff. "I think we're leaving."

"Leaving? But the ball isn't over." While I wouldn't be opposed to an early exit, it's highly uncharacteristic for my stepmother to leave any social event until everyone of importance has left as well. It can't be later than ten o'clock.

"Don't ask me. Ask her." With that, she walks away, only to whirl around and say, "Come on!"

I dart after my stepsister, and she leads us through the ballroom and out into the hall. There I find Mrs. Coleman and Imogen.

My stepmother releases an irritated sigh as we approach. "It took you long enough. Come along."

Clara and Imogen flank Mrs. Coleman as she starts down the hall, and I follow a few paces behind. When my stepmother turns down a side corridor, I'm not the only one flashing confused glances her way.

"Mother, where are we going?" Imogen asks. "Why aren't we heading for the cab?"

Mrs. Coleman's lips flick into a smug grin. "We aren't returning to that rusty old cab. We have rooms at the palace for the rest of the season."

I nearly trip, while Imogen and Clara exchange wide-eyed looks. "How did you do it?" Clara asks.

"When will you girls learn to trust me? You know I have my ways."

"Mother, rooms at the palace aren't given out to just anyone," Imogen says. "Especially not for an entire month. What did you do?"

Mrs. Coleman smiles at her daughter, then slides her gaze to me. Dread sinks my stomach as her expression shifts into something I can't decipher. "You'll see."

MY STEPMOTHER LEADS US DOWN THE HALL, UP AN ELABORATE staircase, then down a quiet corridor before stopping at a set of doors. She raps once, then smooths her glamoured skirts. Her daughters follow suit, patting their hair and adjusting their gloves. All I can do is fight back the unease that's been creeping up and down my spine ever since Mrs. Coleman looked at me so strangely. Whatever she's planned, it can't be good.

Steps sound from inside the room, and Mrs. Coleman whirls back to me just long enough to hiss, "Take off your mask."

Too confused to question the demand, I do as I'm told, untying the ribbon that secures the silver mask to my face. As soon as I'm freed from the disguise, the doors swing open to reveal a male figure.

My heart hammers against my ribs.

It's Brother Marus.

Gone is his mask, giving me a clear look at his face. He appears as young as I first assumed, but there's no warmth in his dark eyes. And that hateful pin remains firmly on his lapel, making nausea turn in my gut.

Marus exchanges polite nods with my stepmother before his gaze lands on me. "How good of you to come," he says, eyes lingering on mine far too long considering the words are meant for Mrs. Coleman.

"No, it is far too good of you, Brother Marus," she says. She takes a step to the side, waving at her daughters to do the same, and in turn revealing more of me. "You met my stepdaughter, Ember Montgomery."

"I'm delighted to see you again," he says with a smile. One that would make him handsome if it weren't for the waves of disgust surging through my body.

I somehow manage a nod when all I want to do is run away again.

"And these are my daughters," Mrs. Coleman says, stealing his attention back to herself, "Imogen and Clara Coleman."

His smile is more subdued for them. "A pleasure. Please,

come in." Extending an arm, he steps to the side and beckons us through the doorway.

My stepfamily enters first, and I hear their gasps before I can make sense of why. As I follow them inside, I find a luxurious parlor with fine furniture one would expect of a fae royal—moonstone walls, opal floors, onyx tables and chairs. The sconces glow with orbs of pale light reminiscent of the moon. Several doors branch off from the parlor, telling me this is more than just a single room.

"These are the apartments gifted to me by the queen herself," Brother Marus says. "I hardly have need for so much space, so I am more than happy to put my extra rooms to use."

Mrs. Coleman's smile brightens with greed. "I can't thank you enough."

"Wait," Clara says, pausing her open-mouthed inspection of the parlor. "We're staying here?"

Imogen elbows her sister for her tactless outburst, but Brother Marus laughs. "Yes. Your mother and I have come to... an arrangement," he says.

Imogen looks him over, as if seeing him for the first time. "What kind of arrangement?"

His gaze slides to me, and the blood drains from my face. The heat in his expression makes me feel suddenly naked despite my modest dress. I get the urge to shove my mask back on, but I can't bring myself to lift my arms. "One of great marital happiness."

I take a step back, but my legs feel as if they're made from water. No. No. This can't be happening.

Imogen's eyes turn hard, her lips pursed tight as realization seems to strike her. Whirling toward her mother, she whispers furiously, "You can't be serious."

Mrs. Coleman ignores her and sweeps over to me. Like the last time I stood before Marus, she places a hand on my shoulder. Claiming. Threatening.

The touch seems to snap me out of my stupor, and I whirl to face her. "I will not marry him."

A crimson flush creeps behind her glamour, and she tosses an apologetic smile at Brother Marus. "She doesn't mean it. It's shock—"

"It is not shock," I say, tearing out of her grasp. "I won't do it."

Mrs. Coleman opens her mouth to argue, but Brother Marus speaks first. "I apologize if I overstepped, Miss Montgomery. I should have waited until we were in private to declare my intentions."

"The answer would have been the same," I say through my teeth, my eyes locked on my stepmother's.

Marus emits a low chuckle. "I'll give you a moment alone." With a bow, he heads for one of the rooms at the other end of the parlor.

Once the door clicks shut behind him, Mrs. Coleman bounds forward, both hands grasping my shoulders. "You ungrateful, wretched girl."

Tears prick my eyes, and a lump sears my throat. "How could you? How could you even *think* I would marry him? You know what he represents. What his brotherhood did to my mother."

"Don't be such a simpering child," she says, giving my shoulders a shake. "You will marry Brother Marus."

I shake my head. "I won't. You can't make me."

She narrows her eyes, a cruel smile twisting her face into something monstrous. Something I've always known her to be. "Can't I?"

Pressure squeezes my chest as her words ring true. Until I'm free from our bargain, she can force me to obey her, to do anything she wants. My only defense would be to suffer the pain my refusal would inflict. Can I endure such torment for two weeks? Or will it kill me first? If I were full fae, it most certainly would.

"Mother, it isn't fair," Imogen says, and for one unfathomable moment, I think she's coming to my defense. "Ember was never supposed to marry before me or Clara."

Mrs. Coleman keeps her grip tight on my shoulders as she swivels her head toward her daughters. "Not fair? What's not fair? An apartment at the palace? Positions at court for an entire month?"

Imogen's chest heaves, but she snaps her mouth shut.

Clara's voice comes out small. "Couldn't you have married one of us to him?"

Mrs. Coleman's gaze returns to me, brimming with bitter rage. "No. He wanted *her*."

Another wave of nausea strikes me. Why would a man of a fae-hating church *want* to marry me? The hidden implications are sinister, spreading panic through every inch of my body. My words come out with a choked sob. "I can't."

"You can and you will." After one final squeeze of my shoulders, my stepmother pushes me away, making me stumble before I can right myself. She points a finger at me, her voice like a growl. "You *will*. Otherwise, you won't live long enough to regret it."

A flicker of pain shoots through me, but I don't know if it's from the weight of our bargain or the realization that Mrs. Coleman just threatened my life. Stripped of words, all I can do is stare, my hands shaking so hard I can't even ball them into fists.

Finally, my stepmother averts her gaze and turns to her daughters. Patting her hair, she says, "Come, girls. We shall return to the ball. Ember will remain here with her betrothed."

My stepsisters join their mother. Imogen's posture is tense while Clara's is defeated.

I take an uneven step forward. "You can't go to the ball without me," I say in a rush. "The invitations—"

"The invitations have been accepted," Mrs. Coleman says. "The enchantment only required you not be left behind. I wouldn't consider you taking a brief respite in a luxurious palace apartment as being *left behind*." With that, she opens the doors, and the three shuffle out into the hall.

I follow hard on their heels, but Mrs. Coleman is already closing the doors by the time I make it to her. My mind spins to come up with something—anything—to keep from being shut in this room with Brother Marus. "You can't leave me with him. It's improper. Our reputation—*your* reputation—is at stake."

She closes the doors until only a sliver of her cold, cruel smirk can be seen. "Then you better make him your husband."

The doors snap shut in my face. I remain in place, my heart hammering so hard it makes my entire body shake. Pressing my ear to the door, I try to make out my stepfamily's retreating footsteps, counting them, visualizing how many they'll take before they reach the far end. If I sneak out once they round the corner—

The soft sound of the door opening behind me announces Brother Marus' reentry to the parlor.

My heart plummets.

I whirl to face him.

# 14

**EMBER**

Brother Marus pauses just beyond the threshold of the parlor. The room he emerged from appears to be a bedroom.

"There's no need to fear me," he says, tone gentle. But there's an edge to it. One I can't place.

I consider fleeing but don't know how he'll respond. Would he let me go? Or catch me? Would he call for guards? Steeling my nerves, I meet his gaze with defiance. "We shouldn't be alone together."

Marus takes a few slow steps toward me. Thankfully the parlor is large enough that there's still vast space between us. Even so, I press myself as close as I can to the door behind me. "It's not improper," he says. "I'm a man of the church."

"Not my church."

He halts his steps, but only for a beat. Then he walks closer. Closer. A hint of amusement dances behind his eyes. "Your stepmother said you were untamed. Is this true?"

Normally, *untamed* would feel like an insult. Right now, it feels like armor. I bare my teeth. "Yes."

He reaches the settee and lowers onto it. "Come," he says, extending an arm toward the chairs arranged around the tea table. "Sit with me. All I ask is that we talk."

I consider running again. The fact that he's sitting could give me an advantage. I could dart out the door before he has the chance to rise.

"I won't hurt you," he says, as if he can read the panic in my eyes. "Whatever wretched things you've heard about Saint Lazaro, I assure you they aren't true. Not anymore. I have no disdain for the fae. Why else would I seek matrimony with a woman of fae blood?"

"*Why* is the question indeed," I bite back.

"Sit and I will answer any question you have," he says calmly, a model of unwavering patience. As if to demonstrate his lack of threat, he settles into a more relaxed position, angling his body to the side and draping an arm along the back of the settee. He still seems stiff, but his effort to set me at ease is clear. "Take any seat you like."

I watch him in silence for a few moments, and he offers me a small smile. The expression paired with his stoic calm has me second guessing myself. Am I overreacting? Am I treating a man like a villain just because he belongs to a faith I abhor? Or is there validity to the way my skin crawls when I look at him and the pin on his lapel?

My gaze leaves him to assess the chairs and couches. Finally, I push off from the door and claim the seat farthest from Marus. Perched at the edge, I ball my fingers on my lap to keep them from shaking.

"What would you like to ask me?" he says.

My mind whirrs, but I can't form a single question. I just want this conversation to be over.

"Then tell me something, Miss Montgomery. Why do you hate Saint Lazaro?"

It takes a few breaths before I can steady my voice enough to speak calmly, and still it comes out with a tremor. "My mother died in the rebellion eleven years ago. She was shot by one of your brothers. Died from the iron bullets your brotherhood smuggled into Faerwyvae."

"How?" he asks, tone neutral. "Was she a soldier? Or a bystander?"

"A soldier." I bite the inside of my cheek to distract myself from the grief I expect to strike me at any moment. It doesn't come. Instead, it's relief I feel—relief at being able to talk about my mother without Mrs. Coleman shutting me up or shoving her own narrative down my throat. For once, I can tell the story the way Father always had. "Long before I was born, my mother was a royal guard of the Wind Court, favored by Queen Minuette. When she chose to marry my father, a human, she was dismissed from her position. She and my father moved here, to Lunar, and I was born. We were happy here. But when the rebellions started, Mother refused to abandon the Wind Court without at least trying to help. Since Wind was the first court attacked and suffered many casualties, the queen welcomed her back. Mother fought with her former comrades and helped them defeat your brotherhood, but she paid dearly for it."

He gives a knowing nod and leans slightly forward. "I do hope you believe me when I say I'm sorry. What my predecessors did was wrong. They may have fought for religious freedom, but they went about it in the wrong way. I was but a boy during the rebellions, just fourteen years of age. I played no part in what happened. After the unrest was quelled by our fae monarchs, I saw the church change into something far better than it had ever been. Our radicals were executed and any brothers who proved to sympathize with their cause were taken out of the upper rankings of the church and replaced by men of peace. Men whose footsteps I have chosen to follow."

I want to believe him. I want to trust that I'm safe, that he doesn't see me as a demon to be put down. Such vile teachings were how the zealots tipped the scales from unrest into full-on rebellion in the first place. They poisoned the minds of the good humans, hardened the hearts of the poor and down-trodden citizens—primarily those who had been displaced by the previous war, people who lost their homes and jobs when the isle was unified. They used the greed of aristocrats to fund their battles, but it was the poor who fought them. Once the radicals had their funds and fighters, they smuggled guns and bullets made of iron—an illegal metal for the fatal effect it has on the fae—and attacked three courts. Wind, Lunar, and Spring.

"What kind of fae was your mother?" Marus asks.

"A sylph."

"What did she look like?"

My eyes unfocus, memories of Mother filling my mind. "She was so beautiful, both in her seelie and unseelie forms. In her seelie form, she looked much like me. Perhaps an inch or two taller with a blue cast to her skin. In her unseelie form, she was incorporeal. She had some humanlike features. A face, arms, and legs. But she was the most beautiful shade of blue. As bright as the sky, but transparent. She could fly, float, dance with more grace than a ballerina."

"You loved her."

I nod, a tear escaping down my cheek.

"And can you...shift forms like your mother could? Do you maintain any fae magic?"

All the grief-tangled-warmth I felt from speaking about my mother vanishes, leaving a chill in its place. "No," I say, an edge to my voice. I wonder if he can read what I'm hiding. It's not that my answer is a lie. It's true about the first part of his question, at least, for I cannot shift forms. Most human-fae hybrids can, but I...I never learned. Without my mother alive to teach me, I doubt I ever will. As for fae magic, well, that's a far more complicated question. "I use no fae magic."

Marus releases a heavy sigh that seems to carry much relief. He leans forward, bracing his forearms on his thighs as he clasps his hands. "I will be good to you, Miss Montgomery. I will love you dearly if you'll have me."

My stepmother doesn't plan on giving me the choice of whether I'll have him or not, but I don't say so out loud. What I do say is, "Why me? We barely spoke and I made my discomfort obvious. Why seek out my hand when you could have wooed my stepsisters with far more ease?"

He says nothing for a few moments, then slowly rises to his feet. I brace myself, but he doesn't approach. Instead, he stands tall. "It is my personal duty to bring salvation to your kind. Not through violence. Not through rebellion. Through example, kindness, and instruction."

"Salvation," I echo, my blood going cold. "You think I need...salvation."

"All fae need salvation," he says, not looking at me. "Saint Lazaro stands against violence. We are men of peace. My mission is to purge the isle of sin in what little ways I can. That's why I've decided to take a fae as my wife. *You.* I will love you and give you a good and honest life, free from sin and magic. Since you already have no connection to magic, you are nearly free from sin. When we are married, we will be an example for others. Together, we will bring goodness to Faerwyvae."

I rise to my feet, a storm of rage blowing through my blood. "I neither need nor want your salvation. My fae heritage doesn't make me sinful."

He turns to face me, eyes alight. "There's that untamed nature. That's where I can help you. How I can save you."

"No, you won't." Head held high, I march toward the door.

In a few long strides, he stands before me, blocking my exit. Like a crack in his carefully curated façade, a flash of hate flickers over his face before he steels it behind a neutral mask. "You will stay with me. We are to wed tomorrow, and you will not leave these rooms until then."

My mouth falls open. "Tomorrow? You can't be serious. I will not wed you!"

"It has already been decided. Your stepmother and I have come to an arrangement that will benefit us both. Benefit everyone in your family. If you love them as much as you should, you will agree to this without a fight. If not for your salvation, then for their wellbeing."

I blink a few times, at a loss for words. There's so much wrong with everything he just said, I don't know where to begin, what to address first. Finally, a cold laugh bursts from my lips. "You have no idea what you're talking about. My stepfamily doesn't deserve an inch of my consideration."

His gaze turns hard. "Your stepmother warned me you'd be difficult. That you have a selfish streak and care only for yourself. I didn't believe her at first, seeing how timid you appeared. I knew you were untamed, yes, but I never thought you'd be so unfeeling. Now I see it. Now I understand why she asked for the promises I gave. You carry far more sin than I realized."

His words turn my stomach, and I want to rage at him. But a question nags at the back of my mind. "What did you promise my stepmother in exchange for my hand?"

"Use of my private apartments. Positions at court for your sisters." He pauses, and there's something smug in the lift of his lips. "A monthly allowance for your family's upkeep."

"An allowance."

"From your inheritance. Something that should have been bestowed by your kindness and goodwill but will now be distributed by me."

"My inheritance?" I grind the words between my teeth. "You have no right to my inheritance, nor does she!"

"After we are married, your inheritance will fall under my control."

I shake my head. "No, it won't. It's not even under my control yet. I don't claim it until—"

"Until you turn nineteen. Yes, I was told. However, marriage overrides that."

Alarm rushes through me. He's right. I remember my stepmother saying as much when I overheard her confessing to Imogen about our bargain.

*So long as that wretched girl remains under my care, my stipend will be paid. Once she turns nineteen, it will be her choice to continue payments. And if she's married...no. She cannot marry. She'd no longer be a valid dependent and her husband would gain control over it all.*

"You're going to steal my inheritance," I say.

"There will be no theft involved. As your husband, it will be my right."

"Under human law, maybe, but I'm half fae! The same rules don't apply."

"You could petition the queen with that argument," he says, "but considering I have her favor, she won't care about the woes of some unknown half-human girl. Besides, once we marry tomorrow, there will be nothing to petition. The prince himself will oversee the signing of our license, and all will be settled."

I frown. "The prince?"

Marus nods. "With Queen Nyxia away, Prince Franco rules in her stead. While we could wed at Saint Lazaro's Cathedral, both your stepmother and I deemed expedience to be prudent."

"I won't do it," I say, taking a step back from him.

"The prince already agreed. We have an appointment with him tomorrow."

"Do you expect to take me kicking and screaming?" For that's what it will take. My stepmother can inflict all the pain she wants with the power of our bargain. Now that I know the depths of Mrs. Coleman's scheme and the darkness behind Marus' kindness, there's nothing anyone can do to make me go through with this.

"Kicking and screaming," he says slowly as if testing the weight of the words on his lips. Then he nods. "If I must."

I open my mouth, a thousand arguments burning my tongue. But what can I even say? My first instinct is to claim the prince would never condone such an obviously forced marriage, but based on my irritating exchange with Prince Franco behind Madame Flora's shop, not to mention his careless, arrogant attitude at the ball…I'm not so sure that's true.

Pinning him with a glare, I take another step back, lips curled in a snarl. "I'd rather die."

He lifts his chin, staring down his nose at me. "I shall pray for your salvation." Then, with a lunge, he captures me in his arms.

# 15

**EMBER**

I scream and buck as his arms encircle me, but it's no use. He's so much stronger than I would have guessed for a man of the church. In the blink of an eye, he has my back to his chest, my arms trapped against my sides. I aim a kick at his foot, but he lifts me off my feet and hauls me to the other side of the parlor, muttering something under his breath that sounds like a prayer.

"Saint Lazaro, Most Holy Above..."

With a roar, I slam a foot against his shin, but he pays me no heed and continues toward a closed door. He reaches it and pushes it open. The light from the parlor reveals a bedroom, but darkness quickly envelops me as he shuts the door behind us. I increase my struggle, trying to writhe from his grasp as he carries me through the room. Then he releases me, heaving me away from him. I hit something soft, and I realize it must be the bed. Fearing more sinister actions will soon follow, I scramble to the other side until I roll off and strike solid ground. I freeze, blinking into the darkness and willing my eyes to adjust. A sliver of light shines to my right where I see Brother Marus' silhouetted form slip out the door. He slams it shut, leaving me in darkness again. The handle rattles with the sound of a key turning in the lock.

I charge toward it, stumbling across the floor, coming up against unseen bedroom furniture again and again as I make my way to where I last saw the light—light that subtly spills in from under the door. Finally, I reach it and test the handle, but it doesn't budge. "Let me out!" I shout, pounding my fists against the door. I pause and press my ear to the wood, listening for clues of Brother Marus' whereabouts.

"I will love you, Miss Montgomery," comes his voice from the other side, startling me. I launch a step back as he speaks again. "I will treat you with kindness. But first, you mustn't fight me. You must seek your better nature and turn from sin toward goodness."

My chest heaves. "Go to hell."

Like he did when he was carrying me, he begins to mutter a prayer. "Saint Lazaro, Most Holy Above, smite the sin from this creature and tame her wicked ways. Stay her hand and purify her with your righteous fire..."

He continues, but I refuse to hear a word more of it. Turning away from the door, I search the room. With my eyes adjusting to the darkness, I'm able to make out the shape of the bed, a cluster of furniture that must be a sitting area, and—there! Another sliver of light glows against the far wall. Curtains. I race toward them and pull the drapes back. Starlight streams into the bedroom, drawing my eyes to the sky. My buzzing thoughts go still at the sight, reminding me of how it looked through the domed ceiling in the ballroom. Back before this night went horribly wrong.

It's enough to make my chest ache. An hour ago, I was so close to freedom. Not just because of the music and the light-hearted feel of the ball, but because I was naïve enough to think I could outlast my stepmother's cruelty. I knew she wouldn't stop trying to claim my inheritance until it was well beyond her reach, but I never imagined she'd do it this way. Now that I realize how close this new scheme is to success, I'm surprised she hasn't tried it sooner. Pride is probably all that ever held her back. Her desire to have her daughters marry before me has likely been equal to her greed for money.

This final ploy ruins everything. All my plans. All my dreams for my future.

Swallowing the lump in my throat, I reach inside my corset and take out a small handkerchief. I unfold it, revealing my secret treasure—my train ticket to the Star Court. At first, the sight of it only gives me pain and longing. Then something shifts inside me, a fiery indignation. It builds and builds from a breeze to a tempest, and I know this isn't where it ends for me. I'm getting on that train in two weeks' time.

Like Mrs. Coleman told Brother Marus, I am an untamed creature. And I'm getting out of this cage if it's the last thing I do.

I TUCK MY TRAIN TICKET BACK INTO MY CORSET, THEN CHECK THE door, peering beneath it for any clue that Brother Marus is nearby. All I find is the uninterrupted sliver of light from the parlor, telling me he must have left his post and his fruitless prayers for my soul. I creep back to the window, examining the closures and locking mechanisms. They are of far finer construction than the window in my attic bedroom, but the function is the same. With slow, careful moves, I flip the latch and gently push against the windowpane. It swivels outward, quiet on its hinge, and welcomes the fresh night air. Then, leaning over the sill, I examine my surroundings.

I appear to be on the third floor, the ground plummeting far below. There will be no dropping to my feet from here. I'll need to maneuver to a much safer ledge. Luckily, I'm an expert climber.

My pulse quickens as I glance from side to side, studying the outer wall. It's constructed of what looks like smooth moonstone, leaving me with very little to utilize as handholds, unlike the ease something like sandstone brick would offer. A few feet below the sill runs a cornice all along the facade. Lack of handholds remains an issue, but every few feet the cornice skirts around a decorative opal pilaster, each column slightly wider than my body. I can already envision the moves required to traverse it—hold, quick step, quick step, hold. Repeat. But what after? If I can drop to a windowsill or balcony on the second floor, I can then drop to the ground with less risk of injury.

Leaning farther over the sill, I study the second-floor balconies to the right and find light streaming out from most of the windows, marking them as most certainly *not* safe places to sneak over to. The same goes for most of the windows to the left…save for what must be a few rooms over. There I find two dark windows and a balcony between. Unoccupied, as far as I can tell. At worst, the room's resident is sleeping. But who would be sleeping on the night of a ball?

I glance back at the bedroom door and the sliver of light beneath it. There's still no sign of Brother Marus, but that gives me very little comfort. Who knows when he'll return? Clenching my jaw to steel my resolve, I remove my gloves, tucking them into my bodice, and swing a leg over the windowsill. My hand-me-down hose with its many patches already appears freshly torn from my struggle with Marus. As I swing the other leg over and gather the folds of my skirt, I wonder if I should strip out of my gown and climb in my underthings. Then again, once I'm free from the room, that's only the beginning of my problems. I don't need the additional challenge of creeping around in my corset and petticoats. At least I wear no unwieldy crinoline, like many of the ladies at the ball have on tonight.

With as careful and quiet movements as I can manage, I angle my body so my front is against the sill. Then, clasping the ledge, I lower my body down, the soles of my shoes sliding against the moonstone wall in search of my landing place. For the first time tonight, I'm grateful not to be wearing elegant heels or dancing slippers.

Finally, my toes touch the cornice, and after securing both feet on the ledge, I begin to creep along, hands still latched to the sill, until I'm able to grasp the first pilaster. With slow moves, I step as far as I can while maintaining hold. I pause here, but only for a moment while I gather my bearings and press myself in close. Then I release the column. My heart leaps into my throat as I step quickly along the ledge, my body flat against the wall, then grasp the next pilaster. I continue like this for several minutes.

Hold. Quick step, quick step. Hold. Quick step, quick step. Hold.

Each time I reach a window, I grasp the sill and check for occupants before creeping past it. Every now and then, I look back the way I came, fearful that I'll see Marus leaning out the window in search of me. The thought makes my heart beat even louder. It riots in my ears while sweat beads at my brow and neck.

Hold. Quick step, quick step. Hold. Quick step, quick step. Hold.

I'm panting by the time I reach my first destination—the balcony on the floor above the one I need to climb down to. Hugging the pilaster that rests just a few feet from the balustrade, I take a deep breath and plan my next steps with precision. Then I'm off with another set of quick steps before I grasp the balustrade. My feet slip beneath me, as I fail my attempt to secure them on the bottom ledge of the balcony. I bite back a scream, gritting my teeth as my feet regain purchase. Once secure, I pause, allowing my pulse to return to a somewhat less terrified rhythm. Then I move one hand at a time from the balustrade to the balusters beneath it. Hands firmly in place, I release my feet—on purpose this time—so that I'm dangling over the next balcony down.

I continue shimmying down the balusters until my hands reach the base. My arms scream in protest, muscles trembling as I struggle to keep my hold. I hazard a glance at my feet, assessing how far I've left to go until my toes touch the balustrade. Unfortunately, the distance is far greater than I'd anticipated from afar.

Damn my short height.

I'll have to swing myself onto the balcony floor instead.

The chance of waking someone slumbering inside—if there *is* anyone in the room—is greater, but it's the best I can do without risking loss of balance.

I move my hands from the balusters to the bottom ledge, wincing at how my muscles quiver and ache, begging to let go already. *Not yet. Not yet. I'm almost there.*

Lifting my knees, I swing my legs forward. Then back. As I swing forward again, I release the ledge.

I try to catch my balance as I land, but instead, find the hard floor of the balcony biting into my hip. At least my fall didn't make much sound. Regardless, I pull myself to stand as fast as I can, ignoring the ache along my side. I brace my hands on the rail and search the grounds, planning where to run once I jump.

*It doesn't matter,* I tell myself. So long as I get away from here, away from Marus, away from Mrs. Coleman—

A sharp pain lances my stomach. I double over and narrowly avoid striking my chin on the balustrade. I bite my lip to keep from crying out, but the pain is almost too much.

Damn it. *Damn it!* It's the bargain. That stupid breezing skyforsaken bargain—

For a moment, I consider throwing myself over the balcony and continuing on despite the pain, but another wave strikes me, stronger than before. I know I won't make it far if I'm able to climb down at all.

I'm hit with an echo of our bargain. It reverberates through my head, bringing a shooting pain with it.

*Until you turn nineteen, you will remain in my care and live under my roof. And you will obey me.*

My heart hammers so fast, I fear it will explode. Gasping for breath, I push away from the railing, and my back comes against the balcony doors. *I'm obeying, I'm obeying,* I think to myself, but the pain doesn't abate.

Why did I have to think of Mrs. Coleman? It's obvious why thinking her name triggered the bargain's punishment; with magic so tightly woven into personal intent, all it took was a flash of guilt on my part. If only I'd been able to make it past the palace grounds before realization dawned. If only I'd gotten somewhere Mrs. Coleman wouldn't find me.

My mind begins to spin while nausea storms through my stomach. Cold sweat emits from every pore. I sink to the balcony floor, my back still pressed against the door.

*I'm obeying. I'm obeying.* But it's no use. I know the words are untrue.

The pain increases and my eyes begin to flutter shut. I can already feel consciousness slipping away. Suddenly, the door behind me opens, and I fall back. The last thing I think before my head hits the ground is, *I'm under your roof again, Mrs. Coleman. I'm obeying.*

# 16

*FRANCO*

My mystery girl has left the ball, I'm sure of it. As has my patience for this night. Music continues to blare into my ears as I lean against the far wall in the throne room, an overfull glass of wine my only companion. My guests appear tireless in their obsession with dancing the same chaste patterns over and over again. Quadrille. Cotillion. Waltz. Gallopade. I recognize them all, for once upon a disastrous social season, I partook in such nonsense. The memory makes my stomach clench...

I swallow the rest of my wine in a single gulp, delighting in the way the liquid warms my chest and buzzes in my mind. What I wouldn't give for a bottle of euphoric Midnight Blush. Or even Autumn Court's hallucinogenic honey pyrus wine. I could go for a nice hallucination right about now.

Although I'm loath to admit it, much of my current vexation results from my fruitless hunt for the mystery girl. My inability to find her has brought about my boredom far faster than if I'd never met the charming pianist or heard her haunting song. I can hardly make sense of what has me so fascinated in the first place. Is it simply that she treated me as a regular person? Is it her music? The fact that I have no idea what she looks like?

I know it's pointless to wonder. It's been over an hour since I last saw her, and I'll likely never see her again. If I do, I won't know it's *her*, and she won't know it's *me*.

That is, unless my first theory is correct.

That she's Princess Maisie.

It's a wild guess, but it's worth considering. Maisie is of the sea and *could* be related to a siren. A siren *could* be capable of producing such enchanting music. Behind our awkward first impression, the princess *could* be hiding a glowing personality.

An idea forms in my mind, one requiring further investigation. And—better yet—freedom from this infernal room. I glance at the throne, finding Augie perched upon it and doing his job. Well, not his *actual* job. As an ambassador, he's meant to act as a liaison between my sister and the Seelie King of Lunar, as well as communicate with our court's human representative, neither of which he's doing tonight. His duty as my friend, however, he seems to be performing quite well. Only several hundred times have I caught him staring longingly across the room at Seri. That's a minor infraction for a male so pathetically and hopelessly in love.

I place my empty glass on a nearby table and leave the throne room. As soon as I turn down the hall toward the Dawnstar wing, a sense of peaceful emptiness comes over me. This far from the flurry of activity, the halls are deserted, giving me a break from sensing others' emotions. But just as I'm nearing the corridor that leads to Maisie's room, I'm overwhelmed with a sudden shock of pain. Not physical pain, and not my own. It's grief and agonizing despair, clashing with jaw-clenching determination.

## Heart of the Raven Prince

It's coming from the same direction as Maisie's room.

I start off again, this time at a jog. The emotion grows stronger with every inch of distance I close, convincing me it's not just coming from the same *direction* as the princess' room; it's coming from *inside* her room. I reach the door, and the emotions suddenly abate.

Bringing my fist to the door, I rap on it. No answer. I knock again. Harder. Still no answer.

"Princess Maisie," I say. "Is everything all right?"

I hear a shuffling sound on the other side, followed by whispered voices. Then comes the telltale clack of Podaxis' claws on the marble floor. "May I ask who's calling?" he asks.

I throw my hands in the air, for the answer should be obvious. After my many failed attempts to call on the princess, the crustacean should be more than familiar with my voice. "It's Prince Franco. I need to see Princess Maisie at once."

More tapping of claws. More inaudible whispers. "Just a moment," Podaxis says.

I fold my feathered arms across my chest—

Oh shit.

Remembering the glamour I wear, I reach for my black cravat pull it from my neck. Just to be sure I'm properly attired, I glance down at myself, relieved to see I'm dressed in black trousers and a white shirt. Thank the All of All I chose to wear pants beneath my glamour. I stuff the cravat into my trouser pocket and settle into a domineering posture. No, that's all wrong. I'm not here to interrogate, I'm here to...investigate. I should look kind. Relaxed.

I shift about ten more times while the sound of footsteps approach, followed by the turning of the handle. The door opens a mere six inches to reveal Maisie—or what I can see of her, at least. She blinks into the dim light of the hall, the room behind her dark. Her updo is just as elegant as it was the first time I saw her, so I know I can't have woken her. Could her pink hair have been hiding beneath the teal glamour of my mystery girl? I glance at the high collar of her blouse, its cream shade not the pale blue I thought I might find. Still, there's every chance the dress had been glamoured as well.

"Your Highness," Maisie says, although she doesn't open the door farther. Nor does she meet my eyes, keeping her gaze on my neck or chin.

"Is everything all right in there?"

She hesitates before answering in a quiet voice. "Why wouldn't it be?"

"I...well, I sensed something coming from your room."

"Excuse me?" Her face blanches, eyes going wide as they flick to mine for the merest fraction of a second.

"I'm a psy vampire," I say, hoping that's explanation enough.

Her expression relaxes before she shakes her head as if to clear it. "Oh, yes, I was told about that."

"I had no intention of spying on you in that way." I sort through my next words before I say them, since I'll need to omit some facts without lying. "I was coming to check on you when I felt it."

"I see."

I wait for her to say more, but she doesn't. "So...is everything all right?"

"I'm all right," she says slowly, carefully, and offers me a contrived smile. I breathe in her emotions, comparing them to what I gleaned from our first meeting. Beneath an outer layer of anxiety, I sense a familiar buzz that must be her energetic signature. If only I'd read the mystery pianist's energy to compare it to. If she is the girl I'm looking for, it could explain her anxiety. After telling me she wasn't coming to the ball, she might want to hide that she attended without my knowledge. Then again, I sensed her alarm long before I reached her door.

I fold my arms. "The emotion I sensed was coming from you, correct?"

"I was afraid for a moment," she says easily. Too easily. "Startled by a sound I heard, but it was nothing truly terrifying."

"And you're all right now?"

She lifts her chin. "I've already said as much."

I narrow my eyes. She's definitely hiding something. "Did you come to the ball tonight?"

"No, Your Highness, I did not. I've been in my room all evening."

My stomach sinks at her answer, my disappointment far heavier than I could have guessed it would be. So, she isn't the mystery girl after all.

"I appreciate you checking on me, but it is getting late," she says flatly. "I should sleep."

"Right," I say, shrugging off my chagrin.

"Goodnight, Your Highness." The words are clipped, her posture stiff as she shuts the door in my face.

I stand there a few moments, eyes unfocused as I sort through the chaos of my thoughts. With the slam of her door still echoing in my ears and the uncomfortable murky energy that lingers in the air, it's painfully clear how much the princess dislikes me. I've never courted someone who didn't at least feign desire. But when we spoke this morning, she seemed upset when I mentioned she could leave. So, what the hell is going on here? If we continue to interact so coldly, no one will believe we're truly courting. Not the humans, not the fae, and certainly not my sister. I *must* convince my sister I'm trying... even if I'm not.

I turn away from Maisie's room, shaking my head. If I am to take advantage of this unwanted pairing, I need to get in the princess' good graces. At the very least, I need to convince her not to hate me. As I make my way toward the heart of the palace, an idea begins to form. I think I know what I can do to set her better at ease around me...

I'll make it right tomorrow.

I expect my new idea to comfort me, but as I continue down the halls, I can't shake a crushing sensation that hums deep in my core. Am I upset at Maisie's coldness? No, that's not it. While I'm not sure what I did to earn her dislike, I appreciate honesty and prefer open disdain over falsified respect.

Then what has me so forlorn?

A blue dress and silver mask flash through my memory, sending another pang of regret. It's her. The mystery girl. Until now, I hadn't realized how badly I wanted Maisie to be the pianist. But why? Was I hoping to discover we're more compatible than I originally thought? And if so, why should I care?

Maybe it's just a distraction I seek. My conversation with the mystery girl was entertaining, and she was certainly easy to talk to, but that's only because she didn't know who I am. If she knew my true identity, it would be different. *I'd* be different.

There's no further my fascination can go. No further I should *allow* it to go.

Besides, she's certainly long gone by now. If I was ever going to find her, I already would have.

Chuckling at my foolishness, I stop at the center of the empty hall and close my eyes. Letting all thoughts slip away, I focus on the sensation of air touching my skin, the way it envelops me in a cocoon of quiet calm. With a shudder, my body contracts, shrinking in on itself, my flesh giving way to feathers, my face elongating into a beak. My mind goes still, my animalistic instincts taking over as I shift into my unseelie form —a raven—and fly down the hall and out the nearest window. Augie can handle the rest of the ball on his own. Right now, I just need the vast open sky to blow some sense into me.

My wings beat the air as I fly over the forest trees, scents of earth and night-blooming jasmine mingling with the wind. All my concerns over cold courtships and royal successions flee, making my heart feel as weightless as my raven body feels against the updraft.

And yet...

In the very back of my mind, a melody continues to play.

# 17

**EMBER**

When I come to, I find myself in a dark room, lying on my side on a cool marble floor. The only light comes from one partially opened curtain that lets in the starlight from outside. My first response is a bone-crushing dread that the last several minutes of my life were nothing but a dream, that I haven't escaped the bedroom Marus locked me in. Heart pounding, I rise to sit. That's when I notice something I hadn't at first—the sound of shuffling movement. Then a shadowed silhouette hurrying about the room. The clearer my surroundings become, the more certain I am that I'm not in Marus' room.

"Who are you?" I call out. "Where am I?"

The voice that answers is female, a frantic undercurrent to her tone. "You've come at a very inopportune time. I know neither why you were climbing around on my balcony nor why you asked me not to tell anyone you're here."

"I...spoke to you?" I furrow my brow, unable to recall doing such a thing.

"Yes, and if you keep quiet about me, I'll do the same for you." She moves across the room from the far wall to the bed. With the room so dark, I can't make out what she looks like, only her hurried motions. "I'm guessing you got locked out of your room and had a dreadful time finding your way back inside the palace."

I swallow hard. "Something like that."

The figure leaves the bed and approaches me with an extended hand. "Come. I'll show you the door and you can be on your way."

I recoil from her, scrambling back. "No, no I can't go back inside the palace. I need to get out of here—"

My words are swallowed by a cry as a sharp pain erupts inside me. With it comes a return of memories.

*Standing on the balcony, ready to run.*

*The pain of my bargain igniting.*

*Falling against the balcony door, my consciousness slipping.*

*The door behind me opening, a frightened shout.*

*Then my voice, begging for help, pleading that no one can know I am here.*

I breathe through the pain. *I'm obeying,* I tell the magic. *I'm not running away.*

"Are you all right?" I open my eyes to find the girl crouched before me. All I can make out is a pleasant face surrounded by tendrils of unkempt hair. "Miss, I need you to calm down. It won't do to draw the prince back with your hysterics."

A spike of alarm cuts through me. "The prince? What do you mean the prince?"

With a grumble, she rises to her feet and strides over to the single open curtain, drawing it shut. She's nothing more than a moving shadow as she sweeps to the other side of the room. A second later, dim light emanates from over several sconces. "Calm. Down." Her words are punctuated with annoyance. "I can't have you ruining this for me."

I glance around the now-illuminated room. It's larger than the one I escaped from, but not quite as extravagant as the whole of Marus' sprawling apartment. Satisfied that I seem to be free from imminent threat, I turn my study to the girl. She looks to be my age, although her pointed ears tell me she's full fae. Her skin is a dark golden tan, her wild hair the pale pink of candy floss. She wears a pair of dark trousers, a cream shirt, and a brown unbuttoned waistcoat. Her state of dress reminds me of what men wear in the Gray Quarter. Next, my eyes rove to the bed, where I see an open trunk next to a smaller traveling bag. A thick gray fur hangs halfway out of the bag. "Who are you?"

She crosses her arms. "The less you know the better."

"She's right." I nearly jump out of my skin at the male voice. Rising to my feet, I look for its source. Then movement—the clacking of two red pincers—draws my gaze to the floor near the balcony door. It's...a crustacean of some sort, covered in an assortment of oddly shaped, multi-hued mushrooms. "You're lucky I didn't just snip your fingers and push you over the balustrade."

"We aren't snipping anyone's fingers, Podaxis," the girl says. "As for going over the balustrade...well, I need to leave. Are you done panicking? Can I go now?" She returns to the bed and finishes stuffing the fur into the traveling bag, then places a brown cap upon her head and tucks her tangled pink strands beneath it. Then, gathering the bag in her arms, she says, "If you need to remain in my room a little longer, fine. I'll ask no questions. But when you leave, be discreet about it. If anyone inquires, you never saw me. We never spoke. You can lie, yes? You're human?"

"Half human, but..." I take in her bag, her state of dress, her hasty way of speaking. "Wait, are you running away?"

The crustacean named Podaxis snaps his pincers again.

"Did you not hear what the princess said? The less you know the better."

I whip my gaze back to the girl. "Princess?"

She shoots a daggered look at her companion. "Damn it, Podaxis. You just gave her the very information we were trying to hide."

"Ah, so sorry, Your Highness." The way he brings his pincers together reminds me of someone wringing their hands. "Shall I snip her tongue, then?"

"You shall not," I say at the same time the girl—the *princess*—says, "Not if she can keep quiet."

I glance at the bag in her arms again, and urgency propels my feet toward her. "Take me with you." Another sharp pain twists inside me, but I breathe through it. "I must get out of here. Please, if you're running away, I need you to take me too." I double over with another wave of agony, stronger than the last. Sweat beads at my brow as my words become increasingly difficult to bite out. "I need you to *force* me to come with you. Even if I cry out in pain. Drag me if you must. Once we're far enough away, you can leave me somewhere off the beaten path."

Her eyes go wide. "Are you mad? I'm going on foot. Am I supposed to carry you?"

"We can get a coach," I say, half spoken, half hissed. "We can…*borrow* a cab. There are many here for the ball. Surely, one can go missing in the fray. Plus, I can pay you for your trouble. In two weeks, I can return here and claim my inheritance. I'll give you all of it. Just get me out of the palace until then."

"I don't want your money."

Another twinge of agony has me sinking to my knees, a trail of hot tears streaming down my cheeks. "Please."

The princess remains silent for a few moments, and I fear she'll brush past me and leave me behind. Then, with a muttered string of curses, she kneels at my side. Her voice takes on a softer tone as she asks, "What kind of trouble are you in?"

My head spins and it takes all my strength of will to focus on the present moment. *I'm obeying. I haven't run away. I'm not running away. It's only words. That's all.* The pain lessens, and I'm able to find my voice again. "I'm trapped in a bargain with my stepmother. I've sworn to live under her roof and obey her orders until I turn nineteen. That will be Sunday two weeks from now. After that, I'll be free. But I can't stay in the meantime. She's using our bargain to try and force me to marry a dangerous man. I...I can't do it." Another twinge of pain. A sharp gasp for air.

She reaches a tentative hand and pats my shoulder, an awkward attempt at being consoling. Her words, however, seem far more genuine. "I know a thing or two about unwanted pairings. Not that mine is with someone dangerous so much as unlikable."

"Please help me. I'll do anything. I'll make a bargain."

"What good is a bargain if you'll be forced to break a previous one? I can't take you with me if you'll be suffering a magical punishment the entire way. You'll slow me down." I'm surprised to find regret in her tone. "My travels require expedience and secrecy."

"We can make it work," I say, my mind reeling to come up with something to convince her to help me. "In my bargain, I'll promise to return the day after I turn nineteen. Our travels will be considered...a brief sojourn. I'll still deem myself living under Mrs. Coleman's roof since she's taken rooms at the palace all month. I just won't be...physically beneath it for the next two weeks." The pain lessens further but doesn't abate entirely.

The princess brings a finger to her chin and taps it. For a few moments, she watches me through slitted lids. Then, with a wide smile, she says, "No, I have a better idea. We will make a bargain, but you won't be coming with me."

"Princess Maisie," Podaxis mutters, scuttling closer to us. "Are you certain it's wise to get involved with whatever scandal this riffraff has gotten herself into?"

Maisie shushes him, and I shake my head. "I can't stay here. If my stepmother finds me, she'll haul me back to Brother Marus. They expect me to marry tomorrow, and the prince has agreed to oversee our nuptials. Even if I were to try and fight it, there's little chance the prince would intervene on my behalf."

She stands and paces before me. "I don't know the prince well, but he has as much personality as dry kelp."

"He's selfish and arrogant," I say through my teeth. "I doubt he'd even hear my petition."

She stops her pacing and smiles down at me. "I'm glad to hear you feel that way about him." Then, turning on her heel, she goes to a stack of chests and opens the top one. From within, she extracts a pair of elegant shoes, then returns to me. "Here, put these on."

Furrowing my brow, I stand and take them from her. The shoes are made of a pale blue silk dotted with tiny pearls. It has a low heel of the same shade, but smooth and sheer and... "Are the heels made of glass?"

"Sea glass," she says like it's unsurprising. "They're quite strong, so don't be alarmed. However, they will break if you are careless with them, so do treat them well. They were designed for dancing."

"Dancing?"

"I'm a selkie," she says with an air of irritation. "My kind are known to take seelie form after sundown and dance on the shore. Despite never having done so myself, Father thought they'd make a nice gift for all the dancing I'm supposed to be doing to woo the prince."

"You're...wooing the prince?"

She shrugs. "*Was* wooing the prince. I've decided I cannot. There's no way I can keep up the charade of liking him, and now that I've seen his psy vampire powers at work, it's only a matter of time before he finds out we're incompatible. It's imperative I leave before he sends me back to my home court."

I sort through everything she's told me, everything I've learned. She's a selkie. A princess. And Podaxis called her Princess Maisie. I've heard that name before. "You're the youngest daughter of King Ronan, the Seelie King of the Sea Court."

She nods.

"If you don't want to court the prince, and you don't want to be sent back home, where are you going?"

"Too many questions!" shouts Podaxis, snapping his pincers.

"He's right," she says. "Enough about me. Go stand before the mirror and put on the shoes."

"Why? What significance do they have?" I can't see how a pair of fancy shoes is supposed to help my predicament.

"Just do it." She gives me a light shove toward the full-length mirror propped next to a dressing screen. I take in my reflection, startled by what I find. I almost forgot I'm outfitted in my beautiful ballgown, and seeing all the stains and tears it has gathered during my trip out the window brings a pang of regret. My gaze leaves the dress to my face, where I find my eyes rimmed red, cheeks flushed, hair in as much disarray as the princess' pink strands—which have already begun to fall out from under her cap. She comes up beside me and raises her brows, arms folded. "The shoes. Put on the shoes. I don't have all night."

While her voice isn't unkind, it snaps me into action. I place the elegant, heeled slippers on the floor before me and step out of my shoes. Then I slide my feet into the new pair.

"Do they fit?" she asks.

I shift my weight from side to side. "They're only a little loose, but it isn't too bad." I lift my eyes to catch her satisfied smile in the mirror but jump back at my reflection. Gone is my teal hair, my pale complexion. I still wear my ballgown, but my skin is a warm tan, my hair pale pink and neatly styled in a formal updo. My ears are pointed and bejeweled with pearls. My cheeks are lightly rouged, my lashes long and black.

The shoes...they hold a glamour.

I bring a hand to my glamoured hair, surprised when it feels exactly like my own. Patting all around it, I find no evidence of my true hair, which I know should be fanned out around my shoulders in disarray by now. I turn my face to the side, studying angles that aren't my own, touching my rounded jawline, my pointed ear. Everything about the glamour feels real. I blink, and my eyes obey. I force a smile, and my lips turn up. I pull a strand of perfectly curled pink hair off my forehead, and it responds as if it were my own.

Whirling toward the princess, I say, "Why do you have a glamour that looks exactly like you?"

"*Exactly* like me?" She scoffs. "Look again."

I return my gaze to the mirror. The glamour I wear is most certainly designed to mimic the girl next to me. The only differences are the addition of mild cosmetics to cover her heavily freckled skin, the rounded jaw, the pearl earrings, the perfect coiffure. Oh, and perhaps our height. She's at least two inches taller. On further inspection, our eyes are different too. Mine retain their bold turquoise hue, while hers are bright blue. It seems the glamour only impacts my skin and hair.

She flips off her cap and gestures to her body from head to toe. "*This* is what I look like. I mean, I don't normally wear clothes I've stolen from my brothers, but do you honestly think I can impress the vain Prince Franco looking the way I do? I'm not like the pretty females he's used to courting. At first, I thought this glamour would be enough, and it's come in handy twice already. The first time, I donned the shoes but forgot I was wearing trousers. I had to cover myself with a blanket before he could see. Thank the shells I had the foresight to put them on when he came to the door just now."

I whirl around to face her. "The prince was at the door?"

"Yes, he's the one who came knocking when you tumbled through my door."

"Did he see me? Did he know—"

"No," she says. "I covered for you without lying, but the exchange was enough to convince me I can't remain. He's probably already thinking of excuses to shorten my visit."

"So...you want to stay, but you don't want to stay."

"It's complicated," she snaps. "I can't talk about it. Just know that I need to get as far away from the sea as I can. That's where you come in. You're going to help me."

"How so?"

She points at the shoes. "You're going to impersonate me, which will give me the head start I need to disappear."

Her words fill my chest with a hollow dread. I narrow my eyes. "Why do I get the feeling you're in danger?"

She stares back, saying nothing.

I fold my arms. "If you are, I'll only be inviting the same danger to myself, won't I?"

"So long as you have the prince's favor, you'll be safe," she says, which isn't entirely comforting. "All you have to do is continue to court him in my stead. Since you can lie, you should be able to do what I could not—convince him you like him enough to keep his attention. As soon as our bargain is fulfilled, you're free to do as you please and leave my sudden disappearance a mystery."

"Why would I agree to this? It's madness. I can't even imagine the punishment if I'm caught."

She shrugs. "Could it be worse than the alternative?"

I nibble a corner of my lip. She has a point. I can't imagine any punishment worse than being forced to marry a man like Marus.

"This bargain would serve you too," she says. "Who would think to look for you *here*? Who would second guess a princess on a royal visit? If you do this for me, you'll be given the perfect subterfuge to wait out the end of your bargain with your stepmother. You'll be under her roof, just like your bargain requires. And we can word our bargain in a way that affirms you'll be obeying her as well."

I consider her words, pulse racing. Her plan is reckless, dangerous for us both.

It is also my only hope. I clench my jaw, fingers flinching at my sides. If only I had a piano and the time to work this all out through song. But all I have is my mind. "How long do you propose our bargain must last?"

"Just until the one with your stepmother is fulfilled. That's all I'm asking. A head start, so that by the time anyone realizes I'm missing, there will be no fresh trail to follow."

"Wouldn't you have had that problem if you'd left tonight without leaving a decoy behind?"

She gives me a tense smile. "Yes. Which means we're both fortunate to have run into each other. What do you say? Do we have a bargain?"

I drum my fingers on my thighs. "State your terms."

# 18

**EMBER**

Maisie paces from one side of the bedroom to the other, muttering to herself. My stomach is a roiling mess as I watch her from where I sit on the bed. I've taken off the shoes, leaving them on the floor by the mirror. I can hardly bear to look at them. Soon they will link me to something I swore I'd never do again—another bargain.

"All right," Maisie says, facing me. "I've got it."

My heart slams against my ribs as I await her words, my mouth painfully dry.

"In accordance with your bargain, you..." She halts, lips dipping into a frown. "I don't know your name."

"Ember Montgomery," I say, voice barely above a whisper.

She nods. "You, Ember Montgomery, will take on my identity. You will court the prince in my stead until your bargain with your stepmother is served. Until then, you must wear the glamoured shoes in public and let no one see you without the glamour. You shall tell no one that I've run away. During this time, you will remain living at the palace, which is currently considered your stepmother's place of residence."

She gives me a satisfied grin, but I can't return it. My mind is tangled around her words, seeking weaknesses, areas needing further expansion. The clause about the palace being my stepmother's current residence lessened much of the lingering pain from my almost-broken bargain, but what would happen if my family were cast out of the palace in the next two weeks? Brother Marus could refuse his arrangement with Mrs. Coleman after I turn up missing. Will the incentive of stealing my inheritance be enough for him to hold out hope that I'll return or be found? Both Marus and my stepmother mentioned my stepsisters now have positions at court for the month. If that's already been settled, will it be enough to keep them here?

The blood leaves my face when I consider what would happen if they were forced to return to the Gray Quarter and I'm trapped between two bargains, one that makes me follow and one that makes me stay.

I swallow hard. The result would be more than pain. It would likely be the death of me.

Whatever happens, I must ensure my stepfamily remains at Selene Palace. Hopefully parading around as a princess will give me some sway if I'm forced to intervene.

"What else shall we add?" Maisie asks.

I force the fearful thoughts from my mind and shift my attention to the terms of our soon-to-be bargain, testing them against the one with Mrs. Coleman. A hum of pain continues to burn through me, and I try to seek out which of her orders I'm still disobeying. I recall our last exchange where she left me with Marus.

*You will marry Brother Marus.*

A stab of pain has me doubling over and I breathe it away. My words come out strained. "For the duration of our bargain, I will consider my engagement to Brother Marus valid. I will do nothing to sever it." My stomach unclenches, and I fill my lungs with air. There's still an ache deep within me, but that's likely as dull as I can make it. In my heart of hearts, I know what my true intentions are. There's only so much one can fool fae magic.

Maisie repeats my words, adding them to our official terms. Then, striding over to me, she holds out her hand. "Do you agree to this bargain?"

Her question makes my heart sink. The last time I heard those words, they came from the mouth of the bargain broker. And I've lived to regret them ever since. Will I regret this too?

*Not if it helps me defeat my stepmother once and for all.*

Setting my jaw, I rise from the bed and clasp her outstretched hand in mine. "I agree to this bargain."

I FEEL NUMB AS I WATCH THE PRINCESS CLIMB OVER THE balustrade, doing the very thing I set out to do tonight and failed. She drops from the balcony to the ground with a muffled *oomph*, then halts in place. With the glamoured shoes secured on my feet, I lean over the rail and look left and right, searching for guards or prying eyes. She looks up at me, her cap back in place to hide her hair, and I nod. In the dark, she looks like a farm boy or a laborer. Nothing like a princess. With a final wave at me, she darts across the lawn toward the line of trees, Podaxis under one arm and her bag clutched in the other. My heart clenches as I watch her disappear into the shadows, to freedom. I watch the quiet lawn several minutes more, until I'm certain no one saw her.

Just like that, she's free. Free from whatever she's running from. Free from her unwanted courtship with the prince.

Free, while I remain imprisoned for two more weeks.

Two more weeks.

I can handle that.

Can't I?

THE NEXT DAY, I STAND BEFORE THE MIRROR LOOKING AT A FACE that is not my own, standing in a room meant for a princess, and wearing clothing that doesn't belong to me. I feel like an impostor as I assess my reflection, studying my white lace blouse with its high collar, the green tartan skirt, and the glamoured shoes that peek from my hem. Beneath the skirt and blouse, I have on a clean chemise and corset. I was surprised to find the latter. Before I looked through Maisie's trunks, I expected to find them full of clothing in the fae style, which usually consists of low-cut dresses in thin, flowing fabrics, designed to wear without corsets. Instead, everything I found was modeled after human fashions, including the undergarments. A pinch of disappointment hit me at first, for I have always admired fae fashions. Yet, this style suits me best. The clothing I wear may be of the finest wool, silk, and lace that has ever graced my form, but it feels more like…me. One less thing I have to pretend about.

If only I could feel as comfortable in my new room.

I turn from the mirror and take in my surroundings. Never in my life have I stayed in such luxurious accommodations. The floor is smooth, glittering opal, the walls pale moonstone. Gilded frames surround beautiful paintings of the night sky, and the furniture is carved of pale birch and black obsidian. The room hosts a bed, a nightstand, a sitting area with a table and chairs, and a dressing area with a dressing table, wardrobe, and screen. When I first awoke, I bumbled around the room seeking a washbasin before I discovered a private washroom behind a closed door.

My skin crawls with the heavy awareness that none of this is mine. None of this is meant for me.

The thought has my fingers drumming against my thighs. For the love of the breeze, how the hell am I going to pull this off?

I shake my head and look at my reflection once more, turning this way and that to ensure it reveals no hint of who I truly am. Even though the glamour only affects my face, hair, and skin tone, one would be hard pressed to find any similarities to my true self, aside from the color of my eyes and my figure, perhaps. But I doubt anyone would notice my eyes, and my form is hidden behind fine clothing no one would ever expect me to wear.

*This will work*, I tell myself, patting my glamoured hair in its perpetual pink updo. *I'll be safe. I can do this.*

I'm about to turn away from the mirror but stop myself when a flash of gold catches my eye. My fingers fly to my locket. I hadn't thought of it until now and had draped it over my collar like I normally do. While it isn't the most noticeable piece of jewelry, I can't risk wearing it. One look between the hinged halves would show my parents' portraits. Not something Princess Maisie would have any reasonable explanation for. I go to take it off, but when my fingers brush the clasp, sorrow sinks my heart. My locket is all I have left of my parents. That's never been truer than now when I don't even have my face or my mother's hair. So, instead, I tuck it beneath the high collar of my blouse, where not even the chain shows through.

That's not the only evidence I must attend to...

Anxiety tickles my chest as I glance at the dressing screen. Behind it, my discarded clothing from last night rests in a pile. I haven't a clue what to do with it, aside from hide it somewhere. There's no furnace in the room, so burning my things is out of the question. Besides, the thought of destroying my lovely gown makes my heart ache. A proper hiding place will have to do.

I make my way behind the dressing screen to collect my gown, underclothes, shoes, and train ticket—still wrapped safely in its handkerchief—and bring them to Maisie's trunks. The top one overflows with the clothes I sorted through to find today's outfit. I pull that one down and begin searching through the rest. It's mostly clothes, including some rather elegant ballgowns, but I also find an embroidery set, a blank sketchbook, and a book on human etiquette. I may not know Maisie well, and yet it's hard to imagine her sitting around doing needlework and engaging in soft manners.

Panic surges through me. Is that what I'm going to be expected to do every day while I pretend to be her? Stich, draw, and read like a proper noblewoman? As nice as it might be to have a break from the constant chores that have taken up every waking moment of my life, spending any extended period in idle time sounds like torture.

I continue rifling through the trunks, pulling most items out and reorganizing them so I can decide which should hide my belongings. The last chest I open contains nothing but hat boxes, but when I open them, they aren't full of hats at all. Instead, one is filled with seashells, another with a collection of tarnished silverware, and a third with various pieces of chipped or broken porcelain dishes.

*So, she likes to collect things*, I think to myself. *Well noted.*

I'm about to rearrange the hat boxes into a trunk with the items I know I won't need when a knock sounds at the door. My heart leaps into my throat. I freeze in place, unable to move as fear seizes me.

Another knock.

I swallow hard and force myself to stand. *I can do this.*

I'm about to head straight for the door, when I recall the reason I'd been preoccupied with the trunks. My things! With trembling fingers, I gather my gown, old shoes, and undergarments and stuff them into an empty trunk. Then I tuck my train ticket into a fold of my gown and toss a cloak over everything before I close the lid.

With a deep breath, I make my way to the door. It takes me a few moments to gather my composure. How would Maisie answer the door? With her head held high like a royal? No, that doesn't seem like her at all. With a smile? A frown? I settle on mild curiosity and open the door.

Standing on the other side are my stepsisters.

# 19

**EMBER**

The blood drains from my face and with it goes all my hope. How did they find me so soon? Was Maisie caught before she could get far enough away? My stomach churns, sweat prickling behind my neck. It's over. It's all over.

"Your Highness," the two girls say in unison in a tone I've never once heard directed at me. They dip into curtsies, batting their lashes when they rise.

For several moments I'm stunned into silence. They don't know it's me. They think I'm really Maisie.

Then what in the name of the breeze are they doing here?

My stepsisters' expressions remain stretched into contrived smiles as I continue to stare at them. When I still find myself unable to speak, Imogen says, "We're your new lady's maids, Your Highness. I'm Imogen Coleman, and this is my sister, Clara Coleman."

"Oh, I see," I finally say, trying to keep my voice slightly higher than normal. Hopefully, they don't hear the slight quaver that comes with it.

Imogen quirks a brow but says nothing.

Right. For once my stepsister must defer to me. My mind reels to make sense of everything. So, *this* must be the position Marus promised my stepsisters in exchange for my hand. A position I need them to keep to ensure they remain at the palace. I grit my teeth at the cruel irony.

"I see you've already dressed," Imogen says. "Shall we take you to breakfast? Or bring a plate to your room?"

"My room," I rush to say. "Yes, please bring my breakfast here."

Imogen bows her head. "As you wish, Your Highness. I shall go and leave Clara with you."

"No, I would like you both to go, for I would also like a fresh pitcher of water. And...and tea with honey."

"Yes, Your Highness," the girls say with warm smiles.

I close the door before they even turn away. Then, chest heaving, I press my back against the wall.

This is bad. This is very, very bad.

I return to the trunk with my hidden clothes, piling a few more items on top of the cloak. Then I scramble around, digging through the disarray I've created in search of the key. Finally, I find a brass ring with a selection of keys buried under a mound of blouses. After fumbling to find the right fit, which I'm sure isn't helped by how badly my hands shake, I discover the key that slides easily into place. Then, with a turn, I seal away the only proof of my true identity.

Relief washes over me, but my head continues to spin. I tuck the keys into the pocket of my skirt and sink onto the locked trunk. With slow, heavy breaths, I force my racing heart to calm.

Well, this is off to a terrible start.

I've barely managed to gather my composure before I hear

another knock at the door. Rising to my feet, I brush off my skirts and swivel to the side to catch my reflection. Still Maisie. Still perfectly disguised. And still very much unready to see my stepsisters again.

I keep my face impassive and open the door. But it isn't my stepsisters I find.

It's Prince Franco.

With one arm braced against the doorframe and the other propped at his waist, he leans forward in a casual slouch. Then he lifts his eyes to mine and grins at me like he's practiced this a hundred times on a hundred different females...and expects me to swoon just the same.

It conjures memories of our encounter in the alley, and all the rage I felt then returns now. Even though his current expression is in stark contrast to the bored, arrogant countenance he wore then, it still sends a torrent of fury coursing through my blood. I clench my jaw, wanting nothing more than to slap that stupid smile off his face, but over his shoulder, I see an even more unwelcome sight—Imogen and Clara returning with their trays of tea and breakfast.

My heart slams against my ribs, my legs threatening to give way beneath me. I'm not ready to face my stepsisters again. Not yet. Not until I gather my wits and figure out how to act around them.

Without a second thought, I say to the prince, "A walk, yes?" I don't give him the chance to answer before I duck beneath his arm, closing the door with me. He's still standing in the same position, brow furrowed at the closed door, when I reach his other side.

He pushes off the doorframe and faces me, looking momentarily flustered. My gaze runs over the length of him, noting his tight black trousers and blue silk shirt. His collar is unbuttoned to the middle of his chest, and his neck adorned with strands of long black beads. He wears no cravat, waistcoat, or jacket. If we were amongst human society right now, he might as well be naked for his improper state of dress. "Did I hear you right?" he asks, turning to face me. "Did you just ask me to take a walk with you?"

"Is that a problem?" I tear my gaze from the indecently tight fit of his pants to his eyes. I nearly wince when I realize how sharp my words came out. For the next two weeks, my safety depends on the prince's favor. I tilt my head and shift my tone, taking on a demure quality. "Should I have waited for you to invite me to walk, Your Highness?"

He opens his mouth but can't seem to find the right words. "Well, yes...I mean, no. I mean...well, I came here to invite you on an outing with me."

I glance to the side, catching sight of my stepsisters. They've paused several feet away, and I glimpse a flash of brutal envy in their expressions. There's no doubt they heard the prince's words. Since Maisie and Franco have yet to make their courtship public, they may be the first to witness it.

"An outing," I say, fully aware of how awkward I sound. "Yes, let's go on an outing."

Imogen dons her brightest, falsest smile as she steps forward and dips into a curtsy, one Clara is quick to mimic. "Would you like us to chaperone, Princess?" Imogen asks.

"No, thank you," I say as warmly as I can manage. "You may leave the trays in my bedroom. I will take breakfast when I return." Anxiety nearly blows me over as frantic questions fly through my mind. Did I leave anything behind before I locked the trunk? Left some clue out in the open? Am I certain I hid everything important? I replay my every move, every item I stashed.

*I'm safe*, I tell myself. *All hints of who I really am have been tucked away.*

I pat the side of my leg, feeling the weight of the trunks' keys in my pocket.

The girls' faces fall, eyes darting to the prince as if they expect him to intercede on their behalf. He says nothing, of course. In fact, he doesn't even look their way, his eyes locked on me. My stepsisters mumble a solemn, "Yes, Your Highness," then brush past us, whispering with their heads close together.

I glance up at Franco, who continues to watch me with unsettling curiosity. Or is it suspicion? I swallow hard. "Shall we go?"

"With pleasure," he says and offers me his arm. Gritting my teeth, I secure my hand in the crook of his elbow. My pulse quickens as my hand makes contact with the smooth silk of his shirt. Not because it excites me to touch the prince. That most certainly could *not* be it.

*It's been so long since I've been this close to a male, that's all it is.*

My awareness of our irritating nearness only grows the longer we walk, but I try to shift my focus to the figures we pass. The halls appear mostly empty, which I'm grateful for. Still, I can't shake the fear that we'll cross paths with Mrs. Coleman or Brother Marus.

"I thought we could benefit from getting to know one another on a personal level," the prince says. There's a hint of hesitation in his tone as he continues. "You know, before we make our courtship known. Are you still...willing? Do you still want to be here and...court one another?"

"Of course," I say quickly. Perhaps too quickly. "Where are we going anyway, Your Highness? You said you were taking me on an outing."

"First of all, enough with *Your Highness*. If we are to court and spend significant time together, you shall call me Franco."

*Significant time together.* Oh, what have I gotten myself into? My heart beats faster. Can he hear it? I swallow hard. "Very well."

"Is there anything you would like me to call you?"

"Me?" I meet his eyes for the briefest moment, unsettled by

the question despite my best efforts to hide it. "You know my name, Your High—Franco." The last word feels dangerous on my tongue. Forbidden.

"All right then, Maisie."

Hearing the name only unsettles me further. I was not prepared for how guilty I'd feel being directly referred to as *Maisie*. At least being called *Your Highness* makes it feel more like a childish game of pretend rather than deception.

Franco stops and faces me, brow furrowed. "You don't like that, do you?"

"What do you mean?" I ask, pulse quickening as I release his arm and take a step away from him.

He watches me for a few silent moments. When he speaks, his voice holds an unexpected softness. "I don't mean to use my power on you, Princess. I just naturally do. And when I said your name, I sensed you didn't like it. I'm sorry if that was too forward of me. We don't need to be on a first name basis if you're uncomfortable with it."

I'm taken aback by his sudden sincerity. It's nothing like the arrogance he revealed in the alley or the bored disdain he displayed upon his throne at the ball. More surprising than that, though, is what he said about his power. He can sense my emotions. That means what Maisie said about him is true; he's a powerful psy vampire. I need to be really, *really* careful around him. And so far, I'm off to a terrible start.

"It's not that," I say slowly, gathering my composure as I weave a new lie. "I just...I miss my family. Hearing you use my name like that...makes me think of my...siblings and how much I miss them."

He tilts his head, and I get the impression he's reading me, dissecting my lie. For a moment, I fear I may have said something wrong. Maisie has siblings, doesn't she? Didn't she mention stealing menswear from her brothers? Before I can panic, he flashes me a grin. "How about I call you something else? Something meant just for me."

Relief settles my nerves, and I force a smile. "All right."

He offers me his arm again, and we return to walking. He taps his free hand to his chin. "What about...May? Zee? Zizi? Em?"

"Em?" I echo, my hand automatically coming to rest over the lump that is my hidden locket. No one has called me Em since my father was alive.

Franco nods. "The first letter of your name. *M*."

A comforting warmth spreads through me. *M*. The first letter of Maisie's name. Or *Em*. Short for Ember. A piece of my true self to keep while I wear another's face. If it will make my bargain with Maisie even the slightest bit easier to bear, then I'll take it. "I like that. Em. Let's make a name of it."

"As you wish, *Em*," he says, exaggerating the name as he playfully bumps his shoulder into mine.

I can't help the way my lips flick up at the corners. *Stupid, foolish lips. Don't fall for his charms.* So what if he showed me a moment of empathy? It's only because he can read my breezing feelings. Besides, he's still the same vile prince who asked if I planned to have a tryst with him against an alley wall.

The thought helps sober me, and I force my expression back to neutral.

We make our way down a staircase that lets out into a hall I recognize—the grand hall near the ballroom. With the hazy daylight coming in through the windows and the quiet emptiness around us, it's hard to imagine it's the same place I was last night.

*Last night.*

For something that started out feeling so magical, it ended so horribly. My stomach turns at the memories. Then, reminding myself that the prince is likely reading my feelings at this very moment, I make myself focus on the better parts of the ball. The dancing. The music. My brief encounter with the fat raven. That sends a wave of comfort through me and even sparks a pang of longing. I know there's no sense dwelling on a stranger. He could have been anyone. A servant or an aristocrat. A human or a fae. Ugly or handsome. It wouldn't matter, of course, for I enjoyed our conversation either way. And his voice...I can't remember its sound, only that it was youthful. Warm.

It's a futile treasure, but maybe one worth keeping—the last delightful moment I had while wearing my own face.

Who knows, perhaps the memory will come in handy. I can use it to alter my emotions next time I want to strangle the prince. Which I'm sure is likely to happen any moment now.

## 20

FRANCO

Today must go perfectly. If I am to convince my sister my efforts with the princess are genuine, I need Maisie—or *Em* as we've agreed I should call her—to not hate me. While I can't have her falling in love with me, it's imperative she at least pretends to tolerate our courtship. So far, things are going far better than I expected. She's kind today. Smiling now and then. She's even managed not to completely shut down when I try to act anything other than boring.

Outside the palace, I see exactly what I hoped to find—one of my best coaches parked at the bottom of the palace steps with two moon mares hitched at the front. The princess and I descend the steps and are almost to the bottom when I find her suddenly rooted into place.

"What are those?" Em asks, a tremble in her voice. Her hand slips from my arm.

It takes me a moment to realize the source of her fear. I cast a glance at the moon mares before returning my gaze to her. "Donna and Dominus? They're my babies."

"Your *babies*? They're...they're..."

"Beautiful?" I say with a chuckle.

"I was going to say terrifying," she mutters.

I look back at the creatures. While I see only the two most adorable fillies ever to have been born, I can sort of see why others would find them frightening. Moon mares are slim and skeletal with a cover of thin, pale, velvety skin over their bony frames. Their eyes are ruby red, and their mouths are lipless, leaving perpetually bared teeth. Instead of a mane, they have a row of spines along the back of their necks. "Don't be alarmed by their appearance. They're as harmless as puca—or maybe a kelpie is a better comparison."

"That isn't comforting."

I quirk a brow. "Do you not employ puca for your own carriages?"

"Oh...yes, of course I do," she rushes to say, eyes flashing toward me, "but I'm not in charge of handling them."

"Well, then, let me show you how harmless they are." Keeping my eyes on her, I make my way to the moon mares and place a hand on each of their noses. They nuzzle against my palms, releasing guttural snorts in request for more pets. I stroke the sides of their faces, an idiotic grin tugging my lips in response. "Donna and Dominus are the sweetest creatures you'll ever meet. They're just over two years of age. This is their first year pulling our coaches. They listen to me. Maybe not as well as their parents." I say this last part under my breath and give them each a kiss on the muzzle.

When I next glance at Em, I see she's taken a few steps closer, some of the terror gone from her eyes. "I suppose they are sort of adorable," she says, but her attempt at a smile looks more like a grimace.

I give Donna and Dominus each a final pat, then turn to Em. "Shall we?"

She stares at the moon mares a few moments more, then

*Heart of the Raven Prince*

reluctantly follows me to the coach. Once we reach the doors, I help her inside and take the bench across from her. She seems to relax a bit as she settles into her seat, smoothing the folds of her skirt. I tap the wall behind me and make a clicking noise in the back of my throat. The coach starts forward, and Em splays her arms out wide. "Wait. Isn't anyone else coming? Footmen? Guards? Where is the coachman?"

"For one, I'm the driver. The mares listen to me. They know where I want them to take us. For another, we can manage perfectly on our own. You've got me, after all." I offer a wink, but she pointedly ignores it. Not that I thought it would work on her. "Besides, you said no chaperones."

Her mouth falls open before she speaks. "I only said that to my...my lady's maids. I didn't want them coming with me."

"Ah. Well, forgive me for misreading things. How do you like them, anyway? The maids, that is? Will they suffice?"

A wave of agitation ripples off of her. "I wasn't expecting new maids at all."

"Neither was I, but apparently I already said yes."

"What do you mean *apparently*?"

I huff a laugh. It was Augie who approved Brother Marus' request to give the two human girls positions at court. Marus approached him at the ball, having no clue Augie wasn't me and asked if Princess Maisie was in want of a pair of lady's maids. The ambassador relayed the conversation this morning when he came to return my glamour. Not that I wanted to touch the string of beads after whatever dark deeds it witnessed overnight. Needless to say, I promptly burned the glamour, both for my sake and the safety of my kingdom. A glamour that allows one to impersonate a royal is a dangerous thing to leave lying around.

I realize Em is still waiting for an answer, but that would require me to confess my glamour shenanigans. Instead, I ask, "Would you like me to send the girls home? I could dismiss them. I believe their entire family has taken up residence at the palace, and I wouldn't mind giving them the boot."

Her expression shifts, brows knitting together. "They would have to leave the palace? Couldn't you just give them...other positions?"

"Do I sense a soft spot for humans?"

She taps her fingers against the sides of her thighs—an anxious gesture. For not the first time, I get the sense she's hiding something. Her words come out slow. "I think you should allow them to stay for the social season."

"As you wish."

Another tapping of her fingers. "But you're sure you don't have a different position to offer them?"

"As hard as it is to believe, I have no other use for two empty-headed human girls. I already know their kind." She glowers at that, but I feel no remorse. I sensed the desperation oozing from the two women the moment they entered the hall carrying Em's breakfast trays. Once they saw the princess and me together, all I could taste was bitter jealousy bordering on hate. Perhaps she'd be better off without them. Then again, she arrived with only Podaxis, as far as I know. Which reminds me...

"How is Podaxis? I didn't see him this morning."

Her mouth hangs open for a few moments before she speaks. Then, turning toward the window in a too-nonchalant sort of way, she says, "He isn't adapting to land as well as I am. He decided to return to the sea."

I lean back in my seat, arms resting on each side of the backrest. Bending my knee, I cross my legs and prop my ankle over my thigh, drinking in the murky flavor of her emotions. "Is that so?"

She nods but doesn't remove her gaze from the passing scenery the window offers.

We fall into silence as the coach takes us through the

woods. She seems to grow genuinely fascinated with our surroundings, and I don't blame her. I've always loved the beauty of my court, the way the sun is never too bright, always tinted with the same lovely quality that only a solar eclipse provides in other courts. I can hardly imagine witnessing such splendor for the first time—especially by someone who's rarely left the sea. While I'm sure the Sea Court is home to wonders that would surely blow my mind, I'm convinced there's plenty here to impress her. Which is precisely why I chose a forest drive for our private outing today.

I take advantage of her distraction to quietly study her, from her long skirt to the beaded slippers peeking beneath it—the same shoes she wore when I first met her on her balcony. My gaze slides up to the high lace neck of her collar, the tendrils of pink hair that frame her face. I take in the turn of her lips, the angles of her soft, lightly rounded face, then land on her eyes. My heart quickens as I realize their color for the first time.

"Aqua," I say, not realizing I uttered the word out loud until she faces me. The hue is even more striking now that they're in full view. "The color of your eyes."

She nods, reaching for a strand of her hair. "The same color as my—"

She stops and lowers her hand with a shake of her head. "The same color as my mother's eyes." With that, she faces the window again. I catch her tapping her fingers against her thighs, but this time, she stills them by gathering them around folds of her skirt.

I breathe in her energy, comparing it to what I sensed when she was distracted with the view. Then I recall how it tasted the other two occasions we've met.

Curious. Very curious indeed.

"We should get to know each other, Em," I say, watching her carefully as she faces me again. "How old are you?"

Her energy erupts in a panicked riot, but her voice comes

out smooth. "Isn't it like the human saying goes? A lady never tells her age, and a gentleman never asks."

"Oh, Em. I'm sure we both know I'm no gentleman."

She pales at that, eyes narrowing almost imperceptibly.

"How are your siblings? You have mostly sisters, am I correct?"

A long pause. Another flash of panic. "Brothers, actually."

"Ah, that's right. And your oldest brother. Is his name Davy?"

Her chest heaves, her emotions spiking so high, I can taste their acidic tang on my tongue. "I'd rather not talk about my family," she says slowly. "I miss them too dearly."

"That's all right," I say. "I know what we can talk about instead. First, let's start with you telling me who you really are."

∽

### EMBER

My lungs feel too tight, and my breaths become ragged and shallow. It's over. He knows. Has he known from the start? Is that what this *surprise outing* is truly about? Oh, for the love of the breeze, he's taking me to the middle of nowhere so he can kill me. My body convulses with tremors, but I refuse to let my fear show on my face. If I am to die, I'll do so with my mother's wild spirit shining through my eyes, with defiance burning my veins.

"Was that question too hard?" Franco taunts. "Let's try this. Where is the princess?"

I force a light laugh. "I don't understand what you're talking about."

He narrows his eyes to slits. "I can make things very bad for you. Answer my questions, and I might be lenient. Otherwise, I will throw you in a dungeon until my sister returns. She won't be so gentle."

My stomach twists. If I'm thrown in a dungeon, they'll surely strip me of my glamoured shoes to dress me in rags. There will be no maintaining my disguise. My bargain with Maisie will be violated. And once he finds out the truth...I'm ruined. Everything is ruined. Tears prick my eyes no matter how hard I try to blink them away. I never should have done this, never should have made another bargain—

"Come here," the prince says, his tone like ice.

My muscles tense, poised against attack. "Why?"

"I'm going to ask you a series of questions and you're going to sit next to me and answer them. I want you as close as possible so I can sense every flicker of deception you try to conceal."

"What will you do to me?"

"That depends."

"On what?"

"On a lot," he says, tone sharp. "Look, you don't have much to barter with. I know you aren't the same person I met twice before, and you've all but confessed you aren't the princess. I also know you must be at least part human to lie so well. Now. Come. Here."

With my fingers curled into fists, I rise from my bench and take a step toward him. All at once, the coach hitches. I stumble forward, arms outreached to catch my fall. Just as I'm about to tumble to my knees, a pair of hands grip my shoulders. The coach lurches again, tipping me to the side....and planting me straight onto the prince's lap. Our eyes meet and his widen with alarm, followed by a flash of disgust.

"Get off me!" he shouts at the same time I push off from his chest.

Scrambling to the far end of the bench, I burn him with a glare. "What is the meaning of this?"

His cheeks redden. "You think that was *my* doing? I don't even know who you are. Why would I want you in my lap?"

"I doubt that's the first time you've had a stranger in your lap," I bite back. If he were anyone else, I'd regret such a response. In this case, I'm prepared to spew any barbed insult I can find. What's the use of holding back now when my own execution is likely just around the corner?

The thought makes me dizzy, and I drum my fingers against my thighs to calm my pulse.

Franco straightens his shirt collar, my fall having set it askew. Then, pinning me with his furious gaze, he says, "Where is the real Princess Maisie?"

I lift my chin. "I have no idea."

"Tell me."

"I. Don't. Know. Read my energy. Am I lying?"

He's silent for a moment, eyes searching my face. "Did you harm her or coerce her in any way?"

"Of course not."

"Does she know you're impersonating her?"

I go over the terms of my bargain with the princess, making sure my answer doesn't contradict what I agreed to keep secret. While I am unable to state that she ran away, it still leaves enough room to tell a portion of the truth. "She knows."

"Is she still at Selene Palace?"

"No."

"Did she leave of her own free will?"

"Yes."

A flash of hurt tightens his expression. "Did she ask you to take her place?"

"Yes."

He quickly averts his gaze, eyes going unfocused. With a bitter laugh, he runs a hand over his face. "Was I truly so repugnant?" he mutters. I don't answer, knowing the question was meant to be rhetorical. When he returns his eyes to mine, something like pain or amusement dances in them. "Who are you to her? Why did she trust you with such a grand deception? And why the deception to begin with?"

I open my mouth to answer but am saved from speaking when the carriage lurches again. This time, it turns sharply to the side, sending me sliding down the bench toward the prince. His arms encircle me, but I can't tell if he means to protect me or shove me away. Probably the latter. Before I can find out, the coach comes to a sudden halt that sends us both careening to the floor.

Franco lands on his backside, his shoulders pinned against the bottom of the opposite seat, while I'm sent sprawling over his chest. His arms remain around my back, and when I lift my face, I find his is an inch away from my own. Jasmine and the distinct aroma of a cool night breeze fills my senses. With a jolt, I break from his grasp and roll off of him, my cheeks blazing like a wildfire.

He recoils. "What are you trying to do, impostor?"

"I could ask the same of you, rake."

He sits upright, a word poised on his lips. Then he freezes.

The hair on the back of my neck stands on end as I'm suddenly aware of our too-quiet surroundings. No birds. No whinnying moon mares. Just the crack of a twig and the slow, rhythmic sound of creeping footsteps.

"What is it?" I whisper.

He releases a grumbling sigh. "Brigands."

## 21

**EMBER**

"Brigands?" I ask, heart thumping a panicked rhythm. "What do you mean, brigands? Who would dare attack a royal coach?" My first thought is Saint Lazaro. That's how the rebellions started, with smaller attacks on ambassadors traveling between kingdoms, taking hostages of royal sons and daughters, nieces and nephews.

"Stay low," Franco says. "They don't always attack with weapons, but if they do..."

"Who's attacking us?"

Franco puts a finger to his lips and shushes me. "If you keep talking, I'll throw you outside to find out." He cocks his head, listening. The footsteps are closer now. Slowly, he shifts his weight to the side and rises to his feet, keeping to the side of the window. A few more beats pass.

"What are you doing?" I whisper.

He flashes me a dark, crooked smile, then reaches for the door. "Let this be a warning for you too."

He shoves the door open. I don't see who's on the other side, but I hear their screams. Franco takes a slow, leisurely step out of the coach, then another, until he has both feet on the forest floor. I creep forward on my hands and knees, terrified of what I'll find. At first, all I see is Franco's back, arms raised, his body cloaked in swirling shadows from head to toe. But as he steps farther and farther away from the door, I catch sight of the figures who surround him. Three are frozen in place with dark shadowy tendrils connecting them to the prince. Two more drop knives at their feet and begin to retreat. Before they can take more than a few steps, the prince sends two smoky tendrils toward them. The shadows latch onto their heads, freezing them alongside the first three.

My mind spins to comprehend what I'm seeing. Is he hurting them? Controlling them? His strange dark cords seem to draw more shadows from each of the five figures.

That's when I realize something. Our attackers aren't Saint Lazaro's minions.

They're children.

Human children.

While each wears a hat and a cloth over their mouths, a few of their coverings have slipped off. I see rounded ears, gaunt dirty faces, filthy clothes. The oldest looks a few years younger than me while the youngest can't be any older than ten. My heart clenches. They remind me of the children of the Gray Quarter. Or worse—the slums.

I pull myself to standing and rush from the carriage. Afraid to get too close to the prince and his strange shadows, I keep my distance and come up alongside him. "Franco, stop! They're just children."

I look up at his face then.

And scream.

Gone are his dazzling looks, replaced with a monstrous sight. His skin is thin and translucent, violet veins pulsing beneath the surface. His eyes are fully black without a single hint of white around the irises, eyelids rimmed with red. His lips are pulled back in a vicious snarl. Where before he had just two delicately pointed canines, he now has an entire mouth full of long, sharp teeth stained with blood.

His head swivels toward me and I shriek again, retreating. Then, in the blink of an eye, the monstrous face is gone. The tendrils unlock from his victims, and shadows absorb into him until they too are gone. Five screams erupt around us. My eyes leave the prince just long enough to see the terrified children darting away.

The prince looks from me to the retreating forms. When his eyes return to mine, they're full of fury. "Damn it, impostor. Why did you have to distract me?"

"What the hell were you doing to them?" I say, voice trembling.

"I don't owe you an explanation."

"You do if you were trying to murder human children. I don't care if you're a prince. You have no right—"

"I wasn't trying to murder them," he says through his teeth.

"Then what was that...that thing you did?" I wave a hand toward his face, where moments ago he looked like a creature from a nightmare.

"It was a glamour," he says. "It's what I do when I feed."

"When you *what*?"

He lets out an exasperated groan. "I'm a psy vampire. I do more than simply taste emotions. I also feed on them. They sustain me the same way food nourishes others. I choose to feed on fear because it's easy to come by. And when I feed on one's fear, it generates more fear. I weave a glamour, it frightens those who see it, and I drink the fear that emerges. I drink fear, I create more fear, and I drink that too. Got it?"

I cross my arms. "So you were terrorizing those children. Devastating them."

"They attacked our mode of transportation." He waves a

hand at the front end of the coach. "They unhitched Donna and Dominus and would have stolen our wheels next and sold them by sundown."

"Our wheels," I echo. "Five hungry children inconvenienced your leisurely ride and tried to steal your carriage wheels, and you found it prudent to traumatize them."

He puts his hands on his hips. "This isn't the first time these urchins have attacked, and it's about time they learned their lesson. Normally, it's the adults who target the royal coaches, hoping they'll get their hands on our coffers after tax collection. The young ones steal wheels and any part of a carriage that can be quickly removed, carried, and sold."

I grit my teeth. "They're poor and hungry. What do you expect?"

"I expect them to not break the law or to at least have the decency to refrain from doing so in front of their prince. I could have rounded them up and thrown them in the dungeon, you know. At least this way, they run home to their parents and perhaps think twice next time about robbing travelers."

"You aren't at all worried about fixing the root cause, are you?"

"What root cause?"

"That they're homeless. From the slums at best. That they're underfed and overworked. That they're probably orphans." A lump rises in my throat at the last word. I know what it's like to be orphaned. While I may have been treated poorly by Mrs. Coleman after Father died, I've lived a life of luxury compared to most children who are left parentless. I can't even begin to imagine the horrors underprivileged orphans are forced to endure every day.

"I'm an unseelie prince. It's up to the seelie rulers to look after humankind. The Seelie King of Lunar should be taking care of the human cities—"

"Well, he's doing a shit job," I say, my voice trembling with fury. "His palace lies in the south, while yours is *here*. I don't care that you're politically unseelie. You're a prince. Your palace is within a stone's throw of Evanston, and yet you act like you have no responsibility for its people."

"Why am I even arguing with you? I have no idea who you really are. *You're* the one breaking the law. *You're* the one I should be terrorizing. Have you any idea what the punishment is for impersonating a princess?"

"Severe, I'm sure. Which means I have nothing to lose by speaking my mind."

He scoffs. "Oh? By all means, speak. Get off your high moon mare and tell me what exactly you expect the Unseelie Prince of Lunar to do for these dear little ruffians you're so keen to defend."

"Well, you could start by entertaining the aristocracy less and try just giving a breezing shit about the starving and the poor. Or anyone but yourself, for that matter."

He tilts his head back. "Entertaining the aristocracy? I'm hosting the social season because it keeps the elite in check. The rebellions were started by Saint Lazaro and the elite families. They took first action in cities and towns closest to the unseelie palaces. Hosting the social season reminds them the unseelie are watching too. That we remember. That they would do best to keep our favor."

I shake my head and begin to turn around, although I'm not sure where I expect to go. All I know is that there's no point arguing with him. I've said my piece and I know he won't take a word of it to heart.

"How dare you shake your head at me," he says, following behind. "What you're saying is potentially treason. Hosting the social season is Queen Nyxia's policy. Do you think she's wrong? You think she's foolish for doing this one thing to placate the aristocracy?"

I round on him. "I think you're focusing on the wrong

people. Yes, the elite funded Saint Lazaro's rebellion, but who do you think they got to fight it? The poor. The hungry. Those who already had nothing to lose. Who do you think lost most at the end of it? Who do you think is *still* losing?"

Surprise flashes over his face, but he steels it behind suspicion. "Who are you?"

I purse my lips, then lift them into a cold smile. My words come out quiet. "No one. Just another nobody far below your notice."

He holds my gaze too long, and I can't tell whether his expression reveals hurt or anger. I wait for him to speak, but he doesn't. He just watches, one tense moment after the next. Then finally, he turns around and starts walking away. "I'll deal with you later. For now, we need to find Donna and Dominus. Come on."

He doesn't wait for me to follow, but I do, trailing several feet behind him. As we walk in barbed silence, I consider whether my outburst dug me a deeper hole than I already had. How is it I'm able to hide most of my ire from my stepmother, but I can't hold my tongue in front of the prince? I try not to think about what repercussions await and focus instead on the dirt road.

After a few minutes, Franco stops. I look up to find the moon mares off to the side, feasting on two large hares.

"Of course," Franco says. "The little bastards have figured out the fillies' weakness. Tempt them with raw meat and they'll forget what they're supposed to be doing."

"I thought you said they listen to you." I keep my voice neutral, not wanting to spark another argument.

"They normally do, but they're still young. The adult mares would bite a brigand's head off before letting them anywhere close to their harnesses, but these fillies..." He shakes his head at the feasting creatures.

"What do we do now?" I ask.

He opens his mouth to speak but snaps it shut. Faster than I've ever seen anyone move, he whirls around and stands in front of me, one arm pressing me close to his back. "I know you're there," he calls out.

I don't dare move as footsteps approach, slow and heavy. Not like a child's. Franco pushes me closer to him again, and terror has me clinging to the back of his shirt.

"What do we have here?" says a menacing male voice.

Shadows obscure my vision, and I hear Franco hiss. My mind fills with memories of his monstrous glamour.

A low chuckle reverberates from not too far away. "That won't work on me, fae. I know a glamour when I see it."

"You dare address me as *fae*? Do you not know who I am?"

"Another entitled creature," the man says. "Another fae noble who feasts on riches while children starve."

"I'm your prince, human."

A scoff. "*My* prince? When have you ever been *my* prince? When have any of the unseelie royals been *mine*? I've never been welcomed to make a petition or apply for aid—"

"That's what your seelie king is for."

He barks a laugh. "He might as well be in a different court for all the attention he gives the humans of the north."

I purse my lips to keep from muttering *I told you so* at the prince's back.

"If you can't be reasoned with," Franco says, tone light and amused, "I have other ways to deal with you." He starts forward but freezes at the sound of a loud click. Franco inhales a gasp. "Iron is forbidden on the isle."

"It's steel. Not iron. There's no law against iron alloys."

Franco's tone darkens. "Guns are forbidden too."

"Then come over here and arrest me."

"What exactly do you want?"

A pause. "I want you to empty out your pockets."

Franco throws his head back with a laugh. "My pockets? I

travel with no purse, you fool. My face is credit enough should I want anything. Besides, aren't my carriage wheels plenty? Take the doors while you're at it. The opal panels should fetch you a pretty fortune."

"What about the girl?"

He stiffens, and for a moment I think he'll shove me at the man's feet. "You're not getting the girl."

"I want her purse."

"You're about to get my teeth buried in your neck in about five seconds."

"And ruin your fine clothing in the process?"

Franco takes a step away from me. "You forget your place, human. I am a prince, and you are threatening me with a gun. I may wear this seelie form, but my heart is as wild and unseelie as those who first fought your kind over a thousand years ago. I have no qualms with bloodbaths. And when I tire of tearing you limb from limb, I'll shift into my raven form and peck out your eyes."

"You don't frighten me. I have worse things to fear when my children are starving."

"You're truly willing to risk going up against me?"

"I'm the one with a gun."

Franco's tone deepens. "But are there even bullets in it? I'm beginning to taste your bluff, human. It's written in every emotion that lurks beneath your valiant posturing." The shadows around Franco begin to darken, writhing faster. "I'm getting tired of—"

"Stop," I say, stepping out from behind the prince. The man's hard gaze locks on me, and I raise my hands. He wears a black cloth over his lower face, but what I can see of his upper half is scarred and dirty. His clothes are torn and stained. There's a fierceness in his eyes in contrast to his gaunt form. He looks like all the men and women I've seen coming in and out of the workhouses in the poorest parts of Evanston. "You want money, right?"

"Aye. I'll take your purse."

"I don't have a purse, but I can give you my clothes."

He furrows his brow. "I don't need your clothes."

"What are you doing?" Franco asks in a furious whisper.

I ignore him, keeping my eyes on the man. "Did you not mention how fine they are?"

He looks from me to the prince. "Aye, but what use are they?"

"You may not know me, but I'm Princess Maisie of the Sea Court. My skirt is made of the finest wool tartan. The lace and pearl buttons on my blouse are enough to feed your family for months. More than that if you say it was worn by a fae princess."

The man scans me from head to toe. "Is that so?" His voice holds disbelief, but his eyes say otherwise. Calculations run behind them, and I have no doubt he's already wondering which stall in Black Square will give him the highest payout. He thrusts his gun and takes a step closer. "Off with your clothes then. Both of you."

Franco puts a hand on his hip. "I'm not taking off my clothes."

"I want your shirt," the man says. "Those dangly necklaces too."

"This shirt is an Amelie Fairfield original made of the finest Autumn Court spider silk. Have you any idea of its thread count?"

"More reason for me to want it."

The prince rolls his eyes and faces me. "Get behind me and let me deal with him. I'll break his neck faster than he can blink."

"No, Your Highness," I say, already unbuttoning my blouse. "He's hungry, just like the children. He's probably their caretaker."

"And he's waving a gun at us. What a charming father figure. I'm sure he'll bring them up to be proper scholars."

I loosen the final button of my blouse. "You said so yourself that you think he's bluffing. Besides, would you be any better in his situation? What lengths would you go to protect your loved ones?"

He glares at me a few moments, then shakes his head. "Fine," he calls to the man. "I'll take off my shirt for you."

I'm about to shimmy out of my blouse when the prince turns toward me and begins unbuttoning his shirt. "Turn around!" I squeal.

With a grumble, he does as told. Back-to-back we strip down. I remove my blouse and skirt, remembering last minute to unclasp my necklace before the man notices I have it. With swift fingers, I tuck it into my corset and adjust my chemise to cover as much of my exposed flesh as I can. Then I turn toward the man and set my clothing on the ground. Franco does the same with his shirt and strands of beads.

"I'd give you my pants too," Franco says to the man, "but I don't wear undergarments. Although, I imagine you could fetch an impressive price for them. I can see it now. A sign in the market square. Here lies the pants that touched the throbbing—"

"I want the shoes," he says, pointing at the hem of my petticoats.

My pulse quickens. If I step out of my shoes, the glamour goes with them. The prince may already have guessed I wear a glamour, but the bargain I'm bound to forbids me from letting anyone see me without it. "You can't have my shoes."

"The shoes look more valuable then all this clothing put together."

"She said you can't have the shoes," Franco says, tone bored. "If you want to leave this little meeting of ours alive, I suggest you accept what has already been so graciously offered to you."

The man strides forward, teeth bared, gun aimed between my eyes. Now that the gun is trained on me, I'm starting to wonder if the prince might have been wrong about the man's bluff. He seems awfully bold for someone wielding a gun without bullets. Perhaps I shouldn't have encouraged Franco to go soft on him after all. "Give me the princess' shoes."

Franco growls and his shadows return. In a matter of seconds, they fill the space around us like a fog. I feel a bare arm pull me close, then the other reaches under my legs. Sudden movement sends my stomach lurching. When the shadows clear, I find the ground has fallen beneath us, leaving only the tops of trees in sight. One glance at Franco reveals a pair of enormous black wings sprouting from his back where moments ago there was only naked skin. They extend behind him, beating the air.

He looks at me with a smirk. "See what happens when I try to play nice?"

The world blurs as he flies us away.

## 22

EMBER

Cool air beats all around us. I cling tight around Franco's neck, my heart slamming against my ribs as he flies high over the treetops.

I've always wanted to fly. Always wished I could shift forms and become one with the wind like my mother could. But in all my fantasies where I soared through the sky, *I* was always the one doing the flying. Not being hauled hundreds of feet in the air by an infuriating prince.

Vertigo seizes me, and I close my eyes, tucking my head under Franco's chin. My cheek comes up against his collarbone. The feel of my skin on his has my eyes flying open, my stomach tightening in a way that no longer has to do with being dizzy. My breath hitches with my awareness of Franco's arm beneath my knees, the other around my waist, holding me close to his bare chest. If that weren't unsettling enough, a secondary realization comes over me—that he could drop me at any moment. On purpose. Because he knows I'm a liar, and after everything I said to him outside the coach, he has every right to despise me...

I pull back as far as I dare. "Put me down," I say, but my words are swallowed by the wind. Not willing to risk my life to remove my arms from around his neck, I tap a finger against his shoulder to get his attention. When he looks down at me, I raise my voice. "Put me down!"

His feathered wings shift and our momentum glides to a stop. We hover in place. Franco remains upright, his wings beating the air at intervals to keep us in place while I continue to cling to him. "What did you say?"

I level a furious stare at him. "For the thousandth time, I said put me down."

"I'm flying you back to the palace," he says, voice rich with agitation. "I'm taking you to safety so I can come back for Donna and Dominus."

Safety? Does he mean straight to the dungeon? "I'd rather walk."

He quirks a brow, an amused smirk playing over his lips. "What? In heels?"

"Yes."

As if the shoes realize they're the subject of conversation, I feel one start to slip from my foot. I lift my leg high enough to catch a glimpse of the offending shoe and see the back has come free from my heel. My pulse races as sweat beads at my brow. "Your Highness, put me down," I say, an edge of panic cutting through my tone. "Put me down *right now*."

He slices me with a glare. "You're not in any position to make demands of a prince."

"Please," I say. "I'm begging you."

"Fine." With a muttered string of curses, we begin to lower.

My breathing begins to calm, but my relief is short lived. Our descent has lodged my shoe even farther off my foot. I shift and squirm to get a better angle, then try to use my other foot to push the loose shoe back on. The ground is still over a dozen feet below us, but if I can keep my shoes in place...

Just when I think my efforts are working, the shoe slips off completely. With a yelp, I tug my head back under Franco's chin, but my shout seems to have startled him, and I feel our momentum come to a halt. "What is it?" He tilts his chin down at me.

But I can't let him see me. If my shoe is gone, the glamour is too. Which means I'm in violation of the terms of the bargain.

*You must wear the glamoured shoes in public and let no one see you without the glamour...*

Has he already seen me? I shove my hand in the prince's face to keep it averted just as a flash of agony strikes my gut. I bite the inside of my cheek to keep from crying out. Franco, of course, must sense my shift in energy, for he again tries to look at me. "Put me down, damn you!"

He squirms against my hand and continues our descent, his flight haphazard as we careen to the forest floor. I keep my hand in his face despite his protests, ignoring the muffled complaints he shouts against my palm. When we finally touch down, I wriggle from his grasp, looking everywhere for a hint of pale blue discarded amongst the bushes and brambles. I catch sight of a glass heel several feet away, and I can only hope it isn't broken. If a glamoured item so much as tears a seam, the enchantment breaks too. Franco releases me, stumbling from my frantic movements, and I take the opportunity to shove him forward in the opposite direction of the shoe. He falls to his hands and knees, and I make a mad dash for the slipper. In a matter of seconds, it's in my grasp, and I dive behind a large bush with it.

Once fully hidden, I scramble to secure the shoe back on my foot, noting how my hands shift from my paler shade to Maisie's dark tan in the blink of an eye. Relief floods me. The pain of the compromised bargain dissipates at once, leaving exhaustion in its wake. Then comes the dawning realization that I just accosted a prince.

A prince who already hates me.

Too soon the sound of his footsteps come tearing across the forest floor.

～

## FRANCO

I stand before the impostor with my hands on my hips, my wings splayed out wide, every muscle twitching with agitation. "What the hell was that?"

With a guilty expression, she slowly rises to her feet, not bothering to brush off the dirt, sticks, and brambles that now cling to her undergarments. "I'm sorry," she says, not meeting my eyes.

"For which part? Where you impersonated a princess? Where you argued with me over my inadequacies as a prince? Where you made me give away my best shirt? Or how about when you nearly blinded me mid-flight and then pushed me over into a cluster of rotting mushrooms?"

"I didn't realize there were mushrooms," she mutters.

I bark a cold laugh. "*That's* the part you're sorry for?"

"I'm sorry about all of it, all right? None of this was supposed to happen."

"What *was* supposed to happen?" She purses her lips and drums her fingers against her upper thighs. I breathe in her energy, expecting defiance, but find only anxiety. Exhaustion. Resignation. I release a heavy sigh, shoulders slumping with my own bone-crushing fatigue. This outing went the complete opposite of what I expected. I was supposed to impress the princess, make her an ally. Not argue with her decoy in the woods after the real Maisie, for reasons unknown, left the palace and willingly plotted to deceive me. I fold my wings down my back and run my hands through my hair. When I speak, my words come out calm, quiet. "I need you to tell me the truth. In return, I promise to hear you fairly. Where is Princess Maisie? Why did you take her place?"

"I can't tell you."

Frustration slices through me, and I nearly bite out an angry response. Somehow, I manage to reign in my annoyance with a slow, deep breath. *Calm. Be calm about this.* "This is your last chance, impostor. Answer my questions."

"I *can't* tell you and that's the truth. I physically cannot."

I breathe in her emotions, strong and full of conviction. She isn't lying. "You have a bargain." Her answering silence tells me I'm right. "What *can* you tell me?"

She wrings her hands, shoulders stiff. "Not a lot."

"What was the goal? Were you supposed to trick me into marrying you?"

"No."

"Was this ploy meant to harm me in some way? Is King Ronan behind it too?"

"No, this isn't about you at all."

"Isn't about me at all?" I scoff. "The princess I was supposed to court fled my palace and left someone else in her place. Forgive me if I'm unable to not take it personally." I wait for the pain of rejection to sink my stomach, but it feels like nothing more than a fleeting, hollow *thud*. For once, I was rejected by someone I care nothing about. I suppose I can consider that a vast improvement to my love life. "So, what was in it for you?"

She nibbles a corner of her lip. "I can't tell you."

"Can you tell me your name? Let me see who you are without whatever glamour you've concocted?"

"No."

"I could force you, you know." There's no anger in my tone, only weary truth. "I could take you to the dungeon and make you spill your secrets, bargain be damned. Give me one good reason why I shouldn't."

She looks down at her feet. "All I can say is it's a matter of desperation that made all of this happen."

I frown. "Whose desperation? Yours or hers?"

She says nothing.

"You never answered the last question I asked you in the coach. Who are you to Princess Maisie? Why did she trust you with this?"

She hesitates before answering. "A friend." I breathe in her energy, finding nothing to suggest that's a lie.

"Did you arrive with her from the Sea Court?"

She purses her lips.

"Are you one of her maids? I never saw anyone with her but…for the love of the night, are you Podaxis?"

Her mouth falls open. "Of course not! Do I seem like a crustacean to you?"

My lips flicker up at the corners. It's the first hint of amusement I've felt since everything went so horribly wrong. "I thought the voice was a little off."

She sighs, expression softening. "I *am* a maid," she says, revealing no spike in her emotional signature. The truth, then. "I am a maid and an ally to Princess Maisie, and that's all I can tell you."

"How long was this deception to last? If you weren't planning on tricking me into marrying you, how was it supposed to end?"

She tenses slightly and says nothing for a few breaths. When she speaks, her energy is calm. "Our courtship was never meant to extend past the social season."

"So, what? You expected I'd be fooled the entire month and we'd amicably sever our courtship at the end of it, leaving me none the wiser that the real princess had hardly ever been here?"

No answer, just a tap of her fingers against her thighs, a mild flutter of anxiety. Does that mean I'm getting close to the truth?

I ponder her words, going over everything she's told me and analyzing every emotional shift I've tasted. The facts I've managed to glean are that Princess Maisie willingly departed Selene Palace in secret because of some supposed desperation, and she left behind her maid who is also her friend and ally as a glamoured decoy to continue to court me but *not* try to marry me.

My mind whirls to comprehend it. What could possibly make a princess so desperate to go to such great lengths?

Then an explanation hits me. I know why she left. I know why the real Princess Maisie was so cold, so disinterested.

"She eloped, didn't she?"

The impostor's body goes still, emotions sparking with surprise. She says nothing to confirm or deny it.

"I'm right, aren't I? She fell in love with some unsavory character her father didn't approve of and needed this pretend courtship to hide what she's really doing. Who's the lucky guy?"

"I don't know," she says quietly.

I put my hands on my hips, feeling like a weight has been lifted from my shoulders. It doesn't change that I've been duped, but at least now I can be almost certain I don't have some grand conspiracy on my hands. I shake my head with a sigh. "I do wish she'd have told me the truth. She would have found me a far more willing ally than she anticipated."

The girl nibbles her lip. "What now?"

"What now, indeed." I look her over with fresh eyes and tap the underside of my chin. She trembles under my scrutiny, her emotions darkening with fear. I extend my hand. "Come. Let me fly you back to the palace."

"Why? To throw me in the dungeon?"

"To take you back to your room. Well, Maisie's room."

"You aren't going to punish me?"

"Oh, I'll punish you." My lips curl up at one corner. "Just not in the way you think."

She takes a step back. "That's far from comforting."

"Committing a crime shouldn't be comfortable. And if I'm going to allow you to continue your ruse, I'll need something in return."

"What do you mean?"

"More on that later," I say with a wink. "Now, come along. Alternatively, you can try and run. In that case, I'll just have to catch you. You can hide, but I'll use your energetic signature to find you. Either way, you're coming back to the palace with me."

Her gaze falls to my bare chest, and her energy turns a delightful shade of panic. When her eyes return to mine, she says, "I don't want to fly again."

"Why? Are you afraid of heights?" I ask, voice taunting.

"Not at all." She lifts her chin, and I can taste that her words are true.

"Then what's the problem?"

Her jaw shifts side to side, eyes flicking momentarily to my chest. A pale blush creeps over her face—or, more accurately, beneath the glamour she wears. She tries to act nonplussed. "I don't want to lose my shoes again."

I glance down at her feet and the pale blue silk that adorns them. It takes a moment for comprehension to dawn. "They hold the glamour, don't they?" Now it makes sense why Augie saw Maisie leaving Madame Flora's room. She hadn't been paying a friendly visit or getting something to wear to the ball, but procuring a glamour to disguise her maid.

"It's imperative I keep them on at all times."

"At all times? Surely, not when you sleep." I kneel before her and reach for the hem of her petticoats.

"No, not when I sleep. Wait—" She steps away from me. "What are you doing?"

I glance up at her. "Making sure you don't lose your shoes again."

"You'll not take them off."

"I'm not taking them off," I say through my teeth. "I'm tearing a strip of cloth from your chemise so I can secure your shoes to your feet."

"You're ruining my chemise?"

"I'm sure the princess left you others." Then, with an exaggerated flourish of my hands, I add, "May I?"

She looks from me to her skirt, then steps closer. "Very well."

I lift her petticoats just enough to gather the hem of her chemise between my fingers. As I tear it, she stifles a gasp, and I'm forced to hide my smug grin. Once I have two long strips of the linen cloth, I take one and pull it under the arch of her shoe, then tie it over the top of her foot. I do the same with the other. With my job complete, I rise and watch as she tests the hold of her shoes.

"Now will you let me fly you back to the palace?" I ask, extending my hand.

In answer, she places her palm in mine. Clasping my fingers around hers, I pull her close. She lets out a surprised yelp as her chest comes up against mine. I hold her gaze because I can tell it unsettles her. Then, releasing her hand, I lift her off her feet, one arm beneath her legs and the other around her waist. Her arms encircle my neck as I launch us into the sky. Her grip tightens the higher we go, and the cool air sweeps away my worries. Soon, new ideas take their place.

I'm only half aware of these thoughts, as the other half of me is fixated on the girl in my arms, her energy that pulses with the strangest blend of discomfort and exhilaration, her frantic heartbeat that pounds against my chest. She may be an impostor, a liar, and a complete stranger. She may be fierce, vicious, and incredibly rude. And yet, I have plans that are going to make her very useful to me. Plans that will surely incense her to no end, evoke emotions of flame and storm.

I must admit, I'm enjoying that thought far more than I probably should.

# 23

EMBER

I grip the prince tightly as he flies us back to the palace. He must be enjoying himself greatly. Every time I hazard a glance at his profile, I see only his smug grin and want nothing more than to slap it off his face. I have no doubt he delighted in my reaction when he tore my skirt, even more so when he pulled me against him. Playboy prince, indeed. He's worse than the rumors suggest if he's willing to take pleasure in stealing gasps from a woman he hates.

The longer we fly, the darker my thoughts become. What exactly does the prince plan to do with me when we arrive at the palace? He said he'd punish me, but he also stated he'd *allow me to continue my ruse*, whatever that means. Will I be permitted to fulfill my bargain with Princess Maisie, and in turn remain safely hidden until the bargain with my stepmother is completed as well? And if so, will suffering the prince's supposed *punishment* be worth it?

I recall what he did to those children, how he conjured his

terrifying glamour and bled shadows from his victims for sustenance. Can I truly rely on his mercy?

If it means freedom from marrying Brother Marus, then it's something I'll have to risk.

The palace comes into view, and at first, I expect him to take us to the front. That's when I remember how I'm dressed. Undressed, more like. My cheeks heat, and my awareness over Franco's bare chest returns, stronger than before.

"Relax," he calls over the roar of the wind that beats past us. "I'm taking you to your balcony."

"I'd appreciate it if you'd stop reading my energy," I say through my teeth.

"And I'd appreciate a bottomless glass of Midnight Blush, and yet somehow I'm always left wanting." He angles his body, and we dip sharply to the side, our descent coming faster and faster. My stomach bottoms out, and I close my eyes, biting back a squeal as I tuck my head under his chin. His chest heaves with laughter, and it takes all my restraint not to pinch him. Then, not a moment too soon, our momentum stops.

I lift my head and open my eyes, finding us hovering before my balcony. Franco's wings beat a steady rhythm to keep us suspended midair. Then, with unexpected gentleness, he sets me on my feet and joins me on the balcony floor. It takes me a few breaths to gather my bearings, and even after I manage to maintain my footing without toppling over, mild disequilibrium remains.

Franco tucks his wings close to his back, but instead of remaining there, they disappear. How is he able to produce wings without fully shifting into his unseelie form?

He must notice my curiosity. "What? Interested in my wings?" He leans his backside against the railing, hands propped on the balustrade. His posture is perfectly relaxed, making him seem far more at home in nothing but low-waisted trousers than I am in my full-coverage undergarments.

My eyes linger too long on his ink-covered abdomen, but I drag them away and try to recall his question. Oh, yes. Wings. "I was just...wondering," I say, hating how awkward my voice sounds. "How are you able to do that with your wings? Sometimes you have them and sometimes you don't."

"I'm able to shift partially into my unseelie form, focusing only on my wings." He says it like it's a simple thing, but I've heard of very few others who can do that. Many fae have seelie forms that maintain some unseelie characteristics, such as feathers, scales, or antlers, but rarely, if ever, have I seen a fae summon and dismiss only a portion of their unseelie form at will. Furthermore, I've seen him conjure wings both shirtless and clothed, and his wings don't affect his clothing. I know fully shifting forms doesn't impact a fae's garments, so I suppose a partial shift would work the same way. Curiosity buzzes through me, and with it comes a pang of regret.

If my mother were still alive, I'd have more firsthand knowledge of fae magic.

"Enough about me," he says, interrupting my thoughts. "Let's talk about you."

I fold my arms over my chest, feeling naked beneath his gaze. "What about me?"

"Do you promise that your bargain with Princess Maisie is of a personal nature, and has nothing to do with politics nor does it pose any threat to me or my kingdom?"

"I promise." On my side, at least. I haven't a clue about Maisie's motives.

His eyes narrow, and I'm certain he's reading my emotions. I keep my breathing steady, willing my energy not to dip into panic. I've come to realize I can avoid his suspicion so long as my intentions align with my words. That's how I got him to believe I'm Maisie's friend and maid. I am *a* maid, after all, according to my stepfamily. And I do consider Maisie to be a kindred spirit, if not a friend. Finally, he nods and pushes off the balustrade. "Very well."

"Very well? What does that mean?"

"It means you get to live another day. Many, if you play your part well."

A flash of irritation has my muscles tensing. Is anything ever straightforward with him? "I ask again, what the hell does that mean?"

He winks. "Just keep doing what you're doing."

I'm about to say more when the balcony doors fly open. My heart leaps into my throat as I meet the stunned faces of my stepsisters. They look from me to the prince and back again, cheeks burning crimson at the sight of our near nakedness. "Forgive us," Imogen says, dipping into a low curtsy. When Clara doesn't move, Imogen tugs her skirt until she too lowers. "We didn't mean to interrupt." With eyes downcast, they begin to retreat.

"Fret not, for I was just leaving," Franco says with a dazzling grin. His wings sprout from his back, and I expect him to leap off the balcony. Instead, he strides over to me. Before I know it, his arms snake around my waist, gathering me close. I place my hands on his chest to keep from making full contact, only to realize how intimate the gesture seems. He stares down at me with mock adoration. His words come out low and wistful. "But how can I leave you?"

I glare back at him. "Easily, I'm sure."

He leans down, bringing his face close to mine. I flinch, my heart raging in my chest. From my periphery, I see my stepsisters' mouths fall open. When I return my attention to the prince, his gaze has dipped to my lips. Without my permission, my eyes fall lower as well, taking in his full mouth as he leans closer and closer. I'm frozen in his arms, unsure what to do, what he's playing at. As soon as a mere inch separates our mouths, he angles his head to the side, bringing our cheeks to touch. His breath stirs my hair, brushing the shell of my ear. "Play the part," he whispers, voice low as he grasps me tighter.

It takes me several seconds to understand what he means. This is all for show. For my stepsisters.

He's letting me fulfill my bargain with Maisie because he... wants me to *play the part*. Continue to court him—or pretend to, at least.

*That* is my punishment.

My conclusion does nothing to ease the tension coursing through every inch of me, coiling in my lower abdomen and heating my blood. Before I can consider what to do, he pulls away, eyes turned down at the corners as if every inch that builds between us is too great. He isn't such a good actor that I believe him, but the way Imogen glowers and Clara swoons tells me they are fully convinced by his performance. He blows me a kiss and says, "I'll see you tonight," before leaping off the balcony and into the sky.

I CAN HARDLY BEAR TO FACE MY STEPSISTERS, SO I TURN AWAY from them to gather my composure. The sound of their swishing skirts announces their approach. "What might we do for you, Your Highness?" Imogen asks, her voice full of forced sweetness.

"Why are you in your underthings?" adds Clara, but a stifled grunt tells me Imogen kicked her for the impertinent question.

I take a few deep breaths to steady my nerves. *They don't know it's me*, I tell myself. *Be the princess.* Forcing my lower lip to quiver, I turn around to face them. "Oh, it was dreadful," I say in a voice I hope sounds much unlike my own. "The prince took me through the woods for a leisurely ride and our coach was attacked by brigands. The man made us give him our clothes." I make the last word come out softer than a squeak, and I grip the balustrade while I pretend to sway on my feet.

Imogen puts a hand on my shoulder, and I do my best not to recoil at her touch. "How awful, Your Highness! Come inside and let us care for you."

I nod, allowing the girls to flank me as they lead me into the room. Once inside, they guide me to the sitting area where I lower into a chair. Imogen pours a cup of tea and places it before me, while Clara hands me a plate of scones. It takes all my restraint not to laugh. My two hateful stepsisters are serving *me* for once. I take a bite of scone, suddenly aware of how hungry I am, and wash it down with warm tea.

"Shall we run your bath, Your Highness?" Clara asks.

"Please," I say with a generous smile.

Clara leaves for the washroom, while Imogen moves to the wardrobe. "Would you like me to pick you something to wear to the opera?" There's a bitter edge to her tone, one I'm not sure anyone else but me would notice.

"The opera?" I echo.

Her expression clouds with annoyance, but she quickly trains it behind a contrived grin. "His Royal Highness said he'd see you tonight," she explains, "and tonight is the opera in Evanston. Everyone knows the prince is planning to make an appearance. Apparently, he's bringing you."

Excitement and panic war inside me. I'm going to the opera. The opera! I've never been before, not even when I was a child, but...I'm going to the opera...with the prince. As the princess. As his *date*.

Imogen opens the wardrobe doors and begins shuffling through the clothes inside. I'm so caught up in my thoughts, it takes me a full minute before I realize something about the wardrobe.

It was almost empty this morning...

And is now full of items that had previously been in and around the princess' chests.

I rise to my feet, stomach turning as I glance at the trunks. Instead of the haphazard disarray I left them in, they now sit stacked neatly against the wall. "What did you do with my things?"

Imogen pauses, looking at me with a raised brow. It takes a few moments for her expression to soften. "We put everything away for you, Your Highness. You left quite a mess for us."

My pulse quickens as I study the trunks. If they found my gown...well, I suppose they would have said something by now. I swallow hard. "Did you put *everything* away?"

She leaves the wardrobe to approach the stack of trunks, words slightly clipped with indignation. "No, Your Highness, not everything. One was locked." She gestures toward the bottom trunk. "Perhaps you have the key?"

My hand flies to my skirt pocket—only to remember I'm not wearing a skirt, just my chemise and petticoats. The keys are long gone now, in possession of a thief. Regret washes over me, but it quickly shifts into relief. If I can't open the trunk, neither can anyone else. I'll need to find a way inside before I make my escape, if only to collect my train ticket. But that's a problem for a future day, not now. "No, I do not have the key. It's been lost."

"I see," Imogen says. "Perhaps I can inquire about a locksmith—"

"No," I say, tone far sharper than I intend. Forcing my posture to relax, I add, "That's not necessary."

"What's inside?" Clara asks from the washroom doorway.

I blink a few times, seeking a valid explanation. One that would make sense for Maisie. A princess. A selkie. Then it comes to me. "My sealskin. I must keep it locked away."

"Why?" Clara asks. After a glare from Imogen, she adds, "Your Highness."

"It smells," I say, and the girls go pale. "Like rotting fish, in fact. Believe me, no one wants that chest to open."

"Won't you need it again, Your Highness?" Imogen asks.

"That's doubtful."

"Because you're courting the prince?" Imogen's smile contrasts with the iron in her gaze. I recall Mrs. Coleman expressing her desire for Imogen to woo the prince. That was before any of us knew there would be a princess to contend with. I can see the calculations in my stepsister's eyes as she assesses me from head to toe, wondering whether she stands a chance.

"Oh yes, the prince," I say with a dreamy sigh and watch Imogen's expression turn hard. If I were a kinder person, I wouldn't take such pleasure from being the source of my stepsister's angst. "He's quite the handsome specimen, is he not?"

"Your bath is ready," Clara says. "Would you like me to wash your hair?"

All vindictive amusement flees at the question. Is that normal for a lady's maid to do? I suppose anything can be asked of a maid when in service to a royal. "No, that won't be necessary. I like to bathe in private. However, while I bathe, you may select fresh undergarments for me as well as something to wear to dinner. After that, please take the evening off."

"Take the evening off." Imogen looks as if I suggested she jump off a cliff. "Don't you want us to help you dress, Your Highness? Accompany you to the opera?"

"Oh, I'm sure I can manage."

My stepsisters exchange a wide-eyed glance and dip into resigned curtsies, Imogen looking positively livid. With as much grace as I can manage, I brush past them to the washroom. Just as I'm about to enter, Clara says, "Your shoes, Your Highness."

I glance down, a surge of terror heating my cheeks as I wonder if something's amiss. Did the heel break? To my relief, they appear the same as they last were, tied to my feet by the two strips of torn cloth.

"Leave them out here and I will have them cleaned," Clara says.

Specks of dirt have stained the toe, but they are otherwise of little concern. "That's all right."

She frowns. "Surely, you don't need to wear your shoes into the washroom."

Imogen quirks a brow from across the room. My mind goes blank as I seek a reply. A princess has no need to explain herself to a maid, but their suspicion is the last thing I need.

Then it hits me.

A web of truth to spin alongside my growing collection of lies.

"As a matter of fact, I do wear my shoes to the washroom. In the bath too."

"Might I ask why, Your Highness?" Imogen says with clear distaste.

"Well, as you already know, I am a selkie," I say, recalling everything I know about selkie lore. "My kind only take seelie form when we remove our sealskins. We are able to maintain this form after sundown, but if we fail to don human clothing by sunrise, we perish." I wave a hand toward the nearest window, curtains drawn open to reveal the daylight. "So long as the sun is up, I must wear at least a single article of human clothing."

"Oh, well, that makes sense," Clara says with a grin.

"But wouldn't something less...unwieldy than a pair of shoes suffice?" Imogen asks.

I lock my eyes on hers, willing my expression to turn serious as I summon the air of a princess. Considering how few princesses I've made my acquaintance, it isn't easy to do. So, I try mimicking the coldness of my stepmother instead. Holding my head high, I say, "Are you questioning me?"

Imogen blanches under my stare. "Of course not, Your Highness."

"Good." I turn on my heel and enter the washroom, closing the door behind me. My body sags at once, the weight of my lies, my act, my deception dragging me down. The aroma of tuberose fills the room, and I breathe it in, allowing it to soothe me. I turn the lock on the door handle and strip off the shoes and undergarments. A metallic clink hits the marble floor as I remove my corset, and a flash of gold catches my eye.

My locket.

I stoop down to retrieve it, grateful it hadn't made an appearance any sooner. If my stepsisters had seen it…

I shudder. After today's events, it's clear I can't risk continuing to wear it. I tear a large square from my already ruined chemise and fold the locket inside. Then I tie a thin strip of cloth around that. Without the key to the trunk, I'll have to find somewhere safe to stash it.

But that will have to wait.

For now, the only thing I want is a bath.

I climb into the enormous moonstone tub and sink below the warm, fragrant waters. Right away, I close my eyes and lower my head beneath the surface until all but my nose is submerged. Sound shifts into a haunting, underwater melody, helping me forget where I am, who I am, and who I'm pretending to be. My mind goes still, peaceful, with nothing but the song of my own heartbeat thrumming in my ears.

# 24

EMBER

With no windows in the washroom, no bells to mark the hour, I lose track of time during my soak in the tub. Hours pass as I wash and doze, disallowing all thoughts and worries to plague me. The tub has become my sanctuary. A place I can wear my own face, free from the eyes of outside spectators. Best of all, no matter how long I linger, the bathwater remains at the perfect temperature as if warmed by some unseen heating element. Or magic. I suppose a fae palace would host the most advanced marvels of day-to-day magic.

My primary motive for staying so long in the washroom is to avoid my stepsisters. Even though I told them to take the evening off, I continue to hear proof of their lingering presence—footsteps, whispers, giggles. I'm about to give up hope that they'll ever leave when Clara announces herself at the bathroom door. My pulse quickens as I glance at the handle. I know I locked it, but I can't help fearing she'll come in.

"What is it?" I ask, voice quavering.

"I've brought your dinner, Your Highness," Clara says. "I was wondering where you would like me to put it before my sister and I leave your company for the night."

"Just place it on the table," I call out sharply, my words still edged with panic. To soften my abrupt statement, I add, "Thank you for your service today."

I hear a shuffle of footsteps, as if she wants to say more. After a few moments, she says, "You're welcome, Your Highness. Good evening."

I train my ears on every sound that follows, every footstep and whispered strain of conversation, until—finally—I hear the bedroom door open and close. I wait several minutes to see if they return, and when silence answers, I gather the courage to leave the delightfully soothing water. My skin prickles against the steam-filled air as I retrieve a plush towel from a peg on the wall. I wrap it around me, closing my eyes at the heady gardenia that wafts from it. I remain like that for several minutes, enveloped in warmth, before I dry my body and step back into the shoes. Lastly, I gather the cloth-wrapped locket, fisting it tightly in my hand.

Outside the washroom, I find my bedroom has fallen under the dusky light of the setting sun. I make a beeline for the table where a tray of food rests. I don't bother sitting down as I take a bite of still-warm bread, richly buttered and decadently soft. My stomach growls and I quickly down several heaping spoonfuls of soup. After the events of today and the night before, with hardly any food in between, it's no surprise I'm ravenous. I make quick work of my meal, then shift my thoughts to the next most pressing matter.

Attending the opera with the prince.

Is that truly what he meant when he said he'd see me tonight? What reason could he have to bring me? Although the prince made it clear he'll allow me to continue acting as Princess Maisie, I still haven't figured out a reason *why*.

Furthermore, why would he want to act like we're courting? I recall the flash of hurt I saw cross his face when he realized Maisie left the palace. After how he acted at the ball—making eyes at that moth pixie—I can't imagine he'd be put out by losing a potential lover. Then again, it's likely not his love life that suffers from being dismissed by a princess, but his ego.

I clench my jaw. Is that what this is about? Does he want me to pretend to court him so others will be clueless he was rejected? I suppose he'll want to be seen as the one who severs our courtship when our alliance is over.

My fingers ball into fists. When one clenches around something soft, I recall the locket that remains in my hand. A sense of urgency has my eyes glancing around to every corner of the room, seeking the best place to stash it. No drawer will suffice unless I can ensure it's well hidden amongst other items. If only I had the key to the trunk, I could hide it alongside my ballgown...

A knock at the door has my heart hammering a staccato beat.

Anxiety pulses in my chest. Have my stepsisters decided to disobey my orders to let me get dressed on my own? Damn them.

"Just a moment," I call out as I stride over to the bed. There I find a spread of clothing my stepsisters laid out for me to wear tonight. I look from the clothing to the nightstand, then back to the bed, where I quickly stuff the locket deep under my mattress. That will have to do for now.

Another knock. "Princess...Em." To my horror, it's Franco's muffled voice that calls from the other side.

I bite back a squeal of alarm, and my voice rises an octave. "I'm indecent." With hurried motions, I gather the clothing from the bed and rush behind the dressing screen.

"The first step is admitting it," comes his taunting voice. "Now we have something in common."

"I'm not dressed."

"There's hardly anything indecent about being undressed. Although, I'd have thought you'd want to wear at least *something* to the opera."

I grit my teeth, sorting through the clothing. I find silk stockings, a chemise, corset, petticoats, a dress, and a collection of ribbons that are probably meant for my hair. "Just...give me a moment."

"Can I wait inside? We should talk."

"What part of *I'm not dressed* did you not understand?" Heat courses through me as I slip my fresh chemise over my head. How could he possibly think it's proper to wait in a lady's room while she gets dressed?

*He's fae,* I remind myself, *and of the unseelie reign, at that.*

Based on how he seems to look down upon humans, I doubt he's had much experience with society's rules of propriety. I wrap my corset around my waist and secure the closures. Luckily, the laces only require a slight adjustment to secure the fit.

He knocks again.

"Fine," I say through my teeth. At least now I'm wearing what he's already seen me in. Not that I'll allow him to see me so underdressed ever again. Thank the breeze for the generous-sized dressing screen. I hear the door open and close, followed by his footsteps. "Don't you dare come any closer." Then, thinking better of it, I add, "Your Highness."

His footsteps halt. "You can still call me Franco."

I don my petticoats and take up the dress that's been chosen for me, a confection of mauve silk damask patterned with seashells. I hardly need to look at it to know I've never worn anything so elegant in all my life. As I pull the gown over my head, I'm painfully aware of the sweat already pooling beneath my armpits.

"Can I still call you Em?" he asks. "Now that I know you

aren't the princess, I can't call you Maisie. It's akin to lying, should I state it like I believe it to be your name."

"Yes, you can call me Em." My voice comes out strained as I fight with the dress. Unlike the simple gown Gemma Bellefleur gifted to me, this one features laces in the back that require much tightening to secure the bodice. I wonder if my stepsisters chose it on purpose, knowing I'd regret dismissing their assistance.

"That's why your energy spiked when I called you Maisie the first time, isn't it?"

"An astute observation," I say dryly as I try to tug the laces. They are far less wieldy than the corset had been.

He takes a few steps closer. "Are you all right back there?"

"Don't!" I shout. "I'm still getting dressed."

"It sounds more like you're wrestling with a nine-tailed kitsune. Where are your lady's maids?"

"I gave them the evening off."

He huffs. "You can't dismiss your maids, Em. You're supposed to be a princess."

I open my mouth to argue but snap it shut before I can get tangled in a lie. I must remember he thinks I'm a lady's maid myself. "I'm not used to being waited upon. It makes me highly uncomfortable." That, at least, is true.

"From now on, let them do their job," he says with a note of annoyance. Then his tone softens. "In the meantime, can I help you?"

"I don't need your help."

"No, you don't *want* my help. I can feel your frustration from here. Are you sweating profusely yet?"

"How do you know it isn't you I'm frustrated with?" But he's right. My neck and forehead are now coated in a sheen of sweat in addition to my armpits, and no matter how hard I try, I can't get the back of my dress tightened while ensuring the bust is properly situated as well.

"Either accept my help or let me call your lady's maids."

Neither option is palatable, but I suppose I'd rather accept his assistance than see my stepsisters' smug satisfaction after I admit my struggle. "All right. You may help me."

He lets out a low chuckle as he approaches the dressing screen. My heart drums a rapid tempo, several beats for every step he draws near, but I force my breaths to remain even. Not that it will do me much good. I'm sure he can already sense how flustered I am. Keeping my back to him, I refuse to so much as look his way as he comes up behind me. His footsteps pause. "What the hell are you wearing?"

My cheeks heat, and I whirl around, grasping the bust close to my chest. "What do you mean? My maids picked it out. Is it not appropriate for the opera?"

His eyes are wide and bewildered. "No, I suppose it's appropriate. It's just so...human. I didn't expect the princess to own such complicated garments."

I turn back around, jaw shifting side to side. "You mean not as simple as the dresses you usually have adorning your bedroom floor?"

"Ouch, you wound me," he says, but his tone sounds far from offended. I feel his hand brush the back of my dress, sending an unexpected shiver up my spine, then a tug as he begins tightening the laces. "I figured we should talk."

I recall him saying as much when he came to my door. "About what?"

"Our arrangement." Another tug of the laces, and the bust finally remains in place on its own.

I lower my arms, trying not to focus on the fact that a man —a prince—is dressing me. My violinist lover hardly aided in removing my clothing during our tryst. For some reason, being laced into an evening gown during casual conversation feels far more intimate than I ever would have guessed. "What about it?" I ask, my voice coming out a little breathless.

"I just wanted to make my intentions clear. I will allow you to continue impersonating the princess until your bargain with her is complete. You mentioned previously our contrived courtship wasn't meant to last beyond the social season. Am I correct to assume you are to leave at the month's end?"

"I can't talk about the bargain," I remind him. Besides, I can't have him knowing the truth—that my stay will be far shorter than a month.

*Less than two weeks. Then freedom.*

Another tug. "Fine. Regardless, I expect you to act as she would. That means allowing your maids to do what their position entails."

"Yes, Franco, that lesson has been learned."

"It also means you should court me as she would. Or *not* as she would, considering she left. I want you to court me as someone giving serious thought to becoming my mate. You will attend public events with me. Since I cannot lie, you shall introduce yourself when Maisie's name must be stated, and you shall answer any questions where direct untruths about you are required. Then, before you leave, you must publicly affirm *you*—as Princess Maisie—are the one who desired for our pairing to go no further."

I blink a few times. Did I hear him right? The breaker of many hearts wants *me* to publicly sever our courtship? That means my first assumption about his motive was incorrect. "I don't understand. You want me to reject you?"

"Yes," he says. "Oh, but you must not give some slanderous reason for why I'm at fault. We shall part amicably."

I consider his words backward and forward and can only find one reason why he'd desire such an outcome. "You want to repair your reputation, don't you?"

He doesn't immediately answer. When he does, his voice is quiet. "In a way, I suppose that's true. Although, I doubt it's for the reasons you think."

I scoff at that.

Franco gives a final pull of the laces and begins to tie them off. Once the duty is done, I expect him to return to the other side of the screen, but when I glance over my shoulder at him, he's still there, fingers lingering at the ends of my laces. His gaze meets mine, and he takes a hasty step back. I quickly return to facing forward. "You can leave now."

Without a word, he moves to the other side of the screen while I gather my composure. Brushing out my skirts, I will my flushed cheeks to cool, hoping the glamour will hide as much redness as possible. To give me a little more time, I gather the hair ribbons up from the floor and pretend to search for a place to tie them. When I catch sight of my shoes peeking from beneath my dress, an idea strikes me—a precaution. Crouching down, I tie the ribbons around each of my shoes, much like the prince had done with the strips he tore from my chemise. For all I know, he plans on flying me to the opera. For the love of the breeze, I hope that isn't the case.

Once my wits are well within my control, I step out from behind the screen. Franco stands several feet away. Taking in my first full look at him since he entered the room, I realize he's dressed far more elegantly than I've yet to witness. Instead of a carelessly unbuttoned shirt, he wears full evening attire with a jacket, waistcoat, and cravat. Not a single article is without some hint of fae flamboyance. His jacket is of the deepest, darkest violet, his brocade waistcoat a few shades lighter. His trousers are slim and black like before, but this time, they are of an iridescent silk that matches his cravat. Despite my elegant dinner dress, I feel like a pauper next to him.

Which means, I suppose, I feel like myself.

His eyes flick briefly over my body, then lock on mine. I avert my gaze and move to the wardrobe in search of gloves. I recall seeing a pair on the bed, but I'll take any excuse to turn my back to him once more. Why does he have me so flustered?

As I search through the wardrobe drawers, feigning indecision, I feel his eyes burning into my back.

"Why do you dislike me so?" he says, tone more curious than condemning. When I turn around, I find him lounging at the end of my bed, toying with the white silk gloves my stepsisters had indeed laid out. He extends his hand, offering the gloves.

I stride over to him and snatch them away. "Whatever do you mean?"

He leans to the side in a lazy slouch. "If I'm correct about Maisie's motives, then I can understand why she wouldn't like me. What's your excuse? We haven't met before—"

I snort a laugh as I pull on a glove.

His eyes brighten with amusement. "So, we *have* met?"

My posture goes rigid. "I wouldn't say that."

"Then say what you mean."

I put on the second glove but say nothing, lips pursed tight.

"Come, you've already insulted my abilities as prince and managed to keep your head." His tone is full of taunting. "I expect you to continue with the same brutal honesty."

Finally, I meet his eyes. "Why?"

His expression shifts, brow furrowing for a shadow of a moment. Then he shrugs, turning casually away from me. "Because it's rare that I hear it." Despite his obvious efforts to feign indifference, there's candor in his tone. Vulnerability.

Could he...*respect* the completely awful way I've spoken to him? If only he knew I'm the same girl he insulted in the alley.

"Come out with it," he says, shaking me from my thoughts. He waggles his brows, lips pulled into a sideways grin, although his eyes maintain a hint of gravity. "What terrible misdeed of mine has so greatly discolored your opinion of me?"

I suppress the urge to tap my fingers against my thighs and fold my hands at my waist instead. If he wants brutal honesty, I suppose I can provide a portion of it. I lift my chin. "I attended last night's ball."

He tilts his head back. "And that's supposed to mean something?"

My words come out slow, careful. "I saw you on the dais."

He grins, rising from the bed and sauntering a few steps closer to me. "Oh? Looking handsome and benevolent, I presume?"

I take a step back, my ire sparking. "More like arrogant, smug, and brooding—"

His mouth falls open. "Brooding? *Brooding*?"

"Yes, brooding. And being rude and dismissive with your guests. For someone who seems to care much about what others think of him, you do nothing to engender a warm opinion. And yet, nearly everyone has endless patience with what sparse attention you give. I must admit, I don't quite understand you or your countless admirers."

He opens his mouth only to snap it shut. For a moment, I fear I've said too much, that my words were too cutting. Despite his request for honesty, I must remember he's a prince and is used to being coddled. I'm about to take it all back and beg his forgiveness when he speaks. "That's what you thought of me at the ball? Upon the dais? You thought I was being rude and dismissive?"

I'm surprised to find his tone is again without condemnation, only open curiosity. It gives me the courage to answer with the truth. "Yes."

His eyes unfocus for a moment. When they return to mine, his expression looks nothing like the prince I saw on the throne, nor does it hold the arrogance of the man I met in the alley. "Believe me when I say that was not my intention. More accurately, I hadn't realized that would be the repercussion. It was supposed to be a joke. A riddle. It wasn't...me."

I frown. What was supposed to be a riddle? Shaking my head, I say, "Prince Franco, I find I still don't understand you."

He watches me a few silent moments, and I think he might elaborate, perhaps reveal yet another layer of the vulnerability I'm starting to glimpse. Then, in a flash, his expression shifts into one that's become far more familiar, full of smug joviality. His words come out light and teasing. "Then understand this. I do not brood. I am funny and clever and charming. Charming people do not brood."

The evasive change of subject sends an unexpected pang of disappointment through me, but I take the opportunity to escape our serious conversation. Evoking the same teasing quality, I say, "Charming? You?"

"Oh, yes, I'm quite charming. Everyone says so."

I dip into a mocking curtsy. "My mistake, Prince Charming."

"Don't ever call me that. Or if you do, don't say it with such sarcasm. Say it like it's a fact, for it is."

"I've never known anyone who had to tell others how funny and clever he is. Usually, it's a lot more obvious. You know, from their personalities."

"Do you take pleasure in insulting me?"

"I must take some pleasure from your company if I'll be forced to endure your presence for the foreseeable future." As soon as the words leave my mouth, I want to swallow them back down. He's right, I do take pleasure from insulting him, and I find myself unable to resist every chance I get. But I must stop. He isn't a friend or a lover but a roguish prince and cold ally. He has the power to destroy me in every way, should he choose to. He may be teasing now, but I've seen that dark power of his. "Forgive me if I've overstepped," I say, bowing my head.

"You have overstepped," he says, words low enough to send a chill to my core. But when I lift my eyes to his, I find laughter written over his face. "You've all but put me out of a job, for it is normally my duty to insult me. Nevertheless, I suppose that means we shall get along *swimmingly*."

I offer him a small smile.

"Swimmingly," he repeats, and I quirk a brow. With one hand on his hip, he flourishes the other. "Because you're from the Sea Court. At least, I assume you are, if you're truly the princess' maid." I keep my expression flat to avoid reacting to his latter statement. Luckily, he seems to take it as my response to his horrendous joke. He shakes a finger at me. "I'll make you laugh, eventually. Truly and wholeheartedly, and not just at my expense. Now, take my arm, you cold-hearted impostor. The opera awaits."

## 25

EMBER

With a deep breath, I take Franco's arm and allow him to lead me out of my room. We enter the hall, which is thankfully somewhat empty. But as we make our way deeper into the palace, I see the halls have grown busier since this morning when we left on our outing. Servants pass. And pause. Dozens of eyes lock on us, trailing our progress down the hall. The significance of this moment strikes me. It's our first public appearance as a courting couple. The realization sends a wave of dizziness to my head. What if I can't do it? What if I say the wrong thing? What if—

"Relax," Franco says, putting his hand over mine. It's then I realize my grip has tightened on his arm. He leans in close. "Tonight is going to go...swimmingly."

His comment eases my nerves, and I latch onto it like a sturdy tree in the breeze. "It wasn't funny the first time."

"But you're smiling."

"Perhaps that's just the glamour. I could be grimacing while I slowly die inside."

His grin widens as if my jab had been the most forward of flirtations. "You, Miss Em, have the sharpest tongue."

The way he says *tongue* has my cheeks reddening, my insides sparking with a strange mixture of delight and annoyance. What is it about him that gets me so easily flustered? One moment, I'm holding my own, the next, I'm suppressing a smile and blushing like an idiot.

Outside the palace, we find a coach parked on the drive, just like this morning. I glance at the front, where two skeletal horses stand hitched.

"Were you able to find them? The...what are they called?"

"The moon mares?" Franco says. "Yes, I found Donna and Dominus and brought those rascals home. These two, however, aren't them." As we descend the stairs, I take a closer look at the horses and realize they do appear much larger than the ones from this morning. He leaves me at the coach's door to give each of the mares an affectionate pat. I'm amazed at how his face transforms, glowing with boyish joy as he strokes their necks. He glances over, catching me staring, and offers me a sly grin. "Care to join me?"

I avert my gaze. "No, thank you."

With a chuckle, he returns to my side and opens the door. Again, there's no coachman, no footman, and he offers me his hand. I take it and hoist myself inside—only to find I'm not alone. Two fae, a male and female, nuzzle close together, giggling on the bench I'd intended to claim. At my startled expression, they pull apart and rise to their feet with a curtsy and bow. My gaze locks on the female, recognizing her short dark hair and enormous black eyes. It's the moth pixie that flirted with the prince last night.

For some inexplicable reason, a flash of rage roars through my chest.

"Princess Maisie," says the male, stealing my attention to

him. He's a slim, youthful fae with charcoal hair, fluffy triangular ears, and amber eyes. "A pleasure to finally meet you."

Franco enters behind me. "Why are we all standing?"

"Isn't that the polite thing to do for a princess?" the male asks. "Stand until the lady sits?"

The prince huffs and takes the empty bench. "Polite? Since when do we do polite?"

The male smirks. "I thought you'd at least want to impress her before she learns what a miscreant you are." He and the moth pixie return to their seat, leaving me the only one standing.

"You should sit before the coach starts moving, Em," Franco says. "Unless you want the same thing to happen that occurred earlier." His brows raise suggestively, reminding me of how I fell on him—*twice*—when our coach was attacked.

Trying not to let my annoyance show, I settle onto the empty seat next to the prince.

The male looks from me to Franco. "Em? Who's Em?"

"That's what I call her," Franco says. "Em, meet my ambassador and friend, Augie."

"I see the two of you have become close in the span of a day," Augie says. "Already choosing pet names."

The moth fae turns to her companion, lips tugging into a pout. "Why don't I have a pet name? I call you Augie-boy."

"How can you say that?" Augie croons. "I'm sure I've called you...something."

"Only when we're in bed."

At that, Franco knocks on the back wall of the coach and makes a clicking sound. The coach rolls into motion, and Franco leans close to me. Pointing at the pixie, he whispers, "If you haven't guessed, that's Augie's lover. Her name is Seri. They're appalling together."

I furrow my brow, looking from the prince to the bickering —and now kissing—couple. I expect to see jealousy spark in the prince's eyes, or some hint of longing or discomfort, but all I see is amusement as he shakes his head at them. I can't be mistaken, can I? Seri is most certainly the fae I witnessed Franco lusting after at the ball.

I recall his words from earlier, when he told me he hadn't meant to come across the way I said he had. *It was supposed to be a riddle.* Surely, that look in his eyes couldn't have been feigned. And if so, why? Could Seri be...a fae courtesan of sorts? Have I barged in between some complicated relationship? I continue to watch the passengers as we continue the ride but can't find a single moment where the prince gives Seri more than a cursory glance. The same goes for the pixie, who can hardly take her eyes off the ambassador. There's nothing heated between her and Franco. Nothing to suggest I hadn't imagined what I saw last night. Could my disdain for the prince have colored my impression of him? I've witnessed his arrogance. His smugness. His annoying sense of humor. But I've also seen that hint of vulnerability. Thoughtfulness when he tied my shoes to my feet. Mercy when he could have thrown me into the dungeon.

The more I think about it, the more confused I am. The more I wonder if there are layers to him that I've yet to see.

～

## FRANCO

"Come now, Augie," I say to my ambassador as the coach comes to a stop. "Extricate yourself from your beloved so we can get on with our night."

With a sigh, he pulls away from what is probably the thousandth passionate kiss I've been subjected to since we left Selene Palace. His lips are pink and puffy, twisted in a crooked smile to give him the distinct look of a drunkard. "What did you say?"

"Your job, Augie. Do your job. Did you think I invited you tonight so *you* could provide the entertainment?"

He leans forward to glance out the window. "Oh, we've arrived at the theater."

"We've been parked for a full minute at least," I mutter to Em, who doesn't respond. She's been in a quiet and contemplative mood the entire ride. No matter what I've said to her, I can't seem to spark conversation. But as she too glances out the window, I sense a shift in her energy. It begins to buzz with a dizzying whirl of excitement and anticipation.

Augie slips a piece of paper from his waistcoat pocket. Scanning it, he says, "You'll be seated in the royal box, which is located on the third floor."

"Has the performance already begun?"

The ambassador glances down at his timepiece. "Fashionably late, as the humans say."

I nod. "Perfect."

Augie and Seri leave the coach first, then I exit and help Em down. Our tardy arrival means no one but a pair of ushers are at the front of the theater to greet us. They open the doors to an empty lobby, and I let out a sigh of relief. I half expected a circus to linger until I made my appearance, but apparently some humans can act with class. Or perhaps Augie succeeded in sending my request to the theater ahead of time that stragglers be banned.

"Why did you want to arrive late?" Em asks, her voice just above a whisper as the ushers lead us through the lobby toward a carpeted staircase.

"Contrary to what you probably believe about me, I don't relish being the center of attention."

She quirks a brow. "You mean, *human* attention?"

"Any attention, if it's in mass."

She seems confounded by that, and I get the impression she's trying to figure me out. The efforts are mutual, although I've yet to learn more than a handful of facts about my new ally. I'm not even sure how much of what I do know is a lie.

The ushers part a pair of doors that lead to a dimly lit corridor. As we step inside, music begins to float upon my ears. My companion's energy surges with a spike that I can only decipher as pleasure or longing. I glance over at her as we continue on, the music growing louder with every step we take. Her lips part, breaths coming faster—a strangely enticing sight that has my lower abdomen tightening.

So, she's a music lover. Good to know.

The ushers open another set of doors and gesture for us to bypass them into the box. It seats four, and I lead Em to the front while Augie and Seri claim the seats behind us. The music is louder now, the orchestra playing a slow, sad tune. I study the stage far below, the elegantly painted sets, the bright lights illuminating the woman who stands at the center of the stage. She wears a many-layered human gown in a deep burgundy, the bodice plunging low at her ample bosom. Her dark hair is piled upon her head in a coiffure of curls adorned with glittering jewels. I've heard of singers such as she, and know the Seelie King of Lunar is fond of keeping such human artisans in his employ. However, this is my first time witnessing such music firsthand. It's unsettling at first, reminding me of a banshee's wail as the singer's voice rises and falls, rises and falls. But the longer I listen, the more beauty I find in the tune.

Em, on the other hand, doesn't seem to need any time at all to appreciate the production. I turn my attention from the stage to the girl seated at my side. Her turquoise eyes glitter with unshed tears as she brings a hand to the base of her throat. Her fingers fumble for a few moments, as if she expects to find something there, then go still over her chest. My eyes unwittingly lower to the modest swell of her décolletage, but I avert my gaze. As much as I've enjoyed the sparse glances I've had of her figure, I haven't the slightest clue how much of her form is morphed by her glamour.

As I return my gaze to the stage, I catch a few eager glances from the audience. Heads lean in close and swivel toward my box. This, of course, creates a ripple effect, as others try to steal covert looks while maintaining as much tact as they can. I shift uncomfortably in my seat, then fling a hand toward Em. She jumps as my hand grasps hers and remains there on her lap. Without meeting her eyes, I lean closer to her, smoothing out her gloved palm until she allows me to thread my fingers through hers. Her hand is stiff for a few moments, then finally relaxes. It feels so small in mine. I hazard a glance at her, but she won't meet my eyes, her jaw set as she watches the singer. Her energy has grown uneven, something like panic now mingling with her pleasure for the music. My emotions have shifted as well, sending a flustered vibration through my chest as an odd tingling runs up my arm from where our hands meet.

"You enjoy the opera?" I ask, voice low enough so only she can hear. Hopefully that will mask my sudden trepidation.

"I was enjoying it," she whispers, her words catching slightly on an intake of breath. "Why are you holding my hand?"

"Because they're watching." When she looks at me, I nod toward the audience. There I find more pairs of eyes, more heads leaning in to exchange whispered gossip.

Em's throat bobs, and she lowers the hand that had been settled over her chest. "Well, it's distracting me."

I grin, a bold warmth propelling my next words. "I suppose that's a proper response to being held by a man you're courting."

She blushes and quickly turns her gaze back to the stage. As the minutes pass, she seems to forget her discomfort over holding my hand and is taken once again by the music. She leans forward as if she would float straight from her seat to the stage. Her eyes glisten again, and I sense a new energetic frequency emanating from her. Resistance. What she's resisting, I don't know, but I see her throat begin to bob, again and again. A chill shimmers down my spine, bringing with it a spark of familiarity. There's something about her energy that feels so...so...

"We're going to get some...refreshments," Augie says, leaning around my seat.

I roll my eyes, knowing exactly what he means by that. He and Seri are going to find a dark corner where they can shove their hands all over each other. I suppose I should be grateful they have the decency to avoid doing so in the theater box. "Just don't be gone too long," I say. If anyone comes to speak with me during the performance, I'd prefer they first be vetted by Augie.

Seri squeals and the two scurry out of the box, closing the door behind them.

I return my attention to Em, realizing my hand is now empty on her lap and she's brought both of hers to the base of her throat. A small smile dances over her lips, and a tear trickles down her cheek. I'm struck by a sudden urge to lift my finger and brush the tear away. Startled by my nonsensical reaction, I remove my hand from her lap. As I bring it to rest over my thigh, I'm surprised at how cold it feels in the absence of her small, gloved hand.

The doors open behind me, and I turn around with a quirked brow. "That was fast." But the figure who darkens my theater box isn't my lovelorn ambassador but one of the last people I could ever want to see.

Brother Marus.

## 26

FRANCO

"Your Highness." Brother Marus bows, then turns to my companion. "And you must be Princess Maisie."

Em stiffens, alarm writhing through her energy as she whirls around in her chair. Her face pales. She says nothing, only looks at our intrusive guest with wide eyes.

"I'm Brother Marus," he says with a bow.

"A pleasure," she bites out before turning to face forward. I frown. Her spike in energy seems like an extreme reaction. Then again, aside from Augie and Seri, who are hardly intimidating specimens, Marus is the first person she's had to pretend to be the princess around.

"Why are you here?" I ask, my voice a slow drawl as I slouch in my seat.

Marus takes the chair that had previously been occupied by Augie. Leaning forward, he speaks in a hushed tone. "Do you recall when I spoke to you last night, Your Highness?"

I grind my teeth. I'm assuming he means when he spoke to

Augie thinking he was me. "You asked me to appoint two human girls as lady's maids for the princess, correct?"

"Yes, and I mentioned they were sisters to Miss Montgomery, my fiancée. I also asked you to officiate our marriage, which was supposed to take place today."

Marriage? Augie promised I'd officiate a *marriage*? He didn't mention that this morning. Since when does the brotherhood expect their prince to perform such menial tasks? "Sorry," I say flatly, "I've been busy today. We'll have to reschedule—"

"She isn't here anyway," he says. "Miss Montgomery...left the palace."

I huff a laugh. "Left? The very day after she agreed to marry you? What a surprising turn of events."

His energy darkens, and I can tell there's much he isn't telling me. I'm guessing it has to do with why his unlucky bride departed. "She will return on the seventeenth of this month. That is her birthday. She's set to claim her inheritance that day, which is being kept by the crown due to the death of her late father's executor."

"Let me guess. You want to secure my services in officiating your marriage the minute this Miss Montgomery of yours returns."

"Yes."

"Well—"

Em rises to her feet and flashes me a tight smile. "Forgive me, Your Highness, but I must find the washroom at once." She doesn't wait for me to respond before she exits the box.

I stare after her, brow furrowed with concern. I'd been so focused on Marus' energy, I hadn't been paying attention to Em's. But I can feel it lingering, even in her absence. Fear. Disgust. Anger.

I rise from my chair and take a step toward the doors, but Marus has the nerve to block me, standing in the narrow aisle between the two rear seats. "I ask a promise of you."

"You have no right to ask anything of me," I say through my teeth, pinning the man with a glare.

"Queen Nyxia assured me I'd have my choice of bride, and I've made my choice. The promise I ask of you is only an extension of hers."

"Fine," I say with a growl. "What promise do you demand of your prince?"

"Only that when Miss Montgomery returns to Selene Palace to claim her inheritance, you will have her turned over to me."

"Turned over to you?" I scoff. "Your kind truly do treat females like chattel."

"She is my fiancée," Marus says, his energy clouded with rage. The kind of rage my sister assured me we must never stir. "I only ask that you turn her over to me so I can speak to her one more time. I vow to you that I will not hurt her, but I will see that she keeps her promises to her family. She has vows of her own to maintain, whether they end in our marriage or not."

I glance lazily at my nails. "I haven't the slightest clue why you find it imperative to involve me in whatever family melodrama you've become embroiled in."

Another cloud of murky rage. "Because she is my promised bride. Your sister wouldn't deny me."

I have about a hundred arguments against that, but I think it might be best if I take them up with my sister first. It seems to me she's given him far too much freedom and power. Too many promises.

And yet, the truth remains that Nyxia is queen. The best damn queen in Faerwyvae. While I...I am nothing like her. I am just a boy playing dress-up as a proper heir. She isn't training me to start a revolution. She's training me to ensure everything she's strived to build doesn't go up in flames the moment I take her place.

My defiance slowly begins to wane until it extinguishes completely.

"Very well," I say, my whispered voice edged with iron. "I promise that if your Miss Montgomery returns to Selene Palace, and I am made aware of her presence, I'll return her to you so that you may *speak* with her."

A corner of his jaw ticks, and I can tell he wants to say more, demand more. Thankfully, he keeps his arguments to himself and takes a step back. With a low bow, he says, "Thank you, my prince."

I brush past him and out the box before he can utter another word.

∼

## EMBER

I make my way to the bottom floor and the hall that leads to the lobby. That's when I realize I have no destination. Contrary to what I said to Franco, I have no need of the washroom, but if I can find it—or anywhere private—I'll take the opportunity to be alone. To escape Brother Marus.

I've known it was possible that I'd encounter him sooner or later, but I certainly hadn't been prepared to see him waltzing into the prince's private theater box. Nor had I anticipated he'd talk about me. About how he assumes I'll return and claim my inheritance. He's wrong, of course. While it pains me to consider my inheritance being forfeit to the crown instead of gifted to an orphanage, I can't risk being confronted by Marus or Mrs. Coleman.

His confidence has one benefit. It means he'll maintain his agreement with Mrs. Coleman—in turn, ensuring they remain at the palace—at least until then. Still, I hate the way he spoke of me like I was property, like I already belonged to him.

Thankfully, he gave no indication that he suspected I was anyone but whom my glamour suggests, but the prince...I can't hide my emotions from him. If *he* finds out I'm only using my bargain with Maisie to evade a primary bargain...

A sharp pain strikes my gut, and I bite the inside of my cheek. *I'm obeying,* I say to myself. *I didn't mean it. I'm not evading a bargain. I still live under Mrs. Coleman's roof. I made no attempt to sever my engagement with Marus.*

The pain subsides to its dull ache, but anxiety takes its place. My chest heaves with panicked breaths, hands trembling, fingers flinching at my sides. I glance around the hall, trying to decide where to go from here. I consider fleeing outdoors but don't want to draw notice by the ushers or anyone passing in the street. The coach could pose as a momentary sanctuary, but I dread the thought of getting close to the moon mares unaccompanied by the prince.

Without a second thought, I head to the left, down a corridor lined with closed doors that must lead to the theater. Strains of the vocalist's beautiful melody snag my attention, and I focus on them, let them calm my racing heart. I'm tempted to reenter the theater through one of the doors and steal a seat in the back, but there's no guarantee I'll go unnoticed. The last thing I need is for anyone in the audience to catch Princess Maisie sneaking around without her date.

But the music! How it calls me.

Before Marus came in and shattered my attention, I'd been fully entranced by the song. Its effect on me had been equal parts pleasure and pain. Pleasure from my thorough enjoyment in the orchestra and the singer's talented voice. Pain because I couldn't join her. Couldn't hum along. Couldn't produce a tune, play a note, or release the emotion it stirred inside me. My throat still burns with my aching need to sing, stronger after my unpleasant encounter with Marus.

I follow the melody's call, not through the doors to the

theater, but farther down the hall. I know not where it leads, only that the music is growing louder. Stronger. My nerves grow less frazzled with every step I take. I quicken my pace, feet flying across the plush crimson carpet. Finally, I come to a plain unmarked door. I hesitate only the briefest moment before I open it.

On the other side, I find not papered walls, elegant sconces, and carpeted floors, but the rustic beauty that is a theater's backstage. It's far more majestic than the quaint space at the back of the music halls I used to frequent, but it's similar enough to know where I am and what to expect. On silent feet, I slowly make my way forward, deeper into the vast underbelly of the opera. My breath hitches as I catch a glimpse of the stage from the side. The gorgeous singer stands in profile as she croons to the audience, while the musicians play in the orchestra pit. The music sounds somewhat muted from my vantage point, no longer amplified by the structure of the main room, but there's a rough authenticity to it that holds a different kind of magic. I tap my fingers against my thighs, feeling some of the tension in my muscles unwind. I stand like that for countless moments, getting lost in the unfamiliar song. With every beat, my pulse calms. My nerves unwind. But there's still an ache that blooms in my chest, one that creeps into my throat and begs to be released. It's my wild fae side, and I know what it wants.

*Sing. I know you want to.*

The taunt comes from deep inside me.

*I don't sing,* I say back to it. *You know that. Not anymore.*

*Just a hum. It won't hurt anyone. No one's around. No one's listening. And it will make you feel better.*

My breaths grow uneven yet again. The temptation is too great. Too needed.

I glance around, finding the narrow hall empty. The only movement comes from closer to the stage where stagehands work rope and pulleys to shift the sets, their labor turning painted wooden waves into a storm-tossed sea. My throat bobs, and I purse my lips, trying to stifle my urges. Marus' face comes to mind. Sneering. Claiming. Rage sparks within me, undoing all the work the music had completed in calming me. Fire burns my chest, my throat. My fingers drum faster against the sides of my thighs, nearly raging at the absence of piano keys. It's too much. It's too great.

So I close my eyes and hum.

# 27

## FRANCO

I follow Em's energetic signature down the halls, uncertain why I'm trailing after her, only that I feel I should. She was upset about something, and I know she lied about needing the washroom. So where did she go? And why did Brother Marus upset her so?

These questions urge me onward as I track the emotions she left in her wake, as potent as if she were at my side. They taste sharp and bitter, tinged with anxiety. I halt at the bottom of the stairs that lead to the lobby, sensing where she went from here. Breathing deep, I catch her signature meandering to the left. I follow it, tasting a shift in her energetic trail. Here, anxiety cools and transforms into longing. I continue down the hall as it curves along the row of doors.

Then I taste something that has me halting in place.

It's a new mix of emotions, and not from a fading trail this time. It's current. It's her. And she's close.

I take off again, faster now, pausing only when I reach the end of the corridor and the door that stands between me and

Em. Her concentration of energy burns bright on the other side.

Then it changes again.

It ripples with a haunting power, one that has me entranced. Peace settles over me, and a fluttering feeling warms the center of my chest. That's when familiarity sparks. I've felt this before. Followed this pull. But when? Slowly, I open the door. At first, all I see is a shadowed corridor that leads backstage, but when I glimpse a tiny silhouette, propped against the wall farther ahead, I know it's Em. Her energy grows stronger, that familiar element weaving brighter around her, tasting like citrus and rose and the breath of a storm wind. I step closer to her. Closer. I'm unable to keep myself away, but at the same time, I'm terrified that one loud step will stop her song and frighten her away like a startled animal. Then she'll take off into the night and I'll never see her again.

*Again.*

I'm certain I've been in her presence before, but not with the face she now wears. As her energy grows and spreads, it conjures visions of a teal-haired girl in a simple ballgown, of a coy smile and dazzling eyes just visible behind her mask.

Then I hear it. A soothing hum that echoes in my bones, tugs at my heart. It mingles with the melody that rings out from the stage, but hers doesn't follow it. It chases it, plays with it, flits around it like a bird on a breeze. I dare to step even closer, and her face comes into view. Her eyes are closed, lips pursed, fingers fluttering at her sides. She looks exactly like the glamoured impostor who fled the theater box, but new energy glows around her, and yes, I remember now. I recall the last time I followed this energy.

My heart flips as my eyes lock on her hands. Hands I've seen anxiously drum against her thighs more than once. A gesture I knew to mean anxiety, but only now recognize for what it is.

Piano keys. She's playing invisible piano keys.

Her tune wraps around me, digging through me, burrowing into my deepest core. I feel a sudden lurch, and something inside me unfurls, spreading outward like a blooming rose. It rises and grows, tingling from my heart and down my arms, eliciting joy, pleasure, desire, and awe. Tears prick my eyes as it nearly overwhelms me. I feel as if I've been dosed with every hallucinogenic fruit in Faerwyvae, and I don't know if I want it to stop or last forever. My head begins to swim in a not unpleasant way, and I close my eyes. As my entire being continues to buzz, I feel as if I'm melting into the floor. My knees start to cave beneath me, and I brace my hand on the wall.

The humming vibration cuts off.

A muffled cry of alarm takes its place. I blink my eyes open and find myself standing far closer to her than I realized, my hand planted on the wall next to her head. Her face is full of terror, her hand to her lips. I'm too overwhelmed with the emotions that envelop me—*my* emotions, for once—that I can't taste hers, nor can I move. For endless moments, all I can do is catch my breath, will my mind to clear. Once I've finally managed to gather my bearings, I push off from the wall and take a step back. Em's eyes are wide and frightened as she watches me in silence. I clear my throat, but it takes me several tries to summon my voice.

"You're her."

She quakes before me, fingers flinching once more. "Who?"

"My mystery pianist."

## EMBER

I stare at him for several moments, unable to blink. Unable to think. Franco's last words were not the ones I was expecting. When I opened my eyes and saw Franco standing before me, all the pleasure and relief I found from my hummed tune fled. I thought for certain he'd come to tell me he'd discovered my true identity. That he and Marus figured it out in my absence. The last thing I ever imagined was what he actually said.

*My mystery pianist.*

Why would he call me that? I shake my head. It makes no sense. No sense whatsoever.

"What are you talking about?" I ask.

His voice comes out barely above a whisper. "You're the girl in the blue ballgown."

Shock runs through me as I try to understand what he's suggesting. He saw me at the ball? Then why would he refer to me as his mystery pianist? The only people who saw me play piano at the ball were the wisps and the fat raven.

And...*no*. That's not possible.

I shake my head. "You couldn't possibly know that."

"You played last night. In the parlor."

"You weren't there," I say, taking a step back until I come up against the wall. "You were on the dais."

"I told you. It was supposed to be a riddle."

"How is that a riddle?"

"I thought you figured it out. You seemed to be the only one who realized the *prince* wasn't wearing a glamour. It would only stand to reason that if the prince wasn't wearing a glamour at a glamoured ball, then he wasn't actually the prince. And he wasn't. It was Augie who stood on the dais. I was—"

"You were the fat raven." My heart hammers against my ribs. The man I spoke with last night, flirted with...that was the prince all along. My breath hitches as I realize what that means.

I've discovered my raven's identity! Then my stomach takes a dive, sending my mind reeling upside down and back again, and my discovery takes on a new meaning. *His identity.* For the love of the breeze, what a fool I was! I thought that conversation had been flirtatious and genuine. But no, he wasn't a charming stranger who enjoyed my company; he was the prince. The same prince who humiliated me behind the glamourist's shop.

"You're angry," he says.

"Stop reading my energy."

"I can see it on your face," he says with unexpected sincerity. Or perhaps it's apology.

I open my mouth, but I don't know what to say. I *am* angry. And embarrassed, and...so very confused.

"What are you?" he asks, brow furrowed as he studies my glamoured face. He takes a slow step closer, his eyes searching mine. "What do you really look like? Were you glamoured last night? Or just masked?"

"I can't tell you," I say, tone sharp. "Besides, why do you care?"

"I...I don't know."

Again, his words are not what I expect. I anticipated something witty, a joke, but my song seems to have unraveled him. Guilt sinks my heart.

Unraveled.

That's what my song does.

It unravels. Upends. Destroys.

"Just answer me this," he says, then adds, "Please."

It's the look in his eyes when he says *please* that keeps me from outright refusing his request. "What?"

"Are you aware you use magic when you sing?"

I lift my chin. "I don't sing."

"How about when you hum?" When I don't answer, he adds, "Are you a siren?"

I'm surprised at the question. For a moment, I've forgotten

he still believes I'm of the Sea Court. I hesitate, preparing to weave truth into my next words. "I inherited fae magic from my mother."

"And your father?"

"Human."

His lips flicker, as if he can't decide if he wants to smile or frown. "Why do you resist it? Singing, I mean?"

Another truth I can give. "It's dangerous."

He nods. "Your song is an amplifier, isn't it? When you sing, you amplify the emotions of your audience."

A pang of grief stabs through my heart. "Yes."

"It's haunting. Beautiful. And, yes, dangerous." A strange look settles in his eyes, one I can't name. Neither of us seem to know what to say after that, so we settle into silence. I want to tear my gaze from his, but I can't seem to move. His eyes brim with questions, and mine beg him not to ask. "Em," he whispers, a quaver breaking that single syllable.

My breathing grows ragged as I await whatever it is he's going to say. I still can't decipher his expression, no matter how I try to read the furrow in his brow, the trepidation in his posture.

He opens his mouth to speak again. "You were—"

"Oy, what are you doing back here?" a male voice calls. Franco and I startle, turning toward the stagehand who stands at the far end of the hall near the stage. He sprints toward us. Franco faces him, standing at full height as he straightens his cravat. The man halts when he recognizes the prince. "Forgive me, Your Highness. You're welcome to go wherever you like. Is it a tour I can give ye? Or is it a closer view from side stage? Madame Cecily is just finishing up the final number right now."

"No, but I appreciate the offer," Franco says with an easy grin, seeming to have recovered most of his composure. "We were just leaving. Thank you for putting on such a fantastic show." Taking me by the hand, he turns around before the man can reply, and leads me back the way I came. His hurried footsteps spell agitation with every beat. Is it because of me?

I curse my foolish self. Of course it's because of me! He's probably dragging me somewhere to punish me for ensnaring him with my dangerous magic. Using magic on a royal without their permission is a criminal offense.

But that look in his eyes before we were interrupted—*No*. I'd be stupid to think it held anything other than disgust. And if he wants to punish me for what I can do, I deserve it. I deserve worse. I've *done* worse than enchant a prince. If only he knew...

The music rises to a crescendo as we rush down the hall past the doors that lead into the theater, the tempo in sync with my pulse. Once we reach the end of the hall, the last note rings out, then leaves silence in its wake. Franco quickens his steps, tossing a glance over his shoulder now and again. His grip tightens on my hand, but not in threat. It feels more like... comfort. Perhaps it isn't me that has him in such an aggravated hurry after all.

We reach the lobby and make a beeline for the doors flanked by a pair of ushers. Several more men await outside, ready to assist patrons to their carriages. Franco pulls me toward our coach, which remains where we left it. Just as he reaches for the door, he pulls up short. I frown, uncertain why he hesitates. Then I notice a slight rocking of the coach. A moment later, a soft feminine moan reaches my ears.

My mouth falls open. I whip my head toward the prince, fully aware of how warm my cheeks have become. "Do you think..."

"Yes," the prince says, then mutters a string of curses that end in, "Damn it, Augie! In the coach? Could you not have found anywhere else to spread your passions?" His words, of course, don't reach the coach's occupants as the vehicle continues to rock. He looks at the moon mares. "You let this happen?"

A sudden wave of sound grows behind us, and a second later, I recognize it as chatting voices. The audience has exited the theater. Franco grows tense next to me. His tight grip on my fingers reminds me that we're still holding hands.

"His Highness," someone whispers loudly. More whispers follow until they build to an excited murmur. I glance over my shoulder at the crowd that pours from the lobby to the street outside.

Franco runs a hand over his face. Then, after a deep breath, he turns us around and flashes the crowd a winning smile. I do my best to follow his lead, acting ever the serene princess, but I'm sure my grin comes across more like a grimace. Bows and curtsies follow. When the people rise, wide eyes dart from the prince to me and back again. I try not to cringe beneath their scrutiny as they stare at our clasped hands.

Franco clears his throat. "Thank you for this wonderful night of entertainment. The…" He pauses and glances up at the marquee. "The Nightingale Theater has been a most generous host this evening. And now I bid you goodnight." He turns to me and lowers his voice. "Are you ready to cause a scene?"

My pulse quickens. "What?"

"How are your shoes? Secure?"

"I've tied ribbons around them."

"Good." With that, he lifts me in his arms and smiles once again for the crowd. "It's been a pleasure." His wings sprout from his back, and he lowers into a crouch. Then he launches upward. I bite back a squeal, arms tight around his neck as we shoot into the night sky.

# 28

## FRANCO

The flight back to the palace feels vastly different from when we left the forest after our coach was sabotaged. Back then, I'd been confident. Playful. Brash. But now...

With the ghost of Em's haunting melody lingering in my veins, I'm left feeling...strange. The air brushing my skin feels colder, sharper. The girl in my arms feels warmer, heavier, her heartbeat louder, her breath on my neck as thick as a caress. It's unsettling how my awareness of her makes my lungs feel tight, my stomach clenching.

I'm not entirely sure why her magic would make me feel this way. Her singing has the power to amplify emotions, but which emotions was it targeting that has me feeling like this? Which emotions made my legs feel weak and my tongue feel like it had been tied in a knot? I can only imagine it had much to do with my shock over realizing who she is.

My mystery pianist.

I still don't know her face or her name, but in that moment

before my emotions overtook my senses, I'd been struck with her essence. Not just her energetic signature, but beyond it. That wild, glowing mass that tasted like rose and citrus.

I glance down at her as we fly. At some point during our journey, she shifted her head from under my chin and now looks down at the scenery below as it passes by in a blur. I breathe in deeply, sampling her emotions, but find them muted. My own are still so present, so strong, I can't get a clear read on her. She does, however, seem less uncomfortable about flying with me this time.

We exchange not a single word as we continue our flight. I'm afraid that if I speak, I'll just say something incredibly stupid anyway. My tongue feels as heavy as it had backstage.

At last, we reach the palace. I set her on the balcony and consider taking off without a second glance. But no, that's a rather odd reaction. It's not like I'm afraid of the girl. Am I?

I blink a few times, realizing I've been staring at her, and she's been looking right back. She hovers before her balcony door, a pained expression on her face. I try to taste her energy again, and after some effort, I'm able to glean a murky blend that must be confusion with perhaps a dash of embarrassment or shame. What does she have to be embarrassed about? I'm the fool who can't seem to get my head on straight.

I don a grin and try to think of something witty to say, but my mind goes blank. What the hell is wrong with me? I retreat a few slow steps toward the balustrade, every step hesitant. "I should go."

Her expression falls, and it makes my heart sink so deep that for one inexplicable second, my only desire is to do something—anything—to remove that hurt. Why does she hurt? And did I cause it? For the love of the night, why do I care? She may be my mystery pianist, but she's still a stranger. An impostor. A woman whose true face I don't know.

And yet…

That citrus and rose emotional cocktail blooms in the back of my mind. I may not know her true face, but I saw something else. Tasted it. And it was unlike anything I've ever sensed before.

She takes a sudden step forward, and her next words come out in a rush. "What were you going to say?"

I shake my head to clear it. "What? When?" Idiot. I can't even form a complete sentence, only clipped words.

"Backstage. You said my name. Then...it seemed like you were going to say something else."

A blush burns my cheeks, and I'm grateful the moon is merely a crescent, keeping my face in shadow. I know exactly what she means, and my first reaction is to brush her off or say something clever and abrasive instead. But the look in her eyes, the murky haze in her emotions, has me shifting awkwardly from foot to foot. I'm about to say something very, very stupid.

Rubbing the back of my neck, I avert my gaze. "Just that... that you were the best part of the ball."

I turn away from her, not allowing myself to witness her response. Instead, I dive over the balustrade and shift fully into my raven form, letting my wings catch the air and take me far from the palace.

**EMBER**

As soon as the prince is gone, I rush into my room and close the balcony doors behind me. Enveloped in the quiet of my empty room, I go to the bed and fall face first upon it. I want to hide. From whom, I'm not sure. From myself? All I know is that a flurry of emotions strike a dissonant chord within me. Humiliation and shame act as dueling conductors, leading all my other feelings in a disharmonious symphony.

I close my eyes but all I see is the prince's wary expression before he left me on my balcony. He couldn't get away from me fast enough. Like I'm dangerous.

I *am* dangerous.

And a fae prince far more deadly than I just looked at me like I could be his undoing.

I release a frustrated groan.

Why did I have to hum? Now that he knows what I can do, he'll...

He'll what?

He said nothing to condemn me, but that doesn't guarantee he won't end our arrangement. He could send guards to my door any minute to throw me out of the palace. Or escort me to the dungeon.

Then I recall the last thing he said to me before he all but toppled off the balustrade in his haste to get away from me.

*You were the best part of the ball.*

My pulse quickens. I still can't believe he was the fat raven. It means all the annoyance I felt for the man on the dais was never meant for Franco. It had been his ambassador all along. And yet, the way he acted in the alley remains.

Unless that wasn't him either.

I groan again, this time striking my pillows with my fist. Humiliation rises higher than all my other conflicting emotions, although it takes me a few moments to realize its source. Then it dawns on me.

I fell for him. I was a fool and I fell for him.

As determined as I was to hate the prince after our alleyway encounter, I fell for him anyway. Not in love, of course, but for his charms. And that son of a harpy probably knows it too. How could he not? He could have been reading my damn emotions the entire time we were in the parlor last night.

My cheeks heat, and all I want to do is disappear and never see the prince again.

*You were the best part of the ball.*

I hate the way my heart flutters at those words. The way it sinks when I consider if he said them not as a compliment but with regret. Or an apology. Parting words before he has me locked away for my dangerous magic...

My emotions rise again, clashing like cymbals as fear joins the fray. I'm so close to freedom. So close to fulfilling the two bargains that must precede the new life that awaits. I can't be thwarted now. I can't have all my plans and dreams upended when everything I desire is just a handful of days away.

I hate being at the prince's mercy. I hate how sorry I feel for ensnaring him with my song. I hate that I now have to question whether he's truly the arrogant rogue I first thought him to be. I hate that he's become a complex mystery I want to both solve and flee from. I hate that his last words continue to echo through my ears. My mind. My heart.

With another groan, I climb under the covers and pull them over my head. Still dressed in my elaborate gown, I leave my raging thoughts behind in search of sleep.

## 29

EMBER

"Do you think the prince will call on you today, Your Highness?" Imogen asks. She glances over at me from the table where she plays a game of whist with Clara. Her eyes don't leave me as she lays down a card.

"I'm not sure," I say lightly, trying to keep my tone higher than natural. In the week that has passed since the night of the opera, they haven't shown an ounce of suspicion, other than what they expressed over my shoes. Still, I want to give them no reason to suspect me further. I've taken Franco's advice in letting them do their duties as my lady's maids, but I've remained as distant with them as I can. Speaking seldom. Playing my part as the reserved princess in their presence. Even now, I'm seated in a chair at the opposite end of my bedroom, my hands busy with needlework.

*Needlework.*

Of all the things I never thought I'd spend my time doing. At least it keeps my fingers moving and reminds me of the mending that was once my daily chore. Something I never thought I'd miss. Then again, it isn't the chores I yearn for. It's feeling useful. Active. A sedentary lifestyle has never been something I've craved. Even my dreams for freedom include activity. Music. Never living a dull moment again. And now that dream is only a week away from coming true.

So long as nothing else goes wrong.

For the first few days following the opera, all I could think about was what could go wrong. My nerves were a tightly wound mess. Every knock at the door had me certain that guards were on the other side. Yet as the week went by and no confrontation came, I began to relax. Well, as relaxed as one can be in my situation. I've still had to keep my composure around my stepsisters.

And Franco...

"Has it only been twice he's called upon you this week?" Imogen says with a smile I know well. One where her lips turn up at the corners while her eyes are keen. Assessing. Calculating. She watches me with her unwavering gaze, seeking any crack in my façade, any opportunity for her to slip past with her cunning plans. Unfortunately for her, she isn't as clever as she thinks.

"Has it?" I say flatly. "I haven't been counting." I have, of course, been counting, and she's correct. Twice he's invited me to take a short walk outside when human visitors come for tours of the palace grounds. These tours are a privilege restricted only to the month-long social season and seem to attract quite the crowds. He seemed mostly back to his confident self during these brief outings, although I could feel a new tension between us that hadn't been there before, one I refuse to read much into. Instead, I've focused on the subterfuge our ruse provides, walking at his side, speaking of only superficial topics as we put on a show for his people. We've talked of nothing personal since the night of the opera. Nothing beyond the weather and whatever else serves to fill our time together.

My stepsisters exchange a knowing glance while Clara lays a card on the table.

"Perhaps you can send me with a letter for him," Imogen says, fluttering her lashes. "Surely, that isn't too forward for a princess."

It takes all my restraint not to roll my eyes. Of course she wants me to send her to the prince with a letter so *she* has a reasonable excuse to interact with him. I clench my jaw as an unexpected heat burns my cheeks. "That's not necessary."

"No?" Imogen quirks a brow. "Are you no longer courting, Your Highness? Or are romantic missives inappropriate for your level of attachment?"

I catch movement under the table as Imogen nudges Clara with her foot. Clara cuts Imogen a glower, then contrives a tense smile for me. "Oh, yes, Your Highness. You should write to the prince and let Imogen deliver your letter. It would be so romantic."

Idiots. Their schemes may be obvious to me, but I daresay a real princess wouldn't be fooled either. And what does Imogen expect to happen? That she'll stroll over to the prince's private quarters, hand him my letter, then be invited inside for tea and a declaration of love? Does she think a single errand will win his affections? If she does, she's a fool and doesn't know him at all.

What am I saying? *I* don't know him at all. And of course she thinks he's easy prey. That's exactly what his reputation suggests. Still, he's proven to have very little patience for human women throwing themselves at him, as evidenced by his sharp words in the alley.

I narrow my eyes at Imogen, wondering if perhaps I *should* send her to the prince. See how she likes being humiliated when her obvious attempts at seduction are rebuffed without remorse. Then my eyes fall on the plunging neckline of her gown, on the haughty turn of her lips. If there's even the slightest chance I'm wrong about him, and she's able to tempt him...

I slam my needlework down and stride across the room, heading straight for the balcony doors. Without a second glance at my stepsisters, I exit onto the balcony and swing the door shut behind me. It doesn't fully close, but I can't bring myself to return to it. Instead, I make my way to the railing and rest my hands upon the balustrade. A trio of wisps dart over to me and circle over my head, but thankfully, they don't bother with their usual teasing. I don't think I could summon the patience for that right now. With a sigh, I close my eyes and let the morning sun warm my face while the breeze calms my racing pulse. What has gotten into me? Why am I so flustered at the thought of Imogen tempting the prince? I've always been upset by her marital schemes, but this...this feels different. Personal.

The sound of whispering catches my ear. I open my eyes, shifting slightly to catch a strain of my stepsisters' words through the door I left slightly ajar. "Are you really going to write a letter in her name and bring it to him?" I hear Clara say. "What if he finds out?"

Imogen shushes her. "Keep your voice down, Clara. I'll do what needs to be done. If we're going to have any success this season, we need to take risks."

"Everything feels like a risk these days," Clara whispers. "What if Ember doesn't return?"

My heart leaps into my throat at the mention of my name. It's the first time I've heard someone utter it since the night of the ball. After that, I've been *Your Highness* and *Princess Maisie*. Or, for the prince alone, *Em*.

"She will," Imogen mutters. "Her inheritance is at stake."

I take a few slow steps closer to the door, careful that my glass shoes don't make a sound. The wisps follow me, still circling over my head, but I quietly shoo them away until they take off with a chortle.

"What if she doesn't?" Clara says.

"Then I will do what needs to be done."

"What does that mean?"

A pause. Imogen's voice lowers even further. "It's not like anyone knows what Ember looks like."

Again, I step closer to the door until I'm just on the other side. Thankfully, the girls are facing in the opposite direction.

"I don't understand," Clara says.

"It's not for you to understand. Trust me. Trust Mother."

Clara gasps. "Wait, are you going to pretend to be Ember and claim her inheritance?"

I hold my breath, but Imogen doesn't answer.

"I'm younger," Clara says too loudly, earning another hush from Imogen. She returns her voice to a whisper. "I should be the one to do it. No one will believe you're nineteen."

"What's that supposed to mean? Are you saying I look old? I'm only a year older than she is."

Clara's voice turns pouty. "My figure is more similar to hers."

"It doesn't matter what I look like," Imogen says through her teeth. Her next words come out slow. "A trip to a certain glamourist's shop in Evanston will do the trick."

My blood goes cold. For the love of the breeze, Imogen is going to get a glamour that makes her look like me. It doesn't even need to be convincing, considering how few people know who I am. The only person in the palace who knows what I look like is Brother Marus, and I doubt he'd bat an eye at such a scheme.

A storm of fury roars through my veins, sending my arms trembling, my knees quaking. I always knew they'd try anything to take my father's fortune, but I never imagined they'd come up with an idea that would work. And I can't let it work. I have to stop them. I must. But how? I can't show my true face here ever again. Even after my bargain with Mrs. Coleman comes to an end, I can't risk her trying something to thwart me. She could drum up false charges against me, or even accuse me of my true crimes—evading a legally binding bargain.

A sharp pain strikes my gut. I bite my lip to keep from crying out. *I'm obeying. I'm obeying. I'm not evading my bargain. I'm not.*

"Where has Ember gone, anyway?" Clara asks. "It shouldn't be possible for her to leave the palace under the terms of her bargain with Mother."

Another wave of pain washes over me, and I close my eyes against it. *I'm obeying. I'm obeying.*

"Mother doesn't think she's left the palace at all." Imogen's words send icy terror through me.

"Then where is she?"

Pain lashes my core, and I brace my arm against the door.

"Being a disobedient rat," Imogen says.

The unlatched door gives way beneath my arm. My stepsisters whirl toward me with wide eyes just as I tumble over the threshold. I stumble to right myself, and for one horrifying moment, I fear I'll slip clear out of my shoes. But as I gather my bearings and look down at my feet, I find them secured in place by the ribbons I've begun tying around them every morning.

Thank the breeze.

Pain continues to rumble inside me, but I force it away, breathing deeply to steady my pulse. *I'm obeying. I'm obeying.* I don't notice when my stepsisters leave the table and only realize they've come to me when I feel a hand on my shoulder. It's Imogen's. I flinch away from her touch.

"What's wrong, Your Highness?" Imogen asks, with only a

hint of true concern in her eyes. Clara, on the other hand, looks wildly perplexed.

"It's nothing," I bite back, painfully aware of how much control I've lost over my voice. It trembles, sounding far too much like my true self. My meek self. The self my stepsisters know too well. Pulling away from them, I weave a lie. "The sun made me dizzy. It appears I'm still not used to being on land."

"You should sit, Your Highness," Clara says, trying to lead me toward the table.

I swallow hard and force my voice to come out as evenly as possible. "No, a walk will do." On trembling legs, I brush past them to my door and rush out into the hall. My mind continues to spin, my vision a blur as I work to breathe away the hum of pain that roils inside me.

"Em." The voice snags my attention, and I blink a few times as I find myself a step away from colliding with the prince. I halt and stare up at him, the abrupt shift in my momentum making me rock back on my heels. His hands come to my upper arms to steady me, his grip firm but gentle as his touch invades my awareness, overriding my anxiety. Even the bargain's spike of pain has returned to the dull ache I'm used to. Aromas of jasmine mingling on the night breeze fill my senses, sending my pulse quickening while calming my nerves at the same time.

What the breezing hell? Since when is his scent familiar to me? Since when does it *calm* me?

"Franco," I say under my breath, shoving the unanswered questions to the back of my mind.

He gives me an easy smile, seeming much like his usual self. "Might I have the honor of your company at Lake Artemisa?"

"Of course, Your Highness," I say with as much polite restraint as I can manage. All I want to do is beg him to take me away from here, away from my sisters and the conversation that lingers in the pit of my stomach.

"Shall we take a coach or fly?" he asks, extending his hand.

I know the right answer. The safe answer. The answer that keeps the proper distance every courting couple—even pretend ones—should maintain. But right now I want to feel the air on my face, tugging my hair, brushing my skin.

I place my hand in his. "Fly."

## 30

**EMBER**

I'm starting to get used to what it feels like to fly. My stomach no longer roils the same way with the dips and turns Franco makes, although I can't say I'm completely settled. There's still the fact that I'm cradled against the prince's arms, my arms encircling his neck, the heat of his chest warming every inch where our bodies touch. Yet it doesn't feel quite so terrifying anymore to be this close. His grip on me feels...safe. The wind streaming through my hair feels exhilarating. And now that I've grown more used to the ride, I'm not as dizzy, which means I get to admire the scenery passing far below.

A warmth spreads through my heart as I wonder, is this what Mother saw when she flew?

I'm surprised to find my disappointment so strong as the lake comes into view and we begin our descent. Not that I dislike the idea of walking by the lake. It's more that I'm not done flying.

I study our destination as we continue to lower. The lake

glistens a blue-green, and I see several small rowboats upon it. On the path surrounding the lake stroll countless well-dressed figures, the women carrying parasols while the men wear their finest walking clothes. I glance down at myself, relieved that I appear to be dressed comparatively well. I'd been so preoccupied with getting away from my stepsisters that I hadn't thought to change before we left, but my blue satin skirt and matching short coat are perfect for walking.

Franco lands us on a part of the path that just so happens to be unoccupied at the moment. I'm guessing he chose it for that specific reason. The closest figures are mere blurs in the distance, slowly rounding the bend toward us. Once I have my feet beneath me, I brush off my skirts and straighten my blouse and coat, ensuring nothing has gone awry during our flight. With a few pats, I smooth down my hair as well. Although, based on what I've witnessed of my glamour in the mirror, my hair is the one thing that always looks perfect no matter what I do to it. Feeling as put together as I can, I glance at Franco.

And find him staring straight at me.

I suppress a start. Has he been watching me the whole time I was fiddling with my appearance? As he continues to stare without a word, I realize we haven't spoken since we left the palace.

"So, why are we here?" I say, breaking the silence. "And what do we do now?"

He shakes his head as if he's coming out of a daze. His posture grows relaxed and he extends his arm. With one of his familiar, winning smiles, he says in haughty mockery, "We must promenade at least once around the lake, my lady. They expect it."

I take the proffered arm, placing my hand at his elbow. Something that's become quite natural, despite how it always sends my pulse racing just a little. "Who's they?"

"The all-seeing *they*, our judges, juries, and executioners," he says with a lazy drawl.

We begin to walk in the direction of the approaching strolling couples. "Aren't the royals the ones who judge, trial, and execute? In other words, you?"

He chuckles. "I'm trying to be melodramatic. Let me have this, won't you?"

His tone makes me smile. It feels like things are back to normal between us. That is, if things ever were *normal*.

We pass the first set of people, who offer nods as they dip into curtsies and bows. As we continue on and fall back into silence, that buzzing tension I noticed earlier in the week begins to form all over again. We make it another dozen or so feet, nodding again at another couple when Franco gestures toward the water's edge and the small rowboats tethered to the dock.

"Shall we take a leisurely boat ride?" he asks.

"I thought we were here to promenade."

He winks. "I'm the prince. I can do whatever I want."

I roll my eyes at that, and the easy feeling returns. Maybe our silences are normal and I'm overthinking things. Imagining a strange energy where there is none.

I follow him to the rowboat and watch as he climbs in first. "Come," he says, extending his arms. "I'll help you down."

I reach for him, but his hands don't clasp mine like I expect them to. Instead, they come to my waist. My breath hitches as he easily lifts me from the dock to the boat. I'm not nearly as graceful when he sets me on my feet. With the boat rocking beneath my poorly distributed weight, I nearly lose my balance.

"I've got you." Franco laughs and brings one hand to my side, just below my ribcage, while the other helps prop up my arm. A squeal of laughter bursts from my lips, but with his help, I'm able to find my footing. My eyes meet his, and I find him so much closer than I expected. The hand on my side tightens the slightest bit, and his expression shifts into something I can't read. I want to avert my gaze, but I can't bring myself to move even the slightest inch away from him. Which makes no sense, for it's not like I'll fall overboard without his stupid help.

I clear my throat to find my voice. "Should we sit?"

Again, he seems to have to clear a daze from his mind, and he tears his gaze away from me. "Yes," he says with a small smile, and I'm almost certain I see a blush on his cheeks as well. He takes my hands in his and holds them while I lower onto the bench. He takes the opposite bench with very little effort.

"I would have thought someone from the Sea Court would have an easier time on water," he says with a smirk.

"Excuse me?" I infuse my tone with mock affront, hoping it will hide the truth. "I've never been in a boat before. What reason would I have to do so?"

He chuckles at that, but his gaze goes steely as it catches something from over my shoulder. "For the love of the night, let's get as far away from here as we can. Fast."

I cast a glance behind me and see a small crowd has gathered near the dock. They do their best to feign nonchalance, but it's clear they came because someone spotted the prince.

I look back at Franco as he reaches for the side of the dock and pushes our boat away from it. "I thought the point of bringing me here was to be seen by others."

"Seen. Not crowded." I expect him to reach for the oars next, but instead, he sprouts his wings and extends them wide. Lightly, they begin to beat the air and our boat moves away from the dock. In a matter of seconds, we're far from shore.

"Nice trick," I say, nodding at his wings.

"Isn't it?"

I look out at the lake, taking in its calm shimmering waters, the other boats interspersed over its surface. The sun is high overhead, but it isn't blindingly bright. It never is in the Lunar Court, which is something I've always appreciated ever since I lived here as a child. I love the way it casts everything in a strange, almost violet glow during the day. Peace settles over me as Franco continues to navigate us over the lake. When I return my attention to him, I meet his eyes, but he quickly flicks them away.

Then more silence. Again.

I resist the urge to drum my fingers on the bench. "Lovely weather today, is it not?"

"Very." He glances around the lake, then pins me with a pointed look. "You know no one can hear us right now, right?"

I take that to mean he doesn't want me to speak to him anymore, so I purse my lips and nod.

Franco throws his head back with a frustrated groan. His wings go still as does our momentum. "Damn it, Em. I can't take it anymore," he mutters.

My heart leaps into my throat. Breezing hell. This is it. This is the confrontation I've been dreading. The one I almost stopped fearing would come to pass. "You can't take what anymore?"

His posture stiffens. "This. Talking about the weather. Pretending we're the two most boring people that ever lived. It's driving me mad."

I shutter my eyes as I process his words. That's not at all what I was expecting.

"Insult me," he says. "Tell me I'm being an ass. Roll your eyes and remind me what a chore it is to be in my presence."

"What? Why?"

"Just do it. I like when you're honest. When you aren't afraid of me. You were the one person who…never mind." He snaps his mouth shut and looks away.

I'm about to let that be the end of it. I *should*. If I don't, I have no idea where this conversation will go. And yet, that's the very reason why I can't let it end here. "If you want me to be honest, then do the same for me. What are you trying to say? I'm the only person who what?"

He opens and closes his mouth several times before saying, "Ever since we returned from the opera, you've been walking on eggshells around me, and it makes my skin crawl."

My eyes go wide as a flood of indignation heats my cheeks. "You're one to talk. You've been avoiding me all week, acting like I'm some...some plague."

He pulls his head back as if I'd slapped him. His words come out small. "Is that what you think?"

A thousand heated retorts burn my tongue, but my defiance is quickly extinguished when I remember how he looked at me after he caught me humming. It was an expression I couldn't comprehend, but it doesn't take much thought to know what it meant. I lower my head. "I don't blame you."

He runs a hand over his face with a groan. "That's what I'm talking about. Don't do that. Don't act like I'm someone you need to cower before."

I lift my eyes. "You *are* someone I should cower before. You're my prince."

"That's never stopped you until now. Not until...until that night. Now you act like I'm going to send you to the executioner's block at any moment."

"Have you not threatened to do exactly that?"

"I thought we were beyond threats by now."

"Why? Because we've spent all of a handful of hours together?" My words come out far sharper than I intend, and as soon as they leave my lips, I don't quite understand why I said them in the first place. All I know is—in the moment—they felt like a weapon.

A flash of pain flits over his face before he steels his expression. "If I was going to punish you for impersonating a princess, I would have done it already."

"That's not what I was afraid of being punished for."

"Then what?"

"My singing. I...I regret what happened. I shouldn't have hummed that day."

He's silent for a few moments, studying my face. My entire being flushes beneath his scrutiny. "Why would you regret it?" he asks.

"You know why."

He leans back slightly, expression wary. "I do?"

"You said so yourself that night. I'm dangerous. I ensnared you with my power. That can't be short of an attack on a royal. A crime."

He shifts awkwardly in his seat. His answer comes out low, barely above a whisper. "When I said your magic is dangerous...that's not what I meant."

I frown. "How did you mean it?"

He says nothing.

"Which is it, Franco? Are we going to be honest, or are we going to flit around each other like...like—"

"Like mating butterflies." He slouches to the side, his wary expression shifting to a sly smirk in an instant.

I clench my jaw. "Now you're trying to evade the question with your charm and humor."

"So you admit it. I *am* charming."

If we weren't in a rowboat, I'd storm away from him right now. Since we're stuck together at the center of a lake, I can only burn him with a glower. He wants honesty? He can have it. "I know you do that in self-defense. You shy away from serious topics and try to act like you don't care. I don't know who you think you're fooling, but it doesn't work on me."

His eyes go wide, expression falling as he slowly slides out of his lazy slouch. For several moments, silence hangs heavy between us. A tingling sensation crawls up the back of my spine, and the meek human side of me urges me to beg forgiveness. I refuse. He asked for honesty.

"You're right," he finally says. "About me. About how I've been avoiding you and treating you differently since the opera. I didn't realize I was doing that until now. All week, I've been focused on how *you* were acting around *me*. I never realized I was being different too. But the reason why I acted that way isn't what you think."

My shoulders relax, and muscles I hadn't realized I'd been clenching begin to uncoil. "You mean, you're not upset with me for using my magic on you?"

"I wasn't upset. I was...embarrassed."

"What would you have to be embarrassed for?"

His eyes flick to me but don't linger, instead hovering somewhere over my shoulder. "I could barely form a coherent word around you after that."

"Which is why I was racked with guilt. I didn't mean to do that to you."

He huffs a laugh, shaking his head with subdued amusement. "I don't think you know exactly what you did."

"What did I do?"

His eyes return to mine, and he smiles. Not a smirk or a sly grin, but a soft, hesitant smile. After a few beats, his face turns serious again. "Why are you so afraid of your power?"

My heart pounds heavy against my ribs, my lungs constricting. I can't stop my fingers as they begin to drum against my seat. "I don't want to talk about it."

"That's all right," he says slowly, his gaze falling on my fluttering fingers. "How about this? We each ask and answer question for question and agree to state only the truth."

My breaths continue to feel tight, but I manage to still my tapping fingers. "That's easy for you."

"Well, yes, I'm incapable of lying. But if you can promise not to lie to me, I'll promise neither to evade nor deceive."

The offer is tempting. There are many mysteries I'd like to unravel about him, but still...

"I can't answer the question you asked," I say. "I'm not comfortable talking about that."

He shrugs. "You have a right to your secrets. You may decline to answer any of my questions. All I ask is that when you do answer, you tell me no direct lie. I'll even let you go first. How does that sound?"

I drum my fingers against my bench a few more times. "I don't have to answer the questions I don't want to?"

He nods.

I swallow hard. "All right."

Another smile breaks over his face. "Very well then. The first question is yours."

# 31

**EMBER**

Franco returns to lightly moving his wings and propelling us over the lake's surface. It takes me a while to decide on my first question. Then it comes to me.

I form each word with care to ensure I give nothing important away. "You told me your ambassador acted in your stead during the New Moon Masquerade. Have you ever had him act in your place outside of that instance? Has he been glamoured as you on any other occasion?"

His answer comes easily. "No."

My heart sinks a little. That means Franco truly was the arrogant ass I met in the alley.

"My turn," he says. "Were you wearing a glamour the night of the ball?"

I pause to consider my answer. Or if I even want to answer at all. He said I could refuse any question I want, but I find myself wanting to tell the truth. It stands to reason that the more honesty I give him, the more he'll give me. Although, that doesn't mean I have to give him the whole truth. "I wore a mask and ballgown that night." Before he can comment, I pose my next question. "Why did we flee the theater in such a hurry after the opera?"

He sighs and looks out at the water. His answer seems to pain him. "I meant what I said when I told you I don't like crowds. There are many reasons for that. For one, being a psy vampire means I can get overwhelmed by others' emotions, especially those belonging to strangers. I have a difficult time tuning them out or shielding myself against them. It makes me feel...defenseless. For another, well, I tend to feel awkward around people I don't know well. Maybe even shy."

His answer surprises me. Even though he agreed not to evade or deceive, I didn't expect him to express such vulnerability.

"My turn again," he says. "Why were you upset when Brother Marus came to our opera box?"

My fingers curl around the edge of my seat, and my blood seems to freeze in my veins.

He must sense my shift in energy. "I don't like him either, Em. If I could do away with him, I would. I just want to know why you have a particular dislike for the man."

I take a few deep breaths to steady my nerves. Again, I could refuse to answer. But that would be far more suspicious than the truth. "My mother died in the rebellion," I whisper.

His expression falls. "I'm so sorry, Em."

Part of me wants to tell him more, but I stop myself from elaborating. My brief answer explains more than enough. Besides, it's my turn again. "Why do you want me to pretend to court you? When I asked if you wanted to improve your reputation, you gave some vague answer about how it was only partially true but not for the reasons I think. What's the real reason?"

His wings brush the air. Once. Twice. Our boat glides a little faster. "I need to show the people I'm trying to be the heir they need and gain the respect of both the humans and the fae. To do that, I need to prove I am capable of a serious courtship. Which, in turn, means I'll make a good king who can produce a proper heir." He says the last part with a flippant wave of his hand.

I furrow my brow and nibble a corner of my lip to keep my response at bay.

He gives me a pointed look. "Come on. I know that expression. Out with it, already."

"It's just..." I take a deep breath and gather my courage. "I don't fully understand you. You say you need to prove you're capable of a serious courtship, and yet you're pretending with me. You say you're trying to be the heir your court needs, and yet you glamour your ambassador to take your place at the ball for the sake of a riddle when you could have taken the opportunity to show everyone who you really are. You say you must gain the respect of the humans and fae, but whenever you get a chance to interact with the humans, you flee from them. Or use me as a shield."

"A shield," he echoes, a note of disbelief in his voice.

I gesture toward the surrounding lake, at the rowboats that maintain their distance while their occupants stare our way with eager smiles. "Yes, Franco, a shield. You use my presence and our false courtship to keep others from approaching us. Instead of coming here alone and stopping to talk with the people you've agreed to host for the season, you're out here, as far away from them as you can be."

His jaw tenses, wings twitching with agitation. "I'm fully aware of what a poor prince you think I make, and trust me, I don't blame you."

"That's all you have to say about it?"

"What else is there to say? I know I can't measure up. I know I don't have what it takes to fill my sister's shoes."

"That's not what I mean. It's not that I don't think you have what it takes, but that you *do* and have chosen not to put in the effort."

"It's not that I haven't tried."

I scoff. "Is that so?"

"Yes, but when I did...it didn't go so well."

His expression has my defenses softening. I lean slightly forward. "What happened?"

I expect him to evade the question and remind me it's his turn. So I'm surprised when he answers. "It was shortly after the rebellions ended," he explains. "Nyxia decided the best way to quell human unrest was to make a marriage alliance between me and a human aristocrat's daughter. She drew up a list of potential brides she wanted me to meet. We planned for me to spend Lunar Court's social season amidst human cities where I would find an acceptable mate. To be honest, I was thrilled. Despite how terrified I've always been of crowds and strangers, I was willing to set it all aside for the new experience. I'd seldom left the palace before this, and I certainly hadn't ventured out to human cities for frivolity. It was a chance I couldn't pass up. I learned all the popular human dances, took rooms at the most expensive hotels, and was outfitted in the finest human clothing."

He pauses, shaking his head. "It was overwhelming but fascinating at first. The admiration I received from men and women alike was unlike anything I'd felt from other fae. And their energy. It was a psy vampire's playground to be amongst such new and decadent emotions, so different from what I sense from faekind. I relished them. Learned what it took to spark certain ones I liked best. Desire became a quick favorite. That's where things started to go wrong."

My stomach clenches, and I wonder if this is where he learned to become the playboy prince. Part of me wants to tell him not to go on, but I'm too enraptured by his confession to speak.

He continues. "I courted the women my sister asked me to meet. There were several different cities I began to frequent with a potential bride in each. I made my rounds, called upon them. Brought them gifts, paid them compliments. I didn't grow emotionally close with any of them, but I could tell I was earning their desire. I reasoned that companionship and affection would soon follow. Since I knew courtship to be a sort of audition that precedes an engagement, I thought I was doing all the right things to help me discover which woman would be the best mate for me. I attended ball after ball, dancing with my potential brides, song after song after song. I grew more comfortable and stopped dressing like a stuffed penguin and began wearing clothes I felt more like myself in."

I glance down at his chest, where he wears yet another open-collared shirt with no waistcoat. I've grown quite used to his state of dress lately, but I still remember how scandalized I first felt by his appearance.

"I should have known better," he says with a dark laugh. "I learned about human etiquette, but I let it go in one ear and out the other, all to suit my own enjoyment. I underestimated how serious humankind can be about their rules and strictures. Halfway through the social season, I started to sense a shift in the energy amongst the women I was courting. They were all smiles and compliments when in my presence, but behind their grins lurked new flavors of emotion—envy, hate, and desperation. No one said a thing to my face, but I quickly learned I'd earned a reputation. One for dancing with women more than two or three times during a single ball. And not just one woman, but a different woman for each city I frequented. I hadn't grasped the significance of what I was doing. Where I thought I was getting to know a potential future mate, to the humans, I was luring multiple women into a sense of attachment I hadn't intended to give. Shortly after my startling revelation, a couple of the women contacted me to make excuses for why they must sever our courtship, while others became more aggressive than ever. Their fathers too began seeking me out, vying for my favor, finding any reason to get their daughters before me more and more. In a few veiled words, they pressured me to make my proposal. All the while, I was shocked because I'd yet to get to know a single one of my potential brides. As tensions grew, it became clear that none of these women wanted me for *me*, and I left. My reputation only grew from there, leaving stories of broken hearts and unfulfilled promises in my absence.

"When I returned to Nyxia, I explained everything. While she claimed to understand, I could tell she was disappointed in me. In less than one month, I managed to disrupt our standing with the very people I was supposed to appease. That's when my sister took matters into her own hands and came up with her plan to host the annual social season at Selene Palace from then on. At first, I think she still held onto hopes that she could pair me off, now that she'd be in control of the environment, but I asked her to stop meddling in my love life. She did, for a time, until she decided it was imperative that I marry a royal. That's where Princess Maisie came in. And, in turn, you."

I hold my breath, waiting for him to finish. Then I realize that's the end of the story. "Wait, that's how you earned your reputation? By dancing too many dances in a row and courting too many ladies at once?"

He nods.

My mind reels. While I know how much the gentry value their rules, I never thought *that* was why the prince was known as a rogue. I thought he'd done cruel and vile things to earn that name. "Have you any idea what people really think of you? Why did you never clear up the misunderstanding?"

"I know what is said about me. I never corrected anyone

because I doubted it would do any good. I broke society's rules. I did exactly what they said I'd done, regardless of my ignorance or intentions. Besides, it's true that I've taken numerous lovers but never a mate. I've never had a serious courtship, just like the people think. The last person I gave serious thought to pursuing—" He clamps his mouth shut.

I sit straighter, my attention fixated on his suddenly flushed cheeks. Curiosity burns inside me. I want to ask him to elaborate, but it's his turn to ask a question, and I'm afraid that if I speak, he'll change the subject entirely. Perhaps I can encourage him...

"I never learned the name of my last lover," I say in a rush.

A corner of his mouth quirks up. "Is that so?"

I nod but say nothing else.

"Why didn't you learn his name?"

"It felt safer that way," I say with a shrug. "Our coupling was meaningless, but it felt like freedom. Like I could be anyone I wanted, so long as we never learned each other's names."

He furrows his brow. "I think I can relate to that."

"So, what happened with the last person you pursued?" I ask with as much nonchalance as I can muster.

"Actually, it's my turn to ask a question."

"Actually," I say, mimicking his tone, "you already asked why I didn't learn my previous lover's name."

His mouth falls open. "Did you trick me?"

"Perhaps."

A wicked grin curls his lips. "I like that. Very well, I suppose I can tell you about it. Just don't pity me, all right? I despise pity."

I nod, then wait with bated breath for him to continue. I'm not sure why I'm so eager to hear about his love life, but I am, with equal parts fascination and dread.

He takes a deep breath. "The last person I gave any serious thought to...was Queen Evelyn."

I cock my head. "The Unseelie Queen of Fire?"

"The very one." His cheeks turn rosy again. "My sister arranged our courtship. This was long before the debacle with the humans, back when meddling with my love life was an everyday occurrence for Nyxia. This time, though, I didn't hate her choice. I liked Evelyn. We quickly developed a friendship, and I was starting to feel comfortable enough to be myself around her. But her heart already belonged to someone else. I could taste her love for him long before she chose him. It was as bright as the moon whether I was sampling her energy or not."

"Are you talking about King Aspen?" Everyone in Faerwyvae knows about Queen Evelyn and her mate, the King of the Autumn Court. They were instrumental in winning the war over twenty years ago. A victory that shaped Faerwyvae into what it is now. An isle where humans and fae live together in peace.

He nods. "I never stood a chance with Evelyn, and it's obvious why. Have you seen King Aspen's antlers?" He sighs. "I suppose I had a crush on them both for a time, but Evelyn was someone I think I could have been happy with. I never felt anything close to love for her, but still...I must admit, it was quite embarrassing."

"Rejected by a queen," I say with a grimace.

"We're friends now," he says with an easy grin. "And yet, it serves as a reminder of how difficult it's always been for me to get close to a lover. I can feel their emotions, sense if their feelings for me are lacking. I can taste the murky waters of their rejection before I have to experience it myself. I can smell one's lies when a lover likes me only for my crown."

My heart sinks. I stare at him, feeling like I'm seeing him for the first time. He isn't the careless rake I thought him to be. Now that I know the tale behind his reputation, I'm ashamed of how I've judged him. How I've spoken to him. He may have said and done many things to spark my ire, but when it comes to prejudice, I've been no better than the humans who spread his reputation in the first place. Just like them, I believed it without question. Without proof.

"I'm sorry, Franco."

"I told you not to pity me."

"It's not pity," I say. "It's...well, I don't know what it is. I just hate the way the humans reacted to you during that first social season." I'm not ready to confess my guilt over my own judgments, but I hope he knows it's laced into my apology.

He chuckles. "Now you know why I resist getting involved with humankind in the same way again."

"So you're just going to keep avoiding them?"

"What else am I to do?"

I shrug. "Show them who you really are, perhaps. Be the real you. Maybe show up to these events without finding creative ways to evade talking to people."

He quirks a brow. "Finding creative ways to avoid talking to strangers *is* the real me."

"You're more than that."

His gaze locks on mine. "Am I?"

My pulse quickens beneath those silver eyes. "I believe so," I say, my voice coming out oddly breathless. He continues to hold my gaze for several moments, and each beat of my heart seems to stretch into an eternity. The silence that falls between us feels different than before. It feels heavier, fuller. For once, I don't feel the need for it to end.

He breaks it with a groan, tipping his head back. "Damn it, Em, now I feel like I must try to prove you wrong."

"About what?"

He waves toward the shore. "About the humans. About this rather troublesome theory you've developed."

"About you being yourself around them?"

He groans again. "I can't believe you're making me do this."

"I'm not making you do anything."

"Oh, very well, but don't twist my arm. Shall we finish our promenade?" With an exaggerated roll of his eyes, he mutters, "And perhaps we can stop and converse with a few people."

My expression brightens, but I try not to seem too impressed. "If you insist."

He wags a finger at me. "We aren't chatting with *everyone*, all right?"

"Breezes, no," I say, mimicking his haughty demeanor. "You're not the only one who can hardly tolerate the gentry."

He lets out a bellowing laugh, one that makes his eyes crinkle at the corners. It's a musical sound, a playful melody that has my heart feeling light. Try as I might to ignore it, there's a very strong part of me that wants nothing more than to hear that melody play again and again.

# 32

**EMBER**

We make it a full round along the path that circles the lake, stopping every now and then to chat with passersby. I'm impressed that Franco manages to speak with them without any outward sign of annoyance. If anything, he just seems a little uncertain, his posture less self-assured than it normally is. We hold no conversation overlong, just enough to exchange pleasantries. By the time Franco suggests we head back, my lips are aching from smiling. I'm more than eager to comply when he takes me in his arms and shoots into the sky.

"That wasn't so bad," Franco says as he lands us near the front of the palace. Part of me wishes he'd taken me straight to the balcony instead, but going through the front doors is another demonstration that he's trying. He's letting himself be seen, and not just from afar.

I give him a sardonic smile. "I'm glad you survived. Now, what's our next mission?"

"The Full Moon Frolic is the next public event of the social season."

"The Full Moon Frolic," I echo.

"Another glamoured ball. And no, I won't force Augie to take my place this time."

I run a few calculations in my mind. "The full moon is…"

"Saturday."

My birthday is the next day. Sunday. The day I turn nineteen and am released from my bargains. That means the night of the ball will be my last in the palace. A mixture of anxiety and excitement turns my stomach.

He leans in close, a hint of teasing in his tone. "Will you accompany me? As my lovely date?"

My heart flutters at the word *lovely*, but I smother the feeling down, reminding myself he has no idea what I look like. Even if he's deduced that I was unglamoured when we met at the New Moon Masquerade, I still wore a mask that covered the top half of my face. Besides, he didn't seem to think I was lovely when we met in the alley.

"Do I even have a choice?" I ask.

"Of course not."

We exchange a smile, but I'm surprised to find my heart sinking. I should be excited for another chance to attend a ball. This time, I won't have to hide from anyone, as I'll already be safe behind my glamour. But at the end of the night, it will all be over. I'll be free.

*Free.*

I should be excited. Thrilled. And I am, truly. So why do I also feel a note of sorrow?

After stopping to talk to a few more guests, servants, and residents, we make it back to the hallway that leads to my room.

We're still several feet from my door when Franco stops and turns to face me.

"I enjoyed today," he says, "so much more than I ever would have thought."

"Because I coerced you into socializing?"

He smiles but hesitates before answering. "Because you were honest. You managed to see me for who I am as well as who I could be. And, yes, talking to the humans on a personal level, well, it was...not bad."

My cheeks warm. "I enjoyed today too."

His eyes lock on mine, and he seems like he's going to say something. He steps closer.

My door flies open, and my stepsisters feign startled gasps. "Oh, Your Highnesses," Imogen says as the two dip into curtsies. When they rise, Imogen's eyes dart between me and Franco, watching us with keen interest. Our conversation from earlier returns to me, and I recall the way she not-so-subtly tried to determine how close me and the prince truly are.

This sends a vindictive boldness through me. Before I can consider what I'm doing, I step toward Franco, rise onto my toes, and plant a kiss on his cheek. It's nothing more than a quick brush of my lips, but as soon as it's done, my stomach bottoms out and turns over in a fluttery mess. My breaths come fast and shallow as his lips part with surprise. What did I just do? I stand back and study his face, but all I can focus on is that spot where my lips just were. My mouth tingles with the feeling of his warm skin. I drag my gaze to his and find his eyes are locked on my lips.

Breezes, what have I done?

A slow smile melts over his face. "What was that for?"

My chest heaves as I try to summon a rational answer. "For our audience," I whisper.

"Right." He shakes his head, his smile slipping away. It's almost as if he's disappointed. He straightens his posture and takes my hand in his. Then, like a perfect gentleman, he bends down and presses his lips to the back of my hand. My insides clench during the split-second the kiss lasts. It's no less fleeting than the one I placed on his cheek, and yet it feels similarly as brave, bold, and intimate. Without another word, he releases my hand and turns away to hurry down the hall. It reminds me of how he tumbled off my balcony after the opera. That night, I was certain he despised me for my dangerous song, but today he confessed he'd been embarrassed. He never did fully explain why that was. And if he's embarrassed now, is it because he felt like he had to return my kiss? Or is it something else?

I continue to stare after the prince while I gather my composure. Once my breathing has managed to settle, I force a neutral expression and turn to face my stepsisters. That's when I see Imogen's stony glare. I purse my lips to keep my smug grin at a minimum.

Kissing the prince's cheek may have been stupid. It may have been brash. But if it puts Imogen back in her place, then I'll deem the kiss had been worth it.

*That's what made it worth it?* the wild side of me taunts. *Not the kiss he delivered in exchange? Not the way my mouth still tingles or how my hand buzzes where his lips were? How my stomach flipped and my heart fluttered like a swarm of butterflies?*

*No*, I think back to the voice. *Of course no*t.

Of. Course. Not.

Lifting my chin, I brush past my stepsisters and march into my room with my head held high.

*FRANCO*

As soon as I turn the corner away from Em's room, I stop and lean against the wall. Thank the All of All there's no one else in the hall right now, otherwise someone would see me like this. Catching my breath. Acting like a fool.

I bring my hand to my cheek, brushing the place that's still warm from her lips. My entire being seized up in that moment when she kissed me, sending a ripple of surprise so bright I thought it would knock me off my feet. Warmth unfurled inside me, like how it did when I heard her hummed tune. It spread down my arms and legs, heightening my internal sensations. The light seemed to grow brighter. Sounds became louder.

It's been like this all week, ever since the night of the opera.

Where normally my own feelings are dulled compared to what I sense from others, this week they've become so strong, it's hard for me to sense anyone else's energy. Or, more accurately, Em's energy. Because this has only been happening around her. When she smiles. When she teases. When her lips touch my cheek...

For the love of the night, what's wrong with me?

I thought avoiding her would help me get my mind straight, sort out how to act around her. But every time I saw her this week, I found myself acting stupid and awkward, just like when I was young. Before I learned to keep others at a distance with charm and humor. Keep them from seeing the real me. From worrying about me. From pitying me.

Then today, when we talked, something shifted again. I managed to break through my own awkwardness and told her things I've never told a lover, much less someone I'm only pretending to court. Only those I'm closest to know what happened during that first human social season. Very few know the truth about my reputation. And yet, I told her all about it and she neither judged nor pitied me. I thought it was pity at first, but it was more like...empathy I tasted from her. When she shared her insights about me, gave me a taste of how the humans see my current actions...it was startling. Humbling. Refreshing.

She shared things about herself too, placing new threads in the tapestry that is her mysterious identity. The more I learn about her, the more I see of her. Not with my eyes, but with my senses. That blend of citrus, rose, and wind that makes up her deepest energetic signature, the one I first glimpsed when she hummed. There's so much more about her that I don't know, but she's beginning to become clear in a way I never expected.

I push off from the wall and rub my cheek again, recalling the moment she stood on her toes to reach me. For the briefest moment, I thought...well, I don't know what I thought, but I thought wrong.

*What was that for?*

*For our audience.*

It's exactly what I asked her to do. Pretend with me.

I relive the stiff response I gave to her hand. That part had been forced, something I figured was the proper reaction our audience would expect. But as my lips brushed her skin, all I wanted to do was linger a little longer, hold her fingertips a little firmer, maybe pull her a little closer...

That hadn't felt much like pretend at all.

# 33

**EMBER**

I can't help but notice the way Imogen continues to watch me for the rest of the day. Even when she's embroiled in gossip with Clara, her eyes continue to flash toward me. Assessing. Calculating. The kiss was meant to disarm her, but I'm starting to wonder if I haven't given her fuel against me instead. The thought sends a storm wind through my veins. She can try to steal Franco's attention. After our conversation at the lake, I'm even more convinced he'd never fall for her schemes.

Day turns to evening, and I send my stepsisters to collect my dinner trays. They move toward the door to do my bidding, but Imogen stops before she reaches it. Turning to face me with a poorly veiled sneer, she says, "Odd how you always take dinner alone."

I cut a glance at her from across the room. "How is that odd?"

She gives an innocent shrug. "It's just strange that the prince never invites you to dine with him."

"His Highness never invites anyone to dine with him." I'm only assuming that's true. I can't imagine him hosting lavish dinner parties when it was such a feat to get him to talk with one or two strangers at a time.

"Surely, he'd make an exception for you."

"Surely, he would," I say sweetly.

Imogen watches me with narrowed eyes while Clara looks anxiously from her sister to me. "Shall we fetch the princess' dinner?" Clara asks in a small voice.

"You go, Clara," Imogen says without looking at her. "Might I have Her Highness' permission to speak privately?"

My muscles tense. I have no desire to be alone with Imogen, especially when she's in such a mood as she's in now, but I have a feeling whatever she has to say will come out regardless. I know how persistent she can be. The sooner I shut down whatever she's concocting, the better. My voice comes out calm and collected in what I've deemed my *princess tone*. "Very well. Clara, you may fetch my dinner. Thank you."

"Yes, Your Highness." With a curtsy, Clara leaves.

I stand as tall as I can while Imogen takes a few slow steps toward me. "What did you want to speak to me privately about?"

She stops several feet away, a smug grin on her lips. Then she reaches into the pocket of her skirt and pulls out something small and glittering. A gold chain. At the end of the chain is a locket, one that houses my parents' portraits. One Imogen has seen me wear every day that I've known her.

"Where did you get this, Your Highness?"

The way she says *Your Highness* is like an iron-laced taunt.

She knows.

She *knows*.

No. She hasn't said that yet.

Breezes. What would Maisie do?

I do my best to steady my breathing and hide the terror

rising inside me, molding it into feigned indignation instead. "My treasure!" I shout and try to swipe the necklace from her.

Imogen dances out of reach, her smirk disappearing. "It isn't yours," she says. "Where did you find it?"

I release an exaggerated gasp. "I'll ask you the same thing, Miss Coleman. Where did you find my treasure? And how dare you steal it from me!"

Uncertainty flashes over Imogen's face. "I...I didn't steal it, for it doesn't belong to you. It belongs to my stepsister, Ember Montgomery." She regains some of her composure. "Why do you have it? Do you know where my stepsister is?"

"Since when do you have a stepsister? You've not spoken of her." It's true. In all the time Imogen and Clara have been in my service, I've only heard them mention me the one time when I was out on the balcony, and I'm determined to maintain the ruse that I hadn't heard them then.

"That doesn't matter," Imogen says. "My stepsister is missing and you have her locket. I want to know why and where she is."

I curl my fingers to keep my hands from trembling. My head spins, making me feel as if I could lose my footing at any moment. But I can't give in. I can't let her see how shaken I am. I need to be strong. I need to be a princess right now.

Franco suddenly comes to mind, and I recall how terrifying he was when he confronted the young brigands, how he spoke so confidently to the man with the gun. I may not know how to conjure a glamour nor have magic shadows that strike fear into the hearts of my enemies, but it isn't just magic Franco uses to disarm people.

Lifting my chin, I work my features into a mask of cold arrogance. My words come out high and haughty. "You're in no place to make demands of me, human. You serve *me*. And you continue to serve me by my grace alone. If I were you, I'd watch my tone."

Imogen pales, her shoulders rising toward her neck. I can almost see the confidence draining from her. "Your Highness," she says, a slight quaver to her voice, "I simply wondered where you found my stepsister's locket. We're looking for her—"

I step forward and snatch the necklace from her fingers, then breeze past her to my dressing table. There I open one of the many hat boxes Maisie left full of seashells and other miscellaneous items. I drop the locket into the box with the tarnished silverware. With my back facing her, I say, "I found the locket the same way I find all my treasures. And like the others, the locket is now mine."

Imogen comes up behind me. "It belongs to my stepsister, Your Highness. I should have it."

I whirl to face her. "If you truly have a stepsister and she's truly lost her locket, then she can come claim it from me."

Her face turns crimson, her jaw shifting side to side. Then she goes still, and her eyes begin to narrow. "You know," she says slowly, "your eyes are the exact same color as my stepsister's."

"You know," I echo, taking a step closer. I have to crane my neck to meet her eyes. "You have the exact countenance of someone who's about to lose her position at court."

Her chest heaves, her defiant gaze locked on mine. I refuse to so much as blink as I keep my focus trained on maintaining my posture. Finally, her eyes shutter and uncertainty fills her expression. She takes a step back and bows her head. "Forgive me, Your Highness. I've been distraught over my missing stepsister, that's all. I thought you could help me locate her."

Lies. I grit my teeth and sweetly say, "I'm sorry I can't help you with that."

She nods, then heads for the door. "If you'll allow it, I'll find Clara and help her with your dinner."

"Very well."

She makes her way to the door, pausing with her fingers on

the handle. Whipping around, she says, "Fall to your knees now. That's a direct order from Mrs. Coleman."

Pain surges through me, scorching my insides. It doubles, triples, made worse by my refusal to bend. To move. To react.

Imogen's eyes widen. "I relay Mrs. Coleman's orders to you. Obey."

Another surge of pain, lashing my insides like molten blades. With a deep, steadying breath, I take one step. Then another. Another. My head feels like it will explode as my vision blurs at the edges. I keep my expression steady, my movements controlled. Imogen's shoulders slump, her face paling with every step I take toward her.

"Forgive me, Your Highness," she says. "It was just a test."

I stop before her. "I don't know what you're playing at, human, but I've had enough. You are relieved from your position. Your sister may remain in my service, but I never want to see your face again."

For the first time, my stepsister looks truly terrified. "Forgive me—"

"No. Get out."

She turns the handle and flees from my room. I slam it shut behind her and run for my washroom. Gripping my stomach with one hand, I lock the door with the other and sink to the floor. Agony pulls me down. Down. Burning. Choking. Slicing.

Tears stream down my cheeks as I curl up on the cool floor. *I'm obeying, I'm obeying,* I repeat to myself, rocking side to side. *Imogen doesn't speak for my stepmother. Her words were false. There's nothing to obey. Nothing to punish me for.*

The pain begins to lessen, but even when it fades back into the subtle ache I'm used to, I'm still unable to move. A while later, Clara knocks on the washroom door announcing she's returned with my dinner. I dismiss her for the night. There's no way I can face her. Not when I'm this broken and out of sorts.

I remain on the washroom floor, sobbing until my tears cease to flow.

# 34

**FRANCO**

In raven form, I fly over the palace grounds, feeling the cool night breeze ripple over my feathers. This is exactly what I needed after the day I've had. First was the lake, then my game of questions with Em. Then the kiss.

*The kiss.*

A nothing of a kiss.

I shake the memory from my mind. No thoughts, just flight. That's what I need, especially after spending the last several hours in talks about the upcoming ball. Normally, I would leave such plans to Augie or Nyxia's advisors, who would then hand it all off to the palace stewards and master of ceremonies. That's what I did with the New Moon Masquerade. Nyxia allowed me to organize it, which meant I put very little effort into it at all. This time, though, I think it should be different. Nothing radical, just...a slight shift.

I circle the lawn a few times. All around the palace, the nocturnal fae come to life. Wisps bob over Lake Artemisa, kitsune chase each other, nipping at the flames that hover over

## Heart of the Raven Prince

their tails, banshees wail in the distance, and the silhouette of a moon dragon flits over the mountain range to the north.

My instincts call me to the forest, where sounds and smells beckon me forth. I'm about to follow them when something else snags my attention. It isn't an instinctual pull, but something else. Something that tugs my seelie side.

I fly toward it, following it to the side of the palace. The closer I go, the more familiar the sensation becomes. It's energy. And I know exactly who it belongs to. A figure stands in the shadow of her balcony, cloaked in a mixture of grief, anxiety, and fatigue. I land on her balustrade, but she doesn't startle when she sees me.

Em turns toward me with a sad smile. "Is that you, Franco?"

With a shudder, I shift out of my raven form and into my seelie body. Leaning against the balustrade, I wink. "Hey there. Why are you still awake?"

"I couldn't sleep. You?"

"I'm partial to being nocturnal. Although, I must say, our recent daytime activities have thrown off my sleep schedule."

She gives a half-hearted chuckle but doesn't meet my eyes. Her gaze remains unfocused as she faces the railing, resting her forearms upon it. She's dressed in a silk floral-patterned robe over an ivory lace nightdress. Her elegant glamoured shoes peek out from beneath the hem.

I furrow my brow. "What's wrong?"

She shakes her head. "I'm just tired."

"But you can't sleep."

"No."

I don't think I've ever seen her so despondent. She's been hesitant, wary, and enraged, but never so downtrodden as she seems now. "You can tell me if something happened."

Finally, she meets my eyes. "I had to dismiss one of my maids from service, that's all."

"Is there anything you would like me to do?"

"No."

I slouch to the side, crossing my arms as I lean toward her with a sly grin. "Are you sure? I'm terribly effective at punishing one's enemies."

Another feeble laugh. "No, it's fine. Please don't make a big deal out of it. I've dealt with it on my own."

"All right," I say, sensing that she truly wishes me not to pry. My voice takes on a more serious tone. "Do you want me to leave?"

"No," she says as she faces me fully. "You don't have to go."

Despite the smile she now wears, I can taste the murky energy that lingers around her. Something happened today, and for once, I don't think it was because of me. I know she doesn't want to talk about it, but...

"Do you want to come to my room?"

"Your room?" she echoes, wrapping her robe tighter around her as if she only now realizes her state of undress. "In the middle of the night and in my nightgown?"

"Yes."

She scoffs. "For someone trying to improve his reputation, you sure have some scandalous notions."

I infuse my tone with a hint of playfulness. "Come on. We've very few human guests staying at the palace who would even care. Besides, I too have a balcony. I'll fly you straight there and no one will ever be the wiser. Plus, I have exactly what you need to make it worth your while."

She raises a brow. "Is that so?"

I inch closer, lowering my voice. "I just so happen to be in possession of a marvelous instrument you can play."

"An instrument?"

"Yes. It's massive. Gargantuan, even. With one look, you'll be begging me to let you put your hands all over it."

Her expression hardens into a glower, and I sense annoyance rippling off her.

"I'm being completely serious," I say with a laugh.

"About..."

"About my big, smooth—"

"Franco," she says through her teeth.

"—pianoforte."

Her mouth falls open, her expression flitting between excitement and suspicion. "Is this still innuendo?"

"See for yourself." When she says nothing, I bellow a laugh. "I promise, I'm telling the truth. I have a piano in my quarters. No other bedrooms are near, so you can play as loud and as long as you want. Will you come?"

Her lips flicker and then draw into a beautiful smile. "Yes."

### EMBER

Just as Franco said, he takes me straight from my balcony to his, one that spans three times the length of my own. At the center stands an enormous set of moonstone doors. After we land, he banishes the wings he'd conjured for the flight and strolls to the doors. I follow behind him, feeling my pulse quicken with every step I take. I've never been alone with a man in his bedroom. The few dalliances I've had happened backstage on neutral ground, not in a man's most intimate quarters...

Wait, this is *not* a dalliance.

Why would my mind go there?

I'm here for the piano. The *piano*. That's all. That's why Franco brought me here. Despite his momentary teasing, which he clearly delighted in, I know his intention is to cheer me up. It isn't a surprise I was unable to hide my mood from him. After what happened with Imogen, I can hardly summon the energy to pretend I'm all right. At least he didn't ask me to explain.

He opens the doors and gestures for me to come inside.

With slow, hesitant steps I cross the threshold and glance at the prince's room.

*Room* is an understatement, for it's more of an apartment, much like Brother Marus'. Franco's, of course, is twice as large and infinitely more elegant. The main room we stand in is large and lush, with walls of moonstone that end in an enormous glass dome, like the one in the ballroom. I can see stars sparkling above, as well as a hint of the waxing moon. Lowering my gaze, I return my study to the room, finding a sitting area at one end, a dining area at the other, and another set of enormous doors left open to reveal what is clearly Franco's bedroom. I don't let my gaze linger there for long, but when I fail to see any sign of his promised pianoforte, my eyes can't help but return.

Hands in his pockets, Franco heads straight for those open doors. "Right this way."

"To your bedroom?" I say, although my feet are already hurrying to follow.

"That's where you'll find what you're looking for."

I glower at the back of his head, but my heart is too full of excitement. It's as if I can feel the piano keys calling my name.

Franco pauses at the threshold and gestures for me to enter. I come up beside him—and freeze. If I thought the main room was elegant, then there are no words to describe his bedroom. The floor is of fiery opal while the walls are pink moonstone. His furniture is jet and obsidian, his bed framed with a sheer white canopy. The blankets are indigo silk and velvet threaded with silver floral patterns, and the pillows are plush and enormous. My heart leaps into my throat when I realize how long I've been staring at his bed. I avert my gaze to the other side of the room. That's when I find the most marvelous sight of all.

Upon a small, raised dais stands a collection of beautiful

instruments. There's an enormous white harp, a violin, and —*yes*—a pianoforte.

His teasing about his gargantuan instrument no longer seems quite so crude, for what I find at the center of the dais is the largest and most lovely piano I've ever seen. It's of a pale, shimmering wood inlaid with opal and obsidian, adorned in gold filigree.

"Go ahead," he says with a light laugh, as if he can feel my desire.

That's all the permission I need, and in a matter of seconds, I'm on the bench, running my bare fingertips over the surface of the fallboard.

"What did I tell you?" He stands next to the piano, his hands still in his pockets. "My big smooth instrument."

I look up at him with the biggest smile I think I've ever worn. "Why do you have these in your room? Do you host musicians often?" Strangely, a flash of envy heats my cheeks at those words, and all I can imagine is a trio of gorgeous fae females sprawled upon the dais, performing some sultry tune for the prince.

He shrugs. "They were a gift from when I was younger. After my..." He shifts his stance and clears his throat before continuing. "After my mother went away, music was one of the few things that could console me."

I've never heard him speak of his mother, but I can tell by that brief hesitation that there's a story there. I wonder if by *went away* he means she died. Like my mother. "And now?" I ask. "Who plays them?"

He grins. "You do. I rarely let people into my room, so they've gone unused far longer than they deserve. Since I haven't any musical talent, all I can do is cherish them. I'll pluck a string now and then or touch a key, just so they know I appreciate them."

A warm feeling spreads through my chest. He talks about

instruments the same way I do. As if they're sentient beings that deserve attention. Respect.

I lift the fallboard. Underneath it, I find the familiar ivory and ebony keys. Like always, I brush my fingertips over the surface, familiarizing myself with the feel of them. Franco stands quietly next to the piano, so still it's as if he's frozen. I place my fingertips over a chord, then change my mind and choose a different one. I press down, and the resulting sound hums deep in my bones. Every worry flees from me at once, every ache drowned beneath the vibration of sound.

Then I play.

## 35

**EMBER**

I play an intuitive tune, a conversation between me and the prince's piano as I learn the voice of each key, the resistance between pressure and sound. My fingers dance up and down the keyboard until I settle into a comfortable rhythm.

"You play beautifully," Franco says. I meet his gaze and find his expression soft and open. "What's the song called?"

"I don't know," I say. "I'm simply playing what I feel right now."

"Is that how you always play?"

"When I'm without sheet music. I love playing existing songs, but I also like to just...play."

"Where did you learn to do that?"

I open my mouth but hesitate before I answer. "I took lessons," I say. The full truth is, while I received ample lessons as a child, the connection I formed with music is my own. With my mother being a wind fae, the air element moves through my veins. One of the manifestations of air is creative expression, especially through voice, speech, and sound. Playing the piano came as naturally to me as climbing did.

But singing came even more naturally...

My song quickens in tempo while my fingers dance toward the bass notes. It takes a few moments for me to regain my composure and return to my previous tune. I don't dare look at Franco to see if he noticed my momentary shift.

"Want to play question for question again?" he asks.

"All right."

He faces me, propping an arm on the side of the piano. "You said your mother died in the rebellion. What was your childhood like before that? When she was alive?"

My pulse quickens at such a personal question, but my heart aches at the thought of my mother. It begs me to speak of her. Honor her. My tune changes into a slow but steady melody, one equally solemn and joyful. "It was wonderful," I say. "During my childhood, we lived on a human estate in the countryside without much fae interaction. Mother was my connection to magic. To my fae side. She taught me ways to experience my wild nature."

The notes I play tell of climbing trees, scaling the roof to study the stars, learning songs on our piano so I could watch her and Father dance. They tell of windstorms and gentle breezes, of bedtime stories and endless smiles.

He breathes in deeply, and I wonder if he's sensing my energy.

"My turn," I say. "What was yours like? Your childhood, that is?"

He pushes off from the piano and begins to take a slow stroll around it. When he reaches the other side, he pauses. His answer comes out soft. "Lonely."

I look up at him with a furrowed brow. My fingers follow the tone of his voice, translating the shift in his expression. "Why was it lonely?"

He continues walking again, starting another circle around the piano. "I didn't make friends easily. When I was younger, I had very little control over my magic. Before I learned to consciously wield my powers, I would drain people of their energy when I fed. They recovered, but you can imagine this left me little in the way of friends."

I nod, playing a backdrop to his every word. I can almost see the small version of the prince, shadows casting all around him, friends screaming as he unwittingly bled their emotions dry.

"After Mother left, it was just me and Nyxia. She's been my best friend ever since."

"Your mother left?" I ask gently. I know it isn't my turn to ask, but I'm hoping he'll answer anyway.

He does. "Once my sister demonstrated her power, my mother was ready for Nyxia to challenge her for the crown. After dealing with the first war with the humans, Mother was more than eager to leave politics behind. She knew my sister would make a perfect queen, so she left as soon as Nyxia assumed the throne. She took her unseelie form indefinitely and never came back."

His tone says more than his words do. My fingers play a low, hollow tune that speaks of a boy being abandoned by someone he so deeply loved.

"My emotions were dark after Mother left," he says with a small, bitter smile. "My shadows were out of control, flooding the halls in darkness while I cried and grieved. No matter how Nyxia tried to hide it, she was unsettled by me, disgusted by my demonstration of sadness. She didn't mean to make me feel bad, but...I felt so guilty for displeasing her. For scaring our residents with my fits of emotion. Day after day, our servants constantly asked if I was feeling better, tried to tell me I had nothing to be upset about. That's when they got me these instruments and brought in musicians to soothe me to sleep. I appreciated their efforts, enjoyed the music, but the pity and disgust were horrible to bear. All I wanted was to be alone and grieve, and everyone else just wanted me back to normal."

A lump rises in my throat at his story. "Franco, you never should have been made to feel like your grief was wrong."

"We're unseelie," he says with a shrug. He finishes another circle around the pianoforte and leans on the side again. "We may take seelie physical form, but we honor the Old Ways. We value our instincts. At least, that's what my sister always said. Sometimes I'm not so sure she feels the same way she once did. She's changed the last few years. I wonder if that's why she's more desperate than ever to cling to our throne, ensure it stays in our bloodline. Maybe she knows we're vulnerable, simply because we've learned to feel too much."

I don't know what he means by that, but I continue to play a song that demonstrates the look in his eyes.

He shakes his head as if to clear it. "Anyhow, it wasn't long before I figured out how to keep all the questioning glances and pity at bay. Instead of wailing and rebelling, I started acting like everything was fine, used humor and flattery to set others at ease. Finally, I was left alone. I was able to feel my sorrow in private when no one was looking."

I can't take my eyes off him as I continue to play. So much about him makes sense now. I already knew he tended to divert attention away from serious subjects using crass comments or lighthearted humor. Now I know why.

"My turn," he says. "Is your father still alive?"

My hands go still, ringing out a dissonant chord. My stomach sinks, my mouth suddenly dry. I bring my fingers to the base of my neck, seeking the locket that isn't there.

He takes a step closer, eyes full of concern. "I'm sorry, Em. You don't have to answer that."

My chest heaves as my eyes rest on the hand that remains

on the keyboard, my fingers clenched over the keys. I don't have to answer. I know I don't.

"It's all right," Franco says softly.

With a few deep breaths, I uncurl my fingers and lay them back over the keys. I lower the hand from my throat and rest my fingertips over a chord. When I return to playing, the song is dark. Deep. Ominous.

"My father is dead," I whisper.

He stands perfectly still, saying nothing in reply. His silence tells me my answer is enough, should I want it to be. He won't push me. Won't coax me. He won't ask me to share the same sincerity he shared with me.

Maybe that's why I do.

"I used to sing," I say. For a moment my song goes higher, lighter, a joyful rhythm like the one I played when I spoke of my mother. "Our dinner guests and visitors would beg me to sing for them. The older I got, the more apparent it was that my song held power. It was an amplifier, Mother explained. When people listened, they felt pleasure. The more I sang, the more their pleasure increased. The more at peace they felt. The more calm and beauty and joy they experienced in that moment. It was a gift. Or so we thought."

My song returns to its deep and haunting melody, the rhythm growing chaotic and uneven. "After Mother died, I continued to sing. Father said using my inherited power honored her. I clung to that magic, let it carry me through the toughest times, especially after he remarried."

My song dips lower again, louder. Tears prick my eyes.

"The last time I sang, I killed my father." A tear streams down my cheek. "It was after a dinner party, and we were all taking tea in the parlor. Upon request, I played. I sang. I remember looking at him, meeting his eyes over his teacup. They sparkled with pride, and I felt my own pride swell up inside me. I was bursting with gratitude that even though my mother was gone, I could still bring him this piece of her. Still bring him such joy. I averted my gaze for just a moment."

Two sharp chords.

"Then I heard the clatter of tableware."

Three sharp chords.

"I leapt from the piano and rushed to his side. He was clutching his heart, the tears I'd sparked still fresh in his eyes. He died before the doctor arrived."

My chest heaves as my hands go still. I can no longer see through the sheen of moisture filling my eyes. My cheeks tingle where streams roll down before splashing onto the keys.

A weight shifts on the bench, and I hear Franco's voice come from nearby, so soft and strained. "Your song didn't kill him."

"It did, though," I say, words rich with emotion. "He'd had heart problems before this. Making him feel that much emotion...it overwhelmed him. Killed him."

"Says who?"

The answer is my stepmother, but I've always known she was right. *You should have known better*, she told me time and time again after his death. *I tried to tell you not to sing. You wouldn't listen. You just had to show off like you always do.*

I hated when she would claim I played music to show off, but she was right about one thing. With my father's heart in such a fragile state, I never should have sung. "I killed him."

"You don't know that. You might never know what really happened, but you can't blame yourself. Your mother was right. Your song is a gift. It's beautiful."

I blink the tears from my eyes and face him. He's sitting on the bench next to me. Now that I can see him clearly, I realize he's so much closer than I expected. "I'm dangerous," I say. "Deadly."

He holds my gaze without waver. "So am I." His words are firm, but they aren't said in threat. It's something so much softer, so much stronger. Like understanding. Camaraderie. Conviction. It's that look that makes my mind go still, soothes my aching heart. I may not believe him about my innocence over my father's death, but he *sees* me in a way no one else has.

Something soft brushes the side of my hand. I look down at the bench to find our hands resting side by side, our pinkies touching. When I lift my eyes, I notice his gaze has fallen to our hands as well. I hold my breath, waiting for him to pull away, but he doesn't. Seconds tick by, and still, he doesn't move. Then, finally, his pinky twitches and wraps around mine. When his eyes return to mine, there's a question in them, as if he's the one waiting for me to pull away this time.

I don't. For some strange reason, the feel of his pinky entwined with mine seems far more significant than the few times he's held my hand. There are no gloves that stand between us. No one to put on a show for.

His shoulder comes against mine, filling me with a steadying warmth. Inch by near-imperceptible inch, he leans closer. His lips are so close I can feel the soft caress of his breath as it mingles with my own.

My heart hammers against my ribs as I realize with a burning certainty that he's going to kiss me. Heat unfurls low in my abdomen, and everything inside me begs him to close that distance. This close I can see every shade of silver in his eyes and the long black lashes that frame them. Across his nose, I see the palest smattering of freckles, and I wonder if he can see mine too...

My breath catches, my blood going cold.

For the love of the breeze, there is no *mine*. I'm glamoured! He only wants to kiss me because I'm wearing the wrong face.

"I should go." I pull away and rise to my feet, not bothering to glance his way as I dart for his bedroom doors.

"Wait," he calls after me, voice flustered, "don't you want me to fly you to your balcony?"

"No," I say. Breezes, if I find myself pressed against his chest right now, I can't promise I won't do something wildly stupid. I reach the main room, looking about to gather my bearings. I spot the open doors that lead to his balcony, then another pair at the other end of the room.

Franco catches up to me. "Are you all right?"

"I just want to walk," I say. Then, remembering everything he told me tonight, the kindness and sincerity he gifted me with, I let my lips pull into a warm smile. "Really, I'm all right. And I'm so grateful that you let me play tonight."

He returns my grin, but it doesn't meet his eyes. "Can I walk you back to your room?"

Quiet corridors fill my mind. Dark alcoves. Him close to me. Our hands brushing as we walk. Him whirling to press me against a wall, his lips coming hard on mine...

I suppress a shudder and blink the imaginings from my mind. My voice comes out breathless. "No, I'll find my way. Again, thank you. Tonight has been...wonderful." So wonderful. Too wonderful. More than it should have been.

"I enjoyed it too," he says, tone wary. He rubs the back of his neck then springs toward the doors to open them for me.

On swift feet, I cross the threshold. Once out in the hall, I turn back to face him, but I haven't a clue what to say. He seems equally tongue-tied, something that draws my eyes to his lips. I blink a few times and sink into an awkward curtsy. "Goodnight." I rise without looking at him, then flee from his room, his echoing *goodnight* caressing my heels with every step.

## 36

**EMBER**

Three days later, I stand on my balcony, staring out at the landscape but not really seeing it. Instead, I'm replaying the moment Franco and I shared on the piano bench. Every time I think about it, my body gets flushed, and a buzzing heat tingles in my core. I haven't seen the prince since that night, which is equal parts disappointing and relieving. Half the time, I can't help but regret that I ran from him like that. Maybe I should have let him kiss me. Maybe I should have let myself enjoy physical closeness for pleasure's sake alone.

Then I remind myself that's all it could be. Pleasure. There can be no future for such a romantic entanglement. For one, Franco doesn't know who I am or what I look like. If he wanted to kiss me, it wouldn't be because he liked me but felt simple desire in that moment. It's not like he has feelings for me, nor could he. For another, he's a prince. I'm...nobody. I'm not a princess. I'm not someone a royal can take as a wife.

Besides, if he wanted a wife, he wouldn't be pretending to court me.

Me.

Someone he can't marry.

Someone he can't love.

Furthermore, in just a few more days, I'll be gone. I'll be on a train heading for freedom and a life of no attachments. So why do I keep thinking about that moment with Franco?

I shake my head. Foolish, foolish girl. This is exactly what I never wanted to happen! I've completely and utterly fallen for his charm. Who cares that his charms are apparently deeper than I ever knew. I still should never have let myself get so close to him.

Close enough to see his freckles.

Close enough to feel his breath.

"Your Highness," Clara says from the balcony door. I turn to face her. She shifts awkwardly from foot to foot as she wrings her hands. Ever since I dismissed Imogen, Clara has been particularly subdued. Uncertain. Best of all, she's been quiet, filling my room with comforting silence. For the first couple days following the incident with Imogen, I waited with bated breath for my stepmother or Brother Marus to arrive and further test out my stepsister's suspicions. But no one has come, and Clara has said nothing to suggest Imogen shared what happened between us with anyone else. From what sparse details Clara has given me, Imogen claimed to have lost her position by unintentionally displeasing me. Of course my stepsister would refuse to take responsibility for losing her position. Then again, it's better than if she told the truth and spread her suspicions far and wide.

*Four more days and I can leave. Thank the breeze.*

I ignore the way my heart sinks at that and don a contrived smile for my stepsister. "What is it?"

She shifts from foot to foot again. "It's just...I was wondering if there's anything else I can do for you?"

I wave a dismissive hand at her and turn back toward the balustrade. "No, thank you."

"Yes, Your Highness," she whispers, but I hear no footsteps to mark her retreat.

I turn back around to face her. Dread sinks my stomach. "What is it *really*?"

She keeps her gaze lowered to the ground, and her words come out tenuous. "It's...well, I know I shouldn't ask. If Imogen was here, she would kick me for what I'm about to say. And she always knows best, so I shouldn't—"

"Your sister does not know best," I say, keeping my voice gentle while maintaining my firm princess persona, "which is why she's gone and you're still in my employ. Just say what it is you want to say."

She takes a deep breath. "Could you find me a husband?" She wrings her hands and glances up at me before adding, "Your Highness."

I furrow my brow. "You want me to find you a husband?"

"I thought that if...if I serve you well, you might reward me with an admirable match. I'll do anything to please you. Just tell me what I can do."

I've never seen Clara so out of sorts. Never seen her beg or plead. She's always been whiny and entitled, always following in Imogen's footsteps, always doing everything Mrs. Coleman says.

Part of me wants to laugh in her face, but it's a very small part. There's another part that urges me to take a step closer. "What's wrong, Miss Coleman?"

Her lower lip trembles. "I'm scared, Your Highness, that I'll never find a husband."

"You have your whole life to find a husband."

She shakes her head. "No, I don't. I...I want to tell you a secret."

"I'll listen," I say, keeping my voice level.

Her eyes flit from me to the floor. "My family is poor. In a matter of weeks, we'll be destitute. Right now, we're living on the generosity of a good man, but I'm afraid that if things don't work out the way he expects, he won't help us the way he promised."

I resist the urge to nibble my lip. It isn't hard to understand what she's referring to. If I don't return to claim my inheritance and marry Brother Marus, he won't keep up his end of the arrangement. There will be no advantageous matches for my stepsisters, no positions at court, no rooms at the palace. They'll be poor, cast out of good society, and left to toil away in the slums.

I've always known that would be the result once I turned nineteen and my stepmother was cut off from her allowance. Not once have I felt sorry. After my father died, my stepmother revealed her true colors. She refused to observe the proper period of mourning and moved us to a new court instead, reclaiming her maiden name to dissociate with me and my father. She spent his money without care, courted new lovers without respect for the man still cooling in his grave.

I may have been the one who killed him, but Mrs. Coleman murdered his memory.

Neither of us deserve my father's inheritance. Of that I'm certain.

And yet, I can't help the pang of sympathy I feel for Clara, something I've never felt for her before. She may have been a willing accomplice in every scheme, and she's never been kind to me. But...she isn't her mother. She isn't Imogen, either.

Then again...

I recall my stepsisters' conversation about using a glamour to steal my inheritance. Clara seemed more than willing to go along with that. In fact, she seemed like she wanted to do it herself.

"Surely, you have alternative means should your current plans fail. Every intelligent woman must have several ways to succeed in life."

She wrings her hands again. "There was another plan, and I think my family still wants to do it, but the more I think about it, the less I like it. When I'm alone, that is. When I'm with my mother and sister, I think their ideas are brilliant. But mostly, like right now, I just want to find my own way."

"By asking me to pair you with a husband?"

Her eyes meet mine, wide and full of pleading. "It's the only way I'll be safe from ruin. He doesn't have to be wealthy or handsome, and I expect he won't be, since I may not have a dowry. He only has to save me from poverty."

"Is that what you want? Marriage to a stranger?"

"That's all any young human woman can strive for. There's nothing else I can do."

It takes all my effort not to scoff. "There are plenty of things you can do, Miss Coleman. You can gain employment, go to university—"

"How can I be employed if I have nowhere to live?" Her voice takes on a note of hysteria. "How can I even fantasize about attending university if I haven't a moonstone chip to my name?"

I purse my lips. She has a point. One I never cared to consider before. Why do I even care now? My stepfamily deserves whatever punishment they get.

And yet, if one of them is the least bit guilty, it's Clara. Clara, who's never schemed on her own, only relished the schemes of her mother and sister. Clara, who's lamented over the loss of friends whenever we've moved to a new court.

"Come, Miss Coleman." I gesture for her to follow me into the bedroom and join me at the table. Lowering into the seat with contrived grace, I say, "Sit. Tell me what you would do if you could do anything."

She takes the opposite seat at the table and places her hands in her lap. "I would marry a kind man who could provide for me." Her answer is stiff, devoid of feeling despite the smile she wears.

I raise a brow. "That's all? If you could have, do, or be anything *ever*, that's all you'd want? Just a kind husband? No friends, no hobbies, no aspirations?"

She bites her lip and rubs her palms over her lap.

"It's all right," I say. "You can tell me."

"Well," she says, drawing the word out slowly, "it isn't something I could ever do, but sometimes I think I might like to attend university like you said. I would go to Maven University in the Fire Court, perhaps stay with my Aunt Marie while I study. I would make new friends, attend university balls." Her eyes take on a dreamy quality.

"What would you study?"

She shrugs. "I've never let myself consider it. It isn't something that can happen."

"Why?"

Her expression falls. "Aside from being poor, Mother would never allow it. She wants to see me wed. She wants me paired with a wealthy man so I can bring wealth and prestige to the family. I, of course, have given up all notions of wealth. I just want to be…not starving."

I think about the hungry children who attacked the prince's coach, the desperate man who threatened us with a gun. Could that be the fate I'm condemning my stepfamily to? The wild fae side of me feels no shame, but my human side looks at Clara with a pinch of remorse.

After everything Imogen and Mrs. Coleman have done—and not just to me, but to others—I hold no hopes for their redemption. But Clara…what if there's hope for her to change?

What if she could become a better person with the right opportunities?

My mind whirls to comprehend how I could make that possible. I'm already determined not to risk claiming my inheritance, but after it's all done, after I'm long gone and far from my stepfamily's reach, maybe I could write to Franco...

*Franco.*

My heart squeezes.

"Besides," Clara says, shifting awkwardly in her seat, "Imogen has assured me I have no admirable talents or qualities worth pursuing, which is why I must put all my focus into marriage, not silly dreams. Do you think you could find me a husband, Your Highness?"

I give her a gracious nod. "I'll do what I can for you."

Clara's answering smile is wide but uneven, her chin quivering beneath it. Then her expression crumples. "Thank you, Your Highness. You don't know how much that means to me. I don't care what Imogen says. You are the most lovely and beautiful person and I hope you and the prince are happy forever." Her last word dissolves into a wail as she sobs into her hands.

I'm frozen in my seat, blinking at her. I've never seen Clara cry without it being paired with a tantrum. Perhaps being away from Imogen all day is truly doing her some good.

A knock sounds at the door, and Clara slowly rises to her feet. Wiping the tears from her face, she gives me a ruddy-cheeked smile. "I'll get it."

She scurries over to the door and sinks into a curtsy when she opens it. "Your Highness."

I nearly trip over my feet as I stand, knowing at once who's on the other side of the threshold. Clara opens the door wide, allowing Franco to enter.

My lungs grow tight, my breaths shallow as I look at him for the first time since our almost-kiss. He smiles shyly at me, then turns to Clara. "May I have a moment alone with the lady?"

Her eyes go wide. "Unchaperoned? In her bedroom?"

"It's all right," I say.

Clara looks from me to the prince and back again. Then she gives me a wide grin, followed by an imitation of her zipping her lips shut. "As Her Highness wishes." She sinks into the deepest curtsy she's ever given me, then exits the room in a rush.

Alone with Franco, my hearts flutters against the cage of my ribs.

## 37

*FRANCO*

My breath catches as my eyes lock on Em's. All I can think is how close those teal eyes were the last time we were alone together, how I was able to study every hue swimming in her irises. Then, like an idiot, I leaned in to kiss her. Before that moment, I felt her desire as strong as my own. It was a rising, unfurling essence that had my heart pounding in rhythm with hers. One moment, she was leaning in to meet my lips, then the next she was three feet away.

I don't know what I did to frighten her, but I know I did something. Yet a fragment of that desire I sensed in her that day lingers there now. Or is it my own? Like always in her presence, my emotions are at an all-time high, making it an effort to single out her energetic signature.

"Hello," she says quietly, a quavering smile tugging her lips.

I open my mouth, but I don't know what to say. For the love of the night, should I not have come? I glance down at the gilded black box in my hands, wondering if I'm making a huge mistake.

She follows my line of vision and takes a few steps closer. "What's that?"

Before I can think better of it, I hand it to her. "It's nothing. Just something I got you. But don't feel obligated to wear it. You probably already have something planned for the ball. It's just...well, I went to Madame Flora's to get my own glamour and I saw this and thought you would like it. If not..."

What the iron-laced hell? Stop talking. Idiot. Stupid. Idiot.

Her brow furrows as she looks from me to the box. "Should I open it?"

I put my hands in my pockets and rock back on my heels. "If you want."

She goes over to her dressing table and sets the box upon it. Then, with slow, graceful moves, she lifts the cover and unfolds the tissue. I hold my breath as I watch her. Once all the layers of tissue are folded back, she pauses, staring down at the box's contents.

My heart leaps into my throat. "I shouldn't have selected something for you without knowing if you would even like it."

"It's beautiful," she says, her voice barely above a whisper. She reaches into the box and takes out the necklace I picked out for her. It's a dainty opal crescent moon flanked by thin cylinders of black tourmaline. They hang on a velvet ribbon with a silver clasp. Her eyes meet mine. "You got this for me?"

I shrug. "I noticed you sometimes touch the base of your throat, as if you used to have a necklace there. Maybe I'm completely wrong, but whatever the case, I thought you might want to wear it to the ball."

"You noticed that about me?" Her hand comes to her collarbone, the same way I've seen her do time and time again.

Heat warms my cheeks as I nod. "Plus, it's attached to a

glamour. Madame Flora assured me it will work over the glamour you already have."

"You didn't tell Madame Flora about my glamour—"

"No, of course not. I simply asked a few leading questions and confirmed whether the glamour would work for its intended purposes. She knows not why I needed it, nor for whom."

Her shoulders relax at that.

"Would you like to see it? The glamour? If you've already chosen a dress, it will work with it. It will simply change the color and pattern."

"Yes, I would love to see it," she says with a smile.

I extend my hand. "May I?"

After a moment's hesitation, she hands me the necklace and faces her mirror. I stand behind her. My hands tremble slightly as I lay the front of the necklace over the base of her collarbone, then close the clasp behind her neck. With her hair in its perpetual glamoured updo, there's no need to brush her hair out of the way, but I do it anyway. She shudders, making my hands go still. My eyes fall to the column of her slender neck and the skin that pebbles over it. Standing this close, it would take no effort at all for me to bend down and place my lips at the spot beneath her ear. What would she do if I did? Startle? Tilt her head? Bring her lips to mine? Heat dances in my core at the thought...

I clear my throat and my fingers begin to move again. Once the necklace is secure, my hands come to her shoulders, and I meet her eyes in the mirror. I can feel how deeply she's breathing as her shoulders rise and fall, rise and fall. Desire pulses between us, but I can't tell if it's coming from me or her. It feels more like a never-ending circuit, with her desire feeding mine and mine feeding hers. Growing. Building.

Shaking my head, I remove my hands from her shoulders and take a step back to assess the effect of the glamour. She does the same, studying her reflection in the mirror. I force myself to ignore the pink that tints her cheeks and drag my gaze to her skirt and blouse. They've been turned a deep shade of indigo patterned with constellations and different phases of the moon. The bottom hem, however, is where its most impressive design lies.

She stares down at it, trying to get a closer look. "Is that…"

"Sheet music," I say.

She lifts her skirt to bring the hem closer, not seeming to care that she's revealing her petticoats. Running her fingers over the three separate staves of music, she says, "What do they play?"

I swallow hard as I prepare my explanation. Will she hate it? Think it's stupid? "These are three songs from three dangerous fae."

"What songs?"

I take a step closer and point to the first staff. "Everyone is familiar with a banshee's haunting death wail, but hardly anyone talks about the melody they sing to welcome the births of their children. A song for new life."

I run my finger over the second.

"A siren's song is known to lure sea poachers to their deaths, but they also sing to guide wayward ships to safe harbors. A song for safety."

I move to the final staff of music.

"A harpy's tune can bring death to lovers they've been jilted by, but they also sing to woo their mates. A song for love."

I take a step back and study her expression as she stares at the lines of music. When she lifts her eyes, they're brimming with tears. "Did you…have this designed for me?"

"I chose the color and the songs I wanted Madame Flora to add. She did the rest."

"Why?"

I frown. "Why wouldn't I? I wanted you to have something to wear to Saturday's ball in case you didn't have anything—"

"No. Why did you choose these songs? Why did you add them to a glamour for me?" Her voice quavers as she speaks.

I take a deep breath to steady my racing pulse. "Maybe I can't convince you that you aren't dangerous, but I'm hoping I can at least show you what good company you're in. That your song truly is a gift, that you're talented and...beautiful."

I meant to say that her music is beautiful, but I make no move to correct myself. It stands true as spoken. When I sense the deepest core of her energetic signature, beauty is all I see. All I feel. I don't need to glimpse her true face to know she's completely and utterly breathtaking.

She brings a hand to her trembling lips, and it takes all my restraint not to gather her fingers in mine.

"Do you like it? You don't have to like it. You don't have to wear it or keep it or anything like that. If you—"

"I love it," she says. "I love it so much. No one has ever given me something like this before."

My stomach flips, a warm, melty feeling spreading over my chest. I desperately want to pull her close—but no. I already scared her away when I tried to kiss her. Stupid, stupid almost-kiss. "I'm glad you like it," I say.

Her lips part, and I hold my breath for whatever she's about to say. It takes all my control to keep my eyes from dropping to her mouth. Then, finally, she whispers, "Thank you."

"You're welcome," I rush to say and begin backing toward the door. It's time I take my leave before I can do something stupid like kiss her hand. Or her lips. Or neck. Stupid. Idiot. "I'll see you on Saturday."

## EMBER

Franco leaves before I can say anything more, and I'm stuck staring at the closed doors for minutes on end. With a sigh, I return to face the mirror. My breath catches as I glimpse the glamour again. Everything about it is beautiful. The color, the pattern. The necklace itself is a gorgeous piece of jewelry. But most stunning of all are the three lines of music that run along the bottom. Not only that, but the meaning behind them.

My eyes prick with tears as I recall the songs he described.

*A song for new life.*

*A song for safety.*

*A song for love.*

I bring my fingers to my throat where they land on the opal crescent moon. I almost wish the glamour could be hidden at will so I wouldn't have to take the necklace off. Reluctantly, I reach to remove it, but when my hand reaches the nape of my neck, I freeze, remembering how his fingers felt brushing my skin before he secured the clasp. I close my eyes and savor the memory, recalling how I shuddered, how my eyes fluttered as I forced myself not to lean into his touch. The moment quickly melds into the one on the piano bench, blending into a fantasy of what might have been had I only…

No. I can't be acting like this. I can't savor this thing between us when it lives mostly in my imagination. Franco is a prince. He's probably used to getting people gifts on a whim. It might not have meant to him what it means to me. And that's all right. I never thought this would go anywhere. Never wanted it to go anywhere.

In four days, I'll be on a train.

In four days, I'll never see Franco again.

I remove the necklace and return it to the box, stroking the velvet ribbon before covering it with the lid. Then I storm over to my chair where I pick up my unfinished needlework with a huff. Clara will be back soon, I'm sure, and I need to keep my hands busy to avoid thoughts better left alone. Yet, no matter how much I train my focus on every stitch, every thread, every pattern, a different pattern fills my mind. One forming three staves of music.

*A song for new life.*
*A song for safety.*
*A song for love.*

Yearning fills my bones. It's almost painful to admit how badly I want to hear those songs.

# 38

**FRANCO**

I stand outside the palace looking over the courtyard where the final touches for tonight's festivities are coming together. The sun is just beginning its descent behind the mountains, painting the sky in rosy hues. It's the evening of the Full Moon Frolic, and as soon as the sun fully sets, the grand event will commence. With every minute that ticks by, I grow increasingly anxious. Did I make the right changes? Am I doing the right thing?

"There's the look of someone who's desperately wishing he hadn't burned a certain glamour." Augie sidles up next to me and surveys the courtyard. "Are you sure you don't want me to take your place again?"

I give the ambassador a sideways grin and wipe my clammy palms over the front of my pants—which reminds me that I still need to get dressed. "I'm sure," I say with as much conviction as I can muster. "If this ends in disaster, I have no one to blame but myself."

Augie shrugs. "I think the changes you've made to the ball will be good ones."

"You really think so?"

"Sure. They've left more room for debauchery."

I chuckle, although that's not what tonight's about. It's about...something else. I can only hope my guests see things the way I intend.

He nods at the courtyard. "What made you decide to do things this way? Was the first ball really so boring?"

I furrow my brow, considering how to answer. My conversations with Em make me want to be more sincere, and the best place to start would be with my friends. Although I consider Augie a friend, we've never talked about anything serious outside of his ambassador duties. Even then, we usually find a way to make light of the subjects.

He snorts a laugh. "You don't need to tell me. It's your princess, isn't it? You're doing this for her?"

"No." The word comes out with a hint of defense. I might have decided to make changes to tonight's ball because of her, but I wouldn't say I'm doing it *for* her. I'm doing it for me. For my people. Slouching to the side, I put a hand on my hip. "She was simply my inspiration."

"I'm happy for you, Highness," he says, slapping me on the shoulder. "I haven't seen you this content with a potential lover for...years. Decades, maybe. Do you think she's the one?"

"The one?" I echo, a tingling warmth spreading over my chest.

"The princess you're going to choose as a mate and bride?"

A twinge of guilt sinks my stomach. Augie has no idea Em isn't the actual princess. "I'm quite fond of her," I say dismissively.

He rolls his eyes. "You're more than fond. That's obvious to anyone who's seen you around one another."

"Oh, and how many times have you seen us together? Once?"

He begins ticking off his fingers one at a time. "In the coach on the way to the opera. At the opera before Seri and I returned to the coach. Twice while you strolled about the palace grounds. And then at Lake Artemisa. What were you even talking about in the rowboat? I couldn't tell if you were about to kiss or yell."

A corner of my mouth flicks up at that. His assessment might not be too far off, although my desire to kiss her has only been a recent discovery for me. "I had no idea you were even there that day. Where were you? Thumping Seri in the bushes?"

"Don't try to change the subject. We're talking about you. You like Princess Maisie, it's as simple as that. There's no shame in it. Isn't that what your sister wanted?"

Another pang of guilt. *Not exactly.* "Of course it is."

"Then she's going to be so damn proud when she realizes you've found someone. And not just anyone. Someone you clearly like. Someone who is exactly what your sister wanted for you."

*Exactly what your sister wanted...*

My throat feels dry. What I'm doing with Em is the opposite of what Nyxia wants. Instead of courting a princess, I'm playing charades with a lady's maid.

My chest tightens.

No, she isn't just a lady's maid. She's so much more than that.

*So* much more.

And yet...she isn't a princess.

I shake the thoughts from my head. "Look at you, getting all sappy over romance."

"I'm in love, Franco. I'm going to ask Seri to be my mate tonight." He dons a grin so wide, I could count every one of his teeth if I tried. With a waggle of his brows, he adds, "You should do the same with Princess Maisie. Females love declarations at fancy events. Besides, it was your idea to forgo masks tonight. What were your words...so we can show our true faces? What's truer than love?"

"Love makes fools of us all," I say with a shrug and turn toward the palace.

"Including you?" Augie calls at my back. "Just admit it. You've fallen hard."

I scoff, but my lungs seem to shrink. It feels like something stirs inside my chest, begging to be released. It's new and terrifying and feels too large for my body.

Augie's laughter follows me, but his prior words are what linger.

*What's truer than love?*

∼

## EMBER

"Your hair always looks perfect," Clara says from next to me as I assess my reflection in the mirror. She's dressed me in a rosy pink evening gown with billowing layers of silk and chiffon. "Although are you sure you don't want me to style it for you? You never wear it any other way. Perhaps something a little more daring for the ball?"

I meet her eyes in the mirror and try to offer her a convincing smile. "That's not necessary," I say. Even though I'm confident the glamour will obey most physical manipulations of movement, I don't want to risk Clara discovering any cracks in the mirage. Besides, I've never known Clara to be proficient with hair. Until Mrs. Coleman dismissed our last servant due to her financial mismanagement, my stepfamily had their hair dressed every day by a maid.

Her expression falls. "All right. Well, is there anything else I can do to make you more...you know...interesting?"

I purse my lips to keep from laughing. The longer my stepsister has been without Imogen's constant interference, the more tolerable she's become. She hasn't learned much about tact, however. I wonder how a real princess would react to her constant slips.

"Please tell me you at least have a glamour," she says. "Now that the prince has deemed the Full Moon Frolic an unmasked event, one's glamour is more important than ever. I'll let you wear mine if you want. It's quite boring, though." She glances down at herself, wrinkling her nose. She wears the same peacock glamour she wore to the New Moon Masquerade, which tells me my stepmother couldn't afford new glamours for tonight's ball. Or perhaps just not for Clara.

"For one, Miss Coleman," I say as haughtily as I can, "your glamour isn't boring. For another, I do have one more thing to add to my ensemble." My pulse quickens as I open my dressing table drawer to retrieve the gilded box I'd tucked inside. I open it slowly, savoring the feel of the box, the tissue, and the delicate beauty of the necklace inside. Clara gasps as I lift it and bring it to the mirror.

"Where did you get that?" she asks, eyes bulging.

"It's from the prince." My voice nearly breaks on the last word. I can hardly look at the gift without being moved to tears all over again.

"Let me help you with it." Clara takes the necklace from me, being surprisingly gentle as she helps me put it on. Memories come to me unbidden of when Franco had done the same, but I shake them from my mind and keep my eyes focused on my reflection. As soon as the clasp is closed, my pink gown turns dark indigo with just a hint of rosy undertones peeking through. The silver constellations and stars stand out in stark contrast, as do the three staves of music at the hem. My gaze lingers on the latter, sending waves of warmth pulsing in my chest.

*A song for new life.*
*A song for safety.*
*A song for love.*

A sniffle breaks me out of my reverie, and I turn to find Clara wiping tears from her eyes. "What's wrong?"

She dabs her cheeks. "You're just so beautiful and kind. And...and I can tell how much the prince loves you."

*The prince loves you.*

A thousand butterflies take flight from my ribcage.

I bite the inside of my cheek to stop myself from replying, knowing if I speak, my voice will come out with a tremor.

Clara sniffles again and gives me a small smile. "Your Highness, I'm sorry if my sister or I ever made you feel...well, I don't know how we might have made you feel. But I'm sorry if I ever acted ungrateful to be in your service. Whatever Imogen did to earn your displeasure, I apologize on her behalf."

It isn't hard to imagine what she's left unsaid—that she's sorry for her mother and sister's secret scheme to have Imogen woo Franco. She, of course, has no idea that I know all about it. I keep my voice even as I say, "There's nothing to apologize for."

A lie, but a necessary one.

"You deserve Prince Franco. Of course you do. Just look at you!" She gestures toward the mirror. "You're a princess. The perfect future queen."

I stare at my reflection, my false face paired with the breathtaking glamour Franco gifted me. I'm no princess. I'm no future queen.

I'm nothing but an impostor.

A fake.

A liar.

I could never be deserving of a prince. My stomach turns at that, but it helps me harden my heart. I have no room for wistful thinking or foolish sentimentality. My bargain with Princess Maisie wasn't about romance but practicality. And tonight, it ends.

Tonight, I'm free.

*Free.*

A knock sounds at the door, and for one ridiculous minute, my momentary resolve collapses, leaving flushed cheeks and heart palpitations in its place.

"That's him!" Clara says in a too-loud whisper as she excitedly clasps my fingers in hers. We exchange giddy smiles, something I don't think I've ever done with her. I'd be more shocked if my mind wasn't fixated on who stands out in the hall.

Clara scurries toward the door, giving me a few seconds to gather my composure. With a deep breath, I remind myself of what I've already decided. Everything that's at stake. Everything that can never be. I lift my chin and watch as Clara opens the door, my expression cold and calm, as if half my heart isn't waiting on the other side.

Then I see him.

Franco enters my room, and his eyes go straight to mine, as if he knew exactly where to find me before Clara even opened the door. He grins so wide, showing me the smile of his that I love, the one that reveals the delicate tips of his canines and makes the corners of his eyes crinkle. Every inch of my stiff countenance gives way, my hardened heart fissuring as warmth seeps through it, fills it, replaces it with a living drum.

Clara slips silently out of the room and closes the door behind her, leaving us alone.

"You're beautiful," Franco says, closing the distance between us until only a fragile few inches serve as a divide.

I delight in the compliment, despite my cynical side's assertion that he has no right to call me beautiful. What he sees now is not what I look like.

*He never said I look beautiful*, I note. *He said I am beautiful.*

Against all my best efforts, I feel my answering smile take over my face. "You aren't so bad yourself," I say, glancing at his attire. He's outfitted in his signature slim trousers, but like at the opera, he now wears full evening attire. This time, however, his waistcoat and jacket are unbuttoned, his shirt is left open at the top, and his cravat is only loosely tied. Every article he wears is a shimmering, iridescent black that reminds me of his beautiful raven feathers. Over the top of the outfit glows with silver constellations and ever shifting moon sliding from one phase to the next. That must be the glamoured portion of his ensemble. The rest of him remains uncovered. No mask. No oversized raven head.

He extends his arms. "The real me."

I raise a brow. "I thought the real you preferred to wear only trousers and a shirt."

"The real me prefers to be stark naked," he says with a wink, "but this is how I can be me while showing the humans I'm respecting their traditions." His expression flickers with uncertainty. "Do you think it's stupid? Am I still demonstrating only partial efforts? You're right, I'm being an ass." He reaches for the buttons of his shirt, but I step forward and press my fingers to his hand to halt his frantic moves.

"No, I think you're being genuine."

His hands go still beneath my touch, and I'm suddenly aware of how close my fingers are to the bare skin of his chest. In this frozen moment, I could imagine he isn't trying to button the collar of his shirt but unbutton it. Instead of stopping him, I could imagine I'm about to aid his efforts, slide open his shirt front, and take in the full view of his ink-covered chest. If I moved my fingers only an inch, slid them off his hand to the space above his open collar...

His breaths go heavy, and his gaze slides slowly from our hands to my lips before locking on my eyes. I'm frozen in place, entranced by the pulsing heat that uncoils low in my core.

His throat bobs. Once. Twice. "Shall we?"

I glance back at my hand over his, certain he's asking me one thing before realization dawns. A flash of disappointment sends a blush to warm my cheeks. I take a step back and lower my hand. "Yes."

With a sly grin, he heads for my balcony. I follow close at his side. Near the balustrade, he extends a hand to me. "Ready to cause a scene?"

I place my hand in his. "Always."

## 39

EMBER

I'm not sure why Franco would find it necessary to fly me to the ball, but I have no complaints. When he begins our descent, I realize what I hadn't guessed before—that the Full Moon Frolic isn't going to be in the ballroom. It's outside. And with every inch we lower, the more awestruck I become. We must be heading for one of the palace gardens, somewhere I've never been. Rows and rows of hedges span out from the palace, leading to dozens of small paths, hedge mazes, and courtyards. At the center of the expansive gardens rests an enormous green dome.

Franco flies us toward the courtyard nearest the palace, which bustles with activity. Every inch of space is filled with chatting guests. Our momentum slows, and I hear several gasps and exclamations come from below. Franco lowers us down and lands us softly at the center of the clearing at the base of a moonstone fountain. He sets me on my feet, and I straighten my skirts. My stomach ripples with anxiety as hundreds of eyes pin us beneath their scrutiny. I'm surprised Franco landed us here at all. Surely, he'd prefer a more secluded portion of the gardens to start off in. For someone who doesn't like being the center of attention, he sure chose the absolute worst possible place.

That's when I realize how stiff his posture has become, the way he fidgets with his hands, alternating between shoving them in his pockets and straightening the hem of his jacket. Gone is the witty, confident prince, the arrogant, lazy male. Left in his place is someone who's on the brink of seizing up.

Slowly, I step closer to him until our sides are nearly pressed together. I reach for him, seeking out the feel of his hand. He lets me take it, and I give it a squeeze, our fingers hidden within the many folds of my skirt.

His chest heaves and I watch him blow out a heavy breath. Then, little by little, his shoulders relax. His expression softens. A smile warms his face as he scans the courtyard from one side to the other. Finally, he returns the squeeze of my hand, brushing his thumb over my palm before stepping away from me.

He climbs up to the ledge of the fountain and addresses the crowd. "Thank you, people of Lunar, for attending tonight's Full Moon Frolic." His voice comes out stiff, quiet. I see him take another deep breath. Another. "Tonight, my kind—the unseelie fae—celebrate the full moon. This phase of the moon represents completion, clarity, and illumination. It is a time for forgiveness, gratitude, and celebration. Of rebirth, renewal, and reassessment."

He pauses, scanning the crowd again. His gaze lands on me, and his smile grows brighter. Finally, the confident version of him begins to shine through. His voice grows stronger. Bolder. "Tonight, I see the full moon as a time of unity and wholeness, which is why I chose to infuse some of Lunar's unseelie beauty into the Full Moon Frolic, to share with you a piece of me, of who I really am. You don't have to celebrate the same way I do, and I don't have to dance the same way you do for us to be unified. And we *are* unified. You may be more familiar with your seelie king, as that is how our isle is structured. But most of you attending tonight are not from the south near the seat of his influence, but here in the north. You may owe your allegiance to a fae in the south, but that doesn't mean you don't have an advocate in the north. We may be different races and standing in separate political spheres, but we are still one people—people of Faerwyvae. And I want to be the prince you need."

The crowd rumbles with polite applause. I study the sea of people in their exquisite glamoured evening attire, their unmasked faces. Some are brimming with delight while others appear bored.

"Join me," Franco says, "and let the Full Moon Frolic commence."

Another wave of applause and Franco jumps down from the fountain ledge to stand at my side. The people break into chatter. "For the love of the night, I'm going to be sick," he says under his breath.

"That was great," I whisper. "I wasn't expecting that."

"That I was great? Or that I made a speech?"

"The latter. Of course you were great. That's not a surprise."

"Was it stupid? Did everyone hate it?"

I consider lying but instead deliver the truth. "Some people truly enjoyed your words. It's a start. Not everyone is here for genuine connection and unity with the fae. Some are just here to rub elbows with the elite and dance."

"Speaking of dancing," he says, extending his arm. "Are you ready to open the ball with me?"

My heart leaps into my throat. I take a step back. "Open the ball? You mean to *dance*?"

He laughs at my reaction. "What else were you expecting to do at a ball?"

Breezes, I don't know what I was expecting but it certainly wasn't dancing. Franco didn't dance at all at the New Moon Masquerade—no. The man I thought was the prince that night hadn't been him at all. That was Augie and Franco was the fat raven.

His brow furrows with concern. "What's wrong, Em?"

I lower my voice. "I've never danced before. Not with a man. I...I was never allowed to practice the formal dances. Not after... after Father died."

He takes my hand and gives it a squeeze. It's the same thing I did for him before his speech. The warmth of his fingers steadies me. "You don't need to know anything about formal dances to do what we're about to do."

I swallow hard. "Somehow, that sounds far more terrifying."

"I promise you'll be fine." He squeezes my hand again, then places it in the crook of his arm. "Are you ready?"

"No," I mutter, but I make no argument as we begin to walk. He turns us toward one of the paths that branches off from the courtyard. As soon as we take a step onto the path, a bright orange light illuminates on each side, high above the tall hedges that flank us. Three more steps, and another illumination. I glance up and study the lights, surprised when I find they're tiny flaming figures. Fire sprites. We continue to walk, and more appear, lighting the way and eliciting gasps from those who follow behind us. Soon, the smell of night blooming jasmine grows heavy in the air. It takes me a moment to realize it's coming from the green dome straight ahead. Our path ends at the dome's arched entryway.

Franco leads us toward it. As soon as we clear the door, a gasp escapes my lips. I'm so enchanted by what I see, I nearly lose my footing. The dome is as large as the ballroom had been, but instead of moonstone walls, its structure appears to be a domed trellis woven with trailing jasmine. The scent fills the space with its heady aroma, and I breathe it in deeply. The floor is of thick, plush grass, while the perimeter is lined with tables and chairs interspersed amongst clusters of pink, blue, and purple bioluminescent mushrooms that give the space a dazzling glow. Closer to the center stands a circle of slim trees that look as if they've been carved from opal. They extend their pale, elegant branches toward the top of the dome. Wisps bob and swirl overhead, bathing the ceiling in blue. An open hole at the center of the ceiling lets in a shaft of pale white moonlight that illuminates the space inside the ring of trees.

We head for this bright spot of light. That's when I hear the first beat of a drum.

It begins as a deep, steady rhythm that rumbles inside my bones. I glance around for the source and find a band set up at the base of one of the opal trees. The drums continue to beat, echoing the pounding of my heart. Then comes the first notes of a fiddle, a light, unfamiliar melody that sparks fire in my pulse.

Franco and I stop when we reach the center of the shaft of light, while the crowd fans out around us, closer to the trees. Excited gasps and whispers rumble amongst the guests. I don't blame them. This is the most spectacular setting I've ever witnessed for a ball. For anything.

And I'm standing at the center of it.

Sweat beads behind my neck as Franco turns to face me. "Might I have this dance?"

I resist the urge to bring my fingers to the base of my neck, eager for the feel of my locket. But no, it won't be the locket I'll find but my crescent moon. The thought roots me to the present moment. *I'm glamoured. I'm supposed to be a princess. I'm supposed to dance with the prince.*

"What do I do?" I whisper. "I don't know this song."

He shrugs. "Nor do I."

"Then how do we dance to it?"

"It's an unseelie melody. It will come naturally to you."

"What will?"

"This." He begins stepping side to side, his movements stiff and awkward. "Trust me, you aren't the only one who feels like they're going to be sick."

"Then why are you smiling?"

"I can't help it. The look in your eyes right now...you should see it!"

"It's not funny," I say, but the corners of my lips are already beginning to lift because now he's shaking his hips.

"Just do what you do when you play."

"How do you know what I do when I play?"

He begins to move his arms, swinging them lightly side to side. "When we spoke in my room, you were somehow able to play a tune that matched what I was saying as I said it. This time, move your body in a way that reflects the song."

A flash of blue darts between me and the prince, weaving around us in a figure eight before coming to a halt before me. It's three wisps. Ones I've become quite familiar with. "You again," I mutter.

"Dance!" one urges. "You know you want to."

"Move! Fly!"

"She wants to. She wants to, I can feel it."

"Why are you always bothering me?" I say through my teeth, taking a few steps away from the prince.

"You're of the wind. You're like us. You want to dance."

I glance at Franco, curious if he overheard the last statement about me being of the wind. He still believes I'm from the Sea Court. At least, I think he does.

Until I leave at midnight. Then what will he believe?

"Come on," Franco shouts over the music, laughing as he continues to move and sway. His movements have lost some of their stiff quality, his arms swinging a little freer, his toes tapping a little lighter, keeping to the beat of the drum.

"Dance," one of the wisps says, "or we'll tell him how many

times we spotted you on your balcony this week, hoping he'd come find you."

I gasp. "I did no such thing!"

The wisps chortle. "She did! She did! She craved a journey."

"But not on land. To a bedroom."

"*His* bedroom!"

My cheeks burn hot. "Hush! Enough of that."

"Then dance. Do it now!" With that, they rush over to Franco and urgency propels me forward.

I tap my feet. "I'm dancing, all right?"

Franco laughs, and the wisps break away to swirl overhead. He reaches for my hand and pulls me closer.

"This is the most embarrassing thing I've ever done," I growl at him. "I'd have preferred to humiliate myself over a quadrille."

"How is this not better? This way, no one knows if we're doing it wrong. Besides, look around."

"I can't."

"Just do it."

With a gulp, I glance around at the crowd...but I can't see them. All I can see is the bright circle illuminated by the shaft of moonlight. It's like all that exists is us. And the music.

The wisps circle above us, releasing excited whoops and chortles.

"You're doing great, Em." Franco lifts his arms. With a crooked grin, he shakes his hips in a way that would be entirely inappropriate for a human dance.

Laughter bursts from my lips, and I find myself moving more in sync with the music. The drums seem to grow louder, heavier, the fiddle faster and lighter. Soon my hips begin to sway, my arms begin to swing. I tap my feet and Franco taps his, and we begin to weave our dance together.

Franco takes one of my hands and guides me into a slow twirl. He swings me away and back in, away and back in. On the third time, his spin is more of a fold, and he tucks me in close until my back is pressed to his chest. He keeps hold of my hand, while the other comes to my waist. I glance over my shoulder at him and find his smile beaming down at me. With the moon glinting off the silver of his hair, he looks more beautiful than ever. More than that, he looks happier. Freer. The smile tugging my lips makes me wonder if I look the same, and for once I don't care that I'm glamoured. Whatever joy I feel in this moment is surely reflected in ways that have little to do with physical appearance. It's in my hips, my arms, my toes. It's in my eyes as they lock on Franco's.

He swings me out again and when he pulls me back in, he releases my hand to grasp my waist and lifts me off my feet. He spins me in a full circle before setting me back down, then brings me in close to his chest. It feels natural to place my hands behind his neck, so I do, and his come to my lower back. We continue to step and sway, somehow able to communicate our intended moves without words. Our eyes rarely leave each other's, and every time he turns me for a spin, I come right back to where I like it best, our chests touching, my hands at the nape of his neck.

Blue light surrounds us as hundreds of wisps join in and play off the song, enhancing our moves with their own as they form pulsing patterns around the shaft of moonlight. If I wasn't so focused on dancing, I'd be amazed by the dazzling beauty the wisps are creating.

Gasps emit from the crowd, but I try not to focus on them. I focus only on Franco, on the music, the beat of my heart, and the sound of his. Or is it the feel? With his chest so close to mine, I can't tell where my heartbeat ends and his begins.

Too soon, I feel the music begin to slow and we match the pace beat for beat. He turns me again, and I feel as if I'm floating through air. Then he pulls me close, closer than he's pulled me before. This time, his hand comes to the back of my head. I angle my face toward his, our breath mingling, his lips just inches from mine. Then he shifts me to the side in a strange sideways dip. There he holds me suspended as the music comes to an end. Applause erupts around us, but he doesn't lift me, not right away. The wisps hold their final pattern as well, hovering in place to form a spiraling column. We remain in limbo, unwilling to face the world outside our moonlight.

But it can't last forever.

And it doesn't.

A new song strikes up from the band, one with far less chaos, less spontaneity. The tune is familiar and human and so muted compared to the wild drums we left behind. The wisps chortle and break away, squealing with mirth as they return to fly about the dome.

Franco lifts me back to standing and we exchange the appropriate curtsy and bow. Then, like waking from a dream, we step out of the moonlight and face the crowd.

# 40

**EMBER**

I blink several times to clear my vision and adjust to the dimmer light. Several faces look at us with scandalized expressions, but others have tear-glazed eyes and slack jaws, as if they're awed or speechless. I catch a flicker of movement—a hand lifted in a wave—and find that Clara is one of these awestruck spectators. My heart lurches at those who flank her. Imogen and Mrs. Coleman.

I sway on my feet, my pulse quickening beneath their hard gazes. Panic has me glancing down to ensure I'm still wearing my glamoured shoes. In the wake of the dance, I feel as if I bared my soul, stood naked for all to see. I'm relieved to find my shoes and glamour intact.

When the applause quiets down, Franco speaks. "Thank you for sharing that with me. This is how we dance at a full moon revel and our dances tend to last until sunrise. However, this is not a revel, but the Full Moon Frolic, and now I turn the night over to you, my respected guests. Please enjoy the ball."

The music changes again, starting another familiar tune,

this one slightly louder than the one played during the brief transition. Franco takes my hand, and we exit the ring of opal trees, while human couples take our place to dance the first cotillion of the night.

I place my hand at his arm, in a daze as we weave around the perimeter of the dance floor amongst the chatting guests. Franco stops to greet them every so often, exchanging pleasantries the way he did after our argument at the lake. Any questions directed at me get only short and automatic answers, as I feel most of my mind still lingers on the dance floor.

It was like a dream.

No, it *was* a dream.

My first and only dance with the prince.

"Are you all right?" Franco asks once we've made a full round of the room. "I'm not able to pick up on your energy as well when we're so tightly packed amongst strangers, but you seem…upset, perhaps."

"It's nothing," I say. When he gives me a pointed look, I add, "I promise. It's just that…I really enjoyed that dance. I've never done anything like that before. It has me feeling…ungrounded, I suppose."

He leans his head close to mine and gives me a shy grin. "You aren't the only one."

"Your Highness." My blood goes cold at the sound of the approaching voice, my grip tightening on the prince's arm as Brother Marus stops before us. "Do you recall our previous conversation?"

"How can I forget?" Franco asks with a sardonic look. For the first time tonight, he's reclaimed his smug façade. "You love to remind me every time I see your face."

Marus ignores the prince's obvious disdain. "As you'll recall, my fiancée turns nineteen tomorrow and will be here to claim her inheritance."

My stomach turns.

"Brother Marus, for someone so keen on ensuring I remember all our prior conversations, you do very little to recall mine. I heard you last time. I hear you again. Thank you and good day."

We turn away from Marus, but he's undeterred. "Do you recall the promise you made me?"

Franco goes still and closes his eyes. I don't need to be a psy vampire like him to sense the agitation radiating off him. He gently removes my hand from his arm and whirls to face Marus. In the blink of an eye, he has the man by the collar of his jacket. Franco's face transforms with his rage, revealing just a hint of the terrifying glamour I saw him conjure once before. "I remember," he says through his teeth, then shoves Marus away from him.

Marus brushes off his jacket, eyes wide. "You forget who I am to your sister. She and I have an alliance."

"And you forget who *I* am. Period."

Marus' fingers ball into fists, his face turning bright red. Then, with a stiff bow, he walks away.

Franco runs a hand over his face, then looks at me. "I'm sorry. I know you don't like him. Now you see why I despise him too. My sister has let him get away with too much. Instead of keeping him close enough to watch with a keen eye, he's grown too proud. Too confident."

I don't know what to say to that so I just nod. Nausea continues to turn in my gut. Midnight. At midnight I'll be free. At midnight, Marus loses all claim to me. As does Mrs. Coleman.

A flash of pain strikes my core and I gasp an intake of breath.

"Em!" Franco takes me by the shoulders. "What's wrong?"

I try to speak but can't find my voice over the pain. *I'm obeying. I'm obeying. The bargain is nearly fulfilled.* One more flash of pain, then it returns to its familiar dull ache. When I return my eyes to Franco's, his brow is furrowed with concern. "Sorry, I don't know what came over me. I'm not feeling well."

He watches me a few silent moments, and I wonder if he'll buy my lie. "Let's get out of here for a bit," he says, pointing his thumb at the domed archway.

Relief unwinds my muscles, and I follow Franco outside the dome and onto the garden path. Outside, a few couples stroll while fire sprites continue to light the many trails. With slow, easy steps, we wander away from the dome, away from the music. Silence falls between us, but it doesn't feel uncomfortable like it once did. It feels full. Warm.

After a while, Franco turns toward me. "You like to swim, right?"

It takes me several seconds to find my words. He thinks I'm a sea fae. My answer should be an outright yes, when in truth, I haven't gone swimming since I was a child. Memories of visiting the lake with Mother and Father flood my mind, filling my heart with peace. "Of course I do."

"Good." Franco pulls me to him and spreads his wings. Exhilaration shoots through me as he lifts me off the ground. We fly away from the palace and the bright bustle of activity, and I press my face close to his chest, breathing him in. I don't care where we're going, only that we're flying. Together.

It might be our very last time.

Soon, the shimmering expanse of Lake Artemisa comes into view, prompting a wave of dread to fill my gut. When he asked if I like to swim, he didn't mean...

Panic sweeps over me as he lowers us to the ground. "What are we doing here?"

He glances down at me with a grin. "Going for a swim, of course."

We land near the shore. As soon as I step away from him, he begins removing his jacket. My eyes lock on his chest. I'm caught somewhere between alarm and desire as I watch his jacket fall to the ground. I snap my gaze to his. "You can't be serious about going for a swim," I say, trying to keep my voice light.

He lifts a shoulder in a shrug, then begins to unravel the knot in his cravat. "I'm a sweating mess after tonight."

"We danced one dance."

"*You* danced one dance. I gave a speech. Two, technically. Then I talked to strangers and had that most hideous interaction with Brother Marus."

I cross my arms over my chest, forcing my gaze not to follow his swift fingers as he moves from the cravat to the buttons of his shirt. "I can't swim right now," I say. "I don't have a swimming gown." Too late, I realize how utterly human that sounds, and the opposite of what someone from the Sea Court would say. I try to think of an excuse to explain away the statement, but fatigue keeps me silent. When I'm this close to freedom, it's exhausting to keep lying to him. Do I even need to anymore?

His hands still over his buttons. "Em, I know you aren't a sea fae." His voice is gentle, devoid of judgment. "You don't have to swim with me. It's what I need right now. Although..." A mischievous glint lights his eyes, and a corner of his mouth quirks up. "You might want to turn around."

"Why?"

He finishes unbuttoning his shirt and tosses it onto the ground. "Because I don't have a swimming gown either." His fingers move to the buttons of his trousers, and I whirl around with a gasp. I hear his laughter behind me. Next comes the sound of splashing followed by movement cutting through water.

I turn around and find Franco's head breaking above the water's surface. "You're really missing out."

I cut him a glare. "Since when do ravens swim?"

"Since they learned to dance."

I roll my eyes and sit on the shore, watching as he dunks

his head underwater. The peace of our surroundings comes to my attention, bringing with it my favorite kind of music—the unseen evening orchestra, something I haven't taken the time to witness since abandoning my rooftop perch in the Gray Quarter. Crickets chirp a soft melody from the surrounding forest, while the light breeze rustles the grass beyond the beach. Nocturnal animals scurry up surrounding trees, their pitter-patter almost too quiet to hear. Franco emerges from the water and waves at me. I wave back, dazzled by the starlight that glints off his wet hair. The moon is bright, making the surface of the lake sparkle all around him. Tiny specks of light draw my attention several feet above the water where hundreds of fireflies flutter about, twinkling a warm glow. Franco dives under the surface again. My lips curl into a smile as I watch him swim and play. I don't think I've ever seen him look so free. Aside from that magical moment when we danced.

My heart clenches.

*The dance.*

Thoughts of spinning to and from his arms fill my mind, bringing with it the feel of him, the pound of drums and two heartbeats combining as one. The memory merges with the beauty of this moment, the brightness of the moon, the starlight in Franco's hair, the music of nature echoing the song from our dance. Longing fills my heart. Longing for him, for the water, for the freedom he feels. It expands until it becomes a storm wind roaring through my veins, my blood, my bones. A burning tempest of need.

I bite the inside of my cheek, clenching my fingers to stop me from pushing off the ground to my feet. *I can't join him*, I tell myself. *I can't swim in my shoes, nor can I remove them. My bargain with Maisie forbids it.*

Or does it?

I go over the terms of our arrangement. I am to wear the

glamoured shoes in public. Furthermore, I must let no one see me without them.

*This certainly isn't what one would consider public*, my fae side taunts. *This is private.*

Besides, I've lost the glamour in his presence before and didn't break the bargain. So long as he doesn't *see* me...

"Turn around," I rush to say as I jump to my feet.

He swims closer, quirking a teasing brow. "Are you coming to join me?"

"Turn. Around." Heat flushes my cheeks. My human side cowers as my fingers move to the clasps at the back of my gown. I had Clara's help to don it, but the back is low enough that I can remove it on my own. My fae side leaps with excitement, quickening my motions to match my racing pulse.

Franco's eyes widen, and he swiftly turns his back to me. "I didn't think you were serious," he calls over his shoulder.

"Don't you dare look at me," I say, my voice higher than normal. "I'll be taking off my shoes too."

Franco's movements go still. "Are you sure?"

"As long as you don't peek."

"I won't," he says.

This is a bad idea. A very bad idea.

*Always be wild. Promise me.*

With a deep breath, I pull down the bodice of my gown and slip the rest of the way out. I consider leaving my undergarments on, but the thought of emerging from the lake in a soaked chemise has another flash of boldness urging me to keep going. I unhook my corset, slip out of my petticoats, and pull the chemise from over my head. Then I untie the ribbons securing the shoes to my feet.

The night breeze pebbles my naked skin, and I resist the urge to bend forward and cover myself. There's no one here. Only me and Franco beneath the night sky. It makes me feel bold. Daring. Maybe even beautiful.

"I'm taking off my shoes now."

"All right." His voice is thick, quavering. After clearing his throat, he adds, "bring my cravat."

"Why?"

"To cover my eyes."

I swallow hard and take a deep breath. Then another. Another.

Finally, I step out of my shoes.

On swift feet, I go to Franco's pile of clothes and retrieve his cravat, then rush to the lake's edge. I squeal as the chill water laps up my bare ankles, my calves, my thighs. Keeping the cravat above water, I dunk the rest of my body beneath the surface until only my head and shoulders remain above it. "Come closer to me, but don't look."

Franco obeys, swimming backward until he reaches the rocky shore in front of me. He keeps his shoulders below water too, and I place the cravat over his eyes.

"I could get into this," he says, voice low and husky. His tone has my knees quaking, but I keep my breathing steady as I tie the cloth at the back of his head. Once his blindfold is secure, he turns around to face me.

I sink a little lower in the water. "You can't see me, can you?"

"No, but that doesn't mean I don't know where you are." With a flick of his hands, he sends a splash of water toward me. I squeal and splash back at him, but he dives under and swims away. My heart fills with laughter as I swim after him. I'm surprised to find it easy to recall the rhythm and motions I learned as a child, how to cut through water, float, tread near the surface. I don't dare go quite as far as he does. Instead, I remain near the shore. After a while, he comes back. The way he swims straight for me has panic whirring inside me yet again.

"Are you sure you can't see me?" I ask when he stops a few feet away.

He laughs. "I'm sure."

"Then why does it seem like you always know where I am?"

"I do know where you are." We hover around each other, treading water to keep our heads above the surface. No matter where I go, he manages to keep his face turned toward me. I'm sure he can follow sound without a problem, but still...

Ever so quietly, I inch back toward the shore and swim to the side. Eerily, his head follows my movements. "Franco," I say through my teeth.

"What?" He laughs and sends a spray of water toward me. It glitters like a thousand sparkling diamonds, sending a cluster of fireflies skittering away.

"I find it hard to believe your hearing is that great, fae or not."

"Then you underestimate me." He swims nearer, closing the distance between us. "Besides, I'm not finding you by sound."

I move closer to the shore until my feet gain purchase beneath me. "What do you use then?"

"Your energy. I can sense it as clearly as if I were seeing with my eyes." There's a note of longing in his voice, one that makes my stomach flip.

"What is it like to sense energy?"

"It's hard to explain," he says, inching nearer until he's close enough to touch, should I try to. The thought makes me shiver. "Sampling energy is a multi-sensory experience. I taste it, smell it, see it. Associate colors, flavors, and aromas with it. Over time, I've learned to identify what certain combinations mean. To me, everyone has a unique energetic signature that I can recognize someone by if I'm around them long enough. Yours is particularly bright, although it wasn't always that way. Not when we first met. I knew your energetic signature by the end of that first disastrous coach ride, but it changed the night at the opera. Or perhaps it was only heightened."

"Heightened?"

"Yes. After I heard you hum, I sensed something deeper about you, and since then it has smelled like rose, citrus, and storm winds. Your colors are bright pink, blue, and yellow. Your taste—" His words cut off and I watch as his throat bobs. He seems robbed of his voice for several silent moments. When he speaks, his voice is a deep rumble that seems to infuse the water around me, caressing me. "It kills me to know your true face is on the other side of this blindfold and I can't see it."

"Don't you dare look," I say, but my words come out far softer than I intend. I'm too distracted by the rise and fall of his chest, the sparkling water beading down his bare flesh, the slowly shrinking space between us as he steps closer. Closer. Every inch he nears is followed by a pause, one I make no move to flee from. In fact, I find myself joining his efforts. We stop when only an inch separates us. My breaths are shallow. If I breathe too deep, our flesh will collide, his torso will brush the tips of my breasts. My heart races at the thought, and it takes all my restraint not to lean the slightest bit closer just to know what he might feel like against me.

He lifts his hand from the water and slowly brings it to rest upon my cheek, fingers trembling at the contact our damp skin makes. "This is your true face," he whispers. Then he glides his fingers up the side of my face to my temple. From there, he runs his hand down the length of my wet hair and lets it slip through his fingers. "This is your true hair."

In the absence of his touch, I feel cold, empty. I angle my face toward his, eager to feel his hand on my cheek again. He complies, lifting both hands to cup my face. One wanders over my jaw, from my chin to my ear, then down the side of my neck. My breaths come in hard and fast, and I feel my chest brush against his. I gasp at the sensation the momentary contact brings, and his hand stills at the base of my neck. I watch as every visible muscle tenses. Then slowly, he brings his other hand to my mouth and brushes his thumb softly over my lips.

"These are your true lips." They part in answer, and he leans down slightly as if to claim them with his.

But he doesn't.

Why doesn't he?

Need pulses deep in my abdomen, tingles my aching mouth, skates over every part of my skin not touched by him.

I lift my hand and place it on his chest. He shudders beneath my palm, and I run my hand up his torso until it winds behind his neck. There I stroke the wet hair at his nape. "Franco," I whisper.

He moves the rest of the way, pressing his lips against mine in a crushing heat. His arms move behind my back, running over my waist, my hips, my shoulders. Mine tangle in his hair. I release a soft moan against his lips, then feel the brush of his tongue against mine. I relish the feel of him, in the firmness of his hands as he lifts me off my feet to encircle my legs around his hips. I press him closer, kiss him deeper, eager for more of him.

His lips move from my mouth to my jaw, then trail down my neck to my collarbone. I throw my head back, panting, wanting his lips everywhere. Everywhere.

His mouth comes to my ear. "For the love of the night, Em."

The sound of my name has my grip on him tightening.

But then I remember what it means.

He called me Em. Short for Ember, yes, but he doesn't know that. He doesn't know *me*. Isn't kissing *me*. He's kissing who he thinks is Princess Maisie's lady's maid. A woman he's pretending to court.

I go still in his arms, and he freezes too. He releases me, and I slide away from him. My insides beg me to return, to leap back in his arms and feel those lips caressing my skin, even if for the last time.

But I can't.

I *can't*.

This is one of our final moments together, and he hasn't the slightest clue.

By midnight, I'll be gone.

And it just...it wouldn't be right to do that to him.

Nor would it be right to do that to myself.

"We should get back," I whisper and turn toward the shore. Can he hear the regret laced in my tone? "Stay here until I get dressed."

"Don't worry," he says, voice thick despite the crooked grin he wears. "I'm going to need a few minutes to cool off."

# 41

**EMBER**

Every inch of me burns as he flies us back to the palace. It's almost painful to keep my arms around his neck, for it only conjures thoughts of my hands in his hair, his lips on my collarbone. I wonder if he can sense the desire pulsing off me in droves. If he does, he says nothing, does nothing to try and convince me to pick up where we left off.

Oh, how badly I want to do just that...

We land in an empty courtyard in the garden, not far from the dome. It's ringed with evening primrose, filling the clearing with their bright yellow hue.

Franco releases me and puts space between us, shoving his hands in his pockets as if that will keep him from reaching for me. He gives me a hesitant smile. "Should we return to the ball?"

My stomach sinks. I try to calculate how much time has passed since I last saw a clock. It must be close to midnight now. Close to goodbye. Close to freedom.

Why doesn't that fill me with the same excitement it should?

"I'm a little tired," I lie. "I think I'll return to my room."

He frowns. "Are you all right? Was the lake too..." He swallows hard, worry filling his expression.

I allow myself to smile, to deliver a fraction of the warmth emanating from my molten core. "Yes, I'm all right. The lake was wonderful."

"Maybe we should do it again sometime," he says with a timid smile. His eyes lock on mine. "The kiss at least. I would kiss you again. Anywhere. Anytime. If you'd want me to."

*Of course I want you to. I want you to kiss me now. I want you to kiss me always.*

But that's not what I say.

Instead, I stand tall, adopting my princess persona. "As nice as that was, we don't need to kiss to pull off this game of pretend."

He takes his hands from his pockets, his fingers curling and uncurling. "What if it isn't pretend?"

"But it is," I say with a too-casual grin.

"It doesn't have to be."

My heart drums a pulsing rhythm at those words. My feet beg to move, to close the distance between us, to wrap my arms around him and tell him how badly I want this to be real. But it isn't. "It *is* pretend, Franco. You can't change that."

He takes a few steps closer. "Yes, we can. I could court you... as *you*."

I shake my head, smothering the hope that blooms inside me. "No, you can't. You don't even know me. I'm not a princess. I'm not someone you could ever court. You know nothing about who I really am."

"I *do* know you. I may not know every fact, but I've gotten to know you more in two weeks than I've ever gotten to know a person in my lifetime. The same goes for how I've allowed you to know me. I've shared things with you I've never told anyone."

A lump rises in my throat. "You're wrong. You only think you know me. I'm sorry. I'm not who you think I am."

"I don't—"

"I'm leaving." The word comes out in a rush. "I'm leaving, Franco. At midnight. By then, I'll have no bargain to hold me back. I never meant to stay."

"You're leaving?" His expression shifts into one of pain. Confusion. "I...I thought you had until the end of the month?"

"I misled you."

He furrows his brow. "I know you'd planned on leaving once your bargain with Maisie was fulfilled, but...hasn't anything changed for you? *Everything* has changed for me. I don't want to lose you."

"Nothing has changed for me. Nothing. I wasn't a princess when I got here and I'm not a princess now. I'm not even a lady's maid." My voice breaks, catching on a sob that builds in my throat. I retreat a few steps. "If...if I was anyone else..."

"I don't want you to be anyone else." He steps forward, and terror runs through me. Not for fear of him, but of what I'll do if he so much as touches me. With one touch, I might unravel. Might open my heart to him, reveal my identity, show him who I am. Someone he'll have no choice but to rebuff.

He can't marry someone like me. If he knew who I was, he'd see at once that I don't belong here. Not with him.

So I unleash the one weapon I know I can use against him. The only thing that will keep those arms at bay, prevent them from wrapping around me.

"And I don't want *you*." My heart recoils at the sound of the words leaving my mouth, at the bitter taste they leave on my tongue.

He freezes, hand outstretched in the process of reaching for me. Slowly, he lets it fall to his side.

My insides scream at me to take it back. To erase the agonized look in his eyes. To tell him the truth.

But what *is* the truth?

That I'm falling in love with someone who could never love me back? That I've already fallen in love with him and all he knows is an illusion?

Swallowing every soft word that begs to be released, I keep my tone firm. "Don't stop me. Don't follow me." With that, I turn and run the rest of the way to the palace while tears stream down my cheeks.

## FRANCO

I watch her go, feeling as if she's taken my heart with her. A searing pain strikes my chest. Shadows writhe around me, making me tremble. My body wants to contract and fold in on itself. I feel as if I'm small again, flooding the halls of the palace with my unruly emotion.

But I'm not small anymore.

With a deep breath, I gain control over my shadows, and the darkness retreats, returning to its proper place inside me. I stare down the trail where Em fled. My heart urges me to follow. Urges me to speak more of the truth I'd only just begun to say.

But her angry words echo through my mind.

*I don't want you.*

*Don't stop me.*

*Don't follow me.*

I reflect on how her energy spiked with regret after she said those things, but it doesn't help soften the blow. She knew what she was doing when she said that. Knew it would keep me at bay. I can't go after her.

I *can't.*

Not when she doesn't want me to.

Not even if it kills me to hold still.

"What are you doing out here?" I startle at the sound of my sister's voice and turn to find Nyxia strolling down one of the garden paths toward me.

With a deep breath, I gather my composure. "I could ask you the same," I say with a smirk. The tug of my lips feels firmly at odds with the pain lancing my chest. "I thought you were on holiday for the entire month."

"I came to see how you're doing with everything."

"Is Lorelei here?"

She purses her lips. "I came alone."

I bark a cold laugh I don't feel. "By that, you mean she didn't approve of you coming to spy on me."

She puts a hand on her hip and pops it to one side. "Can't a devoted sister check up on her dear brother without it being considered spying? I revealed that I'm here, didn't I?"

"Very well, Nyxia," I say, crossing my arms. "What's your grand assessment? How am I doing?"

"You're clearly upset about something." Her eyes dart down the path Em took mere moments ago. "I saw you speaking with Princess Maisie."

Annoyance flairs inside me. If she saw us, then she damn well *felt* us too. "Do you have anything you'd like to say about that?"

Her expression softens the slightest fraction. "All I asked was for you to try with her. If things aren't working out between you, I'll find another royal for you to court."

My heart clenches at that. I don't want her to find another royal. I don't want her to find anyone else. I just want...

*I'm leaving, Franco.*

*I don't want* you.

Shit. There's so much I don't understand. So much I don't

know. It isn't hard to believe Em's feelings wouldn't match my own. I'm not so arrogant to think I can woo any female I like, but when I taste her emotions around me, they spark with desire, joy, and contentment. They reflect my own. Reflect things I'm still too terrified to admit lie between us.

But none of that matters.

Does it?

I narrow my gaze at Nyxia. "Why is it so important that I marry a royal?"

She rolls her eyes. "We've been over this several times, Franco."

"Then what's the harm in once more?"

"Fine," she says with a flippant wave of her hand. "We both know you need to gain the respect of the humans and the fae."

"Because the humans see me as a careless dandy and the fae see me as weak compared to you."

"I wouldn't put it that way."

"But it's the truth."

She huffs. "If you insist. Regardless, if you are to challenge me to the throne, you must maintain a strong enough standing that you aren't challenged yourself. We both know the humans respect royal marriages and the ability to produce heirs while the fae respect strength and formidable alliances."

I shake my head. "Eleven years ago, you were satisfied with me marrying a human aristocrat's daughter."

"That was before I knew I wanted to retire so soon." Her posture tenses slightly. "And that was before that whole debacle with your first social season."

"You never encouraged me to correct my mistakes myself. Instead, you took matters into your own hands."

"I knew you were embarrassed. I wanted to allow you to hide if that's what you wanted."

"The future king shouldn't hide from his duties or his mistakes."

She gives me a sad smile. "Franco, I accept you for who you are. I know you don't thrive on attention the way I do. I know you have a softer heart."

"If I am to be king, the people should accept me for who I am too."

"And a royal marriage will make that so much easier."

"Maybe I don't want to do things easy this time. Maybe I want to do the work for once. Maybe I want to take the time to get to know the humans, and in turn let them know me. Let them know the beauty of the unseelie."

She gives a light laugh. "That's all very sunny and idealistic of you, but we don't need more glittering ideals. We need to demonstrate your standing. Otherwise—"

"Otherwise, what? I'll be challenged to the throne? The humans will start another rebellion? If I'm going to withstand the duties of king, I should be able to handle that kind of conflict as I am. I shouldn't need to rely on false pretenses."

"A royal marriage isn't a false pretense."

I take a step closer, my shadows writhing with anger. "Nyxia, you don't understand. I don't want to marry a princess."

"You don't have to marry a princess. You can marry a prince, a prince's daughter, a royal cousin—"

"Nyxia," I say through my teeth.

"What?" she says, all innocence.

"If you trust me to be your heir, to become king, then you need to trust me to find my own way. If it all goes up in flames, so be it. If I can't keep hold of the crown with my own efforts, then I don't deserve it."

Her expression darkens. "I can't risk it going up in flames. We worked too hard for the Lunar Court for too long. Isn't it already bad enough that we have a seelie king where once I ruled alone?"

I close my eyes and release a sigh. "Sister, you need to decide whether you're truly ready to let go."

"What do you mean?"

"You say you want to retire and give Lorelei the simple life she craves. You say you want to follow your heart and experience what love brings. And yet you desire to maintain a stranglehold on a throne you're leaving behind."

"That throne has been in our bloodline for thousands of years."

I give Nyxia a pointed look. "If you're so certain our bloodline is integral to the successful rule of Lunar, then you should be able to trust me to become king in my own right, not yours."

"That doesn't make sense."

"It does, Nyx. Let me do it my way or not at all."

She purses her lips, and I can feel her resistance, her love for her mate warring with her need for control. Then her energy softens. "Fine," she says, "do it your way, but do not say I didn't warn you."

I stare back at her, disbelieving I've won an argument with her for once. "Do you mean it?"

"Yes, Franco, I mean it. Now, shouldn't you get back to the ball?"

I glance from her to the dome, still bright and bustling with light, music, and dancing. "No," I say, and the word sends a buzz of relief through me. "There's something I need to do first."

# 42

### EMBER

As soon as I reach my room, I seek out the clock on my nightstand. A quarter to midnight. My pulse pounds as I stalk about the room, retrieving the things I'll need to pack—a fresh chemise, an extra blouse and walking skirt. With every move, my heart sinks deeper, aches harder. The last words I said to Franco echo through my mind, searing my very soul.

*It was necessary*, I try to tell myself. There's no future for us.

I rifle through the wardrobe until I find a cloth bag like the one Maisie had taken on her own hasty travels. This one isn't quite as large, but I won't need much where I'm going. Everything else, I can get on the road. I may have left my purse behind at the apartment in the Gray Quarter, but if I sell even one of Maisie's gowns or necklaces, I'll have plenty to fund my journey and beyond.

My mind whirls to solidify my plan. Travel to Evanston on foot. Sell something of Maisie's in Black Square first thing in the morning. Board the nine o'clock train at Evanston Station, just like my train ticket says. Reach my destination in Lumenas.

If my violinist lover—*former* lover, that is—was right, I'll have no problem finding a troupe to join once I reach the city. Then all my dreams will come true. I'll be free of all bargains, all attachments. I can start a new life, have a new name, become a new person...

*I don't want you to be anyone else.*

I shake my head and return to less painful thoughts.

I'll join a band, travel the isle. Every night, I'll play the piano...

Memories of a certain piano bench flood my mind, of lips drawing near. Lips I finally got to taste tonight.

*I don't want you to be anyone else.*

*And I don't want* you.

A sob heaves from my chest, conjuring fresh tears to stream down my cheeks. No matter how I try to shift my train of thought, it goes again and again to those final words we exchanged. Words I didn't mean. Words that severed my heart deeper than it could have done his. Unless—unlike me—he *meant* what he said.

With heavy feet, I drag myself to the dressing table and open the hatbox full of silverware. I retrieve my locket and a tarnished silver knife, placing the locket in my bag and bringing the knife to the locked chest—the one that holds the final remnants of my true identity. I drag it away from the wall and crouch before it.

I can hardly see through the sheen of tears, but I funnel all my hurt, all my rage and pain into slamming the thick handle of the knife into the lock. I'm surprised when it comes loose and the hasp flips open after just three hard blows. Choking on another sob, I flip the toggle latches that flank the lock and lift the lid of the trunk.

I toss the clothing within onto the ground until I find my

hidden ballgown. With trembling fingers, I search through the folds for my train ticket and shoes, but the more I move, the heavier my limbs become. I feel as if my blood has been infused with cold iron. Pushing away from the trunk, I pull my knees to my chest and press my forehead against them. I reach for the base of my throat until my fingers come to the smooth opal crescent.

I breathe deeply for several moments, feeling my heart begin to ease. Then, with all the strength left in my limbs, I rise to my feet and check the clock.

Ten seconds until midnight.

Of course, the clock could be slow or fast...

*Nine.*

But magic is so deeply entwined with intent...

*Eight.*

*Seven.*

*Six.*

What will freedom feel like?

*Five.*

*Four.*

Do I even deserve it?

*Three.*

After everything I said to Franco...

*Two.*

After what I did to Father...

*One.*

My breath comes out in a rush, making me rock back on my feet. A buzz of energy surges from my core, spiraling down my legs, my arms, and out the crown of my head. One by one, my muscles loosen, my jaw unclenches, my stomach settles. The dull ache that's been my constant companion fades completely, taking with it pains I hadn't even realized I'd been harboring. In a matter of seconds, my body feels lighter, stronger. My mind grows clearer, my heart becomes warmer.

Just like that, I'm free.

*Free.*

The absence of two bargains feels euphoric. My chest heaves with the deepest, most tantalizing breaths I've ever taken. The sound of my heartbeat feels like a song, and for several moments all I can do is listen to it. Its rhythm speaks words I can almost hear, words that would become clear if only I'd tune in...

I reach for the base of my neck again and am reminded that I'm still wearing my ballgown and glamour. My heart squeezes as I glance down at my skirt, at the glamoured sheet music that graces my hem.

*A song for new life.*

*A song for safety.*

*A song for love.*

My lips pull into a small smile, one that lifts my heart. But that's not all it lifts. A surge of fear rises alongside it. I glance from the trunk where I've yet to retrieve my train ticket, then to my hastily packed bag.

Freedom is finally mine. I can live the life I've always wanted. Do the things I've always craved. Be the person I've always wanted to be.

*I don't want you to be anyone else.*

A lump rises in my throat.

Franco doesn't know me. He doesn't know who I really am.

But maybe he deserves to.

Without a second thought, I rush to the door and pull it open.

Franco stands on the other side.

I BLINK SEVERAL TIMES TO ENSURE I'M NOT IMAGINING THINGS, but when it's clear the prince is truly there, my heart flutters wildly in my chest. Franco stands with a hand braced on my doorframe, his head lowered, posture slouched. I recall the first time I found him like this. He'd been confident then. So smug. He'd lifted his head with the most practiced, charming grin. One I scoffed at.

This time, though, he seems tired. Defeated. Hurt.

Hurt by *me*.

"Franco." His name comes out like a plea. Everything in me wants to reach for him, comfort him, touch him so I know with even more certainty that he's real.

He lifts his eyes to mine. His voice comes out strained. "I'm sorry I disobeyed your wishes, but please hear me out. I'm not here to make you stay. I'm here to tell you how I feel. You can leave without a word once I've said my piece. You can reject me with all your rage. I'll accept that. I'm ready for it, for every agonizing inch of it. Just please hear me out."

I try to swallow the lump in my throat to no avail. Without the use of words, all I can do is nod. Then, on trembling legs, I move aside and let him in. He strides into my room without looking at me, and I close the door behind him. I watch as he walks toward the balcony doors, then paces back and forth while running a hand over his face. Finally, he stops and faces me.

"I...I think I love you, Em."

My breath catches.

"No," he says, sending my heart sinking. "I don't *think*. That's me still being afraid." He closes the distance between us and rests his hands softly on my shoulders. His eyes lock on mine. "I love you. I know you're leaving and that's all right if that's what you feel you must do. I just want you to know that you are loved. That you are beautiful. That your magic is beautiful."

My eyes glaze over as warmth spreads throughout my chest.

I want to tell him things I've left buried deep in my heart, and yet...the fear remains.

"You don't even know what I look like," I whisper.

"Why does it matter what you look like? Your face could be hideous by traditional standards, and it wouldn't diminish your beauty, for I've seen the tapestry of your emotions. I've felt what you've felt, I've witnessed the kind of person you are. I've heard you hum and seen depths of your energetic signature that might as well have been your soul. I know you're kind yet brutally honest. You're intelligent without being arrogant. You look out for others even though you've clearly been hurt yourself. You've felt ostracized and shamed for your dangerous magic, and yet you haven't become a monster from it. You haven't let it change who you really are, a being of wild feral beauty and strong human determination. Of empathy and rage. Even though I never saw your unmasked face, I saw *you*, Em. And I see you now. I love you. No matter how badly I want you to stay with every beat of my heart, I won't make you. I won't ask you to. But please know that you were loved by me." He holds my gaze a few moments longer, then releases my shoulders and takes a step back. "That's all I wanted to say."

His words send a storm wind through my heart. My tongue feels heavy in my mouth. I could stay silent. I could let him walk away.

Or I could tell him the truth.

"I'm afraid," I say.

"Of what?"

I take a step closer to diminish the distance he placed between us. "That when you know who I really am, you'll take back every word you said."

"I won't."

"Then..." My heart pounds so hard, I feel it might burst as I reach for the ribbon tying the glamoured shoes to my feet. For the second time tonight, I step out of the shoes in his presence.

This time, he's looking.

This time, I don't ask him to turn around.

I stand as tall as I dare, despite the fear that has me wanting to hide my face, my hair. "This is who I am, Franco."

He stares at me with an unreadable expression, saying nothing.

I avert my gaze, keeping my eyes anchored on his cravat. "For the last three years, ever since my father died, I've been living as a servant to my stepfamily because of a bargain my stepmother coerced me into. One day, my stepfamily had some scheme to meet the prince outside Madame Flora's shop, although I didn't learn about it until after. They didn't want the prince to meet them while they had their hideous maid in tow, so they sent me to the alley to keep out of the way. I obeyed."

I dare to look up, to assess Franco's reaction. It's clear when realization dawns in his eyes. His expression falls. "You. *You.* Of course it was you."

My stomach drops. This is where it ends. This is where he realizes he hadn't meant a word he said.

His lips flicker between a smile and a frown. "Oh, Em, I'm so sorry. There's no excuse for how I spoke to you that day. What could I ever do to earn your forgiveness?" His tone is full of regret, but is it regret over the things he said? Or that he confessed feelings he'll have to take back?

"You already have earned it, Franco. I don't blame you anymore. I hated you after our encounter, but now that I've gotten to know you, I understand why you push people away like that. Why you hate meeting strangers. Why you despise being hounded after by admirers who know nothing about who you really are."

His throat bobs. "And?"

"And what?"

"How do you feel about me now?"

A torrent of fear blows through me, sealing my lips.

But no. I am no longer a prisoner. I will allow myself to be free. To speak freely. No matter how much it could end up hurting.

My voice comes out with a quaver. "I love you."

He releases a sigh.

I close my eyes, unable to look at him, to assess what that sigh means. "And you? Now that you know my true self—"

His hands come to my cheeks, and I open my eyes to find his smiling face before mine. "Nothing has changed. I meant every word I said."

"But don't you see? It doesn't matter. I'm not a princess and I won't be your mistress."

He brushes his thumb along my cheek. "How can I make myself any clearer? You have my whole heart. If that means I can't be king, then so be it. If I must sacrifice who I truly am to maintain a stranglehold on the throne, then this is no longer a throne worth fighting for."

"But the queen—"

"Maybe she's wrong," he says. "She might be a powerful queen, but maybe she's wrong about the best way for me to be king. Maybe a marriage to a princess isn't what will earn the people's respect. Maybe our people need someone *real*. Regardless of what my people want, it's what I want. *You* are what I want. Whom I love. Even if you remain determined to leave, wherever you go, my heart will follow. I'll keep away from you in body, if that is what you wish, but you have my heart now."

I allow my lips to flicker up slightly, lifted by the hope that glows warm in my core. It grows brighter, sending the last remnants of my fear burning away. "You have mine too."

"What's your name?"

"Ember."

"Ember." The word comes out with a breath like a gentle breeze. "That's why you let me call you Em. It was never meant to be the letter *M*."

"It's what my parents called me. You can still call me that if you'd like."

"Em. My Ember."

The sound of my name—my full name—fills my heart with the most delectable pleasure. "My Franco."

His lips come to mine, reigniting the fiery passion we left behind at the lake. This time, I hold nothing back. I wrap my arms around his neck, pressing myself close to him. His tongue caresses mine and I moan against his lips. One of my hands weaves through his hair, while the other trails over the front of his shoulder and slips over his silk cravat, still damp from our swim. I trail my fingers down to the collar of his shirt, where I slide my hand over the warmth of his chest. He pulls back slightly, a question in his eyes. I hold his gaze as my fingers come to the knot in his cravat.

My lips quirk into a smile, and his answering smirk sends heat uncoiling from my abdomen. His lips return to mine, but our kisses are slower now, softer. I untie his cravat and throw it on the floor, then slide my hands beneath his jacket until it too drops to the ground. His waistcoat comes next. As I reach for the buttons on his shirt, he bends down to hoist me beneath my thighs and props me onto my dressing table. His lips trail down my neck, and I angle my head to allow him greater access. I continue to loosen the remaining buttons of his shirt while his hands come to the clasps at the back of my gown. Once his final button is free, he shrugs his shirt off completely. I run my hands up and down his torso, tracing the lines of his tattoos until he presses close to me once more to finish unhooking the clasps of my dress.

His hands go still behind me, then slowly move to my sleeves. He holds my gaze as he pulls them over my shoulders, my arms, until the bodice hangs around my waist, revealing my corset and chemise. There he pauses and pulls back to look at me, hands braced on either side of the dressing table.

"You're absolutely stunning," he says. His eyes trail from the neckline of my chemise to my collarbone. He lifts one hand to my hair and runs his hands through the length of it. "This color, it's beautiful." His eyes meet mine. "You're beautiful."

Our lips meet. Softly. Slowly. He pulls back again.

Sitting tall, I bring my fingers to the top hook of my corset and release it. Then I move to the next. The next. He watches my every move, his breaths shallow as his muscles tense. Once free of my corset, I lean forward and claim his mouth. He opens it for me, and I brush my tongue against his. He groans, and his hands come to my chemise. With slow, gentle movements, he slips it down, exposing my skin an inch at a time, until the fabric joins my bodice around my waist. Keeping one hand on my hip, he slides the other up my waist, then over the curve of my breast. His hand feels warm on my bare skin, and I arch into his touch. He draws his thumb in a lazy circle, making me throw my head back and bite my lip.

That seems to unravel him. He lifts me again, and this time he takes me to my bed. As soon as my back hits the soft blankets, I shove my skirts down past my hips, aided by his hands. Then he reaches for the buttons on his trousers. I watch him loosen button after button. I'm eager to see just how far his black ink trails down his torso and am pleased to discover it travels quite far indeed, ending just above the swell of him. Our eyes meet and I scoot farther onto the bed. He steps out of his trousers and lowers himself next to me. With reverent attention, he runs his hand up my calf, my thighs. I explore the planes of his chest with my fingertips, then rest my hand on his hip.

"Your tattoos are beautiful," I say, voice breathless.

His eyes light over the length of me, and a sly grin tips a corner of his mouth. "So are yours."

Confused, I glance down at myself. A bark of laughter escapes my lips as I find my skin speckled with silver moons and constellations. Around my ankles wrap the three staves of music. My fingers move to the necklace. "I didn't realize the glamour would work on skin too."

"Do you want me to remove your necklace?"

I nod. "I don't want there to be any glamour between us right now."

He reaches for the back of my neck and unhooks the clasp. After setting the necklace on my nightstand, he returns to me and cups my cheek in his hand. "I love you, Ember."

The sound of my name paired with his declaration of love sends a euphoric shudder through me. "I love you, Franco."

We kiss again and I arch against him. His hands move over my body, and once he finishes exploring me by touch, he does it all over again with his lips, trailing kisses across my skin, over my breasts, between my thighs. He then kisses down each leg, leaving fire in his wake. The tingling at the apex of my thighs is almost unbearable, searing me to my core. Nothing has ever felt like this. No lover has ever sparked such yearning in me. No *love* has ever had me so enraptured.

His fingers light over my stomach, lowering inch by inch until they reach the place that craves him most. I move against him, but it isn't enough. I want all of him.

Pressing a hand to his chest, I angle him onto his back and climb on top of him. His eyes go wide with surprise, but his smile is pleased. I bend down to taste his lips, positioning my hips over his. I move against him again, then down, until I glide over him completely. He fills me, finally reaching that ache. We begin to move in tandem. I hold his gaze, then watch as his hands move over every inch of me. Beneath his gaze, his touch, I grow bolder, freer. I've never felt so alive, so powerful, so strong. My heart glows with love while my body writhes with pleasure. Every moan that escapes my lips feels like a song, and his sounds of passion are an answering harmony. We continue our duet, creating a symphony. Our melody rises, reaching a crescendo. We become one instrument, one song, one perfectly tuned piano key poised to ring out its final note. When it finally strikes, release unravels through me in sync with Franco's undoing.

We remain in place, several moments after, catching our breath. Our eyes lock, and we break into giddy smiles that say far more than words can. Then, after brushing my lips softly against his, I sink onto his chest and press my ear to the pounding rhythm of his heart.

## 43

**FRANCO**

I wake to the feel of silken hair against my face, to the smell of rose, citrus, and sky. Beneath my hands lies soft, smooth skin. I open my eyes and find Ember nestled with her back against my chest, my arm over her waist. A surge of delight warms me while pure joy radiates down my arms. Memories of last night's lovemaking return, and I feel myself tense against her. It isn't just the physical pleasure I recall. It's the way her energy fed mine and mine fed hers. The way my heart fell gaping open with every kiss I gave her, with every inch of flesh I offered for her to claim.

I close my eyes and breathe her in, sensing her peace, her contentment in sleep. This moment feels both foreign and familiar at once. Foreign, because I've never spent the night with a lover. Not like this. Not with someone whose heart has become woven with my own. But familiar, because Ember's small form, her warmth, her vibrant energy, feels like something I've been waiting for my whole life.

I nestle closer and plant a kiss in her hair. She stirs and

releases a contented moan, one that has my heart flipping. With her eyes still closed, she turns toward me, a smile on her lips. I run a hand over her arm, and a ripple of uncertainty moves through me. What if she opens her eyes, and I find regret in them? What if she takes one look at me, realizes where she is and who she's with, and her energy contracts?

Dark halls flood my memory, reminding me of shadows spilling forth in my grief. I hadn't realized how badly I've feared rejection until I told Ember the story of how my mother left and the sorrow that followed. The experience taught me how to make others laugh, how to turn their attention away from me, how to divert one's pity. But it taught me other things too. Things I hadn't realized weighed so heavy on my soul.

Ember flutters her eyes open and angles her face to mine.

I hold my breath and await whatever reaction she gives...

Her brow furrows for a moment as she searches my eyes. Then she brings a hand to my cheek and greets me with a firm kiss. My hand tightens on her waist and all my fears drain away. She pulls back slightly. "I thought you might not be real," she whispers.

I chuckle. "I am real. As real as you are." My gaze roves over her face, her hair, her bare skin, and I feel as if my heart might fall right out of my chest. "I don't think I'll ever get tired of looking at you now that I get to see your true form."

A smile tugs her lips, one I've seen so many times now, but on a different face. Even though the glamour altered her appearance, I realize just how little it hid of her expressions. Her grin, her frown, her pondering look...it's all familiar to me. With an element of newness to it, of course. A newness I find more than pleasing.

She runs her hands over my chest, and her gaze falls to my torso. "Can I ask about your tattoos?"

"Aren't you already asking?"

She glowers, making me bark a laugh. I know that look. It's

one of the first expressions I ever saw her glamoured face make. "You think you're so funny, don't you?"

"Yes, you know this. I'm funny and charming—"

"Oh, yes, I recall Prince Charming telling me all about his wit and humor."

I shrug. "You didn't believe me at the time. I had to make sure you knew."

She rolls her eyes. "Well, I know now."

"Don't forget handsome. I'm certain I told you I'm handsome as well."

A sly glint sparks in her eye. "Actually, one of the first things you told me was that you thought I wanted to have a tryst with you against an alley wall."

Guilt sinks my stomach. I recall how cold and cruel I was when I met her. Never would I have guessed that the woman in that alley would become my beloved. I'm about to apologize again for my behavior, but the turn of her lips has me smirking instead. "Well, do you?"

She pretends to ponder. "I wouldn't find it appalling."

"Not appalling. I can certainly give you that."

I kiss her jaw and roll on top of her, bracing myself on my forearms. She giggles but keeps her hand on my chest. "You never answered my question about your tattoos."

"You only asked if you could ask about them."

Another roll of her eyes, but her smile remains bright. "Why do you have them?"

I glance down at my torso, trying not to get distracted by the expanse of tantalizing flesh pressed beneath me. "My seelie form bore ink-like designs from the very first time I learned to shift. It took decades for me to realize it was considered uncommon. Other seelie fae were the ones who pointed it out, saying humans referred to such markings as tattoos. Mine aren't placed by ink and needle, but they do change on occasion."

She traces a fingertip over one of the intricate geometric patterns. "Do they hold meaning?"

"Nyxia suggests they represent my connection to the Twelfth Court, the spiritual realm of the All of All, for that is where our energy and form emerge from. As a psy vampire, energy and emotions take shape inside me, transforming into scent, taste, and color. This," I gesture to my torso, "I think represents my energetic signature in physical form."

"Franco, that's beautiful." She continues to trace the patterns, circling the phases of the moon over my ribs, the overlapping triangles at my sternum.

I worry my lip, wondering if I should say what's on my mind. Will she think it's strange? I clear my throat. "I think you'll find yourself there."

Her eyes meet mine. "What do you mean?"

I swallow hard. "There's a new pattern emerging over my heart."

She drags her hand over my pectoral and rests it over the beating flesh. Then, with the softest touch imaginable, she traces the circle that surrounds the new pattern. Once. Twice. Then she drags her finger over the two triangles held within the circle, each pointing upward and bisected with a horizontal line, both representing air. Flight. The sky.

"You're a wind fae, aren't you? *Half* wind fae, I should say."

Her face flickers with surprise. "Yes. How did you know?"

"The tattoo gave me a clue. But…I've known for a while. You use a Wind Court term when you swear sometimes."

She slaps an embarrassed hand to her face, but there's only mirth in her energy. Then she returns her attention to the pattern over my heart, tracing the triangles yet again. One is connected to a secondary triangle, this one pointing down to represent the element of water, Lunar Court's elemental affinity. Finally, she traces both halves of the curved arching line that ends in a spiral, the mirrored image forming a shape that looks very much like a heart.

"You're sure this is new?" she asks.

I nod. "New patterns show up out of nowhere sometimes. This one started forming probably the day we met. I only noticed it after the opera. It's us. Me and you."

She stares back at me, her emotions swelling with awe. Then, sliding her hands from my chest to behind my neck, she pulls me to her. Our mouths meet in a soft kiss, one of honeyed sweetness and emotions too vast to give name to. It's a kiss I wish would stretch on forever, this gentle exchange of wordless promises. It isn't long before heat sparks, starting between our lips. Ember opens her mouth, arching slightly against me. My tongue brushes hers igniting desire to radiate through every inch of me. Like last night, I feel both our energies at the same time. Fueling one another. Combining. Encircling. Heightening. She wraps her legs around my waist and rolls her hips against mine. I shudder as I feel her open for me. Inviting. Begging. Pleading.

I bring myself unbearably close, hovering just above her. She weaves her hands through my hair as I drag my lips down her throat, her collarbone, my tongue flicking over her peaked breast. Her breaths come hot and fast as she brings her mouth to my ear. "Franco," she whispers.

Restraint burns inside me, so intense I fear our passions could be over too soon. Then, little by little, I sheathe myself. She gasps, throwing her head back. The sight is almost too much, but I refuse to let it wreck me. Not yet. Not until we've fully explored the pleasure of this new pattern, this new dance, this new energy we're creating. We move together, a vibrant glow pulsing around us, waxing as bright as the moon. As bright as her smile. As bright as my love for her.

WE LAY SPENT ON OUR BACKS, ENTANGLED IN SHEETS AND SWEAT and limbs. As I look her over, she grins. I roll onto my side and face her. "So, I know we were only formally introduced yesterday—"

"Franco!" She swats me playfully on the arm, but the movement is slow and sloppy, expressing her fatigue in the wake of our passion.

"—and I swear I don't normally do this."

She snorts a laugh. "Do what?"

"Ask someone whose name I only learned the night before if they will be my mate."

"Is that a question?"

Trepidation makes my pulse race. She may have confessed she loves me back, but she never said she'd stay. And...I've never had a mate before. "Yes, Ember. Will you be my mate?"

She turns toward me. "Yes." Her smile stretches from ear to ear, only faltering when a flicker of cloudy energy dampens her emotions.

"What is it?"

"Well...before we can be *anything*, there are issues we should talk about. There remain things about me I haven't told you yet."

"Oh, yes. These dreadful *things* you think might change how I feel. You don't still think that, do you?"

"No, I don't," she says, and I know she means it. But her murky energy remains. "Still, you need to know them because they will impact how we...come out to people. You might have to help me with something."

"I'll do anything. Besides, I'm looking forward to hearing this grand tale of yours. How you came to bargain with a princess." I claim her lips with a light kiss. "How you stole my heart."

"I'll get to the part about Princess Maisie, but more pressingly I should tell you about the bargain that preceded it. The one with my stepmother." She nibbles her lip, then opens and closes her mouth a few times without uttering a single word. Then, gesturing for me to give her a moment, she climbs out of bed and crosses the room to the wardrobe. From within, she extracts a silk robe. Even though it fully covers her, I can still see every curve of her body beneath it, and it takes a bit of focus not to study her tantalizing peaks and valleys. She returns to the bed and perches on a corner of it. "Remember how I told you I've been trapped beneath a bargain I made with my stepmother? Well, the night of the New Moon Masquerade, she used our bargain to force me into an unwanted situation. You see, the terms of our arrangement required that I remain living under her roof and that I obey her. One of her last demands before I ran away was that I become engaged to a man I did not care for. As my guardian, she agreed to our engagement in my name."

A cold dread fills my stomach with iron. No. Please say it isn't so...

"What's your name?" I ask, trying to keep my voice level. "Your surname, that is."

"Montgomery. That's my father's last name."

The blood leaves my face. "You're Brother Marus' fiancée. You're his Miss Montgomery."

"Yes, but I will not marry him," she says in a rush. "I never intended to in the first place, which is why I ran away and took refuge behind a glamour all this time. Now that our bargain is fulfilled, my stepmother cannot make me continue with our engagement."

Her words are a comfort to me, but it does nothing to soothe the agony that begins to writhe in my gut. A sharp pain strikes my heart, and I gasp for breath.

Shit. The promise I made to Marus. One I have no intention of keeping.

*I promise that if your Miss Montgomery returns to Selene Palace, and I am made aware of her presence, I'll return her to you...*

This is bad.

My lungs begin to tighten, and it takes all my effort to leap from the bed and grab my trousers.

"Franco, please don't be upset."

"It's not you," I say, voice strained. I pull on my pants, my shirt, gathering the rest of my clothing as fast as I can. "I promise, it isn't you. There's something I need to do."

Ember reaches for me, but my vision is already growing dark at the edges. It pains me to flee like this, but I'm running out of time.

A broken promise is akin to a broken bargain. A lie.

And for a fae, that means death.

I reach for the door. "I'll be back. I'm sorry." On unsteady legs, I run down the hall.

**EMBER**

I stare at the closed door, perplexed. While I knew he might be surprised by what I had to tell him, his hasty exit was not what I'd been expecting. And yet, he promised it wasn't me he was upset with. He said he'd be back.

Brow furrowed, I stalk the room, then finally throw open the curtains. The morning light is bright despite the Lunar Court's perpetual haze, suggesting we slept in quite late. Well, perhaps *sleep* isn't the most accurate word...

A small smile comes to my lips, and thoughts of his mouth, his body, the pounding of his heart, helps alleviate some of my worry. With a sigh, I open the balcony doors and step between them. It's my first time standing on my balcony like this with my own face. Closing my eyes, I tilt my head back and breathe in the fresh air, delighting in the absence of bargains. There's nothing to weigh me down. Nothing to restrain me.

"She has her old face back," squeals a teasing feminine voice.

I open my eyes, knowing exactly what I'll find. My three menacing wisp friends dart around me, giggling and pointing.

"She found her destination. I can tell," says the second female.

"She did, she did!" says the male. "But not his bedroom. Hers! He came to hers! You owe me ten moonstone chips, Deloise."

"No," says Deloise, "I'm the one who said he'd come to her last night."

"Lies!"

"Not a lie. You're just remembering wrong."

"We helped, didn't we?" says the other female. "It was the dance. The dance! I told you we are excellent navigators."

I shake my head with amusement. "If you're going to harass me all the time, at least tell me your names."

"Deloise," says the first wisp, pointing at herself. Then she points to the other two. "And they are Lila and Jack."

The male shakes his fist. "It's Jacque."

"Jock."

He draws out the name slower, longer. "Jacque."

Deloise shrugs. "I don't see the difference."

I chuckle. "Well, it's nice to formally meet you."

"You should thank us for all our help," Lila says.

"Thank you for...whatever you think you've done."

The wisps spin with a wild chortle, nearly making me miss the rhythmic sound coming from inside my room.

The door.

My heart hammers fiercely at the thought of Franco returning. I all but sprint back into my room and nearly open the door in nothing by my sheer silk robe. Thinking better of it, I throw a thicker robe over it and slip the glamoured shoes onto my feet. Until Franco and I have a solid plan, it's probably best if no one sees my real face. Not until we figure out what to do about my stepfamily.

The three wisps whirl about my head as I make my way across the room, glamour in place. "Will you go away already?" I say with a laugh.

Then I open the door.

Imogen stands on the other side, lips lifted into a smirk. "Hello, Ember."

## 44

**FRANCO**

Pain continues to sear through me as I make my way down the halls. The walls feel as if they're closing in on me, turning, spinning. My legs feel weak. Gasping for breath, I blink to clear my vision of the ever-creeping darkening blur. I reach a staircase, one I know leads to my destination. Agony writhes through my stomach, and I double over, grasping the railing to keep from falling. Then, one trembling step after the other, I make my way up the stairs and down the hall.

When I arrive at the intended door, I slam my fist into it. Every move feels heavy, unwieldy. The door opens seconds later. Or is it minutes? One look at Brother Marus standing on the other side clears a fraction of my pain. I let rage build inside me and erupt in the form of shadows. With a growl, I charge Marus, pressing my forearm against his throat as I turn him toward the wall and pin him there.

"Revoke it," I hiss through my teeth.

Marus' eyes are wide, his movements frantic as he tries to push me off him. "Revoke what?"

Pain continues to tear at my insides, but the taste of his fear acts as temporary fuel, nourishing me, battling the detrimental effects of the promise I know I must break. "Tell me you revoke what you asked me to promise."

Indignation darkens his expression. "No!"

I press my forearm firmer into his throat. "Revoke it *now*!"

"I'll do no such thing," he says between gasping breaths, voice strained. "You promised me you'd turn her over. If you know where she is, then tell me."

I let my shadows darken, send them digging into his skull. I try to summon my glamour, but my magic doesn't seem to obey. Already, my strength is beginning to wane. Especially as his fear shifts into anger, giving me less potent food to take in. My forearm slips, but I feign purpose and dig my elbow into his chest instead. My next words come out tremulous. "Revoke it or I will kill you."

"You must be out of your mind, Your Highness. How dare you threaten me in such a way? I'm the queen's favorite." He tries to push my arm away. I'm only barely holding on...

"You're no favorite of mine, Marus," comes Nyxia's voice, calm despite the panicked energy I sense from her. "I hardly even like you. Now, Franco, get off him and tell me what this is all about!"

I clench my jaw and hold Marus' gaze. Sweat drips into my eyes and I realize my face is covered in a cold sheen of it. Another invisible dagger slices through me. I wince and pull away from him, panting. My strength drains even further. It takes all my determination to remain on my feet.

"Your *brother*," Marus says like a growl, "promised he'd turn my fiancée over to me as soon as he learned of her presence in the palace. And now he's trying to get me to revoke my side of the promise. I won't do it, Your Majesty. She's my fiancée. You said I could have my choice of bride and that you'd support me."

"I did say that." Nyxia's tone is dark, her annoyance swirling against the tides of her concern for me. "Franco, why would you try to get out of the promise you made him?"

"I love her."

Marus scoffs. "You love her? How can you love her? She's *my* fiancée. You don't even know her."

Nyxia faces me, concern shifting into terror. "Franco, you aren't making any sense. If this girl is Brother Marus' fiancée, he deserves to see her. You're overreacting."

I sway on my feet and feel Nyxia's hands come to my shoulders to steady me. My heart pounds hard in my chest, but the beat is slow. Waning. I try to shake my head to clear my thoughts, but it doesn't help. Is Nyxia right? Am I overreacting? Nothing makes sense...

"Just tell him where she is," Nyxia says.

"Talk," I manage to whisper. "That's what I promised."

"Yes, Your Highness," Marus hisses, "I recall, and I have every intention of talking with her."

"*Only* talk." I cut a glare at him, but with my vision nearly black, I'm not sure if it has its intended effect.

Nyxia lowers her voice to a whisper. "Franco, you're dying. Whatever you promised, it isn't worth keeping from him if it means your death."

*My death.* Yes, I am dying. How long have I been dying? Where am I?

"Franco!" Nyxia's voice calls out with alarm, and I feel like I'm no longer inside my body. A second or an eternity later, I find myself on my back, something soft beneath me. My sister stands over me, voice quavering. "Just tell him where his fiancée is."

Fear dances over my tongue—Nyxia's fear—and I breathe it in. It relieves some of my agony and gives me a moment of clarity. "Princess Maisie's room," I say, my voice barely above a whisper. "Only talk, though. Only talk."

"Do you consider his promise fulfilled?" Nyxia's voice is full of rage, but I can't seem to open my eyes to assess her face.

"Not until I see her for myself," Marus says.

My sister's tone darkens. "I'll take you there, but I won't forget this, Marus. I won't forget you let my brother's life hang on the line. I could kill you where you stand."

"And I won't forget that you've both threatened my life in the span of a minute, Your Majesty. If you'd like to make good on your threat, then I promise you my brotherhood won't forget either." There's a warning in his tone, but my mind is slipping again. I can't make sense of what it means. Brotherhood. Death. All I know is pain.

When next I hear Nyxia's voice, it's whispered next to my ear. "I'll be back. Hold tight. As soon as he sees her, your promise will be fulfilled."

A flash of teal hair and smiling lips comes to mind, giving me another surge of clarity. I open my eyes to see Nyxia turning away and grasp her hand before she's out of reach. "Don't let anyone hurt her. Promise me."

She furrows her brow. "I promise."

That's the last thing I see. The last thing I hear. Then nothingness swallows me whole.

## EMBER

With a frightened squeal, the three wisps dart away and fly out the balcony door. My heart hammers, and I feel the blood leave my face at the sight of my stepsister standing on the other side of my threshold. Gone is the uncertainty she revealed the last time we spoke. She's all smug confidence as she narrows her gaze at me.

"I know it's you, so don't even try to deny it." Imogen brushes past me, leaving me gaping at the empty doorway.

What do I do? Try to convince her she's wrong? Keep up the act?

Now that the bargain is broken, there's very little she can hold over me. Before I revealed my true identity to Franco, my greatest fear was that he wouldn't accept me for who I am. That he wouldn't fight for me or defend me against my stepfamily's wicked schemes once he realized what he'd be dealing with. There is still the matter of him fleeing so mysteriously, but I trust him now. Which means there's nothing Imogen can do to hurt me anymore.

I close the door with a slam and round on my stepsister. "What do you want?"

"You don't deny it. Good." She reaches into the pocket of her skirt and takes out a piece of paper, holding it toward me as she unfolds it.

I freeze, recognizing my train ticket. The one I'd stashed with my ballgown and shoes. My eyes flash toward the trunk.

Imogen snickers. "I called on a locksmith to open that thing days ago when you were off playing princess with His Highness."

My stomach roils. I recall how easy the lock was to open last night, needing nothing more than a few quick jabs with a knife handle. Now I know why. It hadn't been locked at all.

She continues. "You may have fooled me after I confronted you about the locket, but I was determined to follow my suspicions to the end. Even once I found your old things and this little train ticket of yours, I knew there was still a chance Princess Maisie was only harboring you. Then, last night, I *knew*."

"How?"

Her lips curl into a sneer. "It was when I saw you at the ball last night. Your face may not have been your own, but your smile was. Your eyes were. No wonder you've been keeping your expression so impassive around me and Clara these past couple weeks. When I saw you smile and laugh with the prince last night, there was no denying who you really were. And when you *danced*," she says the last word through her teeth, "I felt the same way I do when you play your infernal piano. When you *sing*."

I narrow my eyes. "I ask you again. What do you want?"

She takes a few leisurely steps closer, wrinkling her nose at the clothes strewn about the floor—clothes I'd originally had packed for my journey before Franco came to me last night. Without looking at me, she says, "I told Mother where you are. Told her about all the things I found hiding in Princess Maisie's trunk. She's on her way with royal guards to haul you back to Brother Marus. He doesn't know yet. I've told only her."

"Then why are you here? To ensure I don't run away before they get here?"

"No, it's quite the opposite. I want to give you a chance to flee the fate you so desperately want to avoid." She flashes the train ticket still clasped in her fingers. "You can have this back. You can leave here now, and you won't have to go through with marrying Brother Marus. All you need to do is give me whatever glamour you're wearing. When Mother arrives, I'll tell her you fled before I got here, and I'll send her on a false trail so you can get safely away."

She says it like she's doing me a favor, but she isn't fooling me. I bark a laugh. "You want my glamour?"

"Yes." Her answer comes quickly, devoid of even the slightest shame. "I want whatever makes you look like Princess Maisie. It will serve us both well. You'll be free and I'll have what is rightly mine."

"What are you so convinced is rightly yours? Prince Franco?

He doesn't belong to you. Besides, he already knows who I am. He won't believe you're the princess."

Her expression hardens. "You're lying. How could he possibly know who you are?"

"I told him."

"Why?"

I lift my chin. "Because he loves me. *Me.* Not as the false princess, but Ember Montgomery. Orphan and servant."

"I refuse to believe that."

"It's true. He's a psy vampire, Imogen. You can try to take my glamour all you want, but he'll know at once that you are neither me nor the real Maisie."

She shakes her head and whirls toward my dressing table, bracing her hands on its surface. She stares down at the open hatboxes filled with Maisie's treasures. "Don't you dare try to take this from me."

"You don't stand a chance. You never did. Not with him, not with any of your previous schemes."

Her face whips toward me, eyes burning with hatred. "Do you enjoy watching me fail? Is that why you wormed your way into a position where you could charm the Raven Prince? To take him from me when you knew Mother wanted me to woo him? Did you relish my pain when Gemma Bellefleur stole my beloved last year? Have you laughed yourself silly these past three years when I come away from every social season without a husband?"

"I don't laugh, and I don't enjoy it," I say with all sincerity. "I pity you."

"Pity." She scoffs. "How dare you pity me? I pity *you.* You're delusional if you think you have the prince's heart, and I'll hear not a word more about it. Give me your glamour. Now."

"No."

With a roar, she charges me. I dart back in time to avoid the slash of the knife she brandishes. She must have taken it from

Maisie's collection. "Where is it? What holds the glamour?" She eyes me from head to toe, and her gaze locks on my feet. "It's the shoes, isn't it?"

I back up a few paces, looking from her to the knife in her hand. Imogen has never shown a tendency toward physical violence, and I doubt she knows how to wield a knife. Still, I'd rather not get struck by a recklessly handled piece of silverware, regardless of the lack of skill behind it.

She lunges again, and I whirl away from her knife hand. But it isn't that hand that strikes me. It's her open palm. She shoves it into my shoulder, sending me careening to the floor. I bite out a cry as I land hard on my hip. Imogen falls over my feet, wresting one of the shoes from it. Without the ribbons I normally secure them with, she easily frees one. I claim the other before she can take it too.

I scramble to my feet and dart toward the dressing table. She leaps for me with the knife, but I raise the glass heel above the corner. "I'll break it!"

She freezes, understanding sparking in her eyes. If I break the shoe, the glamour will be broken too. "Don't," she says with a gasp. "Give it to me. I'll give you the train ticket and you'll be free."

"I'm already free." I lift the heel of the shoe high overhead and bring it down hard on the corner with all my might. The glass shatters, sending shards to the floor.

With a cry, Imogen drops the knife and dives to the ground, seeking the broken pieces. "What have you done?" she wails. "You selfish, conniving—"

My door swings open. It isn't Mrs. Coleman and the guards that I expect but a beautiful, towering woman with short silver hair. It's Queen Nyxia.

Behind her stands Brother Marus.

# 45

### EMBER

Nyxia whirls toward Marus, her voice like ice as she says, "Is this your supposed fiancée?"

He assesses me with a hard look. "Yes."

"Then do you consider my brother's promise to you fulfilled?"

He nods.

"Say it aloud," she hisses.

"I consider Prince Franco's promise to me fulfilled."

My heart clenches, and the breath flees my lungs. What does he mean by Franco's promise? I recall when Marus confronted Franco at the ball last night. He mentioned something about a promise then, but...

He couldn't have...

He wouldn't...

"Wonderful," Nyxia says with exaggerated sweetness before turning back to the door.

Imogen rises to her feet. "Wait, Your Majesty!"

Nyxia turns around with fire in her eyes. "What now?"

My stepsister burns me with a glare and dips into a low curtsy. "This girl, my stepsister, has been impersonating Princess Maisie. This," she holds up the shoe still grasped in one hand, "is the item that held the glamour. I have discovered her vile subterfuge."

The queen takes the shoe and pins me with a dark look. "Is this true?"

My knees quake and I'm unable to find my words.

She brushes past my stepsister toward me. Imogen stands and staggers back toward Marus as dark tendrils of shadow, much like the ones I've seen Franco wield, emerge from the queen and attach to my skull. Fear lances through me. "Answer my question and speak only the truth. Now."

"Yes," I gasp. "For the last two weeks, I've worn a glamour that makes me look like Princess Maisie. We had a bargain. She asked me to impersonate her." Everything comes out in a rush, and I know it's the queen's magic that compels me. Still, I maintain a sliver of free will, and with that I avoid revealing *too much*—particularly that Maisie seemed to be in danger and used our bargain to run away. I also leave out mention of Franco's involvement with my scheme. Despite how my heart aches from his confounding betrayal, I can't bring myself to condemn him. Not until I have a clear understanding of what's going on.

Nyxia releases me from her shadows, and I inhale a sharp breath. Glancing at Marus, she says, "Are you sure this is your chosen bride? A criminal? I could punish her for what she's done."

Marus gapes before answering. "She obviously got embroiled in some unsavory business involving the princess. You heard her. She said Princess Maisie asked her to impersonate her."

She snorts a dark laugh. "And you're still determined to marry her?"

"I am. All that awaits is the signing of our marriage license."

"No," I say, stepping toward the terrifying queen. My heart riots against my ribs. "I do not agree to this marriage and I never have. Until midnight last night, I've been serving a bargain with my stepmother. She used that bargain to engage me to this man, but I am not a minor. She had no right to offer my hand without my agreeing to it."

Nyxia grits her teeth, closing her eyes for a moment before facing Marus again. "Is this true?"

Marus says nothing, his face a stone mask. Imogen, however, speaks up. "My stepsister has been evading the fulfillment of her bargain with my mother by hiding here. We knew not where she was this entire time. Don't be fooled by her wicked manipulations."

I glower at Imogen and take another step toward the queen. "I was evading the bargain because my stepmother was using it for corrupt purposes. She should not be allowed to force me to marry a man against my will."

Nyxia's eyes are still on Marus. "If she's been evading a legally binding bargain *and* impersonating a princess, she belongs in the dungeon, not a chapel."

"I will not press charges for her previous disobedience, and neither will her stepmother," he says. "Regardless of how she feels about the ethics of our engagement, it stands because *you* promised me my choice of bride, Your Majesty."

She pinches the bridge of her nose. "I don't have time for this," she mutters. "Marus, I promised you your choice of bride, but that does not mean you get to steal whomever you want like you're some storybook barbarian."

My heart lifts, flooding with hope that the queen might take my side.

"Then again, she has committed many crimes," she says, sending my stomach plummeting to my feet. "I promised not to let anyone hurt her, and her only other option is the dungeon."

I step forward. "Then I'll go. I'll do anything but marry him."

Her lips lift into a smirk. "No, my dear. It seems marrying him just might be the *only* appropriate punishment for you."

"Thank you, Your Majesty," Marus says with a bow. "Will you oversee our nuptials? Her stepmother, I'm sure, would prefer haste."

She stares down her nose at him. "Who do you think I am? Take your bride and get out of my palace. Have your wedding at Saint Lazaro's Cathedral where you belong."

"Your Majesty." There's a note of pleading in his tone now. "Once we're married, we will need to return to claim her inheritance anyway. Wouldn't it be easier—"

"Make an appointment with my ambassador. I am not your secretary." With that, Nyxia storms out, leaving me alone with Imogen and Marus.

My breaths grow ragged, defeat tugging my bones. Where is Franco? What did he promise Marus? How could he let this happen after everything he said? After everything we shared...

Marus unties his cravat and pulls it taut between his fists. "Will you come quietly?"

I lift my chin. "No."

He lunges for me.

∽

## FRANCO

I wake up with a start, at a loss for where I am. I find myself prone on a settee in the middle of a large parlor. Pulling myself to sit, I look around, finding no one in the room but me. My limbs feel weak, my mind slow and heavy.

What in the hell happened?

Echoes of pain linger at the edges of my senses, but with every breath, I can feel myself regaining my strength. Then it comes back to me.

Ember's confession.

The pain of my broken promise.

My confrontation with Marus.

Then Nyxia taking him to her...

I rise to my feet, ignoring the tilt of my vision as I stride to the other side of the room and haul open the door. There I pause, bracing myself on the door frame. I breathe deep, seeking sources of nearby emotion. A few subtle strains of mundane energy reach me. It's nothing as potent as fear, but it's enough for me to gather my bearings and refuel even more of my lost strength. Once I feel somewhat sated, I take off down the halls, heading straight for Ember's room.

I gather more and more emotions from behind each door I pass, the nourishment making my feet grow lighter with every step. Finally, I arrive at her door and fling it open...

Her room is empty.

I make my way inside, taking in everything, seeking any clue about where she is. The bed is in the same state as I left it. The floor is strewn with clothing I hadn't noticed last night, but that's not what snags my attention. Near the dressing table, I find a discarded knife and the shards of a broken glass heel. Not far from there, I find the remnants of the shoe, glass heel gone. A lump burns the back of my throat as I lift it gingerly in my hands.

This can't be good.

I need to find her. But where is she?

I breathe in, sensing strains of leftover emotion, but the trail is faint. Old. How long was I out? Was it hours? Minutes? I breathe in again, seeking her energetic signature.

But it's gone.

Nowhere close.

A rush of blue light swirls around me, and I lift my eyes to find three frantic wisps darting above my head.

"The girl of air," one says, her tiny voice filled with a quaver. "They came for her, Your Highness."

"Brother Marus and my sister?" I ask.

"Yes, and the vile human," says another.

"Lady's maid, it's called," says the first.

"No, it's a stepsister."

"She stole her shoe!"

"But the girl of air would not let her take both."

"Broke it, she did!"

"Settle down," I say with as much calm as I can manage. "Where is Ember now?"

"They took her," says the male. "Covered her mouth."

"Tied her hands."

"Dragged her away, they did!"

I hold up my hands to silence them again. "Who's *they*? And where did they take her?"

"The vile angry humans. Gone in a coach."

"My sister allowed this?"

The wisps nod. One says, "She told them to take her and get out."

With a growl, I storm from Ember's room and seek out my sister's energetic signature. I follow it to her study. Without bothering to knock, I charge in with the force of my rage and find her sitting at her desk. "What have you done?"

Nyxia's energy flickers with surprise, then concern. Then sorrow. She rises from her desk. "Are you all right, Franco? I was so worried about you. Why the hell would you put your life at risk like that?"

"What have you done?" I repeat through my teeth. "What did they do with her? Where did they take her?"

"I turned the girl over to her fiancé."

"Was she willing?"

Her expression clouds with uncertainty. "Franco…"

"Was. She. Willing."

"Well, no, but it was either that or the dungeon. She's a criminal, Franco. She's been hiding out to evade a legally binding bargain with her stepmother. Worse than that, she's been impersonating Princess Maisie." She points at the broken shoe in my hand. "She's been using that as a glamour. I had the other destroyed."

I tighten my jaw, my heart pounding as if it will explode from my ribcage at any moment. All I want to do is shout. Scream. Flood the halls with shadows.

Nyxia's expression softens. "Brother, I'm so sorry. The woman you've been courting has been a fake all along—"

"I know who she is," I say. "I've known the entire time. We were in on it together."

She gasps, rounding the desk to approach me, eyes hardening with displeasure. "You can't be serious. You not only knew about this unlawful behavior but condoned it as well?"

"She was hiding from a bad situation." While I still don't know all the details, I've managed to put most of the pieces together in my mind. She was so anxious when she told me about her unwanted engagement. It now makes sense why her energy contracts with fear every time we've been in Marus' presence.

"It doesn't matter. She can't go unpunished—"

"Where is she? Where did they take her?"

"You can't go after her."

"I can and I will. If you know where they went, then tell me. Otherwise, I'll use my senses to track her. I don't care how long it takes. I'm going to find her and get her back."

"Why?"

"I love her. With all that I am, I *love* her."

Her eyes turn down at the corners, but her energy swarms with conflicting emotions. "You...you don't know—"

"Don't you dare tell me I don't know what I'm feeling. I know my own heart and there's nothing you can say that will change that."

"We can't go up against Saint Lazaro," she says, voice firm. "Our alliance with them is tenuous."

I shake my head. "It's tenuous because you've given too much freedom to Brother Marus. You've allowed his ambitions to grow unchecked."

"Are you questioning my judgment as queen?"

"Yes. Isn't that what a future king would do? Shouldn't your heir be bold enough to question the person he'll be challenging to the throne? Shouldn't I have thoughts of my own?"

She pauses, watching me. "If we go up against Saint Lazaro, we could spur on another rebellion. The Alpha Council will hold us responsible."

She's right about the Alpha Council. As the highest form of government in Faerwyvae—comprised of every king and queen on the isle—their support is integral. "We aren't going up against Saint Lazaro. We aren't threatening their religious freedom. We're standing up to one man. Brother Marus. I'll do it with or without you."

Her jaw shifts side to side. "This could end in disaster. One we might have to fight our way out of."

"When have you ever shied away from a fight? Besides, if our roles were reversed, and this were about Lorelei, I'd be fighting at your side without question. I've never asked for anything from you, but I'm asking now. I'm asking you to trust me."

"I do trust you."

"Then prove it." I take a step back. "Or don't. Either way, I'm going. It will be faster if you at least tell me where I might start looking."

"Fine," she says with a groan, her tone equal parts irritated and resigned. She closes her eyes and flicks her fingers one at a time, joints cracking, then rolls her neck. When she meets my gaze, there's a devious glint in her eye, one I rarely see anymore. "Come, little brother. Let's go stir some trouble."

# 46

**EMBER**

Bound and gagged, I sit slumped to the side in the coach. Imogen and Clara are pressed in next to me, while Mrs. Coleman and Brother Marus sit on the opposite bench. She and Clara found us while Marus and Imogen escorted me through the palace. Apparently, my stepmother's attempt to summon guards had been unsuccessful. Her look of indignation shifted quickly to delight when she saw me being hauled her way by Brother Marus. The smug curl of her lips was enough to make my blood boil. I tried to throw every curse her way, but with Marus' cravat tied over my mouth, my words were nothing more than muffled sound.

Now I await my fate. Of course, that doesn't mean I won't go down without a fight. Even now, I discreetly shift my hands in my bindings, trying to slip my fingers free from the hose Imogen tied around them. My jaw clenches when I recall the dark pleasure in her eyes when Marus asked her to help him tie me up. Anger flares in my heart, and I channel that rage into my efforts. If there was ever a time to become incorporeal like my mother, now would be it. What I wouldn't give to know how to take unseelie form...

From my periphery, a pair of eyes burn into me. I startle and meet Clara's gaze, certain she's discovered what I'm doing, but she isn't watching my hands. She's studying my face. There's a strange look in her eyes, but I'm not sure what it means. Is it betrayal? Shame? She hasn't said a word to me since the tale of my subterfuge was revealed.

"This really is the most unpleasant business," Mrs. Coleman says with a huff. "Why couldn't the queen have officiated the marriage at the palace? I thought you were supposed to be her favorite."

Marus shifts uncomfortably in his seat. "She said she didn't have time."

Mrs. Coleman scoffs. "Well, she better have time when we return for Ember's inheritance." She glances at me with a look of disgust.

I scoff behind my gag.

She narrows her eyes. "Was that supposed to be a laugh?"

"She's probably marveling at the cold irony of it all," Imogen says. "After all the trouble she's caused, she ended up losing far more than if she hadn't pulled such a ruse to begin with."

"You're quite right, dear," my stepmother says. "I doubt she'll ever be welcomed at the palace again. I just hope her misdeeds don't taint our reputation."

"Was the prince upset?" I'm surprised to hear Clara speak up for the first time since we began our tense journey.

"Oh, I'm sure he was very upset," Mrs. Coleman says. "What kind of man wouldn't be devastated after discovering the woman he's been courting was a fraud?"

My heart burns. I still don't understand what happened. Why did Franco run from me after I told him who I am? Why did he let Marus take me?

"I can attest that Prince Franco was quite upset," Marus says. "He was so enraged, he nearly lost his wits. You should have seen him attack me."

"The prince attacked you?" Clara says. "How dreadful!"

"It was. He tried to refuse fulfilling his promise. I daresay he would have if the queen hadn't intervened."

I sit straighter, pausing my efforts with my bindings. Whatever promise he made, he tried to refuse it.

Clara frowns. "Why would he do such a thing?"

Marus shakes his head. "Like I said, the prince had lost his wits. It was clear he was confused. He claimed to love the princess, as if he couldn't comprehend that the woman he promised to turn over to me wasn't the princess at all, but a stranger to him."

My heart flips. Questions continue to plague me, but at their core burns hope. Hope that I wasn't betrayed after all. That, somehow, Franco still loves me. My breaths become a little deeper. Stronger.

He lets out a dark chuckle and sits taller, his expression haughty. "Heaven forbid he ever takes the throne. A lunatic like him won't last a day without our generous queen saving him from his own youthful folly. He couldn't even maintain consciousness after threatening me."

"Folly indeed," Imogen says. "I'm willing to bet he'll show us much gratitude when we return to the palace. He'll thank us for saving him from scandal. Can you even imagine his terror if Ember's scheme succeeded and he unwittingly married her?" Laughter bursts from her lips, echoed by my stepmother.

I turn my head toward Imogen and release a string of insults that don't make it past my gag.

"Oh, shut up," Mrs. Coleman snaps. "Your words wouldn't matter even if we could hear them."

I glower.

Clara wrings her hands next to me. "Is this the right thing to do?" Her voice is small, quavering. "Take her all tied up like this to get married?"

Imogen glares at her sister. "Since when do you question Mother's plans?"

"It just doesn't seem...right." She looks from Imogen to Mrs. Coleman. "Why are we doing this?"

"You know why," snaps my stepmother. "This is our last chance to get what we deserve. What should have been ours to begin with."

"Her inheritance?"

"Yes, her inheritance. Don't be daft, Clara. If Terrence Montgomery hadn't so coldly written us out of his will, we wouldn't have to resort to such measures." Mrs. Coleman turns to Marus. "Her father may have been human, but he was just as cruel and sinful as his daughter."

I shout *it's a lie* against my gag, but only muffled sound makes it out the other side.

"I don't remember him being cruel," Clara whispers. My heart softens, and I slowly turn my gaze to her, surprised when I find tears in her eyes. "He was kind. The only time he was upset was—"

"Quiet," Mrs. Coleman barks.

A chill runs through me as I continue to study Clara's face. She purses her lips, but I can tell there are many things she's trying not to say. When I meet my stepmother's gaze, I find a flicker of guilt behind her eyes. I try to speak again, but my attempt turns into a groan. The groan feels so much like a hum as it vibrates in my throat that it sends a surge of panic through me. Then yearning. Everything in me wants to hum. To sing. To play my frustrations and rage away. I strain against my bindings harder now, wishing my hands were free so I could at least drum my fingers.

I release another frustrated groan, and again that yearning to hum burns within me.

This time, it makes me freeze. I take a few deep breaths, exploring the craving.

*It's dangerous*, one part of me says. *I'm dangerous.*

But an answering voice emerges from memory—Franco's. *So am I.*

My chest tightens.

I think of Franco's gift, the necklace bearing the glamour. The three songs sung by three dangerous creatures.

I've spent so much time hating my singing, resenting the power it holds. Resisting it. Suppressing it.

My song may be dangerous.

But in this moment, it just might be the very weapon I need.

So I hum.

It starts as a quiet rumble in my throat, then builds into a tune, growing louder and louder. All eyes turn to me as I continue to weave my hummed song, letting its sound fill the coach. My hair stands on end as I feel the magic swirling around me.

"Stop the coach!" Eyes haunted, Marus hammers a fist on the wall behind him. When the coach rolls to a stop, he all but leaps out the door.

Mrs. Coleman darts forward, leaning halfway outside. "Brother Marus! What are you doing?"

"You said she had no magic." I hear his voice, although I can't see his face. "She has far more sin than you claimed. If she proves too tainted by fae darkness, I cannot make her my wife."

"It isn't what you think!" Mrs. Coleman says, voice panicked. "Just give me a moment to speak with her alone. I'll get her under control."

"Pray that you do," he says, his voice sounding farther away now. "Otherwise, our deal is off."

My stepmother returns to her seat. "Out," she barks at her daughters. They rush to obey without question. Once the door is closed and we're alone, she narrows her eyes to slits. "You will marry him, Ember."

I reply, but my words are still trapped behind the gag.

Gritting her teeth, she leans forward and roughly pulls the cravat from my mouth. Her nails scrape my cheek in the process. "Say your piece, you vile, wretched girl."

I take a steadying breath. "I won't marry him. You can't make me. All of this is futile."

She purses her lips, and I can tell she's fighting to keep a tight grip on her composure. "There are other ways, you know," she says. "If you're so determined not to marry Brother Marus, then promise to continue paying my stipend. Enter a new bargain with me, and I will allow you to break off your engagement."

"What don't you understand?" I say with a dark laugh. "You don't control me anymore. There's nothing you can force me to do. It's over."

"I can do worse. If you refuse to comply, I'll sell you to a brothel."

"You can't sell me, for you don't own me. I'm of legal age and not bound to you in any way."

"Do you think that will stop me? There are plenty of establishments that won't hesitate to take you, legal or not."

I shrug. "Do what you must. It still won't get you your money."

She snickers. "How have you not learned? I always have a plan. Always."

"How have *you* not learned? You may always have a plan, but each one is destined to fail again and again. You've already lost, Mrs. Coleman. No matter what you try to do to me, you've lost. I can weather any storm. Can you say the same for yourself?"

"How dare you speak to me like that! If you won't comply, I will purchase a glamour for Imogen to wear and we'll claim your inheritance in full. Then you'll have nothing, and we'll have everything."

"If you really thought that would work, you wouldn't have resorted to this. Besides, I'd love to see you attempt to fool the prince. If you'd like a ticket to the executioner's block, by all means, try it."

She rolls her eyes. "What are you spouting off about?"

"Franco knows who I am. He's known all along. He never thought I was Princess Maisie. If anyone enters Selene Palace wearing my face, the prince will know it isn't me. He knows my energetic signature."

"Why would he care?" She waves a flippant hand, but I see panic growing in her eyes.

"Because he loves me."

She pales. "You're lying." She tries to laugh it off, but her knuckles have gone white.

"Are you willing to risk it?"

She slams her fist into the seat. "You just had to take that from Imogen too, didn't you?" Her voice trembles, edged with iron. Tears fill her eyes. "You've taken everything from me. *Everything.*"

"Everything you've lost has been of your own doing."

"Are you so sure about that?"

I snap my mouth shut. She has a point. She may be responsible for her own financial woes, but I'm the one who killed Father.

Guilt threatens to drag me under, but I breathe deep to keep it at bay. I allow my heart to ache, to burn, but I don't let it weaken my resolve. No matter what it costs me, I will not let Mrs. Coleman win.

She averts her gaze, eyes going unfocused. "You may think you've suffered," she whispers, "but you haven't a clue what it's like to lose all that I've lost. I was made for greatness, trained for success since I was a girl. Everything I ever wanted was within my reach, but it was all ripped away, one thing after the next. I was made to be a queen. I was the wife of a king."

I've heard this tale before, how she was once married to a fae king. She's never mentioned who it was. Never explained what happened after they were married. I always shrugged it off as nonsense, especially since she would change the subject when asked to elaborate. I hold my breath, wondering if she'll finally spill the truth.

"I was supposed to marry King Aspen," she says, "but he preferred to start a war rather than marry me, all so he could be with his true love, that insufferable know-it-all, Evelyn Fairfield."

I startle at this. She means Queen Evelyn—the woman Prince Franco admitted to having courted. Could Mrs. Coleman be telling the truth? Was she once engaged to King Aspen before he and Evelyn became mates?

She continues. "When that marriage alliance fell through, I was given to King Aspen's brother, another fae king. One who claimed my hand without falter. I was a queen. Did you know that? A queen for all of a handful of days. Do you know what happened to him? He left me to fight in the war his brother started and died in his beloved's arms—Amelie, another Fairfield harlot."

I know who Amelie is. She's a well-renowned dressmaker I had the pleasure of meeting last year.

"After that, I married a human," she says. "A wealthy solicitor I thought I was truly in love with. He sired my beautiful daughters. His eyes tended to wander, and before long, he began spending more nights with his mistress than with me. When he was home, he preferred to be deep in drink, and that made him violent. I poured cyanide in his tea before he could turn that violence on our daughters."

My blood goes cold at how casually she admits to pouring cyanide in her husband's tea. Did she just confess...to murder?

"Then came your father." Mention of Father has my mind going still. Her voice is soft, almost wistful. "That man was everything a good and gentle husband should be. He doted on me and my children. Almost as much as he doted on his half-fae daughter. It wasn't long before I saw just how much he favored her, though. And she relished that attention. Every chance that little girl got, she upstaged my daughters time and time again. Always playing her piano, singing for praise. I was the only one who saw her filthy fae magic for what it was. A plague infecting our home."

I swallow hard, my lungs feeling too tight to breathe.

She shakes her head as if to clear it, and her voice takes on a harsher quality. "It was your fault. It was all your fault." I expect her to bring up the night I sang, but her words follow a different path. "The first time your father witnessed me striking you, he wrote us out of his will, set up new conditions. He went so far as to threaten me with divorce. I was fearful for my daughters, for our future. I was so angry at him."

That must be what Clara was referring to when she tried to bring up the only time she saw my father upset.

My stepmother sighs, and her eyes turn down at the corners. She rubs her chest as a tear rolls down her cheek. After a few silent moments, she drags her hand back down to her side, fingers clenching. Her gaze turns steely as her eyes lock on mine. "You just had to play that night, didn't you?"

My muscles tense.

"Your song put the devil in my heart," she says through her teeth. "I never would have done it if it weren't for that black magic you carry."

A chill runs through me. Dread makes my stomach bottom out. "What did you do?"

"It's what *you* did, you wretched girl. You played that song. Used your filthy magic on us all."

Memories invade my senses, and with it comes a sob that heaves from my chest.

*The clatter of tableware.*

*Father's lifeless eyes.*

*His hand clenched over his heart...*

I close my eyes against the visions, but they replay over and over.

The clatter of tableware.

The clatter...

Of tableware...

Of teacups...

My eyes fly open as understanding dawns. My voice comes out barely above a whisper. "You poisoned him, didn't you? Just like your previous husband."

"No—"

"We were taking tea when I played. The last thing I remember was him looking at me over his teacup."

"You're wrong!"

My voice rises to a roar. "You poisoned my father during my performance! You blamed it on me!"

"You made me do it," she says in a rush. "It was your fault. I never would have done it if your song hadn't amplified my anger. I found out about the change of his will just that morning. How could I not be enraged?"

My chest heaves. "No one made you pour cyanide in his tea. No one made you carry it on your person to begin with."

"It was for my own protection. Ever since my second husband—"

"That's no excuse. You murdered my father."

"No! It was your fault."

My vision turns a strange shade of violet as a torrent floods my body, fills my blood and bones. Every inch of me seems to grow lighter. My hair lifts off my shoulders as a breeze begins to stir around me, coming from...me. I hover a few inches above my seat, barely aware that it's happening.

My stepmother's eyes go wide as she presses herself against the back of her seat. "Ember," she gasps.

My words come out in a roar of sound, bursting from my lips on a storm wind. "You did this!" My words shift into a scream, and that scream becomes a song.

The coach bursts into splinters of wood.

# 47

*FRANCO*

Nyxia and I fly above the road that heads east from the palace. Both in our unseelie forms, I travel as a raven while Nyxia soars at my side as a shadowy wind. Despite being siblings, our unseelie shapes are quite different. I can easily be mistaken for a regular bird, while my sister looks anything but benign, with her shapeless, ethereal body, her red eyes, and sharp, gnashing teeth—perfect for striking fear into the hearts of those she emotionally feeds on. I've been envious of her terrifying unseelie form ever since we were young. My only hope of eliciting terror is to don a glamour, one I'm already poised to conjure as soon as we find our targets. I doubt I'll be able to control my rage once I find Marus.

With my sister's intel that he's most likely heading straight for Saint Lazaro's Cathedral, I'm able to pick up Ember's energetic trail far faster than if I'd sought her out without a starting clue.

Her energy grows stronger with every beat of my wings.

"She's close," I say to Nyxia.

"Remember, don't act too hasty," comes her voice, an edge of warning to it.

"I'll try," I mutter.

A sudden shift emerges in Ember's trail, spiking with citrus, rose, and wind. Even as a raven, I feel a chill run over me, rustling the base of my feathers.

I know what that energy says.

She's singing.

It doesn't last long, and her emotions shift again. She's closer now. So close I can taste her energy as if she were at my side. My wings beat the air, driving me faster. Faster.

Several minutes pass before I spot a dark shape on the road ahead. A coach.

Another shift in energy, another spike of Ember's magic. This time, there's a deep note of sorrow. Grief.

Then rage.

The coach seems to ripple. A hard wind blows against me, momentarily halting my momentum. Once it passes, I train my attention on the coach...only to find it's no longer there. Instead, there's a swirling vortex of wood and debris.

Nyxia and I surge forward to close the distance and begin our descent. My heart pounds with every breath, then clenches as the view becomes clear.

Only splinters remain of the coach, and it's carried on a rapidly swirling wind that surrounds two figures.

*Ember!*

She stands at the eye of the vortex across from a woman I'm unfamiliar with. The woman is on her knees, hands over her ears. I glance to each side of the road. On one side, sprawls a man in a coachman's uniform, scrambling away from the fray. Four horses, still tethered but disconnected from the coach, gallop toward the woods. On the other side, I find Brother Marus and the two girls I know as Ember's lady's maids.

Nyxia's voice comes from beside me. "Did you know she could do this?"

"Not exactly." In fact, it hadn't occurred to me that Ember was responsible for what I'm seeing until just now. But of course she is. Her magic is everywhere, filling the air. If I listen carefully, I can even hear her voice. It isn't a hummed tune or a sung melody. It sounds more like a…scream.

Another chill runs through me. With a shudder, I shift into my seelie form while maintaining my wings.

"What are you doing?"

"I have to help her." I breathe in deeply, tasting fear and confusion. "She doesn't know she's doing this."

"You'll get hurt! Let me go. I'm incorporeal in this form. I can get through the whirlwind without injury."

"No, she's scared," I say. "I can calm her. I know I can."

"How will you even get through without being impaled?"

I assess the vortex again. It's a cylinder of shattered wood, torn leather, and fractured metal, about three times Ember's height. "I'll fly above it and drop in through the eye."

"This is a terrible idea."

"You know I'm full of them." I offer her a crooked smile, but I feel no mirth. No amusement. Only fear. Not for myself, though. For Ember.

"Be careful, Franco."

I nod and head closer to the vortex. The nearer I draw, the faster the wind beats against me, and the harder my wings must work. I gain greater height to outfly the draft. Once I'm over the eye, I begin to lower inch by inch, stopping once I feel the tug of wind again. This is as close as I can get without risk of getting caught in the whirlwind. I assess the distance between me and the ground. It's far, but I'm low on options. My only hope of getting to Ember is to drop straight through the eye.

My pulse quickens, and I taste my own flash of fear before I swallow it down. Then, with a deep breath, I dismiss my wings. In their absence, I fall fast. I plummet down, quickly gaining momentum as I drop through the center of the vortex. When just a dozen or so feet stand between me and the ground, I summon part of my unseelie form, like I do when I sprout my wings. This time, however, it's feathers I conjure. Thousands of feathers that fight the pull of gravity without getting fully caught on the surrounding wind.

I land in a partial crouch between Ember and the woman. Pain shoots up my legs, but not as much as I'd feel if I hadn't softened the blow with the resistance of my feathers. I seek out Ember at once, dismissing my feathers as I dart toward her. A searing pain ripples through one of my ankles, but I don't falter. My fae healing is already taking place, knitting bone, connecting sinew. I take another step. Another. The wind speeds around us in a deafening roar of sound.

I stop just in front of Ember. She hovers a foot off the ground, her teal hair whipping wildly around her. Her skin has taken on a similar shade as her hair, but her body is no longer solid.

It's ethereal.

Her eyes are wide, but she doesn't seem to see me at all. Lips parted, she looks to be screaming, shouting. That's when I realize the roar of sound is coming from her. It's a solemn never-ending wail that fuels the wind.

I dare to step closer. "Ember! Can you hear me?"

She blinks, but her gaze remains unfocused. Unseeing.

"Ember, it's me. It's Franco. I'm here."

Slowly, her eyes move to mine, a plea in them. Her chest heaves. "I don't know what's happening." Though she speaks, her wail continues, laced through every word.

"It's all right," I say.

"Who's doing this?"

I swallow hard. Keeping my voice gentle, I say, "You are, but I can help you."

She shakes her head. "I'm not doing this. I don't know what's going on."

"You've shifted forms, Ember. You're unseelie right now, and I'm guessing this is your first time. I can help you shift back."

She glances down at her arms, blue and transparent. Panic clouds her energy. "I don't know how to shift forms! I don't know how to stop this!"

"You're just upset, but it's all right. I'm here. Just look at me. Focus on my eyes."

Her eyes lock on mine and she gives me a shaky nod.

"Put your hand over mine."

She does, then cries out when her hand falls through my palm.

"Don't try to touch my hand yet," I say. "Just lay your hand over mine."

She tries again, and this time, she simply lets her hand hover.

"Good. Don't look at anything but my eyes. Now, think about what it feels like to hold my hand. Think about the warmth of my palm. Think about the firmness of piano keys beneath your fingers. Remember how it felt when we danced last night? Remind yourself how it feels to have your feet upon the ground. Imagine the sensations."

Her energy calms, and the whirlwind begins to slow.

"Focus on the beat of your heart, then the feel of your breath. Feel it entering your nose, filling your lungs." I watch as her form slowly darkens, shifting from blue to warm skin. Little by little, she lowers to the ground until her feet land softly on the earth. "Take my hand."

She does, eyelids fluttering as relief lightens her energy. With a sob, she wraps her arms around my neck. I pull her close, caressing her back, making soothing sounds in her ear.

But our work isn't done. The whirlwind continues to blow around us, the sound of her eerie scream still filling the air.

Gently, I pull Ember's arms from around my neck and hold her gaze. "Ember, you need to stop the vortex."

Fear darkens her energy. "I can't. I'm not controlling it."

"You are, my love. Magic is fueled by personal intent. If the vortex still spins, it's because something inside you wants it to." I shift our stance so that we face the other figure. The woman still crouches close to the ground, hands over her ears, head tucked into her knees. Shards of wood knock into her again and again, and I see several open cuts over the backs of her hands.

Ember's emotions flare with rage. "She murdered my father," her voice comes out with a tremor. "She confessed in the coach. For three years, she blamed me for it, let me believe it had been all my doing."

"She will be punished," I say, tone firm, "but not like this. You may feel angry now, but if you kill her, I know you won't forgive yourself."

"I hate her," she hisses, tears streaming down her cheeks. "I hate her with every inch of my being."

"That's all right." I place my finger under her chin and gently return her gaze to mine. "Your hate is valid. You hate her because of what she did. She killed your father."

She nods.

"And you loved him."

Another nod. Her energy begins to soften.

"Focus on that, Ember. Focus on how much you loved him. How much you loved your mother. Think how proud she would have been to see you take unseelie form."

She holds my gaze a few moments longer, then falls to her knees. All at once, the vortex goes still. Shards and splinters, all that remains of the coach, come crashing to the ground, forming a circle of debris. Her eyes flutter closed, and I catch her before she falls on her side. She's unconscious, drained from such an expenditure of energy. One's first shift into unseelie form can do that to a fae.

"Monster!" shouts the other woman as she rises to her feet on trembling legs. Her skin is covered in a thin layer of dirt, shards of wood, metal, and glass clinging to her hair. Her hands and cheeks are crisscrossed in numerous tiny cuts. The two young women I'd spotted earlier run forward, as does Brother Marus. Based on their appearances, I can tell the three women are related. So, this is Ember's stepfamily.

Nyxia floats down as a dark wind, then lands in her seelie form beside me.

Ember's stepmother points a shaking finger at the sleeping form cradled in my arms. "Monster," she says again. "Arrest her! This vile girl almost killed me!"

My sister takes a forbidding step forward, but I hiss her name to stop her. "This is my problem," I say, laying Ember softly on the ground.

She clenches her jaw. I can tell she wants to argue. Take charge. Clean up the mess I've made like she's done so many times before. But if she truly wants me to be king, if she trusts me as much as she's claimed, then she must let me do this.

She holds my gaze a few tense seconds then finally relents. "Go ahead, then."

I stand tall and take a step closer to Ember's stepmother—the woman who murdered her own husband and blamed her stepdaughter's magic. Trapped Ember in a bargain and buried her beneath mounds of guilt.

Rage boils my blood.

She takes a wary step away from me. "Why aren't you listening to me? Arrest that monster at once."

"There's only one monster here, and it isn't your stepdaughter."

She scoffs. "Oh, then who is it? Me? I've wasted three years on that wretch, and how does she repay me? I've done nothing but—"

"You mistake me," I say, my voice low, cold. Shadows seep from my fingertips and writhe around my shoulders. "When I said there was one monster here, I meant...me."

My face transforms with my terrifying glamour, lips peeling back from my teeth.

I lunge toward the three women with a hiss.

Their shouts pierce the air.

# 48

### FRANCO

Hours later, after day sinks into evening, I stand on my balcony waiting for my sister to arrive. She sent a request to speak with me, and I asked her to meet me here. I dare not leave my quarters. Not when Ember is dozing in my bed. She's been asleep ever since she lost consciousness. If I couldn't sense her energy, I'd be worried, but her life force is strong. I can feel her healing, her energy building and repairing after such a shocking experience.

A dark shadow flies toward me and materializes as Nyxia. She folds her arms and leans against the balustrade. With a nod toward my balcony doors, she says, "How is she?"

I prop myself next to her. "Still recovering."

"I hadn't realized the girl human was so powerful."

"Half human. You should hear her sing. When she isn't enraged, that is."

Nyxia attempts a smile, but it looks more like a sneer. She still isn't fully convinced I'm making the right choice with my heart.

"What did you do with everyone else?" I ask. After I donned my glamour, I immobilized all three women with my shadows. Nyxia summoned her guards, so all we had to do was wait for reinforcements and transport. I can't say I didn't enjoy every minute I held the women in place, feeding off their fear.

"Mrs. Maddie Coleman is secure in the dungeon," Nyxia says. "I compelled her to give her confession. She admitted to poisoning both her second and third husbands."

My heart sinks. Ember was right, then. Not that I doubted her. It's just chilling to hear it confirmed. Even more so to think I've had a murderer in my palace, and the woman I love has been under her care for years. "What about her daughters?"

"Imogen and Clara Coleman are being kept under guard in Princess Maisie's room. They've confessed to no crimes, so until we know what to do with them, there they will stay."

"And Brother Marus?"

Her energy clouds with hesitation. "I sent him back to his brotherhood."

I stand straighter, irritation flashing through me. "You didn't punish him?"

She fixes me with a pointed look. "Stripping him of his position is the most I can do. Technically, he did nothing unlawful. His only crime was ambition. As a man of the church, it is up to his brotherhood to deal with him now."

"He may have broken no law, but he did worse than simply try to gain our favor. He wielded what little favor he did have like a weapon and built lies around it."

"I know," she says with a sigh, "but we must tread carefully with the church. Is there anything else we can do to avoid making Saint Lazaro's Church our enemy?"

I already know my answer. I've been pondering that very question ever since we returned to the palace. I'd held hopes they'd be preceded by a far more satisfying demise for Brother Marus. Then again, perhaps his loss of position *is* the worst kind of punishment for a man like him. "We'll invite another brother of Saint Lazaro to act as their church's representative. Perhaps someone younger. An acolyte, even. We'll give them one more chance to prove they're worth keeping around."

"And if we discover no one from Saint Lazaro can be trusted?"

My voice comes out cold. "We end them."

"Franco, the Alpha Council will never agree to human extermination on any scale."

"We don't have to kill them to end them. We can banish them from the isle. Whatever we do, we cannot let their power grow. However," my tone softens, "I'm willing to believe Brother Marus might not define Saint Lazaro. Perhaps if we get to know others from the church, we can learn what they're really about. What it is they truly want. Their zealots may have preached that fae are demons, but we can change how the brotherhood and the humans see us going forward. And if they refuse to change their misguided perceptions and continue to view us as sinful demons, then...well, they don't belong in Faerwyvae."

"You've thought a lot about this."

I nod. "If I'm going to be king someday, I need to start thinking about the hard questions and the even harder answers."

"You've accepted it, then. Being my heir."

"Yes, but I'm not ready to take your place yet. You were right to have me interact with the humans, but I must go about it in my own way. There's more I need to do before I can gain their respect. And before they can gain mine. Just like with Saint Lazaro, I want to learn more about them. I want to understand what troubles they face, their plights and concerns, not just entertain the elite once a year. Can you give me time? And the freedom to choose what I do with it?"

She watches me for a few silent moments, then reaches for my hand and gives it a squeeze. "Yes, Franco. I can give you that.

As difficult as it is for me to turn over control, it's something I need to work on. Perhaps I too need more time."

"Will Lorelei be all right with that?"

Her lips pull up in a small smile. "I think so. She's the most patient female when it comes to love. Although..." She pushes off the balustrade. "I better return to my mate before she bites my head off for leaving so long. She may be patient, but she's no gentle dove when she's annoyed."

"Go on," I say. "I can handle the rest of the season on my own."

"I know you can." Her words hold conviction, but there's a wariness to her energy. She glances at the balcony doors. "She's the one? You're sure of it?"

I swallow hard. "Yes, she's the one."

My sister's eyes crinkle at the corners. "Good, Franco. I'm happy for you. If you love her, I'll learn to love her too." With that, she shifts into her unseelie form and flies away.

EMBER

I wake in an unfamiliar room. No, not unfamiliar. Just unexpected. I sit up in the bed, eyes lighting on the piano I played just days ago. But why am I here? How did I get here? Then something snags my attention.

An elegant shoe with a broken glass heel, resting on the piano bench.

My memories awaken in a whirl of color and sound. I remember being taken by Marus. I recall the confrontation I had with my stepmother. I remember her dark confession. Then the vortex that burst around us, one I'd somehow managed to conjure.

Then Franco.

*Franco.*

My raging heart begins to slow, and I take in a few heavy breaths to calm myself.

"You're awake." Franco enters the room and comes straight to me. He moves stiffly as he lowers onto the bed, and there's trepidation in his eyes. I'm not sure what it means, but my first instinct says he's...afraid of me. Nausea turns my stomach. After what he saw me do, of course he's afraid.

"Whatever you're thinking, stop." His voice comes out firm. "Say it out loud instead."

Part of me wants to close up, say something to keep him at arm's length, but I stop myself. The impulse may be strong, but it's the response of a frightened girl, not the woman I want to be. The woman I've become. I take a deep breath. "Do you feel differently about me? Now that you've seen what I'm capable of?"

He furrows his brow. "No, Ember. My love is as whole as it was this morning."

"Then why are you acting so distant? So hesitant?"

Worry creases his forehead, and it seems to take him a while to find his words. "I was afraid perhaps *your* feelings had changed. It was my fault you were taken by Marus. You must have realized that."

I recall the sense of betrayal I felt when Marus first found me and Nyxia mentioned Franco's promise. "What happened?"

"It was at the opera," he says quickly, as if eager to explain. "After you left the box, Marus talked about his missing fiancée. I had no idea it was you. He asked me to promise him that if I became aware of your presence in the palace, I'd turn you over to him. I added the caveat that it was only so he could talk to you. As soon as you told me who you are and what your stepfamily was making you do, I knew I couldn't trust him with you. I tried to break my promise but...it almost killed me. I'm so sorry, Em. I never would have made that promise if—"

"It's all right," I say. Relief floods me. All the missing pieces surrounding his betrayal now fall into place. "I don't blame you."

His posture visibly relaxes, and he turns more fully toward me. Scooting closer, he takes my hand in his, running his thumb over the back of my hand. "I feared you'd never forgive me."

"I forgive you, Franco, but...how can you not see me in a different light now? If you hadn't stopped me, I would have killed my stepmother. I wasn't in control. She was right all along. My magic is dark and dangerous. We just never knew *how* dark it was until now."

"No," he says. "You cannot blame yourself for this. You're a powerful half fae who's never been given the means to explore her magic. You've been suppressed, raised without fae guidance. Of course your first shift into your unseelie form brought about a new level of magic. Do you think this is unusual for our kind? You can learn to control it, Em. I did."

My heart flutters, fixated on three simple words.

*For our kind.*

No one has ever referred to me as belonging to faekind. Ever since Mother died, I've felt so lost, so disconnected, so confused about who I am and where I fit. I thought I'd live the rest of my life belonging nowhere. I've always been too fae for gentle society, and too human for fae acceptance. A life on the road was the only place I imagined feeling free. But what if I was wrong? What if there's a better place for me? A better future? One where, instead of running to leave my identity behind, I can simply grow more into the person I already am.

"You aren't afraid of me?" I ask.

"Afraid? Don't you recall what I told you about my first experiences with magic? I leached my friends' emotions for years until I mastered control. I'm not afraid of you, Ember. I'm amazed." He leans in closer until our arms touch. I lay my head on his shoulder.

We sit like that for several quiet minutes, while I gather the courage to ask my next question. "Where is my stepfamily and Brother Marus?"

He tells me where they are, what happened after I lost consciousness. I shudder when he mentions his plans to give Saint Lazaro another chance to prove themselves, but I trust he's doing the right thing. "What will happen to my stepsisters? To Mrs. Coleman?"

"That's up to you," he says gently. "Your stepmother already confessed to her crimes. She could be executed without trial, should you wish it."

I ponder that for a moment, recalling everything she told me. Every way in which she made me suffer since Father died. Her lies. Her abuse. Her manipulations. Part of me wants her to endure the same fate she delivered my father. Another part of me has a different solution in mind.

"I want her to stand trial," I say. "I want her to confront the full weight of judgment for everything she did. I want her to live with the consequences."

"And your stepsisters?"

I furrow my brow. "Imogen is dangerous, even without her mother's scheming, but she's committed no crime."

He gives me a crooked smile. "What if I just don't like her? Is that not a grave enough offense to have her shipped off the isle?"

"As tempting as that is, no. Instead, let's set her up in a workhouse. Without money and connections, she'll come to understand her own insignificance soon enough."

He nods. "We can do that. What about the younger girl? Clara?"

"She's never treated me kindly," I say, "but I saw a different side of her when she was my lady's maid. I want to send her to live with her aunt, Marie Coleman, and enroll her at Maven University in the Fire Court. If her aunt won't have her, I want her set up in a dormitory at the school."

He quirks a brow. "Enrollment at an elite university. Now that's a luxurious punishment."

"I'd like to give her the chance to demonstrate whether she deserves it." Another thought crosses my mind and I sit upright. "Please don't think I'm expecting you to orchestrate this yourself, Franco. I'll do whatever needs to be done. I'll pay her tuition. There is the matter of my inheritance…"

"Oh yes," he says with a roll of his eyes, "this great inheritance that has your entire stepfamily and a man of the church acting like vicious beasts."

I release a heavy sigh, another hard question poised on the tip of my tongue. "How important is my inheritance to you? I imagine it makes me a more admirable match."

He locks his eyes with mine. "Your fortune has nothing to do with how well matched we are. You are my mate because I love you. That's all there is to it."

I nibble the corner of my lip. "So, if I give it away, will you still accept me?"

"Yes, Ember, but why would you want to?"

I shrug. "It was always my intention to give it to charity. I never planned on keeping it. It makes me uncomfortable to consider benefitting from my father's demise. That discomfort originated from the guilt I felt over his death, but even now that I know the truth, it's still hard for me to consider claiming his fortune." I'm quiet for a few moments, pondering. Then I lift my chin and infuse my tone with certainty. "I'm going to refuse my inheritance. I'll accept just enough to cover Clara's education, but I want none of the rest. I want it donated. I want it to support Lunar Court's orphanages, and perhaps help fund assistance for the poor and downtrodden people of Evanston."

He leans in close with a grin. "I approve of this. However,

let's not use your money to do it. Let's use mine. Whatever you were planning on giving, I'll double it with my own. We'll come up with ways to more evenly distribute wealth, ways to care for the hungry and poor living in my court."

My heart fills with warmth, and yet my stomach still feels heavy. "Why are you so determined that I claim it? I thought you said it didn't matter if I was wealthy?"

"It doesn't, and that's not why I want you to keep it. I want you to keep it because it was a gift from your father, something he left for you with all his heart. He wanted you to have it. You need to learn to accept that. Accept that you're worth his love, no matter what these three years of guilt have done to you. If you claim your inheritance and still want to give everything away, then fine. I won't stop you. But do it because it's yours. Not because you fear laying claim to it."

A lump rises in my throat, but with it comes an overwhelming sense of peace. He's right. My father wanted me to have his fortune. *Me.* I'm the reason he stood up to Mrs. Coleman. I never even knew he saw her cruelty, and yet, he defied his own wife to defend me. To protect me. To assure my wellbeing. It might take time for me to truly accept the truth and heal from the guilt I've carried for three years, but I think it's something I can do. "All right," I say. "I'll accept it. For now."

His grin spreads wide as he leans closer. "You do deserve it, Em. I hope you believe that. You deserve everything wonderful."

My gaze falls on his lips and I shift myself toward him. "Does that include you?"

"If you'll have me."

I lean in and claim his mouth with mine. His lips are soft and warm, and his hands come to frame my face. Tugging the collar of his shirt, I lean back and pull him to me. We lose ourselves in each other's arms and lips, breaking away before things get too heated.

"Then there's the matter of us," he whispers, running a hand over my arm. "I have every intention of publicly courting you from now on."

My heart flips, but logic dampens my joy. "I don't know, Franco. I don't even exist in the public eye. To the people, you've been falling in love with Princess Maisie, not some unknown commoner. We should weave a story to explain why things didn't work out with Maisie so no one thinks you slighted her. Then, with time, we can go public with our courtship. Besides, I never told you the truth about Maisie. I don't know why she left. She never said she eloped. In fact, she acted like she was in danger." My pulse quickens at the thought. It dawns on me that I'll now have to deal with the repercussions of our bargain, something I hadn't anticipated. I grimace. "I thought I'd be long gone by the time anyone realized Maisie had run away."

"We'll deal with that together. Perhaps I'll send a discreet message to King Ronan."

"It must be *very* discreet. I'm worried about her."

"I'll make sure of it. But...about the other things you said." He takes one of my hands and brings it to his lips. After planting a kiss on my knuckles, he says, "Ember, I'm tired of pretending. I never want to spend a moment faking anything with you ever again, not even for the sake of public opinion. I want it to be real. I want to show everyone *this* is real."

"You'll risk a lot of gossip. Your reputation could very well be destroyed."

"Then I'll tell the truth to anyone who will listen. Besides, I'm not afraid of facing my reputation this time. I'm ready to show my court who I really am. Even if it terrifies me. Even if they reject me."

Trepidation ties my stomach in knots, making my pulse pound.

He must sense it, for he furrows his brow and holds my gaze

with intensity. "What about you? Are you ready to show the court who *you* really are? The half-fae, half-human woman I love? One with dangerous, beautiful magic? One with blue hair and eyes to match and a heart as wide as the moon?"

Warmth floods my chest, but fear sends my heart skittering. For so long, I thought I wanted a life of no attachments. No bonds. Love seemed dangerous. Something that either left too soon or made people into monsters. Something that either caused me pain or killed those I cared for. Intimate relationships seemed no better than a bargain.

But now that I've let myself experience love, it isn't as restrictive as I thought it would be. It's freeing.

But with Franco, love brings responsibility too.

Attention.

Renown.

Judgment.

For three years, I've been invisible. Forced to cover my hair in a bonnet, hide my heritage. Stay quiet. Don't show off. Don't spark notice.

Being Franco's mate will change all of that.

It will change...*everything*.

The thought is both agonizing and thrilling. His question echoes in my ears. Am I ready? Am I? My answer teeters on a ledge over a dark chasm. On one side is familiar obscurity I've always known. On the other side are vast possibilities I can't begin to comprehend. Terror and excitement battle for supremacy.

But which melody should I follow? Which song calls my heart?

*Always be wild. Promise me.*

I press my hand to Franco's chest, thinking of his newly formed tattoo. Like that tattoo, our love developed by surprise and our new lives will take shape the same way. Emerging. Shifting. Growing.

"I don't know if I'm ready," I say, speaking the truth. I lean in. Brush my lips against his. Wrap my arms around his neck. Feel his heart pound against mine, a new rhythm for this new endeavor. One we will journey together. A duet. A harmony. I pull away just slightly. "But I can't wait to find out."

# EPILOGUE - ONE YEAR LATER

**EMBER**

With a deep breath, I place my fingers over the keys and press. A soft sound emerges from the pianoforte, reverberating through my bones. My magic responds, whirring inside my heart like the wings of a hummingbird. It rises to my throat, begging for release.

Against the fading sound of the single chord, I sing the first note.

Then I play. My fingers flutter over the keyboard as my voice rises and falls, ringing out over the crowd. I dare not look at the figures gathered before the dais for fear I'll get distracted. I've grown so much more comfortable singing this past year, but I still haven't gotten used to doing so before such large crowds. With tonight being the start of this year's New Moon Masquerade, it seemed appropriate that I play. Each ball during Lunar's month-long social season now hosts human and fae guests alike, with an emphasis on unity. My song is a demonstration of fae magic.

Where danger meets beauty.

I'm no longer afraid that my singing will harm anyone. In the year that has passed since I destroyed the coach with my wayward magic, I've learned to control my song. There have been several mishaps, of course, but in the end, I've learned to accept my singing for what it is.

A gift.

And—should I ever choose it to be—a weapon.

I continue my performance, feeling the music sweep me away as my fingers flutter faster, my voice rising higher. There are words to my song, but beneath them lie layers and layers of story. Emotion. Magic. In word and tune, it tells of love and heartache, fear and loss. It speaks of dark motives, desperate escapes, and dangerous bargains. Then it shifts, turning playful, and illustrates secret smiles, unexpected romance, and bold declarations. The melody darkens again briefly after that, conveying danger and dark magic.

Then forgiveness.

And love.

My tune slows, shifting into something bright yet mellow as I draw near the final notes. I linger over them, letting my voice ring out. Then it fades. My song comes to an end, but in the absence of sound, it relays the opposite of ending. Instead, it's a new beginning. Possibility. Hope.

My magic hangs in the air for several moments.

Then I release it.

The throne room erupts with applause. I rise from the piano bench and face the crowd. Hundreds of smiling faces look back at me, some with tears in their eyes, others with awestruck expressions. A few seem wary, which is understandable. Not everyone feels so warmly toward fae magic, but that's what Franco and I are working toward. That's why we choose to show them who we really are.

I move to the front of the dais and curtsy, then make my way down the steps to the floor. A band of musicians take my place, and the New Moon Masquerade commences with a traditional cotillion.

I move to the side of the dais, where Franco awaits. Unlike most of the guests, he wears neither mask nor glamour. The same goes for me. I've chosen a simple blue ballgown tonight, in honor of the first one I wore a year ago. He and I have had our share of disguises and find contentment being...us. His silver eyes glisten as I approach, and the sight of him sends a rush of delight through me. I don't know if I'll ever tire of his roguish beauty. Tonight, he wears full evening attire in shades of pink and black, although his shirt remains open at the collar and his cravat is simply draped around his neck. I can see just the slightest hint of his tattoos peeking above his neckline. "You were wonderful."

I laugh. "I was terrified."

"I couldn't tell. Your song had me too transfixed by every feeling you conjured inside me. You told your story."

I nod. It's the most honest song I've written, and I've written many this past year in all my efforts to explore my magic. Ever since I agreed to open the ball with a song of my own, I agonized over what to share. In the end, the answer was clear. Me.

I take a step closer to him and grasp his collar in my fingers. "I played *our* story too."

He shrugs with feigned nonchalance. "A minor portion."

"A significant portion," I correct. "One that's still just beginning."

With a soft smile, he lowers his lips to mine. "One that grows every day." When we part, he releases a resigned sigh. "I should go make the rounds. There are several pig-headed aristocrats I'm trying to squeeze a contribution from. They're trying to act like they weren't aware this was a charity ball."

"And when you say pig-headed..."

"One is actually wearing the glamoured head of a pig," he says with a chuckle. "I'm serious!"

"And if they refuse to contribute?"

"Then I'll *convince* them." He lets out a low growl, his face flashing briefly with his terrifying glamour.

I playfully swat his chest. "You will not!"

He catches my hand and brings it to his lips. "No, I won't, but that doesn't mean I can't thoroughly annoy them until they beg for torture instead."

"If you plan on charming them with that wit of yours, then torture can be all but guaranteed."

He puts his arm around my waist and pulls me to his chest. His eyes swim with desire. "There's that sharp tongue of yours."

My lips pull up at the corners. "Perhaps later you can find out just how sharp it can be."

He groans. "You make doing my duty so hard."

I wink. "That's not all I make hard. Now, pull yourself together before those smug aristocrats think you're too fond of them." I stand on my toes and light a kiss on his cheek.

"My cruel beloved," he says with mock wistfulness as he releases me. Then, straightening his jacket, he returns my wink and saunters off into the crowd.

I too begin to weave amongst the guests, skirting around the dance floor in search of the faces I'm eager to see. Finally, I spot a tall woman with a head of dark hair. My chest grows warm, and I quicken my pace. "Gemma Bellefleur," I say when I reach her.

"Ember Montgomery," she says with a wide smile and leans forward to lightly embrace me. I'm a little surprised, as I never knew her to be physically affectionate, and belatedly return the hug. Something hard and round comes against me.

We pull away, and my mouth falls open as I study her. She wears an elegant gown in emerald green velvet that does nothing to hide the curve of her belly. "Oh, Gemma, congratulations." I turn to the figure next to her, a broad-shouldered male with golden-brown hair and ruby eyes. "And to you, Your Majesty."

"Thank you," the King of Winter says. His bearing is regal and stoic, but the sparkle in his gaze reveals his joy. It only grows brighter when his eyes lock on his mate. "Our first pup is on the way."

"A pup," I echo, before reminding myself King Elliot Rochester is a wolf fae. When I met him and Gemma last year in the Winter Court, I'd known he was fae but not that he was a wolf in his unseelie form. And I certainly hadn't a clue he was king, not until word of his broken curse spread through town. By then, Imogen was spreading her own tale, all about how Gemma had betrayed her and stolen Elliot. With Gemma having the heart and favor of the king, her popularity grew, and the townspeople began to admonish every hint of scorn directed at their king's beloved. Mrs. Coleman moved us far from Winter after that.

"Either a pup or a bookworm," Gemma says with a wry grin.

Elliot places a hand on his mate's belly. "Perhaps both."

She turns and meets his adoring gaze. "Perhaps. Although, by the way it kicks, I'm thinking it will be the former. There's most definitely a tail in there."

Elliot laughs and plants a kiss at Gemma's temple.

"And you, Ember," Gemma says, returning her gaze to me. "You sing so beautifully. I had no idea you could do that. It was magic, wasn't it?"

I nod. "It's something I've been honing this past year."

"It was stunning," the king says. Such a compliment—as short as it was—from the gruff Elliot Rochester has me filling with pride.

"Thank you," I say. "However, it's the two of you I want to thank. Gemma, I know I've written to you several times now, but I won't feel my gratitude is properly conveyed until I say so in person. Thank you for the ballgown you sent me. Not only was it lovely, but I wouldn't be here right now if it hadn't been for those enchanted invitations to last year's ball."

Gemma gives me a knowing smirk. "While I'll admit my interference hadn't been made with a love match in mind, I'm glad it brought you happiness." She looks behind me with a subtle nod.

I follow her line of sight to where Franco stands chatting with a pair of gentlemen. Again and again, his eyes flash toward me as if he can't keep his gaze off me for long. I smile and turn back to my friend with a sigh. "It has brought me much happiness, so please know you have my undying gratitude. If there's anything I can ever do—"

"There is something you can do," she says. "Visit with me more often, won't you? Let's be true friends from now on."

For a moment, I don't know what to say. When we first met, I knew she was kind. I liked her. Even though she asked me to write to her after I moved, I struggled to believe she truly wanted me to. For why would someone so refined, so important, want to be my friend?

But if this last year has taught me anything, it's that I must first accept myself. Only then can I see in me what others see.

I reach for her hand and give it a squeeze. "Yes, Gemma. Let us be friends."

As the night wears on, I grow weary of so much activity. There are countless people to speak to, eager strangers seeking introductions, familiar faces pulling me this way and that. I stop to chat with Seri and Augie, who can't keep their hands off each other, not even as Seri invites me to take a turn about the halls to enjoy a glass of wine with her. After I extricate myself from their company, Brother Hans—Saint Lazaro's new representative at court—seeks me out to tell me how much he enjoyed my music. While I still don't fully trust his church, I must admit Hans does give me hope for his brotherhood.

Finally, I find Clara, who has come with a couple friends from university. She seems much changed this past year. Happier. More mature, even. There remains a rift between us, one I doubt will ever be erased. Nothing could diminish the fact that I am undoubtedly responsible for her mother's exile from the isle. During Mrs. Coleman's trial, Clara learned the entirety of her mother's guilt—that she not only murdered my father but hers too. Mrs. Coleman fought tooth and nail to try and convince the court that neither death was her fault. She claimed the first was in self-defense and the second was spurred on by dark magic. In the end, she was able to sway no one. She's now serving a life sentence of hard labor in the country of Bretton. She'll never again step foot in Faerwyvae. Never feel its magic. She'll age and work and die.

"How is Imogen?" I dare to ask.

Clara shifts awkwardly from foot to foot before answering. "She struggled in the workhouse, so my aunt took her in. Aunt Marie has very little patience for her. She gives her no allowance and has her working outside the home to earn her keep. My sister is changing, though. For the better."

"That's good to hear." Again, I feel the rift that stands between us. We were never true sisters before, and I doubt we'll ever be anything more than uneasy acquaintances from now on. But I'm all right with that. I have true friends now, and she has hers.

The pair she brought with her tonight chat not too far from us, and she glances longingly at them.

"Go ahead," I say. "Enjoy the rest of the ball."

Clara starts to dart away but stops mid-step. Turning back to me, she gives me a curtsy and a smile, then leaves to join her friends. With a tired sigh, I seek the exit in search of a respite. Just when I'm nearly to the throne room doors, someone steps swiftly from the wall to intercept me.

It's a man with blue skin and gills at his neck. He clears his throat. "Miss Montgomery, I am ambassador to King Ronan."

A wave of shock runs through me. King Ronan is Princess Maisie's father. Last year, Franco sent a letter to inform him of his daughter's absence from Selene Palace, but we never heard back from him.

He lowers his voice. "I'm here to deliver a message from my king. He wants me to tell you that if you've heard anything from Princess Maisie—and please, do not tell me if you have—then keep that information to yourself."

I furrow my brow. "Is she all right? Is there anything I can do?"

"The best thing you can do is keep her whereabouts a secret."

"I promise." It's an easy promise to keep, considering I have no clue where she is.

"Thank you." He offers a stiff bow, then disappears into the crowd.

I exit into the hall, worry tugging my mind. I may not know Maisie well, but I've thought of her often. Where did she go after we made our bargain? What kind of danger is she in? Where is she now?

I shake my head. Apparently, it's safer for her if I never discover the answer to those questions.

## FRANCO

I'm relieved when the ball comes to an end and my guests finally leave. Beneath the open night sky, I stroll through the gardens, letting the gentle breeze cool my cheeks. I feel like I'll need to nap for ten days straight just to recover from all the talking and mingling I've done. And that's on top of all the social interactions I've immersed myself in for months on end before this.

As fatigued as I am, I regret nothing. I've spent the past year getting to know both the humans and fae of my court on a personal level. Ember and I have dined with aristocrats, danced in the woods with brownies and sprites, had luncheons with dragons in caverns and caves. We've also walked through the slums, visited orphanages, assessed the needs of the people in surrounding cities. Ember was right when she told me there are humans living too far north to benefit from the seelie king's reign, and there's only so much Lunar's human representative can do. But there are things *I* can do. Things I'm already doing.

And more I can soon begin...

I pause as I catch sight of movement nearby. It's Nyxia and Lorelei in one of the garden courtyards. Lorelei's arms are draped around my sister's neck as Nyxia gazes affectionately down at her. They turn and sway slowly over the obsidian floor to music only they can hear.

Keeping my steps quiet so as not to disturb their romantic moment, I continue down the garden path in search of the energetic signature I know is out here somewhere. Finally, I find her, wandering leisurely through a maze of bright, glowing mushrooms. Three wisps float over Em's head, and I hear their tiny, animated voices as she chats with them.

She hasn't noticed me yet, so I stop at the entrance to the mushroom maze, taking the opportunity to observe her beautiful smile, the elegant sway of her steps, the breathtaking glow of her energy. Without even trying, she's become a favorite of our court, and it's no surprise why. She's kind yet unafraid of facing conflict. She's empathetic yet bold. I harbor no doubts that she'll make a wonderful queen.

I step onto the path, and one of the wisps spots me, making all three turn. With a chortling squeal, they taunt, "Kissy, kissy," then fly off.

Ember turns to face me with a grin. "Is everyone gone yet?"

"Finally," I say, closing the distance between us. "How long have you been hiding out here?"

"An hour, maybe," she says with a shrug. "I'm starting to understand why you chose to spend last year's New Moon Masquerade disguised as a fat raven."

"It was truly a moment of underrated brilliance."

She throws her arms around my middle. "Can we go to bed now?"

The glint in her eye makes me want to lift her in my arms and take her straight to my room. But there's a specific reason I came to find her. One I've been agonizing over for days. Perhaps I should wait...

Yes, I should wait.

Another day.

Any other day.

"Franco," she says, a warning in her tone.

I glance down to find her studying my face. "What?" I say with as much innocence as I can muster.

"I may not be a psy vampire, but I know when you're keeping something from me." She takes a step back and clasps my hands in hers. "Out with it."

"Fine," I say with a grumble. I shift from foot to foot, then meet her eyes. "I'm ready to take the throne, Ember."

Her eyes widen, and her energy sparks with surprise. "You are?"

"Yes." My voice trembles a bit, but I force myself to speak the truth. "After everything I've seen and learned this past year, I'm eager to put our plans into motion. Not just as a prince, hosting fundraisers and charity balls. I'm ready to do more. Things I can only do as king."

"Does your sister know?"

I nod. "She's ready, although she fears my heart has grown too seelie. She worries my rule could face challengers."

"And how do *you* feel about that?"

A corner of my mouth lifts in a sly grin. "I'd like to see anyone try. Between your magic and mine, there's enough intimidation to keep others at bay."

She blushes. It's taken a while for her to grow comfortable with her magic, to use it without fear. To own it for what it is.

A wave of trepidation washes over me. "But I want to know how *you* feel about it."

She doesn't answer right away. I keep myself from reading her energy; I want her to relay her feelings in her own way. After a while, her lips break into a wide smile "Proud. I feel proud, Franco. I truly believe you're ready to be king. Not only that, but you'll be incredible."

My heart flutters with relief. "Thank you," I say. "But there's something else..."

Her brow furrows. "What?"

I rub the back of my neck, feeling sweat prickling at my nape. "Let's go back to the throne room."

We walk in silence down the garden paths and into the palace. Once we reach the empty throne room, I guide her up the dais toward the piano. Instead of leading her to her usual place upon the bench, I claim the seat for myself. The room is dark aside from the glow of starlight shining down from the glass dome overhead. It's all the illumination I'll need. Just enough that maybe she won't see the terror in my eyes.

I face the keys.

My stomach churns. I don't know what she'll think about this. She'll probably think it's stupid. Offensive, even. I shouldn't—never mind. All I can do is try.

I press one finger over the appropriate key, then move to the next. The tune comes out slow and clunky, and I'd be surprised if she can even recognize it. I'm about to stop myself halfway through when her energy reaches me. It's pleased. Elated. From the corner of my eye, I watch her bring a hand to the base of her throat, first to the locket then to the opal moon that rests just above it.

After Ember insisted on wearing her gifted necklace every day, we had Madame Flora remove the glamour from it. Well, most of it. All that remains is a secret enchantment. One that marks Ember's skin, hidden beneath her clothing. Something only I see when she graces me with the glorious masterpiece that is her naked body. When she does, I find three lines of sheet music dancing over the side of her ribs.

Three beautiful songs from three dangerous fae.

I finish the clumsy tune and turn to face her.

Tears glaze her eyes, catching on the starlight shining down from the dome, filling her irises with glittering jewels. "A song for love," she says, voice breathless. She's right. It's the harpy mating song, the one they sing to attract a partner.

"There wasn't a song that expressed what I wanted to convey," I say, rubbing my damp palms over the front of my pants. My heart hammers hard against my ribs. "Turns out there's no harpy engagement song."

Her energy expands, but again I refuse to read it. This is too important. Her response should come straight from her lips.

On trembling legs, I rise from the bench and take a knee, just how Augie assured me the humans do. "I know you're already my mate," I say, taking her hand in mine as I meet her tear-glazed eyes. "I've already given you my heart, but will you do me the honor of becoming my wife? My queen to rule at my side?"

She reaches her free hand to her quivering lips but says nothing.

Doubt plagues me, sending words tumbling from my mouth. "If you aren't ready to be queen, I understand. You don't have to be unless you want to. And I know I'm supposed to have a ring, but I wanted us to pick them out together. It's stupid—"

"Franco," she says, her voice brimming with equal parts amusement, joy, and admonishment.

"Right," I say, shaking my head. I take a deep breath and try again. This time my words come out slowly and with care. "I want you with me, Ember. To face the years ahead of us together. To journey the unknown and brave the wilds of our future. Will you?"

She sinks down and wraps her arms around my neck, nearly bowling me over in the process. "Yes, Franco. Yes, I'll marry you."

My joy is so overwhelming, I think I might burst. Our hearts thrum together as she covers my face in kisses. Soon we dissolve into laughter mingling with happy tears.

Ember pulls back, framing my face with her hands. "There's something I want to show you. A surprise of my own." Anxiety darkens her energy, but there's excitement too.

"All right. Show me."

She moves to the center of the dais. I lean against the piano, watching as she closes her eyes. Her chest rises and falls, rises and falls. Then a shudder runs through her. In the blink of an eye, her form turns incorporeal, tinged with blue as she hovers a few feet off the ground.

My mouth falls open. "You've learned to shift at will." When she first began learning to hone her magic, only intense emotion could pull her in or out of her sylph form. I step closer to her. "That's amazing."

"Your sister has been teaching me," she says. Her energy turns timid. "Will you…fly with me?"

A lump rises in my throat. Ever since I learned of her sylph heritage, we've shared dreams of flying together. She as the wind, me as a raven. Over the last few months, she stopped letting me witness her attempts to shift, and she seemed to grow discouraged with her progress. I was starting to think we'd never share the skies like we dreamed.

But now...

Now everything we've dreamed of awaits. Our life. Our future. Our love.

I'm so ready to experience all of it. The ups and down. The trials and challenges. I'm ready to be brave. To show the world who I am. And to have the love of my life at my side.

The girl of wind.

The servant in the bonnet with the blue hair.

The queen with the sharp tongue and beautiful, tender heart.

"Yes, my dearest Em. Let's fly."

# NOT READY TO LEAVE FAERWYVAE?

Keep the magic alive! The next book in the *Entangled with Fae* series is a Little Mermaid retelling that follows Maisie's story. Continue the romance in *Kiss of the SelkIe*! Or read all about Gemma and Elliot (whom you met in the epilogue) in *Curse of the Wolf King*. It's a Beauty and the Beast retelling you won't want to miss!

You can also take a trip to Faerwyvae's past with *The Fair Isle Trilogy*, which takes place twenty-one years before *Heart of the Raven Prince*. The second book in this series introduces Franco! Read what he was like long before Ember came into his life.

## ALSO BY TESSONJA ODETTE

ENTANGLED WITH FAE - FAE ROMANCE

Curse of the Wolf King: A Beauty and the Beast Retelling

Heart of the Raven Prince: A Cinderella Retelling

Kiss of the Selkie: A Little Mermaid Retelling

— And more —

FAE FLINGS AND CORSET STRINGS - FAE ROMCOM

A Rivalry of Hearts

—and more—

THE FAIR ISLE TRILOGY - FAE FANTASY

To Carve a Fae Heart

To Wear a Fae Crown

To Spark a Fae War

STANDALONE FAE ROMANCE NOVELLA SET IN FAERWYVAE

Married by Scandal

PROPHECY OF THE FORGOTTEN FAE - EPIC FANTASY

A Throne of Shadows

A Cage of Crystal

A Fate of Flame

YA DYSTOPIAN PSYCHOLOGICAL THRILLER

Twisting Minds

# ABOUT THE AUTHOR

Tessonja Odette is a fantasy author living in Seattle with her family, her pets, and ample amounts of chocolate. When she isn't writing, she's watching cat videos, petting dogs, having dance parties in the kitchen with her daughter, or pursuing her many creative hobbies. Read more about Tessonja at www.tessonjaodette.com

        instagram.com/tessonja
        facebook.com/tessonjaodette
        tiktok.com/@tessonja
        twitter.com/tessonjaodette

www.ingramcontent.com/pod-product-compliance
Lightning Source LLC
LaVergne TN
LVHW041208250326
834689LV00022BA/174/J